A ROPE OF THORNS

GEMMA FILES

CZP

ChiZine Publications

FIRST EDITION

LIBRARY AND ARCHIVES CANADA CATALOGUING IN PUBLICATION

Files, Gemma, 1968-
       A rope of thorns / Gemma Files.

(Hexslinger series ; v. 2)
ISBN 978-1-926851-14-3

       I. Title. II. Series: Files, Gemma, 1968- . Hexslinger
series ; v. 2.

PS8611.I39R66 2011   C813'.6   C2011-900683-9

CHIZINE PUBLICATIONS
Toronto, Canada
www.chizinepub.com
info@chizinepub.com

Edited and copyedited by Sandra Kasturi
Proofread by Chris Edwards

 Canada Council **Conseil des Arts**
for the Arts **du Canada**

We acknowledge the support of the Canada Council for the Arts which last year invested $20.1 million in writing and publishing throughout Canada.

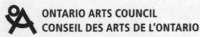 **ONTARIO ARTS COUNCIL**
CONSEIL DES ARTS DE L'ONTARIO

Published with the generous assistance of the Ontario Arts Council.

To Steve
who is the absolute best support
a writer of "repulsive trash" could ask for.

But also to Callum, my monkey-boy,
simply because he exists.

And to Elva Mai Hoover and Gary Files,
for much the same reason.

A ROPE OF THORNS

Do not hate me
Because I peeled the veil from your eyes and tore your world
To shreds, and brought

The darkness down upon your head.

—Gwendolyn MacEwen

No faith without blood.

—Philip Ridley

TABLE OF CONTENTS

PROLOGUE

A DISPATCH
Received from the Field & Personally Penned
by Allan Pinkerton, Founder and Establisher
of the Pinkerton National Detective Agency,
is now Available for Inclusion
in any American or International Newspaper
willing to pay Top Dollar.
A Précis of Material contained therewith, as Follows:

FROM TAMPICO, MEXICO TO YUMA CITY, ARIZONA, BY PRIVATE TRAIN; Legendary successes of the Conquistadors confounded!—Gods of Old Mexico apparently returned—Mexico City in ruins—Earthquake, Fire & Rioting—At fault: Hexslinger "Reverend" Asher E. Rook, lately of Arizona and parts thereto adjacent—His unnatural alliance with a long-dormant Mexican Goddess—Human Sacrifice! Degraded Rites, Bloody & Gruesome Mutilations!—Mexican authorities Outraged; Juarez government view Rook's hexacious meddling as American Incursion into their sovereign territory, only just freed from Austrian Rule—Fresh War on verge of declaration between that country and our own New-founded Democratic Federation?

As always, the Agency stands vigilant, ready to protect both interests and citizens of these United States. . . .

Our Motto: **We Never Sleep.**

In other news, from the Daily Letter of Hoffstedt's Hoard, New Mexico:

A MAGICAL EXODUS?
Witches and Wizards, Shamans, Up Stakes—
Hexaciously Inclined No More to be Found
"Good Riddance to Bad Rubbish"

RED WEED OBSERVED IN ARIZONA
Reports Place it Further Southwest and East
"Better to Burn than to Fight"

Homesteaders & settlers on the U.S. side of the Border complain of a sudden yet utterly pernicious crop-scourge they call "Red Plague-Weed," while rumours from Mexico way have whole farms destroyed in its wake. The Weed grows overnight, very fast, & cannot be easily extirpated through ordinary means (i.e. hoeing, salt or fire). If seen, it must be reported forthwith, and the afflicted lands abandoned until Federal attention can be gained.

Telegram transcript, sent from the desk of Allan Pinkerton to Agent Frank P. Geyer, Chicago, Illinois:

Meet Yuma City soonest STOP Need reliable help of purely natural kind STOP No reply necessary STOP Leave immediately STOP

From a handwritten missive, sent by Express, to meet Geyer on his way:

My dear colleague—

Forgive my previous missive's more-than-usual brusqueness; things are moving quickly here, and kicking up far too much hexation for us ordinary folk to handle without banding tightly together. In this matter, however, I am caught between the proverbial rock and a place too soft to stand—that Chinese sorceress from 'Frisco known as Songbird (a truly poisonous specimen of her kind, allied with us solely out of self-interest, yet still driven blindly by her cannibal instinct to uncover and consume all other hexes) vs. the good Doctor Asbury, whose skills in the area of sorcery-mapping are as unmistakable as they are invaluable, yet whose personal resolve I doubt.

Knowing my disgust for cheap rhetorical tricks, you will know I do not flatter by terming you one of our best Field Agents. You may therefore take this to be my primary motivation in charging you personally with the pursuit of two more adjuncts to the Rook Case, at large and fugitive even as we speak somewhere in this great State—men whose names and involvement we have so far been able to keep suppressed, especially as regards the intelligence of the Mexican government. This state of affairs must be preserved at all costs, for the security of our Agency and America alike.

They are: Rook's former Lieutenant, Chess Pargeter—a notorious desperado to begin with, rendered only more dangerous by his recent expression into full hex status—and Ed Morrow, a man I once trusted almost to the same degree I do you, whose infamous betrayal of his oath to this Agency I fear to be a mere foretaste of what's to come. As you know, in the matter of Rook and Pargeter, our original intent was to capture both through Morrow's services as undercover infiltrator in their gang, then use the latter to force the former's acquiescence in becoming part of Dr Asbury's studies—perhaps even recruit him to our cause, later, if all went as planned. God knows, I'd far rather have hitched my wagon to a tame sorcerer of my own race, especially one schooled in Bible-learning, than the heathen harridan we now employ in the same capacity. But by the time Pargeter fell into our hands (if only briefly), things had changed—Rook had cut some Devil's deal with the thing he calls his Rainbow Lady, and kicked off a campaign against all non-magicals by submitting his own catamite to a particularly awful form of human sacrifice aimed at opening the very gates of Hell itself (a Hell, at any rate).

Now Frank, I know you to be a good man in any crisis, confident and commanding, and that—having dealt with magic before, to good effect—you may make the mistake of assuming yourself already equipped to deal with the likes of young Mister P. Let me warn you, however, that Dr Asbury believes Pargeter to be now at least as powerful as Reverend Rook, if not far more so—in Asbury's parlance, he has become "a little god," an avatar of some other Old Mexican demon known as He Who is Flayed Like Corn, and leaves in his wake a virulent crop of scarlet growth, necromantic activity and various other monstrosities.

And since I myself have recently had direct dealings with the bastard, only to come off substantially at a loss, I can tell you that unless you go into battle with Asbury's latest gimmicks up your sleeve, your chances of escape—let alone success—will be rendered effectively nil. Nor can I promise the support of numbers, even though I know you are as like as not to prefer solitary operation in any event; after Morrow's betrayal, and the recalcitrance I have endured recently from those whose obedience was once absolute (George Thiel, amongst others), I find I cannot bring myself to take loyalty for granted as I once did, or to risk you being betrayed, as I was, by men weaker than ourselves.

One way or another, Pargeter is untaught, vicious, and his first inclinations are always to violence, making him far too dangerous to approach directly. So do not come at him like any other outlaw, hexslinger or no: track, monitor, but leave alone unless absolutely forced to engage (at which point, prepare for heavy casualties).

Information on both targets is attached, to be distributed as you see fit.

I remain, yr. most obt., etc. etc.

Name: Chess Pargeter.
Age: Perhaps twenty-six years (approx.).
Height: Five feet and seven inches.
Hair: Red.
Eyes: Green.
Identifying Features and Marks: Aquiline nose, longish face with high cheekbones; pale-complected with high colour and tendency to sunburn; favours a beard to cover a long scar tracing his right-hand jaw-line. Left ear pierced to hold a lady's ear-bob (Hospitaller's cross done in gold, set with turquoise). Distinctly slight-made. A dapper dresser with a taste for brightly coloured clothes (most often in the range of purple).
Place of Birth: San Francisco, California.
Biographical Details: Pargeter formerly held the rank of Private in the Confederate Army, serving with Lieutenant Saul Mobley's Irregulars before being sentenced to death for battlefield desertion of duty in the latter days of the War; he is equally notorious as an uncannily skillful pistoleer and a known degenerate, and stands wanted for murder, mass murder, robbery, assault and battery, consortation with known criminals, illegal acts, destruction of property exceeding the value of one thousand dollars.
Nota bene: Since Pargeter and "Reverend" Rook shared both a sodomitical and professional connection throughout Rook's career as a hexslinger, as Rook's Lieutenant of long standing, Pargeter may be considered retroactively (yet fully) implicated in most of the same crimes as Rook himself, especially since he has also been identified as the de facto leader of Rook's gang

during those few periods of Rook's absence. Pargeter is a crack shot and knifester, well used to close-quarters infiltration. A good if inexpert rider, he displays no fear of personal injury or retribution when executing his crimes. Left to his own devices, he is said to avoid cities and frequent a series of outlaw bagnio-groggeries scattered throughout Arizona, but his current notoriety may have forced him to abandon such hidey-holes. Be on the lookout for a suspicious rise in the sale of absinthe liquor to saloons in previously uninclined towns.

Asbury's Manifold Scale Measurements: Still being reckoned.

Name: Edward Rumsfield Morrow.

Age: Thirty-four years.

Height: Six feet and two-and-three-quarters inches.

Hair: Brown.

Eyes: Changeable (variously described as brownish or greyish, depending on light and colour of clothing).

Identifying Features and Marks: Wide-faced with a firm jaw, pronounced nose, slightly cleft chin; tan-complected; markedly hirsute and low-browed, with a short yet heavy beard; affects mutton-chop sideburns (when shaved, may look startlingly respectable). Short yet substantial scar from ill-mended bayonet wound between second and third ribs, on left-hand side; bullet-pock through right biceps, with visible marking on both sides; Morrow has arthritis in his right ankle, and walks with a limp when exhausted.

Place of Birth: Marianna, Kansas.

Biographical Details: Served with distinction as a Sergeant in the Union Army at Mine Creek and Marais des Cygnes, mopped up after Quantrill's raids at Baxter Springs and Lawrence; twice wounded; discharged with commendation. Joined the Agency in 1866, and did laudable work on five smaller assignments (guarding shipments, bank duty, labour disputes) before going undercover with "Reverend" Rook's gang.

Nota bene: Since Morrow's violations of Agency policy mean he has effectively resigned his position, and the privileges thereof, he too may be considered retroactively guilty in whatever crimes Rook and Pargeter committed during Morrow's tenure. Morrow is a fair hand with a shotgun, adept at dissembling, and clean in his habits. It is possible that his current demonstrated attachment to Pargeter may be magically generated, though this does not excuse his actions hitherto. Do not simply expect him to switch allegiances out of shame or regret, especially in the heat of combat.

Asbury's Manifold Scale Measurements: Inapplicable.

From the dream-book of Yu Ming-ch'in, aka "Songbird":

Fourth week of night visions which call me to Rook's "New Aztectlan," tugging me as though fish-hooked. I am unable to sleep longer than a few hours at a time yet unwilling to medicate myself, even were I close enough to San Francisco's Gold Mountain to obtain good opium; Asbury, oblivious as he is, dares to look at me with sympathy, for which insult I may (one day) kill him.

These dreams contain all the many Elements of Lesser Yin, taken in their most classic conjunctions: rain in winter, a black flag to the north, mortification, distance and suffering, the number six. A bad taste in the mouth, salt and rotten; a smell of fear, like dead pigs unearthed. Your liver squirming inside you, fluid and untrustworthy, like mercury. And a recurrent series of images, variously observed, in endless combination—

Crossed bones at the crossroads. A dog with human hands, dancing in empty places.

A man of salt walking upright, allied with shadows, and seeking for revenge.

English Oona's red-haired son raging through the wilderness, wearing a coat made from black scorpions. They only sting those who draw close; to him, their venom is like wine.

That traitor Rook, still studying over his empty Bible: a lesson ill-learned, and fruitless. While at his left hand, leaning over one shoulder, I see her, the one all this should truly be blamed on—his lady wife, She Who Goes Adorned With Bells—the moon with a serpent's mouth, who labours before dawn. . . .

BOOK ONE:
PRECIOUS BLOOD

May 5, 1867
Month One Crocodile, Day Nine Water
Festival: Toxcatl, or Drought

This *trecena*, or thirteen-day period, Cipactli ("Crocodile"), is ruled by the great earth monster, who floats on the sea of stars. Since this is the first *trecena* of the sacred year, these days are governed by a primordial urge to create order out of chaos. These are good days to participate in the community, bad days for solitude.

Day Atl ("Water") is governed by Xiuhtecuhtli, God of Fire: a day for purification through subjecting oneself to the ordeal of conflict. Water brings out the scorpion, who must sting its enemies or else sting itself. It is a good day for battle, a bad day for rest—at worst, the day of holy war.

The Lord of Night associated with this day is Tlaloc, the God of Rain, Lightning and Thunder. He is a fertility god, but also a wrathful deity. He is the ruler of Tlalocan, the fourth heaven. Tlalocan is the place of eternal spring, a paradise of green plants, and the afterlife destination for those who die violently from phenomena associated with water, such as by lightning, drowning and water-borne diseases. Tlaloc once ruled over the third world, which was destroyed by a fiery deluge. He is the ninth and last Lord of the Night.

CHAPTER ONE

THEY WERE ONLY A scant day or so over the border, riding horses "paid for" in lead, when Morrow woke with a jaw so puffed it hurt him to talk—swole up like mumps, head clammy with fever. Chess was just strolling back into camp after his traditional morning piss, but the very sight of it brought him up short.

"Hell's wrong with you?" Chess demanded. "Looks like you're storin' nuts."

Morrow went to shake his head, but thought better of it.

"Hurts," was all he could manage. "Real bad."

They both knew what a toothache this sudden could mean, or cost them. Chess looked at Morrow askance, hissed like a cat, then looked away again, cursing: "Shit-fire, Ed! I damn well wanted to stay *out* of towns, not—"

"I know."

More to himself: "And the bitch of it is, I could probably cure you, I only knew how the hell to do it. If anybody'd ever bothered to school me in this damn thing I'm carryin' 'round with me . . . if *gods* were anywhere even halfway trustworthy, let alone lying, cheating, Goddamn *men*."

As always, anything which sent Chess's thoughts back toward Reverend Rook had immediate repercussions. Morrow saw the smaller man's hands fist spasmodically, knuckles white, and felt *something* ripple up through the sand-topped earth beneath them both—almost too quick to track, a shiver echoing from everywhere at once. Like their very presence had just started to irk the world's hide bad enough it was tensing, bracing for imminent trouble, and unsure itself whether it wasn't worth the effort to simply flick 'em clear, like a pair of mosquitoes.

Though Chess might seem "normal," most times, he very much wasn't. He had the Rev dancing naked behind his eyes whenever he shut 'em, no doubt, enticing him to make for some dark city high on a hill—and that phantom siren's call had to be damn strong indeed, considering how even a non-magical sort like Morrow could overhear it on occasion, back-washing through the embarrassingly intimate bond he and Chess had shared ever since fleeing Tampico together.

As a result, whenever Chess got riled, it was like being back in proximity *with* Rook . . . except worse, since Chess was far more volatile, and always had been. Apt as not to spit up whole poisonous toads, or stamp and bring a flood of amorously seeking bones, if he didn't get his way; shoot spells that dissolved or transformed things on contact, throw away harsh words like bullets, only to watch them ignite in mid-air: concussive and gunpowdery, horridly random.

And yet, for all that—for *all* that, Morrow found he still trusted Chess more than he'd ever trusted the Rev, even at his most charming or soft-spoken. Their dalliance continued, even now; Chess wasn't one to deprive himself of pleasures, and if it was a choice between fucking or fighting, considering the power disparity involved, Morrow knew which one he'd keep on choosing.

One way or the other, Chess and Morrow had drifted with odd swiftness into what Morrow could only deem some variety of demented battlefield camaraderie—a bond only accentuated by Chess's damnable facility in applying himself to a man's tenderest places: shameless, inventive, with Spartan revelry his favourite type of relief from the barest moment's boredom. And though it was never a taste he'd looked to acquire, the truth was, Morrow could no longer (in good conscience) deny how he very definitely *had* acquired it—as regards to Chess, at any rate, if nobody else.

Would it stick, though? Morrow wondered. Wondered if Chess—opaque as ever—wondered, too. From mere observation, Morrow already knew how he could be a jealous little sumbitch, if and when things got a bit deeper than a passing *Hey you, c'mere, I got somethin' for ya—now you gimme somethin' too, you big bastard.*

Even with all they'd done together, however, Morrow didn't exactly know if they'd reached that stage, as yet. Or if he even wanted them to.

"Am I queer now?" he hadn't been able to stop himself from asking Chess, just the night before.

To which Chess had shrugged, and replied, "Halfways, at best. Why? Worried you'll be doggin' after every other man you come 'cross?"

"'Course not."

"Exactly." Chess turned over, stretching, and fit his head to the sweat-slick hollow of Morrow's chest with creepish casualness, for all the world like it'd been made to act his pillow. "Then again, I *am* a special case, by anybody's reckoning. Most men ain't been to Hell and back, queer or not; most ain't had their hearts cut out and ate by a damn god, and lived to tell the tale. So I figure you're safe enough, regarding frolics with anybody else . . . 'less you don't want to be."

Morrow snorted. "No fear," he said.

"Still," Chess had blithely continued when they were up and dressed the next morning, just as though they hadn't paused to sleep—and screw some more—in the interim, "it's probably best we keep things light, anyhow. 'Cause much as I hate to admit so, seems my Ma was right, all along: love really *is* a damn disease."

"Going by the Rev, you mean? But what makes you think she even knew what she was on about? And 'sides that, what makes you think—"

Chess shot him a shrewd look. "Think what?"

"Nothin'."

"That Rook's the only one I'll ever love—was that it? Why ex-Agent Morrow, you sad sentimental. Or was that your clumsy idea of offerin' an alternative?"

Morrow didn't bother to answer, blushing to his hat-hid ears. And Chess laughed, off and on, throughout the rest of the day— almost from the time they mounted up right to the time they made camp once more.

All of which maybe proved Morrow either far too lust-struck to think straight, too punch-drunk on hexation-overspill to be reliable, simply plain stark crazy, or all three at once. But it had to count for something, didn't it?

"Chess," he made himself say, back in the here and now, "it's . . . okay. I'll be fine."

"No you won't." Chess gave an angry sigh. "Tooth-rot'll kill you, fool. Gets in your blood. Saw plenty die that way, back in the Lieut's Company."

Morrow set his lip, mutinous—tried to, anyhow. "Look, Chess— I'll be *fine*. Don't need no damn tooth-puller. I'll just—"

Ride it off? Was that what he was going to say? Sounded ridiculous, even to him. And it didn't matter, anyhow. Having made up his own mind, Chess just rolled right over Morrow's protestations.

"Big man like you, 'fraid of a pair of grabbers—that's pure foolishness, son. We'll get it looked to, maybe put some gold in your smile . . . now, how'd that be?"

"Aw, stop tryin' to bribe me, you damn fancy-dancer! Call *me* 'son,' when you're half my age."

"Yeah, there we go. Get mad, Goddamnit! Act a man." With a grin: "'Sides which, I really wanted to *bribe* you into anything, I could do it a sight more cheaply—and amuse myself while doin' so, too."

Morrow couldn't keep himself from flushing at the implication. "Rate your services pretty damn high, don't you?"

"Sure. But then again—I'm worth it. Ain't I?"

Morrow couldn't argue with that, literally.

"Saddle up," Chess told him. "Next shit-hole's . . . Mouth-of-Praise, or some such, I seem to recall, from the last time the Rev and I rode through here. Should get there roundabout suppertime—and if the sawbones does his duty, you should be fixed enough to eat it, too."

"Chawin' down with a raw socket ain't my idea of fun," Morrow muttered, heaving himself haphazardly into the saddle. "Man, I wish old Kees Hosteen was here."

Chess, already seated, tossed his head just the once at their dead friend's name, like he was flicking flies. "Well, he ain't," he replied, shortly.

Morrow sighed. "I know. It's just . . . he had a way of makin' things go smooth, is all."

Not the world's best epitaph—but one he thought Kees might have appreciated, was he still in any way able to.

Chess shot him another look, this one almost completely unreadable.

"Talked a sight less than some people, that's for sure," he said, at last. And kicked his horse forward, hard as it would go.

AS ONLY SEEMED FITTING, Mouth-of-Praise was mainly false fronts, with every house and shop jacked up twice its actual size with an overhanging façade meant to mask the disrepair within. They rode in slower than Chess usually liked, with what seemed like an inordinate number of eyes on them right from the get-go. Probably didn't help that Morrow was drooping like he'd been shot, or that Chess's coat was brighter than most of the ladies' dresses.

"Might be they recognize us," he said.

Chess didn't even bother to look 'round. "Oh, ya think?"

Most places, the local barber did what extraction or patch jobs were needed—but here, perhaps as another mark of greatness yet to come, they'd somehow managed to attract an honest-to-goodness certificate-holder with university bona fides. His shingle, hung beside the expected red-and-white pole, read: *CURRER GLOSSING, D.D.S. Painless Process Practised!*

Morrow, who'd had two teeth yanked already, doubted the claim on sight—but damn, if it wasn't getting difficult to even keep his left eye open. He slid down heavily while Chess tied up their horses, and immediately felt a wave of vertigo so intense he almost wanted to thank Doc Glossing—a plump little thing, blinking meekly up at him from behind gold-rimmed glasses—just for opening the door.

"Gentlemen," Glossing said. "You two appear to be in sore need of denticular assistance."

He took one of Morrow's arms, as Chess shrugged himself under the other. Together, they managed to wrangle him over the threshold, and laid him down onto a red plush couch that wouldn't've looked amiss back in one of the 'Frisco whorehouses Chess had grown up in. In similar style, cash changed hands almost immediately—and where Chess had gotten it from, Morrow wasn't quite sure, given they hadn't exactly stopped to rob any banks since leaving Mexico, but he wasn't about to ask. Could be dead leaves dressed up, like in them fairy tales his Ma used to tell. Or dirt, more likely.

One way or the other, deal done, Chess took up a stance near the window, watching the street as Glossing went about his business: Moistening two pledgets of cotton with a tincture of aconite, chloroform, alcohol and morphine, then packing them firmly 'round the afflicted section of Morrow's gum, where he fixed them in place with a spring-wound clamp.

Morrow groaned at the feel, so pathetically it caused Chess's head to whip 'round, hand on one gun-butt. "Can't you do nothin' more for him?" he demanded.

"Well now, that has to set a good five to fifteen minutes, in order for the full effect—"

"Ain't too like to set at all, he keeps on squirming like that. So pour a fresh shot of the same down his throat, and let's get the hell on with it."

"Um, uh*kay*, Cheh," Morrow broke in. But just at that moment—

"Chess Paaaaaaargeter!"

Fuck, Morrow thought. *I knew it.*

The voice came from up the street a ways, brazen-clanging, impossibly loud; it fairly seemed to make the storefront's window jump in its frame. Chess swiped the doc's curtains aside, trying for a better view, and got a shotgun blast over the shoulder for his pains, punching a shower of glass onto the surgery's floor.

"Shit!" Chess cursed. "That son of a mother—"

"Chessss Paaaaargeter!" the voice repeated, yet louder, and the next bunch of pellets peppered higher, some through Chess's hat-brim. Chess cross-drew, firing back blind 'til he ran dry. At the same time, Morrow reared up, automatically grabbing for his own gun, only to be astonished—make that horrified—by how easily Glossing managed to press him back down to the couch.

"Sir—*sirs!*" the dentist protested. "Pargeter—Reverend *Rook's* Chess Pargeter?"

Not anymore, Morrow felt like telling him. But the tincture was definitely starting to work, in that the general cacophony made his head ring swoonishly. Swallowing, he squared his jaw, and managed—"Who *ih* thah?"

Chess was down on the floor now, "reloading" his empty guns—chamber by chamber—with fiery little clots of spell-work that dropped from each fingertip in turn. "Can't damn well see, Goddamnit." To Glossing: "And as for *you,* just keep on goin'. I want my money's worth."

"I believe I asked you a question, Mister—"

From the street: "—*PAAAAARGETER!*"

Chess turned, fixed him with a narrowed green glare and rose to his full height—which, though nothing much comparatively, gave him a good half-inch on Glossing.

"Yeah, that's right, Doc: I'm Chess Pargeter, he's Ed Morrow—this is a gun, and so's this. Now, I'm just gonna go outside and kill that big bastard, and if I come back in here and find Ed ain't been fixed in the interim, you best believe I *will* end you. Got that?"

The dentist drew himself up in turn, primly. "We take an *oath,* Mister Pargeter, the same as any other school of medicine. I aim to honour mine."

Chess shrugged. "Guess we'll see," he replied, and went slamming out the back.

Morrow tried to angle himself so he could see the street—then let loose with a startled yowl as Glossing grabbed his head by the swollen jaw, moving it firmly back to the vertical.

"Quite enough of that," the dentist told him. Adding, kind but strict, like a horse-breaker at work: "I'd rather have had a few more minutes setting time to give you, but this will have to do. Hold as still as you can, Mister Morrow."

More cold metal wedged his mouth open. Morrow braced himself for agony as the pliers made contact with the bad tooth—but the only thing he felt was the featherlight stroke of soft fingertips on his forehead. A split second later, a warm, fuzzy, gluey feeling took hold, like thick treacle coating every nerve; the faintest pressure, for all that Morrow knew the grabbers and brace dug equal-deep. Glossing's face, above him, was a blurred black featureless mask against the light.

This ain't natural, Morrow thought, stupidly. *More like . . .* super*natural*.

Which meant—hexation. And hexation meant a trap.

Aw, crap.

Chess! Morrow yelled, or tried to; least he owed him was a warning. But all that came out was a harsh rasp of breath, a bit too much like a death-rattle for comfort.

Glossing might have shaken his head—hard to tell, at this angle. "Save your strength, Mister Morrow." His voice sounded like bubbles bursting in deep water, far away. "I guarantee my clients painlessness, but you're far from the first to dislike the side effects. Silence really is golden, it seems, especially when fitting a man for gold teeth. Though I admit—" and here he let his own show, in a sly flicker of discoloured porcelain "—they're seldom quite so lucky for me, either. Now, before I forget . . ."

He leaned in, twisted and yanked, hard—'til something gave with a wrench, snapping away with a dull, concussive string of throbs Morrow was thankful to barely feel. Glossing dropped the tooth into a nearby ceramic bowl, then turned to peer out the window, pliers still in the hand he used to shade his eyes.

"Yuh . . . y'r uh hhhex!" Morrow managed to gargle, through a mouthful of blood.

Glossing looked back at him with a raised eyebrow, nodded. "Yes. I do apologize for the impacted molar curse, Mister Morrow, but I couldn't think of a better way to guarantee you'd pay a visit to my poor establishment." Gazing out the window once more: "No point in sending anything similar Mister Pargeter's way, of course; it'd've simply bounced off and come back in my own direction, no doubt rendered considerably . . . harder, for the journey. Now, let's us just wait and see how my friend is doing. . . ."

He appeared not to notice as Morrow, summoning every ounce of effort, pushed himself up on his elbows in order to finally get his head above the windowsill. He spat all down his shirt-front, bright red, and squinted.

The streets had emptied with the first gunshot, though Morrow thought he could catch the occasional cautious head or pulled-low hat-brim lurking here and there. In the centre of the street, a pale, heavyset, rag-bearded man in filthy tattered buckskins snapped the fresh-loaded shotgun in his hands shut and turned slowly in place, his own gaze casting about fruitlessly.

"CHESS PARGETER!" the man bellowed once more, abruptly, and Morrow felt a cold trickle in his belly. There was something innately . . . *wrong* . . . with the man's voice, an odd disjunction which added an inhumanly thick echo to his monotonous, repetitive cry. As though he was literally unable to say anything other than Chess's name—to form any other thought, let alone express it aloud.

But now the silence broke open again, a barrage of thunderous cracks, rapid as hammer blows. The yelling man staggered, buckskins bursting open in a blood-dust spray, as Chess strode up the street, emptying his revolvers into his back.

They ran dry once more; Chess holstered and struck a pose, looking smug. "That's just what happens when you make free with a man's name, and you ain't even been introduced," he hollered—then folded his arms, and waited to watch the man fall.

Which . . . he didn't.

The realization came attached to a sound, strange yet familiar, spurring Morrow to turn his head. It was Glossing, chuckling in his throat; greedy, playful, instantly reminiscent of Rook—and Songbird. Songbird *with* Rook, pulling him down to her level and kissing him hard, sucking magic from him like a damn mosquito. Like it tasted so good she didn't care whether she killed herself doing it, just so long as she got her fix.

Chess, back over his shoulder, running headlong to Rook's rescue: *Don't you know nothin' 'bout hexes, fool? They can't take just a* little—

Morrow fair felt his balls clench as he watched Glossing raise his free hand, fingers twitching, a puppeteer pulling strings. Thought, helpless: *Shit—move, Chess, move—*

Chess saw that the stuff gurgling from the man's exit wounds wasn't blood, but some horrid, blackish goop, a second before the shotgun came up. His eyes widened.

With a yelp more of surprise than fear he dove to one side, not quite fast enough, and spun as the blast caught the barest edge of his shoulder. He howled in pain and hit the ground hard, scrabbling in the earth for something, anything to throw. The gun centred on Chess, and sickness crawled up Morrow's throat as the trigger tightened—

In sheer, futile defiance, Chess snatched up a handful of grit and hurled it, snarling. Only to see the stones multiply and fracture in mid-air, become a howling jet of razor-edged shards flashing from Chess's palm to burst against the gunman-thing's front, like the deluge from a perforated water tank. Rotten buckskins and pallid flesh peeled back from the thing's body, sending it staggering backward. The shotgun fell from one disintegrating hand, flipping to discharge again as it hit the ground—right up into its former owner's groin.

Stunned, Chess made the mistake of letting his own hand drop. At which point the earth-jet instantly ceased, leaving the truth laid bare most awfully.

The body beneath those buckskins had never been human; did not even *look* human, now. By the low-slung hips, black mouldy fur and short thick legs, its bottom half seemed mostly bear. The long wavering spine and deep ribs looked like the remains of a powerful bull's, while the arms . . . scaly and undersized, their gloved-over paws' "fingers" actually long nails made for digging, hovering foreshortened up around the creature's belly. A lizard? Armadillo? Only the head bore any resemblance to a human's, though slackly mask-like, and that was spoiled by the weird letters incised—black and smoking—on its white brow.

Glossing pressed his fingers to his mouth, looking absurdly dismayed. Then his rabbit-eyes tightened; with another subtle gesture, he sent the corpse-amalgam lumbering forward, ready and willing to crush by sheer weight what it had failed to shoot dead.

But Chess had the measure of his foe now, and this was hardly the first dead thing he and Morrow had dealt with. So as it approached he dropped below its clumsy swing and spun, planting a spurred heel square in the thing's knee. The rotten joint burst, bones snapping; gravity took over and brought the thing down to the ground hard—

—and Morrow's head was abruptly crystal clear, while Glossing was doubled over, clutching his own knee, screaming.

Before the dentist could recover, Morrow had already flipped himself off the couch, cursing as he crashed to the floor—the numb-spell was still on him, crawling back up his body even as Glossing regained his senses. He quick-humped toward the door and down the front steps, out into the street with Glossing on his heels. Yelling, as he did: "Cheh! Issa doc! Hessa hex—damn thing's 'is puppet! Glossinssa *hex*—!"

White pain burst through Morrow's head, blinding him; abruptly, he found himself on his back, insect-scrabbling with all four limbs at once. Glossing drew back his boot for another kick, face distorted in a snarl of rage—then buckled once more, grabbing his side as if knifed. Morrow rolled his head, just barely able to glimpse how Chess threw kick after kick into the thing as it twitched feebly on the ground. With each one, Glossing shrieked again, crumpling until he too lay helpless in the dusty street, barely able to watch as Chess dragged the whole huge, stinking mess of his creation over to him by one swollen leg.

Kneeling, Chess traced an invisible line from the thing's letter-carved skull through the air, 'til his hand made contact with Glossing's chest. So intent was Chess's gaze that Morrow was fairly certain he wasn't even noticing the small black shotgun pellets steadily work their way from his wounded shoulder, vanishing in tiny puffs of flame before they could even hit the ground.

"This," he said to Glossing, hand moving like it was following a rope Morrow couldn't see. "Little silver string—that's how you make it dance, huh?" Without waiting for an answer he rose, then stamped down hard between puppet and puppeteer, like he was snuffing a fuse. Glossing groaned. The dead thing stopped moving. Chess stared at it, sick fascination plain on his face. "What the hell *is* that thing, anyway?" he demanded. "What do you even call it?"

Pain and dread had drawn Glossing's face tight; his grim smile made him look like someone else entirely. Again, Morrow was reminded inexorably of both Songbird and Rook. "He's . . . my friend. The proper word is golem. But I call him—*Emmett*."

As the name echoed thickly in the air, Chess and Morrow both found their eyes snapping all unsummoned to those four alien letters on the monster's skull; caught and held by black power, mouths agape, as the thing suddenly reared back up. Behind the word, a thunderous, brazen sound, like sheeting shook off-stage at the theatre—as though each letter had been embossed on the air.

Whether the spell was actually so strong it affected them both— or Morrow was just inadvertently sharing Chess's senses again, through whatever connection Rook had bound upon them—they could all see it, now: A web of black cable strung from golem to hex, then leading back from both of them into the far distance, stretching across miles, toward—

"Rook," breathed Chess. "That house-sized sonofabitch."

On the floor, Glossing coughed. "I lie down every night," he rasped, "with *that* sunk deep in my dreams, calling me; I rise up every morning knowing Reverend Rook'll give me all the power I could ever want, if I only sign away my soul and follow it to its conclusion. And the best joke of all is, it isn't even *me* he wants." His eyes burned. "It's *you*."

"No, doc." Chess shook his head. "This ain't my doing."

"But it *is!*" Glossing pushed himself up slightly, trembling. "Every hex between here and the Mississippi's been bleeding power like a stuck pig for weeks, all so your 'good' Reverend can bring us to help serve *you*! He says he'll make us gods, but he's just one more like you, like me—all he wants is *food*, and *I will not be his meal!*"

Here he flung out a hand, grabbing for Chess's; the power flare between them was so bright, hot and immediate that Morrow cringed back with a yell, hands over his eyes. He felt the sickening pulling even in his own gut, the nauseating wrench of power being sucked away, and knew it must be a thousand times worse for those who had power to lose. Chess's startled cry was a shrike's, so full of rage and pain it made him want to both cringe and weep.

Then—fury, red and sizzling, as the blazing stream reversed itself so suddenly that Morrow felt it rush right up into his throat: a gag, a noose, fit to strangle and choke. And saw Chess's eyelids flutter just a tad, at the taste of it, hot and fresh, like heart's-meat done up sizzling, straight from the spectral grill.

With dread Lady Ixchel's voice crooning alongside, an ill refrain, from the darkest depths of Morrow's memory: **Jaguar Cactus Fruit, so flowery, little husbands. So precious. So . . .**

(beautifulbeautifulbeautiful)

"Often as you claim to've been in consort with Rook," Chess told the dentist, "don't seem like you quite got the bulk of the message. I ain't just *any* hex, to be sucked dry and dropped. I'm *different*."

Glossing gave a bitter laugh. "Oh, you're that, all right."

He waved at "Emmett" one more time, like he couldn't help it; it jerked forward, growling. But Chess just shot again, as if by way of reply—off-hand, without even looking. The final spell-bullet exploded out of Chess's barrel, all bat-wings and squid-legs, writhing and snapping. It ripped the golem's face right off, revealing a perforated horse's skull whose long jaws were set with dog's choppers underneath.

"Naw, I don't think so," Chess said. "'Cause for all you got some fancy tricks indeed, you *still* ain't hex enough to mess with *me*."

Glossing gulped and tried to scuttle, arm flopping hapless, like he'd momentarily forgotten he and Chess were still holding hands. And Chess gave a mean, familiar predator's grin at the sight, gripping so hard his knuckles flared up white—drew in even *harder*, as though he meant to drink every last drop of the fat little man up through a rye grass straw.

It was sad, in its way—for both of 'em. Chess Pargeter, battle-proven killer of men, reduced to a child stepping on ant-hills. Doc Glossing, reduced to meat.

The dentist hissed, a near squeal. Then went all at once a-droop, overwhelmed and withering—a popped pig's bladder.

"So powerful," he gasped, giving way. "*So* strong, and yet . . . you don't know anything. Not a *damn* thing. Not even . . ."

An unintelligible mutter followed, resolving itself into: ". . . was right, 'bout you . . ."

At this, Chess's eyes—already lit up with the surplus—literally snapped and flared. "*Who* was? Rook—that deathless bitch of his? Goddamn *Songbird*?" The man just shook his head, defeated, taking refuge in silence. "*Tell* me, shithead! I'll yank your soul out through your eyeballs, see if I don't!"

"Won't get . . . a stitch more from me, Mister Pargeter. I'm done."

"Oh, you got *that* right," Chess snarled, pulling all the harder, 'til Glossing's entire plump visage seemed about to cave in. "Question is—you want the end of it to go quick? Easy? Or anything Goddamn but?"

"*Cheh*," Morrow said, warningly.

Too late. Glossing slumped, emptying himself into Chess in one foul gush. When Chess looked up once more his pupils blazed like lamps, slitted and triangular; a ghostly cat's gaze, touched with Hellfire.

Across the street, doors were opening—citizens either stood frozen and staring or went scattering off to find guns, the Law, the nearest preacher equipped for a long-distance exorcism. At the sight, power crackled between each of Chess's ten spread fingers, so sharp it made even him jump.

"And what're *you* all lookin' at?" He demanded.

"Cheh, I seh less go. Less juss—c'mon, now. *Go*."

"We're lookin' at *you*, you hex from Hell!" Some brave soul yelled, meanwhile, before ducking back into the town's one saloon.

"Damn straight; we heard your story, Chess Pargeter. Wrecking decent folks' homes, destroying respectable businesses."

As the only mundane combatant here engaged, Morrow could sympathize with their simple human outrage, even when a few started tossing horse-apples along with the abuse.

"Invert! Vandal!"

"For *his name shall be called Abomination, and his place made desolate!*"

"That a jacket, or a damn circus-rig?"

Above, the clear sky growled, like it was getting hungry. Chess flushed, furiously; jacked up on Glossing's stolen juice, his own anger reached out wider, causing the shattered store-window glass to run and drip, mercurially refusing to merge with the street's dust around it.

"You motherless bitches," he said, the lightning flashing 'round his palms rising wrist-high. "Dare to quote the damn Bible at me— I've *had* that, from the best! So c'mon over here and try it to my *face*, you lily-livered—"

"*Chess*, fuh shissakes—"

Chess blew out a snarling breath, and shook his head. "Hold on," he told Morrow, knitting his still-sparking fingers painfully in the bigger man's shoulder.

And—they were gone, popped out and back into existence in a half-second, the town erased like blown-off mist. Nothing but empty rock, scrub and equally empty overhang of cloudlessness, sun the colour of a struck match.

Chess stumbled back a pace, then sat down, heavily, like he'd been gutted. Morrow collapsed on his side, hands automatically gone to his maimed mouth . . . only to find the raw hole plugged once more with a bare rim of new tooth—man-sized, smooth as china plate—poking up, impossibly, through tender flesh.

He wondered how long it'd take to grow out fully, and whether keeping himself drunk throughout would help or hinder the process.

35

"Crap," Chess exclaimed, suddenly exhausted. "I left the Goddamn horses behind."

CHAPTER TWO

THAT NIGHT, SPARKS FLEW upward from the fire only to die halfway, like lightning bugs with aspirations to be stars throwing themselves skyward, heedless of their own hubris. That last was a word Ash Rook had once taught Chess, Grecian in origin—idolators same as those Mex fools who'd once worshipped "Lady" Ixchel and her like, though with the added appeal of having apparently thought it a tad strange for a man *not* to lust after his own kind. Which made 'em a sight more worthy of respect than any One True God Almighty-worshipping Bible-thumper Chess'd ever met with . . . 'side from the Rev himself, of course.

Here, however, Chess felt a shiver at the very name, and grimaced. Just no getting away from Rook when the man's betrayal ran all through him like a bruisy pain, far too fresh to touch directly.

Across from him, Chess saw Ed Morrow look up sharply, like he could hear what Chess was thinking. "You all right?"

"I look like I'm not?"

Morrow frowned. "All seriousness? Well . . . yeah."

There were a fair few replies Chess might have made to that, but he well knew Morrow'd done nothing to warrant them, 'sides from offer him support in ways he hadn't thought to ask for.

So he simply sighed, and answered: "Just tired, is all. How's that tooth?"

"Better. Listen, though, Chess—that calling the Doc spoke on . . . you feel it too, don't you?"

Here the fire gave a punctuational *crack*, as though some unseen wooden knot had suddenly flared through. Chess felt it ring straight through the space where his stolen heart should beat, Dentist Glossing's stolen power galvanizing him with a current of pure arousal fit to make every last nerve pop at once, in similarly spectacular fashion; it *hurt* him so's he had to forcibly restrain himself from grabbing poor Ed by both ears and shutting him up, mouth-first.

"Every night," he replied, instead. "But I'm stronger than he was, Ed—so I don't aim to go there 'til I'm good and ready."

To which Morrow just nodded, sagely. And yet—

When'll that be, exactly? Chess heard him think, nevertheless, no matter how he strained not to. The way he "heard" almost every damn thing around him, these days: two girls strolling east as Morrow and he rode toward the dentist's shop, one of 'em sorting cake recipes, the other wondering when she'd have to start tying her apron higher (and how fast she could catch herself a Joseph-husband, 'fore what she was cooking in *her* oven started to show). An old man cleaning spittoons on the lodge-house stoop, hoping that pain in his stomach was last night's stew, not cancer. A muscle-bound farm-hand moving west to trade for feed at the general store, casting eyes on Chess's backside with the same interest Chess would have shown his, had their positions been reversed.

Hadn't been for all that yammer, Chess might've seen Doc Glossing for what he was at the outset. Which was bad enough, and explained why his natural urge to shun even smallish cities had grown so almighty strong—get him and Morrow back out under a clear sky with enough miles 'round him to see horizon in every direction, and Chess felt immediately easier, if not a damn whit safer. But then things would start going in the opposite direction, a telescope reversed; every particle of "empty" country growing porous-sharp, leaking information like water, leaching memory like chalk. And letting in a whole new flood of voices which settled on him locust-loud, showing him things he didn't know how he knew, and didn't *need* to, either.

Songbird scrying in a dish of mercury and fingering the scar he'd given her, bright red on her ghost-pale face. . . .

Some band of Injuns riding fast enough to raise dust, with a warrior at their head whose face he almost felt he *should* know, if only from someone else's memory. . . .

Doc Asbury in his travelling laboratory, throwing lightning between two steel balls—Pinkerton in his private train-car, scribbling dispatches—faceless agents dispersed to the wind, carrying all Chess and Morrow's particulars in their pockets—red Weed growing wild, constantly turning its many floral heads at once to search out Chess's scent, and re-orienting itself accordingly. . . .

While deep underground, Mictlan-Xibalba roiled like a crockpot, throwing up cracks and sickness . . . and to the north, that *city* grew: dark spires rising, mortared with spells and pain; Lady Ixchel looking down on it all, her empty face the moon set high above. While at her side stood an amused shadow, tall as some blood-watered tree.

This was how things had been for Asher Rook, Chess now understood—*just* like this, the entire Goddamn time. No wonder he did them things he did, with all this forever poking at him, never letting him rest.

Across the fire, Chess could see Morrow fixing him slant-eyed, with what was getting dangerously close to outright pity. To prevent himself from punching him right in the stupidly sentimental face, therefore, Chess broke off conversation entirely and lay down, trusting the annoying bastard to eventually follow suit.

TO SLEEP, HOWEVER, WAS always to lay oneself even further open, the way healing and infection both cracked a wound beyond its own stitchery.

Chess'd never been much of a one for reading—could do it in a pinch, but never for fun. But the dream began with words spilling out into the air before him—silver-white on black, reversed, thorny-twisted in the Gothic style. They hung there glinting, a spray of flickery nails. And next came the voice, as ever: Rook's rasping tones, echoing straight down into a man's groin. Reciting, while Chess felt his unwilling gaze pulled along those floating letters—

. . . HIS CHEEKS ARE LIKE BEDS OF SPICE
YIELDING PERFUME
HIS LIPS ARE LIKE LILIES
DRIPPING WITH MYRRH

HIS ARMS ARE LIKE UNTO RODS OF GOLD
SET ABOUT WITH CHRYSOLITE
HIS BELLY IS LIKE UNTO POLISHED IVORY
SET ABOUT WITH LAPIS LAZULI

HIS LEGS ARE LIKE UNTO PILLARS OF MARBLE
SET ON BASES OF PURE GOLD
HIS BODY IS LIKE UNTO LEBANON
CHOICE AS ITS CEDARS.
—SONG OF SOLOMON, *5:13 to 5:15.*

Adding: *That's you, Chess, sin and ruinous doom incarnate. And quite the prettiest thing I ever saw in my whole life, too—before, or after.*

Chess saw the sky peel away in front of him all at once, present becoming past with one quick rip, like lifting a scab—thrusting him back from this moment to that, from dream to memory, right into Rook's fond embrace. The two of them set up in front of some roadhouse cheval-glass, Chess perched on Rook's lap while the Rev hugged him hard from behind, curled into the bigger man's all-enveloping heat like a purring cat; stripped almost to his skin, with proof of desire pushing hard out the front of his small-clothes as he let Rook puppet him 'round, one hand grazing up through the red-gold fleece of Chess's chest to tweak at a nipple even as the other sank steadily lower, always travelling the other way . . . widdershins, counterclockwise. The broad and pleasant road to Hell.

FOR HE HATH MADE EVERY THING BEAUTIFUL IN HIS TIME; ALSO HE HATH SET THE WORLD IN THEIR HEART, SO THAT NO MAN CAN FIND OUT THE WORK THAT GOD MAKETH FROM BEGINNING TO END.—ECCLESIASTES, 3:11.

Chess frowned. *Wouldn't be puttin' a spell on me, would you, Reverend?*

Aw, now, Chess. Would I even have to?

Probably not, Chess realized, already defeated.

And even though just recalling how he'd once loved the man now sickened him . . . to have Rook's hands back on him, even in a dream . . . hell, it shortened Chess's breath. Made his chest's hollow squeeze like the bastard's fist was thrust deep inside, Rook's phantom pulse beating hard enough to light the both of 'em up like fireworks.

Missed you, darlin', Rook rumbled, into his neck. *You miss me?*

Not . . . as such.

Liar.

Well, you'd know, wouldn't you? 'Sides—you got her.

A dark laugh as answer. *Oh, now, don't sell yourself short. Maybe she missed you, too.*

You fuckin' son-of-a—

But Rook just stroked him, grasping at all Chess's most betraying spots—thumb and forefinger skinning the swollen head of Chess's cock, callused palm slicking briskly up and down, clever and inescapable. Chess arched, cursing his own response.

Uhhhh, shit, God fuckin' damn. . . .

Yeah, that's it. Just . . . like . . . that.

And now Rook too seemed caught up on the same wave of sensation, the same damnable trap—panting a bit himself, unable to quite keep from grinding against Chess's body. Both hands kept equal-busy, with one dipping lower still—right into the sweaty nest of him, to probe at its leisure for that oh-so-familiar entry-point.

Chess gritted his mental teeth, bit his equally mental lip. *You really think this is goin' to go that way, after all you done? Please.*

Rook laughed again, muffled into the sweaty nape of Chess's neck. *Still fussed over my methods—I understand that. But I do believe you'll thank me for it later.*

Hell I will!

Hell you won't. *You uncivilized, rude, improvident young man.*

Improvident—that mean selfish?

Rash, thriftless, not providing for the future. Which you don't much, do you?

Hell, no. I'll be dead long 'fore I gotta worry about that.

Into Chess's ear, a hot breath chased with a gentle bite: *Not if I can help it.*

And now you think you got me well *in hand, don't ya?* Chess thought, anger and desire messing with each other all through him, the way laudanum could be used to cut liquor. So he raised his chin to pin Rook fast with a backward glance, felt the Rev huff in quick, and smiled just a touch at the rush of power that reaction afforded him: *See? Still got it.* A quarter-turn more and they were staring straight at each other head-on, without the mirror to mediate; Chess felt it like a touch of fever, mildly vertiginous.

But then the whole scenario slid sideways, as it so often did in dreams, 'til Rook and Chess stood together on a balcony overlooking what Chess could only think must be Rook's new home. All around reared up buildings slapped together from rock, mud and magic, black and strangely shaped; smoke billowed up from a hundred chimneys, limned in heat-shimmer. The sky was the colour of sugared absinthe.

So, Rook "said," weirdly sociable. *Since you don't seem all too eager for my regular blandishments . . . here we are.* He swept one hand out, leaning back 'gainst the balcony's oddly sharp railing, its wrought iron curlicues reminiscent of those Chess had seen on row house verandahs. *Gaze upon New Aztectlan, o pilgrim, and wonder.*

Chess snorted. *Uh huh. This where you and her are supposed to be rulin' all America from, one of these days?*

That's the plan . . . part of it, anyhow. How's Agent Morrow, by the by?

We have our fun. Chess shot him another look. *Jealous?*

With a tiny tilt of the head: *Should I be?*

Just another mask, smirk and all—another prepared face, be it Good Man Gone Wrong, High Priest of Darkness or Unflappable Mastermind with a plot for every contingency, surprised by nothing. Might've even fooled Chess, he hadn't already seen its like so damn often. And maybe it was just the smoky gloom around them—the dream-sick unreality of everything that green light touched—but for a moment, Rook's face really *did* seem bone-hard, frozen in something more grimace than smile, its eyes dark as glass.

You're not lookin' too good, Ash. The words came out flat and quiet, wiping Rook's visage further, a scrubbed slate.

And after a moment, the answer came back—his mouth's utter stillness betraying this whole illusion, almost absently: *Probably not. But . . . I made my bed.*

Sure did, Chess thought, whip-quick—not *at* Rook per se, the way he had thus far. But not caring all too much if he happened to overhear, either.

Turning away, he saw the city's black blur immediately resolve, as though it felt his attention—ripen all over with squirmy detail, like a dead dog bred maggots. A raw smell struck him, all gunpowder, vomit and hot blood, like Chinee New Year in a San Fran slaughterhouse. Crowds reeled through the streets, their ruckus peculiarly muted, even as magic spilled brilliantly off them. Shapes blurred in flux; power arced from open mouth to open mouth; men and women danced and fought on empty air, easy as though it were solid ground.

Around them, meanwhile, buildings even larger than the front line could now be observed overhanging in unnaturally rock-smooth drapes, and it took Chess a moment to figure why: not a one of them bore the lines of brick and mortar, or even daub-sealed log palisades. Instead, every structure was a single seamless piece, some of granite, some marble or sandstone, some of wood still lined with bark and dripping with sap—as if they'd been raised up like clay out of living rock, or force-grown from tortured tree roots. And the tallest of all reared high directly opposite them, a step-pyramid temple with a great bonfire blaze at its peak, black column of smoke pouring upwards into the green clouds, an unending river of night.

What you got on the grill over there, exactly, makes it go so hot and bright? Chess demanded.

Oh, this 'n' that. Care to see?

Chess gave an angry sigh. He felt Rook work on him unceasingly—a pull like falling, the inexorability of sheer mass—and fought it, the only way he knew how: dirty.

I'm thinkin' it don't matter much to you, whether I do or don't, he snapped back. *But let me take a guess—that's your Moloch, ain't it? The Satan-hole you throw your own children down, on her command, and watch 'em as they burn to flinders.*

He'd known it soon as he laid eyes on it, from the very stink of the smoke. Tasted the power in the back of his throat, burnt and burning, the way that last drink you guzzled before puking left behind a taste you couldn't quite seem to part with.

The lure of it pulled at him like fish-hooks, so horrid, so profane. So . . . delicious.

And you did that to me too, you big bastard, Chess thought, dizzily nauseous with rage. *Gave me your disease, like you were dolin' out the clap; made me into just another hop-head. Put your jones into me and let it fester, knowing once I'd took my first jolt, I'd never be able to pull it back out.*

But Rook just shrugged. *Oh, it's only the stupid who go to feed the Machine. Those as can't keep control long enough to be useful.*

Chess felt that space under his ribs clutch again. *You doing them same's you did me?*

Hell, no. Think the Lady and me want more little gods runnin' 'round? No, they kill 'emselves, mainly—jump in the cistern, or throw ten-at-a-time necktie parties in the yaxche forest, down where the big roots grow. Seems they somehow got the idea it'll complete their 'transition.'

'Cause you told 'em so.

Well, we sure don't tell 'em any different.

Chess clenched his hands on the iron rail and he felt its edges press into both palms, vaguely flaky, as with rust or rotting paint. So *real*, and yet . . .

A dream, he told himself. *That's all this is. He can't touch me, not really.*

Not him. And not *her*, either.

Yet even as he formed the thought, he knew it in error. Because now he could feel the darkness clotting all around him, swallowing him whole. Shadow like mist to his waist and a disembodied mouth nuzzling at his parts, sweet-dreadful, rousing him like no other woman's ever could; wrong, Jesus, so damn *wrong*. A rising buzz. A rustling of papery wings.

Look down, risk just the quickest glance, and that black at his belt became her swirling hair—she looked up, smiled in welcome, her jade-chip teeth sharp.

I have waited so long to greet you again properly, my husband's husband. Poor, angry little warrior . . .

Oh God, get the hell AWAY—

Rainbow Lady Ixchel taking shape, summoned the faster by his fear, in all her awful glory. To wrap herself 'round him just like she'd done that endless night at Splitfoot Joe's, screwing down onto him and riding him for her pleasure. When he'd been at her mercy, and Rook hadn't done a damn thing to help—just pushed them closer together with one hand on Chess's sick-sweaty back, so she could have her will.

Watch how our holy city comes to life, she murmured, almost fondly, licking at his ear. *This is what was meant to be, what must be—and you should be here to see it, so they can lie prostrate before you, do you due worship. So they see for themselves the God for whom all this was made.*

Chess shrugged himself free of her, well aware he only had the juice to do so because of what she—and Rook—had wrought him into, and bitterly resenting it. But damn, it felt fine to do so, anyhow. Far too fine to stop.

And here he felt it again, all over, unwilling but undeniable: that *power*, Glossing's and otherwise, torrenting down into him from every direction. Making him fume and spark out every pore at once, as though his whole body were a fuse lit by some unknown hand.

Don't want none of your . . . tribute, damnit! He snarled, lips fletched back to the canines.

Yet it comes to you nevertheless, she pointed out. **It all goes to you, so you can do what you must. Intent does not matter; your blood cries out, and theirs answers. The river flows in only one direction.**

Chess tried to spit in her mocking face, but the dragonfly cloak she wore whisked her away, depositing her neatly out of range. So he did the next best thing, and drew on her instead—cocked back the hammer, snarl sliding straight to grin.

Uh huh. Well, stand still a while, bitch—'cause for all I ain't much of a debater, I think I maybe got you a suitable rebuttal right here.

Ixchel considered him, her chill gaze moon-calm. The venom-green sky behind her gave her olive skin the tint of verdigris, made her face a tarnished copper mask. **There is nothing you could do to me, little killer, even were your weapons real. As we all three of us know.**

Goin' by history alone, I could probably at least perforate that carcass you're wearin'—just like Ed Morrow did, down in Hell's half-acre. Or did you forget about that?

She clicked her tongue. **Unruly! You should have been beaten with nettle switches.** Throwing her eyes Rook's way: **Must he always be so difficult, husband?**

Rook's mouth twitched, fond and rueful. *Must, I don't know about. Is, though, usually.*

You'd know, Chess thought.

But Rook was already talking at him again—voice affectionate, a laudable parody thereof—*Listen, darlin'—remember back when I first woke up, after they swung me? How I was stuck working from the Bible, as though if I didn't quote Verse on what I had in mind, then nothing was like to happen? Well, that was my mistake. What I knew best, so I wouldn't let it go . . . assumed I needed it, when really . . .*

. . . he does not. And never did.

Magic ain't a gun, Chess; you can't treat it as such, or it'll blow up in your hand. And I know that eventually, you'll outgrow thinking life's a problem best solved with a bullet . . . but we can't wait for that.

Chess guffawed, nastily. *Oh, spare me. Think all you got to do is feel on me some in a dream, and I'll do your damn will from then on? That's some cheap ride you 'spect to take on me, Reverend; thought I taught you better that-a-ways, at least 'bout how my Ma told me to reckon myself.*

Rook contemplated him a heartbeat, with what almost looked like—sorrow? Insult?

I'll never love anyone like I loved you, Chess, he said. *Believe it or don't.*

That'd be 'don't.'

Ixchel gave a laugh of her own, eking up slow as if it came from deep down under-earth, where all Mictlan-Xibalba's horrors lurked. The cogs of some 'quake-engine cut from stone and greased with bone-dust, grating against each other.

Your prerogative, Rook allowed. *Consider this, though. For all Ed's a decent sort, he ain't like you or I. The longer you stick with people like him, whether it's for fancy or to pay us back, or just to stick your thumb in God's eye awhile—the more you'll bring down on their heads. You're a plague to normal citizenry now, Chess, even more so than you ever were. Hexes will come and dash 'emselves against you, go up like rockets, and catch everyone else around in the back-blast.*

Unable to stop himself, Chess saw Glossing's dying face—those rabbit-eyes closing, lids twitching dimly, like he was almost *glad* to bid farewell to any world held Chess in it. Heard those townsfolk yelling trash at him, and felt his free hand fist, itching to blast 'em where they stood.

Which is why, Ixchel put in, **you must accept what you are: our Flayed Lord, red god of red Weed, Opener of our Way. Fight this, and you only fight yourself.**

Chess bristled. *So now you come at me both together, I'm s'posed to just roll over? Screw that, and screw all them other motherfuckers, likewise! You put this shit on me—hoodooed me into sayin' yes, then went* on and did it anyways, even when I stopped. Which is where you both fucked up, or so your Enemy tells me. . . .

Oh, be silent! Even Rook took a step back as the air around Ixchel blazed, stone thrumming beneath her bare feet; the city itself seemed to shimmer and recede. **Do you think yourself special? We were all of us ixiptla, once upon a time—**

(even me, even)

(HE)

A flood of images behind his eyes—or did that work, seeing his eyes were closed already? Chess saw blood and bone and stone knives tearing, heard alien words and *knew* their meanings before she was done speaking them, before their vowel sounds had scratched his ears' drums. *Tlacacaliztli*, piercing with arrows. *Tlahuahuanaliztli*, gladiatorial combat. *Tlacamictiliztli*, extraction of the heart . . .

(His breastbone aching in sympathy, cleft and barely re-sewn, each no-beat of his own missing organ a hammer-blow echoing from the *inside* out.)

Cold crush of drowning. Dirt in your lungs, from burial alive. A drawn mouthful of searing heat, as skin-girt priests swung you over the sacrificial fire. Crunch and *chunk* of separation as your head was wrenched free, placed high in pride on the *tzompantli*, before your body was thrown down an endless flight of steps to slam square at the apex of a far smaller pyramid made from limp, cooling human meat.

(And that was worse, somehow. To feel even a moment's sympathy—not for *her*, so much. But for the girl she'd once been.)

And now the city was gone again, the sky once more a starless but honest black, leaving he, Rook, and the Lady alone on a flat grey plain. Chess reholstered his guns, lifted his hands up between him and his tormentors, palm-out, half shield, half absolute refusal.

Get outta my dream, he told them, hard as he could. *You ain't makin' me do nothin'—I won't be rode, let alone broken. Goddamn you both! I will* not *do what I won't!*

Rook was a towering, fading silhouette, recognizable only to one who knew the shape of his features in the dark. *Okay, darlin'. But, see—problem is—*

*—you will, **Chess Pargeter**. As we all must, eventually.*

IT WAS A MOMENT before Chess realized he was finally awake, for good and true; the smoky smell of campfire embers rose in the desert chill, unblurred by furnace-reek or magic's stinging tang. He held his breath, and waited.

The world stayed as it was, unchanging.

Chess let out a huge sigh, and was struck abruptly with an almighty need to piss, which drew a laugh. Cheered immeasurably, he rolled to his left, away from the campfire, hit something rough, then looked up—and up, and up.

Twelve feet tall, black as tar and shiny as glass, head and shoulders blazing with blue fire, the Enemy—Ixchel's, Rook's, his, the whole wide world's—grinned back down at him, its teeth like knives.

She is right, of course, it said.

Chess crab-scrabbled backwards so the fire was between 'em, anything to get away. Then glanced down himself, all unthinking, and screamed out loud.

CHAPTER THREE

"SEEMED NOTHIN' OUT OF the usual, when we went to bed," the man—Yancey Colder thought his name might be Frewer, but wasn't sure—began, eyes kept careful on the teacup he held balanced on one skinny knee. "I mean . . . sure, that business with Dentist Glossing, earlier, but—everything'd been already took away, street swept clear of bad rubbish. Was warm and fine that night, red skies for a clement morning, not one cloud on the horizon. . . ." He trailed away, head shaking slightly. "And then . . ."

"Then?" Yancey's Pa encouraged.

"My woman woke me, 'round about four of the clock. Said she heard this sound like something tearing, off in the distance. But when I went to take a look out the window, I couldn't get the shutters open, 'cause they were weighted down with all sorts of . . . *bugs*, and other awfulness—grasshoppers, chiggers, furry-winged moths. Devil's darning needles the size of pie-plates, rubbin' 'emselves together 'til the hum went up too loud to yell over."

"How long'd this-all go on?" asked Sheriff Haish from his place in the corner, leaning back in his chair. Up 'til now, he'd seemed far more interested in his chaw of tobacco than in Mister Frewer's story, but Yancey guessed that was mainly for show.

"A goodly piece after dawn." The cup trembled between Frewer's long hands, thin china squeaking dangerously. "We just sat there with our arms 'round the children, hangin' on for dear life. Noise got so loud near the end, by God, it like to've drove us mad."

Pa and the Sheriff exchanged a glance, but seemed to agree to let him set his own pace.

"When I *was* able to wedge the door," Mister Frewer said, at last, "the street was *gone*, all of it. Like it'd never even been. Nothin' left but this low rut through a tangle of roots, and every other house just slick with crawler-juice, and this *smell* in the air—Christ Almighty, like when that whole farm died of Yellow Jack in high summer, but nobody twigged 'til a week and a half later. All it lacked was for maggots."

He took a shallow breath. "Happened to glance east then, where the tooth-pull shop used t'stand, and it was one big green knot, like kudzu. 'Cept for it had little red bell-flowers hung on it every-which-where, gaped wide, like snappin' mouths."

"I never heard tell of Weed grown up that fast," a fresh voice—Mister Mergenthal, Hoffstedt's Hoard's only butcher—piped up, nearer to the room's back end, where Yancey had made sure the half-open door blocked Pa from any sudden view of her eavesdropping. "So . . . what'd y'all *do*?"

Frewer shrugged, hapless. "Might've come about from them hexes havin' a shoot-out in the middle of Main Street, I s'pose, the day before—"

"Who and who?"

"One was Doc Glossing, the dentist, like I already said—not that most've us knew he was hexacious before that, at least not for sure. And the other was that new-turned 'slinger, Reverend Rook's boy—"

Sheriff Haish scowled, and let fly into the spittoon. "Chess damn *Pargeter* shot up your town, and you didn't think anything would come of it?"

"Well, he left, right after. So . . . no, we didn't. Not like *that*, anyways."

Pa frowned too, but refrained from expectoration. "Hold up, though. Pargeter's a pistoleer only, I'd always heard."

"Don't know why the Doc would'a tried to take a pull on 'im in the first place, he wasn't good for the effort. And believe me . . ." Frewer shook his head again, as though to clear it. "Seemed like Pargeter gave just as good as he got, in that direction."

Haish blew out a breath. "Well, *that* ain't good news. Damn little redheaded . . . *creature* was touched enough, back when he was only humanish. And how'd two mages get cleft together in the first place anyhow, even with one of 'em not yet at full effect? 'Don't meddle,' my ass."

The other conclavists looked each-to-each, equally unhappy. "Maybe it really *is* catchin'," Mergenthal suggested.

"Highly unlikely, I'd think," Pa began, in reply, colliding headlong with Haish's: "Goddamn, man, shut your hole! Think we most've us all know a happy load'a horseshit, when we hear it. . . ."

"As it turns out—yes."

Marshal Uther Kloves normally spoke so deadpan that most folks tended to suspect him of jesting, whatever he said. It was one of the things most endeared him to Yancey, but it did make for difficulty in terms of figuring out exactly where he was headed, in public addresses.

"I've had telegrams from all the other Territories," he explained. "Utah, Colorado—far north as Wyoming, even west of the Colorado River. Always it's the same: once the Weed gets a foothold, there's only one thing makes it die."

"Fire?"

"Blood."

"*Any* blood?" Mergenthal said, his interest suddenly piqued— he'd his share of back-stores, after all, Yancey knew. And if perhaps there was money to be made . . .

Yancey could imagine Kloves giving that near-imperceptible little shake of his head. "Human. Fresh-spilled."

A beat of silence, eventually broken by Pa, bewildered: "But . . . that don't make any *sense*."

"Hexation's at the bottom of all this, Lionel," said Kloves. "Don't go holdin' your breath, waitin' for things to add up square."

Someone else cleared their throat. "Well, they do say the Weed

doesn't usually grow up so fast as Mister Frewer tells of."
Incongruously light and pleasant, this voice, though Yancey thought
she recognized it as belonging to the mysterious Mister Grey, a tall,
youngish fellow just starting on a serious walrus moustache, who'd
rode into Hoffstedt's Hoard only a few days ago. "But that may
indeed be overspillage from this hex-battle 'twixt Pargeter and—
Glossing, was it? The blood part, however, that's true. I've seen it.
Bleed a cupped double-handful from, say, five or six folks, spill it
over the Weed and it dries up to powder inside of three days." He
paused. "Even heard a few claim their soil was the richer for it, after."

"That so?" Frewer's mouth twisted, teacup slipping to thump
the thick carpet, thankfully unbroken. "So all's we have to do is
offer up abomination, like the damn Philistines and Pharisees, and
hey presto? Good Christ above, let *that* rumour fly free and folk'll
be pulling bad neighbours in off the streets, tellin' 'emselves it's
better to cut one to save ten! You ever *seen* Weed-infected livestock,
Mister?"

Yancey hadn't—but recalled all too well accounts she'd read,
sprinkled over every news-sheet the Cold Mountain Hotel received.
A cattle drive coming up through Bisbee had stopped in the wrong
place for the night; the cowboys had woken to find their thousand
head staggering 'round like they had worms—kicking, falling,
dying. And then, once the renderers arrived to do due diligence,
they'd found turkey vultures scattered dead every which way, wings
and beaks entangled with fibres . . . after which the first tentative
cuts had loosed a flood of guts stuffed with Weed, whose blossoms
raised themselves up like snails' stalk-eyes to the sun, seeming to
peer 'round for fresher prey.

Excise such places by fire, to the ground, then salt them over as
Biblically prescribed, that was the common-held wisdom. Or wait for
the government men to do much the same, under strict legality—but
people seldom did. Most, like Mouth-of-Praise's former citizenry,
this ragged band of new-made refugees now shivering in Pa's first-
floor saloon-cum-parlour arrangement, simply fled.

"We had to burn near everything, in the end," Mister Frewer

said, at last. "'Fore it seeded. And since blood won't bring that back, I don't hold it'd do the rest of us any manner of good, to know we might've saved ourselves the trouble."

A long tick of Pa's desk clock passed, before Sheriff Haish spoke again. "Mister Frewer, just how many of your fellow townsfolk came with you, after the fire?"

"All of 'em, near as I figure. A hundred and twenty, thirty—fifty? We didn't take no census."

Kloves nodded. "Hard to fault you. All the same, Mister Frewer, we *are* going to have to talk this over somewhat. So, your kind permission . . ."

"Yeah—yes. 'Course." Though stumble-footed, Frewer still made the door fast enough that Yancey barely had time to duck into the linen closet, reduced to watching him stagger back down to where the rest of his delegation waited, through the half-cracked door. Then, soon as he'd vanished, she counted herself safe to take up station outside Pa's doorway once more.

". . . can't just let 'em *in!*" Hugo Hoffstedt, the tobacconist, was saying; a distant cousin of the town's founding family, he was a coward and a snob, but wealthy. "Am I the only man here not a fool?"

"Now, Hugo," Pa protested. "Christian charity—"

"Don't you preach at me, Lionel Colder, with Miss Yancey set to marry and your son-in-law-to-be right here within earshot—*your* family's jeopardized, just as much as mine! What if the Weed chases after their stink and we have to burn down the Hoard, too?"

Sheriff Haish rolled his eyes. "There's no proven evidence the Weed *follows* folks—"

"There's no *proven* evidence it don't!"

An argument impossible to pursue, let alone rebut—but the Marshal, often the coolest head in any room, didn't even try.

"Mister Hoffstedt has a point," he allowed. "In these disordered times, might be all too easy to think Mouth-of-Praise's 'misfortune' a tad convenient, a good excuse to get 'emselves dug inside our borders, so they could kill us in our beds and take all we have . . . but lookin' at poor Mister Frewer, how likely does *that* seem?"

A murmur of agreement ran through the room, and even Hoffstedt had the good grace to look a tiny bit ashamed for something he hadn't actually stated directly. Easy to see how Kloves rose so quickly to his current position, by the relatively young age of seven-and-twenty; he'd parlayed leadership skills hard-won in battle into a peacetime efficacy. Yancey knew all too well he had already impressed her Pa as worthy of every support he could afford . . . including the boon of her own hand in marriage.

He's a good man, gal. I have to think of your future, what with your Mama gone—don't want to work my hotel 'til you're staring at spinsterhood, do you? All I want's your happiness.

She felt her head dip at the truth of it, automatic. For there were no fairy tales in this life, only patterns of supply and exchange—rules, regulations, methods and manners of payment. And she knew all *that* well enough, too; had the very job Pa thought to save her from, to thank for it.

"No," Kloves said, "the Weed's undeniable, as both fact and threat. 'Sides which, you don't want to back rats into a corner, when they're desperate . . . not if it's a whole bunch of rats, armed, and it's *your* corner."

Hoffstedt said: "Well, that's your job, ain't it? To keep us safe."

Pa: "Easiest way to do *that* is act like we ought. Right, Sheriff?"

"Right."

"Then let's put it to the vote, shall we?" Kloves said. "Just so nobody thinks what I suggest carries—this bein' a democracy, same's every other part of these United States."

You diplomat. Yancey shook her head, amused despite herself. *Albeit one with a nice shiny tin star, and a gun to back it up.*

Seemed that shame counted for just as much as fear, however. The vote was unanimous, letting Mouth-of-Praise's stragglers stay—for now.

"All right, gents," Pa said, rising, "I believe we'll end in the loungerie, with drinks on the house. And Experiance, don't think

I don't see you there, gal. Gonna be a sight of extra toil to do today, so go finish up with your regular chores, will you? I expect I'll need your help most of all."

Flatterer, she thought; *costs* you *nothing, ties* me *up all day.* But merely said, out loud: "Yes, Pa."

He snorted, unimpressed by such acquiescence. To Kloves: "Cute little missy, she is—too much so for her own good, or mine. I do believe you've got your work cut out for you, Marshal."

Kloves, meanwhile—Uther—looked full at Yancey, mouth tightening in something which might as well be a smile as a frown. *Am I work for you?* she felt like asking.

"I know," the man who would soon be her husband replied, with preternatural aptness—to Pa, supposedly, though Yancey knew better. So she turned away, dropping a little bobbed half-curtsey to them both, yet still unable to avoid smiling a bit herself, as she did.

Oh, she supposed she *did* feel for him, after all, "arrangement" or not. And most 'specially so at times like these.

Then again, wasn't as though there was any other option.

HOFFSTEDT'S HOARD HAD GOTTEN its name from the wealth its founder used to build it, the yield of an early strike of '48, after 'Frisco's *California Star* set off what folks now called a Gold Rush by trumpeting the find near Sutter's Mill. Built around a grouping of strongly fed wells, it formed a natural way-station in the midst of the Gadsden Purchase of '53, near-exact between Las Cruces and Tucson and close upon the Arizona border. The Cold Mountain Hotel was one of its oldest buildings.

'Course, Yancey herself never had quite gotten a clear answer from Lionel on the question of why a promising young clerk in Boston would suddenly up stakes, hauling his new wife and baby girl clear across the continent and headlong into a vocation she wasn't even sure *he* derived all that much enjoyment from. But her Mama had let slip some hints, and Yancey'd made some guesses.

Considered closely, Lionel's claim to Christianity seemed an absentminded, perfunctory thing at best, and this skill with finance had often provoked the odd angry mutter about "moneylenders"—mutters she would have disregarded entirely if Lionel himself hadn't always flushed and changed the subject, and gained context once she'd heard a few sermons from Pastor Cambrell on the Bible's low opinion concerning usury.

For herself, whatever the Pastor might say, Yancey'd long since learned to appreciate any system made folks want to keep their word. But she'd also begun to glean why Cardinal Dagger John Hughes' Boston wouldn't've seemed the friendliest town twenty years back, not as a flood of even more Church-rode Irish poured in. Couple the burden of secret Jewry with falling hard for a half-gypsy girl from the Old World's darker parts—a girl whose disquietingly apt predictions would draw eyes anywhere, but particularly amongst those attuned for witchery's traces—and Yancey thought Lionel might well have been just the sort of fellow to broach the idea that perhaps the West would offer a far more secure future than the East.

Experiance (thus named due to a drunken clerk's misspelling, which Mala Colder had refused to correct) having been less than a year old when they arrived in the Hoard, it was safe to say she knew literally no other place. The town, and the hotel, had grown as she had; she could track her years as well by recalling when certain chairs had first begun to grace the lounge or china patterns to fill the shelves as she might by reckoning her height's increase through those faint marks Lionel cut into the kitchen door frame.

In an odd way, this familiarity mitigated that restlessness Yancey knew stirred in the breast of most young folks—she felt too close to the Cold Mountain and the Hoard, too much a part of them, to ever feel easy at the thought of leaving. Oh, she dreamed of seeing the world; who didn't? And that yearning'd grown only more acute after Mala's passing, two years previous . . . along with another class of future vision entirely, the kind you didn't tend to talk about, except with those who shared the same facility.

On the cold April night after her first courses—a cause for quiet celebration, seeing her schoolhouse friends had all passed that milestone some time hence—she'd gone to sleep happy, only to wake shuddering with cannon-fire images ringing through her head. Thunder, broken walls above a moonlit ocean, a falling flag. When she'd asked Mala what it meant, Mala had said only, *Wait and see*. Three days on, papers began to ship in with the answer as their headlines: FORT SUMTER ATTACKED, varying tales of predawn bombardment, the Carolina outpost's capture. The War Between the States, begun at last.

It *wasn't* hexation, Mala had hastened to assure her; something less powerful but also far less dangerous, in the main. Still, these sudden flashes of insight (nighttime and otherwise) did come with a perilous knack for attracting the strange, as well as knowing it upon sight.

We are nothing so grand as they, Mala had said, *yet these . . . hexes . . . may be drawn to us, nevertheless. And though they can't batten on us as they do their own, the younger may kill you by trying before figuring that out, while their elders may decide that to brook no competition is always the better policy. It behooves us to know how to spot them, therefore—so we can run the other way.*

Remembering, also, she'd added, after a pause, *that to most without even a touch of the strange, such difference in degree means nothing. What they'll do to hexes they'll do to us as well, if we give them reason.*

An image had flashed between them, then—shared memory made visible, something Yancey'd never thought unusual, until that day. Didn't *all* mothers and daughters occasionally know what the other was thinking, after all? But here it came, spilling out palpable as if Yancey'd lived it herself, with no prompt but Mala's cool hand on hers:

A rake-thin girl, half-naked and bruised, fleeing her hovel while the rest of the village celebrated, unaware / a smaller child turning to see, alerted by some unstruck bell—Mala, as was / fire, flaring from the girl's blood-stained palms as a drunken man emerged after her, setting both him and his home ablaze / screams rising as light leapt from roof to roof, hungry-searing, eating *everything*—

And then, what was left of the village smoking black, the witch-girl bound fast amidst a pile of kindling, too tired even to weep.

As the headman declaimed hoarsely, black coat flapping in a frosty wind: *We burn* her, *or they burn* us. *No other way. You* all *know it!*

Were those tears frozen to his face?

The torchbearer, approaching. Mala's parents stood elbow-to-shoulder with the rest, mouths resolutely shut, her mother trying to angle her away. But the witch-girl's eyes sought her out, needle-through-cloth deft, to stitch their minds together just as the torchbearer's hand dipped down—telling her, without a sound—*Watch them burn me now, sister, like the* gadje *will burn them anyhow, half a year on. Like they'd burn you too, if only they knew what you are.* . . .

Yancey'd wrenched herself free, then, knowing—as Mala already knew she knew—that this was the one possible future they could never flee; that even poor, adoring Lionel, only half-aware of his wife's true talents, could never be allowed complete comprehension, lest he admit his doubts to the wrong person.

At Mala Colder's funeral, everyone had praised Lionel for raising such a self-possessed daughter, so strong and steady, her tears kept decorously muted. But what none of them understood was that Mala's fatal sickness had been no surprise to Yancey, or to Mala. It had been long months since they'd noticed a shadowed figure first standing by the Cold Mountain's saloon door, then at the end of every hall, reflected in every mirror's middle distance. Far more sad than menacing, oddly enough, but as inexorable as any laid pyre. So Mala and Yancey had said their goodbyes already, long before the doctor ever broke it to Lionel, who would never be quite the same again.

Still, nothing in this world came entirely unleavened by its opposite. It had been at the wake following that Uther Kloves, then but new-come to town, hesitantly asked her and her father both at once—a courtesy she'd found impressive—if he might court her for a time, see if they suited. Yancey had become honest enough with herself by then to admit she was flattered: the Marshal, undeniably pleasant to the eye, seemed decent enough, an impression borne out by his patient and gentlemanly behaviour. And so . . .

And so.

She crossed briskly through the parlour, doling out smiles and taking orders.

Near the window, she observed Hugo Hoffstedt deep in whispery congress with Mister Frewer—or Hugo talking *at* Frewer, rather, while Frewer sipped his shot. "Bein' a family man yourself, I know you understand," he said. "So just tell me *nothin'* followed you, and I'll be well-content."

"Never said that."

". . . what?"

"Out in the desert, ridin' hard to get here . . . might be I saw something then, far off, with a sort of glister to it. All white, like snow—or salt."

"Keeping pace with you?" Frewer nodded. "And you didn't think to mention this, upstairs?"

"Thing is, Mister Hoffstedt, I don't think it was *us* it was following. Just that we happened in between it and whatever it *was* after, is all. And given how fast it travelled, I reckon it could've caught up pretty easy, we *were* what it wanted. So . . ."

That same weary shrug, one more mystery in a string of mysteries. Yancey reckoned that was how a surfeit of miracles hit most folks—just plumb wore 'em out.

"But what *was* it?"

"As to that . . . hope I never come to find out."

She sensed Uther a second before his hand touched her shoulder; could almost hear his smile as he leaned close, to murmur in one ear. "I'd tell you not to fret about this, but you'd just give me that look, wouldn't you?"

Yancey let one corner of her mouth quirk up. The Marshal did sometimes let his chivalrous inclinations get the better of him, but he could usually be relied upon to be straight with her; too much the pragmatist to pass up any fresh perspective, no matter its origins. Which meant he'd tell her what she needed to know, sooner or later.

Yet another reason (as Pa kept on reminding her) it'd be so advantageous to find herself this nice young man's wife. But she couldn't think too long about that, in any great detail, or she might figure out exactly what affections she had for Uther, beyond the sadly practical.

By Mala's own admission, there'd been a fair bit of flat calculation in her choosing Lionel Colder—a charming man with his own secrets to keep, who'd have little inclination to paw through his wife's metaphorical lock-box. Whatever detachment she'd brought into the marriage-bed had long since vanished by the time Yancey was old enough to look for it, however. Her parents had loved one another deeply, by the end—a bond all the stronger for having been forced to grow steadily, rather than flare high and fizzle.

The Marshal, meanwhile, was solicitous, brave, fair set up for future prosperity. But the difference between his love and her parents' was like a rope bridge set against an iron-girdered train track. Though both would get you over the gaps, one felt merely . . . adequate.

Nevertheless, she leaned forward, eyes crinkling. "Do I *need* to fret, Uther?"

"Can't really say, as yet. The Weed *has* seemed to cut itself a path, though I don't know . . ." He stopped. "Yancey? You all right?"

She shook her head, knowing the smile she'd worked so hard over must be abruptly gone. "Just realized there's a whole other round of chores needs doing—gotta swap out the linens." She stretched up on tiptoe to gift him with a brief peck. "I'll see you tonight."

"Yancey! Enough canoodling!" Pa was trying for a glare, but his voice held that slight crack she knew proved him more jocular than angry. With a wave to them both, she ducked her head and slid from the room, soon halfway to the second floor, where her true errand awaited.

Avoiding the hall's creakiest boards, she eased her way down to the door of what Pa still optimistically insisted on calling the Bridal Suite—their largest bedroom, refurbished with an excess of lace doilies, fine quilts and pomanders. Certainly, the two guests who'd checked in a half-week back didn't meet anyone's definition of a honeymoon couple.

'Cept for their own, perhaps, she thought. And blushed for herself, at the very idea of someone of her tender age being well aware what that euphemism might mean.

A hotel was no fit place for a lady of true delicacy, she'd always heard. But then—from Yancey Colder's point of view, safe was better than sorry. And to *know* was always safer, by damn far, than not.

Took one moment more for her to find the nerve she needed. Then she lifted one brisk fist to rap on the door—only to see it cracked open with unexpected abruptness, grey-brown eyes peering down hard at her through the narrow gap.

"Don't need any towels," growled the man, who'd given his name as "Chester," on registration. ("Mister . . . Chester, that is. Senior." "And your brother, sir?" "Well . . . he'd be Mister Chester too, 'course. Junior.")

But Yancey, who could tell the ostensible irritation masked wariness, felt suddenly that much more confident.

"Not what I'm here for, sir. Would you let me in to check the levels in your oil lamps?"

"Would *you* go away, I tell you no?"

"Honestly? No." Yancey didn't smile, holding his hazel eyes with her own similar-coloured gaze. "Because, you see—I know who you really are, Mister Morrow. Both of you."

At this, he just stared, open-mouthed. While she, in turn, indicated the unseen room beyond—along with its other, equally unseen, occupant.

"May I come in?" Yancey Colder repeated, patiently.

"Might as well," Chess Pargeter replied, from inside.

CHAPTER FOUR

Five days back:

THE DREAM TOOK HOLD without warning—one moment Morrow was alone in his own skull, sunk deep in darkness and not missing all too much, so long as the pain in his jaw stayed gloriously absent. Next, however, he found himself sat up alongside Reverend Rook in one of a matched pair of chairs cunningly cobbled together from what looked—and felt, horribly—like bone: slim, slick, yellowed like ivory, bound haphazardly together with sinew and hexation alike.

What hit Morrow like a knife through the gut, though, was the *where* of it all: a wide plain, acres in size, wheat rippling like a wind-tossed sea. At the far edge, Morrow knew, a zigzag splinter-board fence divided their lot from its neighbour; a tall man silhouetted against the sunset light was using the day's last hours to continue scything there, slow and steady. Morrow felt the land's faint slope under his feet, rising gradually to the three-roomed farmhouse and silo behind him. The air smelled of grain, woodsmoke, and autumn.

Rook breathed deep, smiling. Huge, black-clad, framed in jagged yellow bone, his very presence made a tangible hole. "Now *this*," he said, "is a place for the righteous, Ed. No wonder you got so much do-gooder in you." He leaned back, hands behind his head. "I wonder if you even know just how lucky you were."

Morrow shut his eyes a second; he didn't want to remember those chairs, or Rook, in this place. "Ain't it strange," he said, carefully, "how the friendliest thing you ever said to me comes out like you mean it to insult."

Rook chuckled, deep in his throat. In the distance, unseen, Morrow's father kept on cutting. "Well, well. Guess you ain't quite so scared of me as you used to be, after all. How's the tooth?"

Morrow's hand went to his face, involuntarily. "This's just a dream, ain't it? So I don't reckon it matters a damn what it's like, *here*."

"Dream world, real world—no border's exactly what it used to be, given what's passed. You've already seen how hard it is to hurt Chess now, and make it stick; well, stand by him, stay close, and that'll be you, too. Can't have the Skinless Man's prophet kickin' off premature from something as stupid as tooth rot, either, even hex-imposed."

Morrow considered that. "So . . . nothing can kill me?"

"*Chess* could."

"He's had more'n enough chances to, he wanted." Morrow faced Rook square on, no longer afraid. "Which means . . . he don't. And he won't."

Rook shook his head, chuckling again. "Ed, Ed! And you the one who pointed out to *me* how Chess'll do any damn thing at all, the moment he thinks somebody expects the opposite. Oh no, believe you me, 'Agent' Morrow—" The smile faded. "He *will* turn on you, sooner or later, like he does everyone else. Won't even be able to stop himself."

"I think that's yourself you're thinkin' of, Reverend."

"We'll see."

Morrow felt a rush of something unfamiliar spill up from inside him, hot like bile, and only realized at the last possible instant it must be rage not on his own behalf, but on Chess's.

"As for me actin' Chess's John the Baptist, or what-have-you," he went on, refusing to be drawn, "I ain't done all too much to spread that bloody gospel of yours as yet, if you've been watching."

"Noticed that, yes." A dark grin: "Feelin' guilty?"

"Not as such. You . . . feelin' mad?"

Rook fixed him again, longer this time, like: *Not as such.*

"There's one or two things you can't know, Ed," was all he had by way of an answer. "And 'fore you ask, what I mean by that is—you can really only see half the show, from where you're sat."

Morrow's heart stuttered, just a bit. "And Chess . . . how much can *he* see, exactly?"

Rook shrugged again. "More than he wants to, I'm sure. But less by far than he knows he needs to."

Morrow took a deep breath, mind whirring like Asbury's shattered Manifold. "What is it you want, Ash Rook?"

Rook sighed, and suddenly the sky was black as his coat, star-studded, cold. Blue fire flickered like heat lightning along the horizon. "Something's comin', and nothing of mine, or my Lady's. More to do with that Enemy of Chess's, I reckon."

Which one? Morrow thought, confused.

"'Course, for all you know, I *could* just be spinnin' you more tales." Rook spread his hands. "But like I said—ain't as big a difference between the two of you as it used to be. Or all three of us, for that matter."

From somewhere else, Chess Pargeter screamed out loud.

AND HERE WAS WHERE Morrow rocketed straight back up into the debatably real world, only to find it deformed by yet another nightmare. Across the dead campfire's smoking blister, Chess thrashed and kicked beneath an undulating blanket of amorously seeking Weed that'd obviously followed them 'cross the desert, tracing Chess's delicious spoor, and now snuggled against him from every angle, stroking him with its many tendrils. In far too many spots to count, Morrow saw its meaty red-green furls broken up with dull ivory bone fragments which must've swum up through the dirt to get there, drawn by a similar hopeful hunger. These fought against each other like puppies at the teat, desperate to bury 'emselves once more *inside* him.

"Jesus!" Chess cursed, his voice skewing frighteningly high, scrabbling them away with both fists while they leaped and snapped in successive waves, quotidian, inexplicable. "You filthy little bastards—Goddamn fucking *magic*! Motherfuck damn Hell shit-ass *Christ*!"

Without thinking, Morrow caught one of Chess's flailing hands between his palms; he hauled 'til his shoulder popped, bracing his boot against the fire pit's rock-set rim. At last Chess came slithering free with a juicy rip, right into Morrow's embrace. The vine-bone mélange turned, seeking eyelessly, and swarmed its way after; when Morrow stomped a few of the tendrils into muck, the others hissed at him, spitting acid that made his boot-tips smoke.

Now upright, Chess had already slipped behind him, using the bigger man's bulk as a shield. "*Do* something!" he demanded, as Morrow whirled and swore.

"Hell, *you* do something!" Morrow swung his duster off his shoulders and used it to lash at the Weed, whipping it back. "Make it go away, like before—"

"'Begone'? That's exactly what I *been* telling it! It just don't damn well listen!"

And this, an amused voice said, inside both their skulls at once, ***is what your priest-king spoke of, little brother, when he warned you that you must learn a better way to deal with such matters or suffer the consequences . . . along with everyone else.***

Who said that? Morrow thought. But Chess's eyes had already flicked straight to the left, and Morrow followed them, automatically. To see something looming there in the dark beyond, born from it, birthing it—something grinning, bigger than a house, a pitch-smeared hulk whose brow leaked fire and mouth leaked smoke. Whose teeth, like the interior of the Rainbow Lady's perforated head when Morrow'd shot her in the Moon Room, were a wailing forest of tiny red faces, generation on generation of those killed to keep her all-fired Blood Engine going.

Oh, this creature said, admiringly, *so you can think. Then he does well to keep you by him after all, soldier.*

Under its gaze, the Weed had pulled back, finally, and now lay cowering in a lop-shaped circle, all a-tremble like pilgrims at the Rock. Morrow swallowed, mouth suddenly so dry he could barely taste his own tongue.

"You . . . you'd be that Enemy the Rev was talkin' 'bout, wouldn't you?"

I would.

"Same one we call Satan, that it? Or is that somebody else entirely?"

The hulk shook its grinning, smoking head, just once, with surprising dignity.

I do not know this name, it told him. *But you and I have met before, albeit only briefly; certainly, you have heard my progress through the dark, if nothing else. Remember? Like this.*

It straightened, spreading great columnar arms and more, as the thing's ribs swung back as well, charcoal-hued glass doors gaping wide into nothingness: the hole, the crack, a wound between reality and Hell. For a second it yawned, then clapped shut, a club smacking home against bone, hard enough to fracture.

Unfolded, in a gust of freezing wind; clapped shut: *whoosh-crack! Whoosh-craaack!*

He *had* heard this before: in a Tampico hotel room, heralding Rook's appearance in the mirror before Morrow went in to face Chess. But no, even further back still—that shuttery pounding, a massive wood-slat heartbeat keeping time all the way up from Mictlan-Xibalba, dragging what he'd thought was Chess's denuded corpse up through that endless tunnel, the cold, wet, impossible dark.

Aghast, Morrow suddenly realized why the feel of the power boiling off this thing was so familiar. He twisted to stare back at Chess. "Rook wanted to make you into . . . into *that?*"

Partly only, little meat-thing, to both your benefits. The Enemy gestured at Chess. *For this is the aspect of mine which loves*

to breed, to grow, to make things rise out of life and death alike.
It loves, as well as hungers. It kills, but with a smile. Everything
yearns for its embrace.

An almost diffident stroke along Morrow's instep made him jerk,
provoking a squawk. Under cover of the Enemy's presence, the Weed
had inched its stealthy way back toward the object of its adoration,
now massed 'round him and Chess both to near a foot deep. Noticing
almost simultaneously that he was once more surrounded, Chess
cried out again, and started dancing, crushing the red blossoms
wetly beneath his boot-heels while Morrow whipped his duster left
and right.

Insulted, the Weed set up a general hiss. A stray shard of bone
raked the back of Morrow's hand, spraying blood; he cursed it,
volubly.

Over Morrow's shoulder, meanwhile, Chess yelled back,
irreverently: "Goddamnit, then—if I'm part'a you, or you me, get off
your bony ass and *help us!* Or was *that* all bullshit, too?"

The Enemy cocked its head, unmoved. **Perhaps . . . I only want**
to see what you will do.

"Aw, you useless *son of a bitch*—"

So childishly outraged, so flat-out helpless and just plain *fed-
up*; how *young* Chess was, after all! More stuck on his own idea of
himself than even the Bible-bound Rev had once been, before the
drop. And here, as if summoned, came that rumbling voice once
more, lapping at Morrow's inner ear: *Spread the Skinless Man's word,*
Ed, 'fore perdition takes hold. Tell folks the only way is to . . . let blood. In
his name.

Well, Morrow thought, abruptly calm, as he looked down on his
spurting cut. *No point wasting a perfectly good wound.*

Chess was still ranting on, scraping the Weed from arms and
shins. "—damn Rook, damn *men,* Goddamn GODS, you ain't none
of you worth a shit in a sandstorm! Fuck *all* y'all!"

My power does not yet flow directly into this world, little
brother, said the Enemy, grinning horribly. **Anything I do will only**

widen the crack between our worlds further. It widens, even now.

"Well, that ain't—" Chess spat, bit at a tendril. "—*my* fault!"

No fault at all, merely fact. How much of this world must die, however, before you allow yourself to care?

"This *world's* a shit-pit anyways! So it burns now, or it burns later—what's the damn difference?"

Morrow laughed, the sound wild and startling enough to silence even Chess's fury; the pistoleer stared at him, as Morrow turned his way. "No difference at all, right? So *why not* save it, just for fun? Might as well hang for a sheep as for a lamb, Chess—saviour or destroyer, you're still Chess fuckin' *Pargeter,* so *shut this down.* While you still can."

Ah, but nothing comes for nothing, the Enemy pointed out. *Were you truly never taught to pray correctly?*

I *was, at least,* thought Morrow grimly. And held out his wounded hand to Chess, canted sidelong, to let the blood flow even more freely.

Chess blinked, bewildered—until he saw the Weed recoil, writhe, twisting toward Morrow as the blood fell upon it, turning brown even as it thirstily drank of the crimson moisture. Some current of self-destructive desire seemed to ripple through the green strands, up along Chess's skin and straight into both his eyes; a hot green pulse went thought-quick from iris to iris, the kill-flash's distant cousin.

Then Chess grabbed Morrow's hand and fastened his lips to the wound, sucking like a babe at the teat.

The Enemy made a deep, rattling sound, laughter's furthest cousin. *Man's dew, juiced from bright heart's fire,* it mused, in far too familiar fashion. *Aaahhh, precious blood, so flowery. So—*
(bbbbeeeaaauuuutiful)

Morrow grimaced. It hurt, but not badly; what was worse was that sense of *pulling,* like Chess had grabbed a loose thread of his very being, unravelling him compulsively. It couldn't be hex-power he was gulping at, not from Morrow—something far more vital, perhaps? Less easily renewed?

Or was this stinging, slimy feeling nothing but Morrow's own fear and disgust writ large, a swarm of insects set crawling on his soul's tender places?

Weakness invaded him; not fatigue, or blood loss . . . more like dread, or despair. A deep, dizzying urge to crumple up and hide his head, to—

—fall on your knees, lowly dog, grind your own face into the dirt in worship. As is only proper before the Night Wind's red aspect, He By Whom We Live, We Are His Slaves—

It took everything Morrow had just to stay on his feet. But whatever was being taken, it was working; Chess's frenzy had faded, the writhing Weed settling to the earth. The two swayed now almost in rhythm, as if equal-drunk on the same thing.

Me, Morrow thought. *Drunk on* me.

Asbury's voice in his head, half-imagined, half-recalled, pedantic as ever: *No, Mister Morrow. Drunk on sacrifice freely offered, all "gods'" only true food. For even the Almighty can save no soul without that soul's consent.*

A wave of power, half-visible, similarly green, suddenly rippled out from Chess, and the mound of red-flowered Weed collapsed, flattening in every direction. Chess released Morrow's hand with a small belch, lips crimsoned, eyes a-glow like candled glass. He licked greenish saliva roughly along Morrow's wound, sealing it shut in one hot stab; favoured Morrow with a look up through his lashes and a goony, purring little smile, a cat stroked from every side at once.

Morrow's pulse leapt in sudden quickstep under a wave of gum-mouthed arousal, jerking him a half-pace forward—'til he felt the texture of the ground beneath his boots change, that was. Which sent him jolting back with a startled yawp—eyes gone wide, heart hammering only with fear.

Sometime during Chess's vampire indulgence, the sky had begun to pale, the east going indigo, then grey. Predawn light fell across the plain, showing how ground that had once been stony Arizona desert was now, for near fifty yards in every direction, a rich, thick, rolling grassland. Even as Morrow stared, more leaves from no plant he recognized came pushing up out of the soil, bursting into blossom with a puff of soporific perfume—the verdant scent of springtime, run rampant.

Onward and outward the greenery crept, freshly brilliant, utterly alien. And how the Enemy grinned to see it go, as 'round its skeletal feet the foliage rippled and grew, strange trees shooting up like fountains, hideously animate. Life, wrenched sap-dripping raw out of dead earth—but *wrong*, core-down and further, for all its vivid wonder. While dawn light slowly brightened on the spreading field of green, Morrow could almost hear a general phantom choir screaming in each new breath.

"Oh, shit, Chess." He found he'd buried both his hands in his hair, yanking painfully, as if hoping the pain would clear his head. "What did we do? Christ, what did we *do*?"

But Chess wasn't listening. He was abruptly all a-droop, down on one knee, left hand buried deep in this strange rich earth and crumbling it 'tween his fingers, like he wanted to inhale it whole— while the other hovered somewheres near his belt-buckle, within easy reaching distance of either weapon.

"There, now. Thasss . . . better."

His voice thick with sleepy languor, like he'd just had the almighty best fuck of his entire screw-happy life.

No no no, it ain't better at all, Morrow thought, suddenly sick. *This . . . this is just* wrong.

God help him, he'd made sacrifice to a false idol, following the counsel of a sorcerer and the urgings of a demon—how could he have expected anything else?

For lack of anyone else, Morrow rounded on the Enemy, demanding: "Did *you* do this? Or did you *make* him?"

I compel no one. The creature's empty grin never altered. ***True sacrifice cannot be taken by force. You sought salvation from***

danger, and made offering to the Flayed One; it was accepted.
His power renewed the earth. All by your will, and his, as such
things always go.

"'Renewed'? Aw, give me a damn—look, this is *Chess's* power,
right? So why can't he make it do what he wants? Why won't these . . .
things . . . obey him?"

Because they are him, conquistador. The Enemy swept one
arm in an encompassing arc. *All this is born of Xipe Totec, and will*
return to him, for he is the remade Land. And just as his deepest
nature is to run wild, to reject any rule so furiously he will not
even rule himself, so things born of his power reject even that
power's rule.

Glancing down at his hand, Morrow was legitimately startled to
see how faded the scar had already become—like years had passed.
"So blood's the key, then. Feed Chess a little, and he can get a handle
on this shit? Control it?"

The Enemy gave a great sigh, like a cold wind. *Yes . . . and no.*
With blood enough, my brother may turn back our sister's
sendings, shape his spells according to will, rather than whim.
But each time he does, this—a glance from horizon to horizon—
is the cost. A winding back, a change, deep in the earth itself. A
widening of the crack between worlds.

"So we're fucked either way, is what you're saying."

"And ain't *that* news," Chess remarked. The pistoleer lay on his
back, all a-grin like a cat in catnip, buried almost to the eyes in
ferns and orchid blossoms; he looked up at Morrow, and winked.
Concluding: "Y'know, Ed, occurs t'*me* that you might'a forgot this
one fact: gods, and 'godly' folk alike—*they damn well lie.*"

He rolled over on one side to face the Enemy, grin sharp once
more with the wild edge that was pure Chess Pargeter. Adding, as
he did—"So I don't see any reason we should trust what *you* say,
neither, come to think on it."

Well, 'at's yer privilege, love. The thing's voice was suddenly
thick with the cooing accent of a Limey whore, though horribly, it
stayed cavern-deep and rasping; recognizing it, Chess lost his smile.

You never did listen to anyfing I 'ad to say, so why start now? But might be as someone else is headin' yer way, wiv 'is own fings to say on the matter. You might even like 'is ideas somewhat worse'n mine.

"Don't talk like her no more," Chess told it, dead-voiced.

Very well. Its voice changed once more, clarifying, a sharpened obsidian blade. *But do not wait so long to play your given part, next time. For next time, your acolytes' desires may not be so easily denied....*

A moment later it was gone, with only deep indentations in the freshly arable earth—bare of green, when everything 'round it shared the same viridian hue—to show where its massive weight had once rested.

Abruptly, Morrow found himself sitting down. "Well, damn if I know what *that* was," he said, more to himself than Chess, not really expecting an answer.

Yet Chess surprised him. "*The* Smoking Mirror." He lolled again, exhausted, barely able to twist Morrow's way. "You saw him the once already, Ed. When the Rev put you on like a shirt, and I had to shove everything I'd seen straight through your head. Must'a caught on then how him and me had a little powwow when I first woke up, after . . ." He trailed off. "After."

Morrow nodded slowly, remembering the storm-flood of images. "He's like that Lady Ixchel, then. A . . . god, for real." That word still felt strange on his tongue, especially when spoken outside of church. "But does that mean he's on our side, or what?"

Chess yawned and stretched, movements kicking up rich-smelling pollen. "Aw, hell, Ed, don't think any of 'em's on any person's *side*. Does seem like he wants to fuck up whatever the Rev's tryin' to pull, though. That's good enough, for me. . . ." He stopped at Morrow's frown. "What?"

Wordlessly, Morrow pointed. Chess turned.

A glitter moved on the western horizon, pale and sharp in the twilight still lingering there. Something about the pattern of its motion reminded Morrow inexorably of a man, running, but too impossibly fast for anything human. And it threw light back in ways no flesh ever could.

Morrow was abruptly on his feet, knowing they probably had only minutes. Chess made his as well, if a great deal slower than Morrow had. Rolling his eyes again, more drunkenly amused than exasperated, he observed: "Christ, it don't never end, do it?"

"Chess, you really *do* need to do somethin'." Morrow's hands clenched; though he suspected his guns would be useless, he still itched to draw them. "That thing's gettin' way too close, whatever it is."

Chess shrugged. "Bet you eights to aces I can kick its ass."

"But *I can't*." Morrow moved to look him straight in the eye. "Now—do you care?"

Chess met his eyes; his mouth twisted, still bright with Morrow's blood, hungry for more. But after a second: "Screw it," he said, and squooched up his face with a grunt.

The air slapped blunt against them both, a phantom bedroll swung hard. Morrow staggered, boots connecting hard onto dry earth. All of an instant, there was a whitewashed two-storey building towering up above, a sign over the main doors proclaiming it the Cold Mountain Hotel. "Rooms to Let," said a smaller one, beneath. Though light leaked from inside, the street around was thankfully empty, the whole town apparently still catching up on their last few minutes of good night's sleep.

Easier than last time, by far, Morrow realized, *for him to jump from here to there; by the look of it, he ain't even breathin' hard. That can't be good.*

The world reshaped itself to Chess's liking now—tried its level best to anticipate his whims, however fleeting. This was what godhood maybe meant, in its most casual sense—godhood without responsibility, writ small and mean, with all the parts of that state that might possibly be of some benefit to others extracted and thrown away, replaced with nothing but vengeful idleness.

Unaware or all uncaring of his companion's train of thought, Chess grinned wide; seemed like the journey'd sobered him some, at least. "Think I might be finally gettin' the hang of this mode'a transportation," he said. "Hell, I don't even feel like pukin' my guts out. Just thought how I wanted someplace safe to sleep, and what do you know—"

"Got any cash?" Morrow asked, cutting him off. "'Cause . . . we left all our gear back there, just like the last go-round."

"Aw, *crap.*" Chess shook his head. "Money. Well . . ."

He turned out his pockets one by one, yielding nothing but dust and grit. Then shrugged, and fluttered his fingers—and watched a stone four yards away pry itself from the ground, skipping right to his hand, as if summoned. He closed his eyes and ran his other palm over it, opening his fingers.

The stone shone under dim lamplight, seamed with purest gold.

Chess smirked. "Close enough."

CHAPTER FIVE

Now:

THOUGH THE GIRL AT the door—innkeep Colder's only daughter—barely came up to Morrow's armpit, that fact seemed not to bother her at all. Those wide-spaced grey eyes held his gaze, mild but level, utterly unafraid.

Something 'bout her, Morrow thought, not knowing exactly what. Yet more hexation? Or had it just been that long since he'd stood so close to something in a skirt wasn't a drab, whore, witch, or some ancient god unconvincingly dressed up in lady-meat?

"Hey!" Chess broke in, from behind. "I *said*, come the fuck in, if you're comin'. And shut the damn door, while you're at it."

She nodded, and did. Observing, at the same time, "That's quite the dirty mouth you've got on you there, Mister Pargeter, for a man in dire straits."

"Oh, do tell. Well, as to that—I've got a whole raft of *other* bad habits, to boot. Care for a demonstration?"

"Not tolerably," the girl replied, shifting her stare to his. And Chess's initial half-smile became an outright bark of laughter, less insulted than oddly impressed.

"Find I halfway like this one, Ed," he announced. "Yourself?"

Morrow shrugged. "Think we should probably ask Miz Colder

here what it is she wants, if you're done admirin' the sound of your own voice."

Chess laughed once more, and swept her a mocking bow.

SAD THING WAS, THUS far, Morrow'd liked his stay at Colder's better than any other place he'd been since last year. Certainly helped that Chess'd spent the first three days deeply asleep, exhausted by his arcane overexertions. If Morrow'd been a different sort, in fact, he might've thought hard on cutting out while the getting was good, and seeing just how far that took him, 'fore Chess came hunting after.

But he wasn't—and besides, he knew better. Wasn't Chess, alone, who wanted him in his current place. And he sure didn't hope to see either Rook's ghost-self or that *thing* again—the Enemy, horrid chest-doors all a-clack—anytime soon, if he could help it.

So he ate civilized food, drank sparingly, and enjoyed the sadly unfamiliar chatter of perfectly normal people for once, while he had the opportunity. Right up until the morning he came halfway down to breakfast, then froze on the landing at the sudden realization that Colder's front rooms were jammed chock full of the exact same folk had chucked trash at 'em down Mouth-of-Praise's main street, a mere week previous.

Morrow busted back in and turned the lock, only to find young Mister P. abruptly awake once more—lounging 'round their room, a mysterious bottle in hand.

"The hell *you* been?" he demanded.

"Tryin' to figure how best to get us both out of here 'fore the wrong folks catch sight of us." Chess stared. "You *do* know there's most of Doc Glossing's neighbours down there right now, takin' our names in vain to Sheriff and Marshal alike?"

"No, I didn't know that."

"Thought you knew every damn thing, these days."

"Yeah? Well . . ." Chess made a face, took another long swig. ". . . not today, I guess. My head hurts."

Which made it Morrow's turn to stare, because—now he thought to think about it—his travelling companion bore the hangdog, hungover demeanour of somebody just coming down off a too-long bender. Leaning far enough forward to catch a whiff from the bottle, Morrow wrinkled his nose: aniseed, heavy enough to cure leather.

"Didn't know they served absinthe here," he said.

Chess hefted it, considered the sloshing green liquid. "Don't know as it was, when I first started in on it," he allowed.

"So you do got some mojo left in you, at least."

Chess bridled. "Damn straight! I just . . ." And here his angry eyes wandered off again, lost focus in a creepish fluttery way that reminded Morrow of Chess's own dead Ma, "English" Oona, pulling hard on her Hellfire-filled junk-pipe. With effort: "That stuff, in the desert . . . turnin' the Weed to vine, and whatnot . . ."

"Yeah, that *was* something, wasn't it? Just did what the Rev said to—gave you blood, made my prayers."

Chess shook his head, and winced. "Felt real good at the time," he muttered. "A bit too damn good, entirely."

He scratched at his beard's fresh scruff, absent; not like the Chess Morrow knew to be so ungroomed, and heedless of it. But here he sat nonetheless, sweat-slicked, smelling of turned earth and dead flowers. Too distracted even to bother flirting, embarrassed and itchy, yet palpably jonesing for more . . . yeah, a *lot* like Oona, from what little Morrow had seen of her, 'fore the Rev cooked her insides out on Chess's say-so.

Morrow thought hard on what he was going to say next, strategizing. Hoping Chess was far too distracted to even bother with picking the words from his brain before they could tumble out his mouth.

"Don't look too rested, for all you been laid up in bed so long," he began.

Chess took another pull. "I *ain't*," he agreed, fairly pouting.

"Bad dreams?" Chess shrugged. "Well, shove on over, then; make some room for a man to sit. And—maybe, you know, we put our heads together, might be we can figure out . . . *somethin'* to do about it."

Jesus, he was bad at this! But it was all he could think to offer: get Chess's mind off new hungers, and back to his old ones. So he gave up on words and sat down as well, forcibly nudging Chess over with his hip. Uncharacteristically, however, Chess merely gave way—went limp and made room, without even looking up.

Morrow bit his lip. "You should think about keepin' the beard longer a while," he said finally. "Fair-to-middling sketch of you up at the trading post, but it's got you close-cut. Might be that's the reason they keep askin' if I'm really your brother."

At least that made Chess snort. "Oh, you poor innocent," he replied. "That ain't it at all. Thing I want to know is, though, why's it always *my* face on those Goddamn playbills? You were there just as much as I was, every step of the ride."

"Uh huh. Good thing that with you there, nobody ever remembers *me*."

"You feeling ill-done by, *Mister* Morrow?"

"Not hardly. But they do got my name, even if there wasn't room left for my mug, and five grand for any as brings me in. . . ." He trailed off. "But not alive," he finished, stomach abruptly cold.

Oh, he'd *known* his bridges were well and truly burned, but somehow the sight of that explicit figure—black typeface smeared on crackling yellow paper—had finally brought it home how there really was no going back. Because those men he'd once counted closer than his own brothers really would gun him down if they felt they had to, rather than take him upright.

Chess's eyes were on him now, sharper than he'd looked to find them. "You know," he offered, "once I'm ace-high again, I could glamour *you* up some too, you wanted to stick 'round. Wear a new face, take a new name . . . get jobs, even." At Morrow's startled snicker: "Hey, might be I got skills you're not privy to. Running a faro table, for example."

"Faro's a nincompoop's pastime."

"'Course it is—the crookedest game around. But seein' how I was raised up, I *can* deal it, in a pinch. We could take these up-stood fools for everything they got." Chess glanced sourly out the window. "The whole lot of nothin' *that* is."

"These're good citizens, Chess. You got no call to twit 'em behind their backs."

"Oh, these fine law-abiders can kiss my queer ass, Ed—yours, too. Hell, I could probably make 'em."

"I'd take it as a personal kindness if you didn't," Morrow said, stiffly.

Chess grinned at that, brief but dirty. "What'll you trade me?"

And soon enough, Chess was dripping whiskey-turned-absinthe in Morrow's mouth, those deft shootist's hands busy on every part of him—doing things he'd never looked to, but certainly couldn't claim he wasn't enjoying, now circumstance had put him in their path.

A minute or so in, however, Chess drew back—sat up straight in Morrow's not-uninterested lap and regarded him, somewhat sadly.

Morrow blinked up at him. "What?"

"Who is it you're trying hardest to convince here, Ed? Me, or you?"

Morrow flushed, half-insulted, half-guilty. *It seem like I'm uninclined?* he wanted to retort. Yet he still recalled Chess saying, of Rook: *He ain't queer all the way to the bone, like me.* Dismissive, but with a sort of rueful hurt hid underneath. An understanding that no matter how fast he and the Rev cleaved together, there was always a possibility they might yet be cleft apart—rent from each other by sheer distinction of nature alone.

As, indeed, had happened.

But she'd been a special case, had dread Lady Ixchel. No regular siren, no mere provoking drab. The Rainbow Lady pulled hard, over unfathomable distances—and those she called *came*, without delay, or recourse.

Maybe Chess *would* meet a man entirely like him, one day—like enough to help, yet not too alike to hinder. God knew, pretty little fellows didn't seem to be any more his meat than pretty little ladies.

"Just tryin' to help, is all," Morrow said, finally.

"Aw, Jesus—" Chess rolled his eyes, torn between laughter and irritation. "Well, thank you kindly. But . . . it's more than simple frolics 'tween us these days, ain't it? You're a pal, Ed, close as I've come to in my whole life. A good man."

Which was . . . flattering, in its way.

Thought the Rev a good man too, though, once upon a time. Didn't you, Chess?

Chess looked at him again, green eyes gone dull. "Don't," he said.

A sliver of ice, just touching Morrow's pulse to its quick: *Never forget he can* hear *you, Ed—whether he wants to, or not.*

He brought his mouth back to Chess's, then—anything to keep from thinking further on that subject—renewed his efforts, doing as he'd been taught Chess enjoyed, by experience and example. And when the vibrations began to roll up both their spines, he let himself enjoy them, in that brief moment it still felt merely like nerves firing at the smaller man's skilled touch . . . right up 'til he realized he was *hearing* the juddering quivers as well, a buzz emanating from walls, ceiling, floor at once, as if the whole room was a reed in some gigantic instrument.

Startled, he pulled back. "Christ, what the—this an earthquake?!"

Chess stared at something past Morrow's head, mouth open. "I don't . . . think so."

Morrow twisted, and gasped.

Behind the bed's headboard, the wallpaper's calm pattern was sliding like unfired clay, blurring from a vague mesh of curlicues to a daguerreotype-sharp tangle of leaves which began to twine even as they resolved, adding a steam-engine hiss to the walls' bass thrum. Red flowers blossomed and withered, strewed shrunken petals, as grinning skulls pushed themselves up out of the print's white gaps.

Smell of bruised greenstalk, flowing sap, a meaty sweetness, honey brewed from carrion: sticky edge-of-stench perfume, signalling growth and decay. Birth. Rebirth. Morrow felt it chime in his pulse like it was trying to get out, reverberating through Chess's empty chest like a great bell's tongue, a hollow chigger-skin cocoon.

Prince of Flowers, Songbird crooned, in both their ears. *Does your new skin itch?*

And yeah, he found—*him*, or Chess?—it did. Just a bit.

Rip it off, then—run naked, green-bleeding, through this awful world. Run free. . . .

But the vines were stilling now, voice and buzz alike winding down to silence. Morrow gaped down at Chess, both of 'em breath-caught with hearts hammering, equally off-put.

"Did . . . all *that* . . . just happen?" He asked.

Chess opened his mouth to answer; God knew what, but the point proved moot. Instead, a knock at the door caused him to swear, vociferous as ever. "Shit-fire! What damn *now*?"

WITHOUT ASKING PERMISSION FIRST, the Colder girl sat down on their single rickety chair, legs neat-crossed at the ankles—almost laughably prim-looking, given the circumstances. Then again, Morrow supposed it was more *her* room than either of theirs, and always had been.

"'Fore we go any further, might it be possible for Mister Pargeter to, uh . . . reassume his shirt?" she asked Morrow, keeping her eyes firm on his.

Chess hissed. "Oh, all things are 'possible,' gal," he said, and a single finger-snap saw him safely "decent" once more; so much so as a mere set of clothes might make him, any road. In return, the girl just nodded—hiding her reaction damn well, if such casual miracles weren't her daily bread.

"Thank you," she said, simply. Chess shrugged.

"What *I'd* most like to know is how you spotted us, in the first place," he replied.

"Should've picked a better fake family name than 'Chester,' might be, you wanted to stay inconspicuous."

"Might be; Ed ain't all too quick on the draw, sad to say, when it comes to mendacious matters. But that's not the whole of it—is it?"

She took up a fold of her skirt, drew it between two fingers.

"It's true how when first I checked you two in, you and him—" she nodded at Morrow "—seemed just about the same height, same colour hair, eyes, and whatnot. Same arrangement of whiskers, even. But something tickled me even then, and I recalled a tip my Mama taught me. . . ."

She held up one hand—her left—and slipped the slim gold band off her little finger, a ring custom-made for one whose bones must've been even more delicate.

Holding it up, she explained: "Look through one of these, sidelong, and it shows things as they really are; magical creatures, or those you s'pect may be so. That's 'cause matrimony's sacred bond peels away all falsehoods." At Chess's grin: "Go on ahead and mock. But when I did, first thing I saw was *you*, Mister Pargeter, the tintype of all she'd warned me 'bout. A Judas-head with poison eyes, walking widdershins through this world, whose wishes all come true. A man with no shadow."

"I got a shadow."

"Not all the time, you don't."

This last revelation didn't seem to surprise Chess quite as much as Morrow might've thought it would. Instead, he stopped short—appraising her with simple objective interest, all other passions momentarily suspended.

"What *are* you?" Chess asked. "Not a hex—not quite. But still . . . something 'bout you I recognize. A . . . taste."

He sniffed hard at her, mouth halfway yawned open—as though she smelled so delicious, he wasn't sure *what*-all to do. Yet she just faced him down, resolute.

"Different, is all," she said. "No good trying to feed off me, though. I know *that* much."

"Oh no?"

A tiny head-shake. "All's you'd do is kill me—that's what my Mama always said. Wouldn't like the afterglow too much, either."

"Sounds like a lamentable smart woman, your *Mama*."

"I like to think so."

"All right. Then . . . what do you see *now*, lookin' at me full-on?"

Miz Colder inhaled delicately, let her eyes drift from his as the lids slid faintly to, mimicking the bare beginnings of what quack Spiritualists called a trance. And suddenly, Morrow felt the same prickling chill he'd had on first coming face-to-face with Asher Rook, more than a year ago—like watching a snake slide slowly 'cross your path: This was no mere confidence-show, some drab provoking ghosts for profit, telling sad and frightened folk what they most wanted to believe, but the truth behind a thousand pretty lies made flesh.

For years, investigating frauds at Pinkerton's behest, Morrow'd heard tell of people who saw things both true and inexplicable, secrets too painful to sell but too accurate to ignore. Those who saw trouble coming in dreams, or talked to God, and actually seemed to get *answers* . . . like Rook never had, but long-dead Sheriff Mesach Love—once champion of Bewelcome, itself turned not exactly miraculously to salt in Rook's wake—had claimed to. Not hexes, but nowhere near normal folk, neither.

Seemed like Miz Colder's absent Mama must've been one such rare creature—and if so, no surprise her daughter shared those same gifts. For blood did tell, they said.

(Yes, soldier. Indubitably.)

Once more, he braced himself internally against that awful rib-slat noise.

But heard only Miz Colder's voice dim down, shedding its humanity by cold degrees, saying, ". . . somebody . . . standing behind you." Only a hint above a whisper, yet the room so abruptly silent her words struck low, toneless notes, like rag-muffled hammers on a Chinese gong. "Yes. In the dark, behind the Black Mirror—his name a door, unlocked. Opening.

"*Tez* . . .

cat . . .

li . . .

poc—"

Without thinking, Morrow leaped forward and slapped her 'cross the face, hard enough Chess actually started; the girl herself staggered back and blinked, holding her jaw. But when her eyes found Morrow's again, they looked more bemused than angry.

Morrow flushed deep. "Ma'am—I'm very sorry. But I just didn't feel I could let that go any further."

"No," Miz Colder agreed. She massaged her jaw a moment, grimacing, then added: "I understand, I think. Though . . . you'll forgive me, I hope, if I don't thank you for it."

"Son of a bitch never told *me* his damn name," Chess muttered, at the same time, half to himself. 'Cause it always had to be about *him*, Morrow thought, exasperated.

He glanced back Miz Colder's way a moment later, and was shocked to see her drop a tiny little shrug, as though in sympathy: *Oh God, here's another one.* But no confirmation followed, one way or the other; she simply took a further moment, avoiding his eyes while working blood lightly through the fine skin 'long her profile with two fingers, so it'd be less likely to bruise.

Before starting over, eventually: "Well, be that as it may, Messrs. 'Chester,' though those downstairs may not read much, *I* do, and daily. That's how I ascertained what your real names might be, and how I know something you might not already've figured out, likewise . . . that—rumours and superstition aside—the Weed really *must* follow people, since it's sprung up overnight in just about every place you two've been reported."

Chess stiffened. "Not here, though," he countered. "Think I'm right, on that account."

"No. Not *yet.*"

Not much to say to *that*, though knowing it'd never stopped Chess anytime previous. Still, when he went to rebut, Morrow shushed him; Chess cast his eyes up, and let him.

"We're listening," Morrow said.

"First choice—I don't guess you know how to send it on its way again, do you? Rumour has it you can kill Weed by spilling blood. That true?"

Chess laughed harshly. "For all the good it'll do your pissant little town, yeah. In a manner of speaking."

The girl's mouth thinned, and Morrow jumped in. "It's a pagan working, a prayer in tribute to that thing you saw: let blood in the name of the Skinless Man, and the Weed turns brown, green grass grows fresh over wherever it's spread. But . . ." He heard his own voice crack, and forced it steady. "I've seen it happen. It's . . . no natural thing. Better it never comes to that."

Miz Colder considered, and nodded. "All right, then. Second choice—you need to get out of here, just as bad as all of us need you gone. So let's work on that a minute." She rose, hands clasped, and began to pace. "I'm not too like to report you to the authorities, since odds are, you'd do damage on your way out. I don't want that. You either, probably."

Chess snorted. "Hell, I don't mind. Ain't like we ain't shot our way free before."

"Maybe. But what you probably don't know is there's going to be a wedding all day tomorrow—Marshal Kloves', town law, with all his friends come in to celebrate."

Morrow rubbed his forehead. "Aw, God damn . . ."

"Town was nearing full already," the girl went on, "and with Mouth-of-Praise's flux set on top, we're stuffed to bursting. Not to mention the Sheriff's got constituents panicked Weed will set in any moment, so there's patrols everywhere, eyes well-peeled for any hint of green and red, which makes trying to sneak out unnoticed probably a foredoomed endeavour." She paused at the window, twitching the curtains close-to. "And so . . ."

Chess shrugged. "So? Your hootenanny goes off as planned or not, don't mean a damn thing to me, little girl, or Ed, besides. Though you sure must play a mean hand of poker, given your skill at schemin'."

Miz Colder fixed him, voice even, eyes cold. "I don't believe you've cause to condescend to me, Mister Pargeter."

Chess's eyes narrowed, and Morrow jumped in again. "It's, uh . . . it's nothin' personal, Miz Col—"

"Yancey."

Morrow blinked. "Pardon?"

"Experiance, that's my name. Yancey to my friends—or to those I share secrets with." She gestured. "You were saying?"

"Yeah, Ed, what *were* you sayin'?" Chess turned Morrow's way, mouth still set in that mean little knot. "'Bout to plead pardon from Miz *Yancey* for my manners?"

Morrow gritted his teeth. "Look, Chess here don't deal too well with those of the fairer persuasion, in the main," he told her. "Which might be 'cause, uh . . ."

"I know 'bout him and Reverend Rook, if that's what you're wondering."

"Um, well . . . good, but no. I meant 'cause his Ma was—uh—"

Here euphemism failed him, polite or otherwise.

Chess laughed outright. "Oh, don't be shy, Ed; if this one's smart enough not to choke on the word 'queer,' 'whore' can't be far behind." Abruptly, Chess was off the bed, backing Yancey up swift 'til her shoulders met the wall. "My thoughts on pussy aside, though, gal—just how you plan on workin' this particular miracle, exactly? 'Cause I can make gold outta shit, these days, and I'm fairly stumped."

Yancey had to moisten her lips. "A far larger glamour," she suggested. "Same's when you checked in, but bolder: hide in plain sight. Come as guests, then leave with the rest."

Chess scoffed. "Or get found out and swung, whichever comes first."

"Well, that's where the hexation comes in, I'd guess." Yancey stepped away from the wall, smoothing her blouse down, and the way the fabric tightened around her put a sudden dryness in Morrow's mouth bid fair to confirm that Chess's bed-play, however enjoyable, hadn't entirely spoiled his original tastes. "Accounts of the Reverend's exploits suggest he was capable of remaking whole towns, if he needed to—am I right in guessing you're more than his match, in that direction?"

"I don't recall him doin' anything like that, and I was there. But yeah, for myself, I could probably cast up something damn enduring, long as it was simple."

"All right, then . . . how 'bout you magnify the headiness of the spirits being served out—get 'em fuddled so extra-quick, extra-potent, the Good Lord himself could ride through on a white horse and they wouldn't notice." Her mouth slanted slightly, cutting a wry angle which came surprisingly close to some of Chess's own favourite expressions. "I can assure you, you won't have to exert yourself too strongly in order to end up with a full day's head start, at the very least."

"So your *plan* is for me to do all the work, in other words."

"Why, yes, given you're by far the more powerful, 'tween the two of us. Would that be too much of a problem?"

Sweet, tart, final: Chess goggled a half-instant at her, then couldn't quite stop himself from exploding in more laughter—of a far more genuine variety, this time 'round.

"Oh, you really *are* somethin'," he allowed, finally. "Must be some damn good friend of yours this lawman's marrying, I suppose, for you to go to so much trouble keeping her bride-day blood-free."

She already had one hand on the doorknob, but that turned her back, nodding. "Oh yes," she said, "the very best imaginable. By which I mean myself."

With no hint of preparation, it was like Morrow's slap had been returned to him six-fold, and again, she seemed to know it.

For she paused, looking up from under her lashes—those clean grey eyes so deceptively mild, for the clockwork mind he now sensed lurked behind 'em—to say, lightly enough, "For all I'm the only one who knows what we'll owe you, I'll make sure my kin and kin-to-be welcome you kindly, Mister Morrow . . . Mister Pargeter. And I'll expect to see you in the throng, tomorrow."

She nodded over at Chess, who returned the favour, if begrudgingly. As though impressed, in the end, by his own inability to scare her—or her inability to *be* scared, even under such trying circumstances. And she was gone a second on, with a switch of skirts, a rustle of petticoats, the discreet click-to of door meeting jamb.

Chess looked back to see Morrow's mouth hung far enough open to catch flies, making him laugh yet one more time, long *and* loud.

"Oh *ho*," he said. "Well, well."

Morrow drew himself up, shrugging it off. "Well *what*?" He demanded.

"Might be you got sorta sweet on her, all those days I was sleepin' it off."

"Wasn't *that* long, and you know it. 'Sides which . . ." Morrow coloured. "Well," he wound up, "that wouldn't make a lick of sense, if so. Would it?"

Chess shrugged, glancing over at the dresser drawer where his belt and guns lay hid; Morrow saw his fingers quiver, palms itchy like he ached to hold 'em, if only for practice—or comfort, of a kind.

"Rarely does," he replied.

NIGHT FELL LEAD-HEAVY, uneasily abrupt, as though the sun might never rise again.

Hoffstedt's Hoard lulled itself to sleep by degrees under its darkness, murmuring slumberous, a beehive awaiting the morrow's stick. Elsewhere, the world's newer terrors came clambering up through Mictlan-Xibalba's widening crack: Songbird's dog with human hands, sweatless empty men made from the wood of the coral tree, their wives carved from the chalky cores of bulrushes. Small female gods swarming in the moon's darkness, like gnats; weeping women giving birth to jade-scaled monsters at the crossroads. Eddies of all kinds, flurrying back and forth across the desert—blood mixed with mud, poisons breeding. The drought which precedes a flood. Ash, falling from the sky.

And salt, too, snaking through the desert toward Hoffstedt's Hoard—hotly calcinate, scorching to the touch, turning sand to glass. Salt, flowing from one more creature's whitened footsteps like an awful road, drawing ever closer.

This glistering vision paused at the town's limits, found a likely enough spot, knelt to make its prayers. Then settled in, to wait.

CHAPTER SIX

YANCEY COLDER'S WEDDING WENT the way those things mostly did, from what little Chess had gathered on vague scattered report. Her and Kloves stood up before a mixed congregation in the clapboard-walled church, local preacher officiating, checking his Bible every few words—not even a pale shade on how impressive Ash Rook'd once loomed, intoning verse from memory, voice a crack-less iron bell. The vows went by in a babble: cleave together, sever never—have and hold, faithful always, by God's grace, amen. Y'all take each other? Ring, kiss; done.

After, a crew of hotel workers hauled the pews back against the wall while others brought out tables bearing platters of cold meat, soup tureens, battered but polished pewter tankards brimming with ale, plus bowls full of sliced fruit in so much spirit Chess could practically smell it from here. Lionel Colder went 'round pumping hands like he was getting paid for it, 'stead of the reverse. Though Chess and Morrow stood a bit back from the press, they still caught him on the swing-by; Chess made sure his hand was where Lionel's glamour-fuddled mind put it—his hex-guise as "Mister Chester Jr." being a foot taller, to make him match with Morrow—and let Yancey's Pa wring it back and forth with a will.

"Lovely, wasn't it?" he burbled.

Ed, creditably grave: "Sure was, Mister Colder. Same's I'd like my own to go, one day."

Lionel looked to Chess, then, like he expected further support for this judgement, and Chess tried to give it him. "Very . . . likely so, I'd guess," he hazarded, at last.

Lionel thanked him kindly enough, blinking an odd look out of his eye—but moved on fast, and didn't look back.

"What'd you have to say *that* for?" Morrow complained.

Chess hissed through his teeth. "I don't know, Ed—'cause this's the one and only time I ever seen this done, in my entire life?" He folded his arms, glowering over at the punch-bowls. "Or maybe it's just 'cause I got a job to pull that'd go a fuck of a lot smoother without me bein' badgered all up and down each side while I stand here tryin' to figure out how it works, in the first damn place."

Ed took the hint and shut up, though Chess suspected he'd be hearing more about this later. But even that small irritation was almost too much of a distraction, right now.

Last night's boasts to Miz Colder (Missus Kloves, that was) aside, however, this was the very first working Chess had ever chosen to do, deliberately—a harder task than it seemed it should be, at least for him.

So he closed his eyes, wiping away everything but the cold clarity of the moment, thinking, as he did: *You were right and wrong, Ash Rook, like always. This* ain't *a gun, and I don't aim to treat it as such. But one thing you did teach me 'bout hexation. It comes out the way means most to a person, no matter who. You and your Bad Book, Doc Glossing's Jew-homunculus—all in how you, and they, was raised up. What you learned, deep down. What's you.*

Well, I never knew too much: killing, fucking, shooting, drinking, etcetera. But I do know how to hook somebody's eye, like I know what it feels like to drown your own mind in something—liquor, smoke, fleshly pleasures. So let's slap 'em together, see what's like to happen. . . .

It was less like taking aim down a barrel than throwing a glance some man's way 'cross any given tumult, casting deep, 'fore reeling the poor sucker in. Chess's favourite recreation, once, aside from killing—and he had to admit how it still made him a bit stiff himself, even now, just thinking on it.

Shrouded in the false face he'd patterned after Ed's own, Chess meandered through the crowd, spinning a cloud of invisible spider's-webbery out through the top of his skull. He could feel it latching on to everyone he passed, too, linking brain-pan to brain-pan; by the time he'd covered the church, the pressure of some twelve-score minds on his was a tangible ache. But . . . it'd worked, Goddamnit, in spite of everything. He *had* them.

The sensation itself was a wonder, too. Same as the way he'd somehow always known where everybody else was in a throw-down, he only now realized, but raised to a whole new order. He could barely resist the impulse to flood those strands with power, take hard hold of 'em and *yank*. Make all these petty, tiny people know just who they had amongst them, so's they might render him his due *reverence*.

But here Chess paused to breathe deep, checking to make sure he'd tied no similar thread to Ed, or to Yancey, and warmed himself again with that little self-congratulatory jolt. Best to keep his eyes firm on the road, lest it lead straight into the Rainbow Lady's own meshes, where Chess would be trapped by his own blunderings like any other foolish insect.

Then, down those thought-strands, he carefully dripped his memories like hot wax on a candlewick: absinthe's sour tang; Oona's eye-watering opium pipe-stink; ether's blissful lassitude, from those rare occasions a Confederate sawbones had drugged him up; the twitchy punch of good chaw. Spreading, fading, dissolving like ink in water as Chess kept up a gentle but inexorable pressure, casting slow darkness over the whole.

All's he'd needed was to fire up, by just a smidgen, a place in their brains most of 'em were already hightailing toward at best speed anyway.

The drinks flowed free, and all 'round, an ungodly mess of a hobbledehoy boiled up: every man present spouting frippery to anything in a skirt, with those same skirts batting their flirtatious eyes and cooing 'til Chess fair ached to yell how money should change hands already, before he puked outright. But then, he supposed this ridiculousness was just how "normal" folk comported 'emselves, when struck by the urge to revelry; just too bad for him he'd no one to share that opinion with aside from Ed, who'd no doubt try his best to talk him out of it.

And that, right there, was where he felt the Rev's loss worst once more, an unset bone. He wasn't drunk enough yet for it not to discomfit him, and unlikely to become so, if he wanted to stay fit to do his part.

Over at the table's mid-point, Miz Colder as was—Missus Kloves now, he reminded himself—caught him looking, and gave him a brief smile before turning back to her cunt-struck bullock of a brand-new husband.

Thinking as she did, knowing damn well he'd be able to hear: *Your patience's laudable indeed, Mister Pargeter; I'm very sure it costs you something, to sustain. Yet soon enough, you and Mister Morrow'll be on your way, unnoticed—all you have to do is just let 'em all get good and snookered, and they'll mind nothing on the morrow but that they had the world's best time. And even if any of 'em were to figure out who-all they might've missed capturing, later on, the hangovers alone will make 'em think twice about coming after.*

So thank you, for that. Thank you for not bringing my home down around my ears, or sinking us all hip-deep in Weed. I sure do appreciate your restraint, seein' how hard—how unnatural—it is for you to practice....

Meant no insult by it, either. It'd be uncharitable to think so.

When'd you ever reckon things by their charity, though, darlin'? the Rev whispered to him, a lick deep 'cross his inner ear, hot and honey-slow. *Woman's got you tied up tight, doing her will like a dray-horse. That ain't the Chess I know.*

Just shut the fuck UP, you house-size sumbitch, he shot back. *I'll do what I like, and like what I damn well do. Like Goddamn always.*

Oh, and now he *felt* the drunkenness he was bringing forefront in

everyone else fine enough, but with no release, no real enjoyment—a
ticking timepiece, a lit fuse's hiss. *Decency* all 'round him, like an
insult by proxy.

On his left a kid sat crying, all by itself, 'til seconds later its
dam swept down to pick the little monkey up, cuddling, soothing,
stroking. Chess watched the kid latch on like a drunk does to his
poison, and felt *something* inside him give a painful click, like
tumblers falling.

He elbowed Morrow in the ribs, hard, hissing under his breath,
"Let's just get the hell gone from this place, Ed—'cause, 'fore God
and man, it's gettin' so I want to *shoot* something."

Morrow gave his head the slightest shake. "Give it another hour,"
he murmured back. "They ain't far enough gone yet. Someone might
still remember us, we left now."

For what minuscule consolation it was, he didn't look all too
much like *he* wanted to stay, either; more like he had a bee crawling
'round in his britches, fixing to find just the best place to sting. And
Chess soon found he well knew why, just from the way he kept on
stealing cow-glum glances back in the newlywed Kloves' direction.

"Christ, Morrow," Chess snapped, "you want this gal so bad, I
could lay the Marshal out under the table for a good few hours, while
she thanks you proper." Which actually got Morrow to throw a glare
at him, flushing—as much in embarrassment as in anger, though,
which cut down on the entertainment factor considerably.

Across the room, a mob of dancers were yelling suggestions at
the band: "'*Rake and a Ramblin' Boy*'! Naw, hell—'*West Virginia*'!"
"'*Buffalo Skinners*'!"

"I ain't too like to make you fear I'll bail out to chase some girl we
both of us just met, let alone one new-hitched in holy matrimony,"
Morrow told him, at the same time, "and not being *quite* so stunned
as I look, I got no desire to get Chess Pargeter mad at me, either.
'Sides which . . ."

"'*The Red-Head Pistoleer*'!" That one got cheers.

Here Morrow cut off, reconsidering his next sentence. But Chess simply nodded, and finished it for him anyhow: "'Sides which, you might get *her* killed," he said, nodding to Yancey, now looking over at the band in dismay. "Right? Oh, Christ's sake, Ed, don't take on— who you think I am, your gal back home? So long's you're there for me when it counts, believe me, you can get gay with whomever you choose to."

"Really?"

"True dish. Think *I* want a damn ring, from anyone? A church full'a fools and some combine playing clog-step crap like—" He turned, frowning. "What the hell *is* that song, anyway? Tune sounds familiar."

"Think it's 'Two Dimes and a Nickel,'" said Morrow, eyes narrowed. "Lyric don't seem quite right, though. . . ."

"Oh, no, *that* ain't 'Two Dimes'!" The man standing by them was one of Kloves' deputies, Chess vaguely recalled; reflexively, he tightened his glamour, and Ed's as well. "It's a whole new reel entire, from someplace back Arizona way—'The Red-Head Pistoleer'!"

Chess froze.

Morrow: "I, uh, never heard that before."

"Oh, don't worry yourself, Mister Chester—take ya home humming, you'll see, 'specially the way Joe sings it." And, slamming back the last of his punch, he hurried for the dance floor, calling over his shoulder: "It's a right toe-tapper!"

Which seemed to be true enough, the way the dancers were now singing enthusiastically along.

Chesssss . . . Pargeter was a pretty little man, his hair was red as flame,
His Ma she knew no better, and she raised him up the same.
The ladies he liked little, the men he liked too well.
Mere repetition of his sins might send a man to Hell!

He danced with men for money, but he'd kill 'em just for fun,
And the only thing he truly loved was the barrel of his gun.

In the army he met Reverend Rook, who tried to pray him 'round,
But Chess sunk in his wicked hooks, and pulled that good man down.

Me, Chess realized. *It's about me. And—*

He drew a long breath, thick-burning, gullet suddenly a-heave. Felt Morrow's touch on one shoulder—all five fingers, strong and warm yet far too brief: *appearances,* don'tcha know. So's not to fright the horses. "Chess . . . ter, Junior: buck up, little brother. Just hold on, now."

Now, one sin leads to every sin, or so you may have heard—
And sodomy and sorcery are almost the self-same word.
He'd been a saint by all accounts, right faithful to God's ways,
But once stuck fast in Chess's toils, the Rev begun to change. . . .

Chess swallowed yet again, spit flavoured with bile. Said, slowly, "So . . . what they're sayin' is—*I* turned *him* bad?"

"It's a *song,* is all. Wrote by some idjit in a saloon five states over, probably drunk, couldn't even think up a brand new tune to set it to. Like the penny-papers, or them Dreadfuls done up on rag-pulp—all the lie that's fit. You know for yourself they always get it wrong."

The chorus rose up overtop, twice as strong, drunken-riotous:

The Good Lord wrote the Bible, Lincoln freed the slaves,
But the Devil made Chess Pargeter to drag fools to their graves.
He made him small and pretty, as bright as any pin,
And set that red-head pistoleer to tempt weak men to sin!

I could kill you, Chess thought, head at once blessedly clear, if aching. All *of you. Each and every damn one. It'd be easy. Pleasant, almost.*

All he had to do was pour every last drop of his rage down the web, turn booze-sodden cheer to the same killing fury burning up his spine, let them all loose on one another and then just sit back, while the blood pooled at his boots. Or maybe he'd just let it rip in all directions at once, unguided: a barrage of grapeshot, grinding everything into chuck— meat on meat blended together to make one red flurry, like it was raining screams. All guts, no glory.

You . . . think you know, 'bout Rook and me? You don't know shit.

"Chess, fucksake—" The light turned strange, and Chess realized Morrow had stepped close between him and the crowd, shielding the one from t'other. "We can't, not now. Jesus Christ Almighty, *look* at yourself!"

Since there was more panic in Morrow's voice than Chess had heard, well . . . ever, he did. And found that the sight did not ease his fury in the slightest, though it did come wrapped in blessedly dispassionate curiosity: A sweaty crimson sheen was leaking from his pores, slick and coppery, backlit by the subtle green luminescence outlining his bones. He turned his hand over and back, yet more sick light spilling forth like he'd cupped his hand on a green-flamed candle, so hard he'd bled in the cooking.

Now if he'd never met him, the Rev might still be right,
But Pargeter, that red-head tramp, a-turned him from the Light.
The Devil gave Rook magic, those mocking him were slayed—
And thus the Rev was proved a hex, and stays one to this day.

They scoured the state from east to west, a-robbing as they went.
Good men they killed, their widows left, ignoring their laments.
They took both trains and coaches, good folk were all appalled,
And the whole town of Bewelcome, the Rev, he preached to salt. . . .

What must his face look like, by now? Chess wondered, idly— some unholy mask, going on Morrow's horrified look alone: raw meat and cut vines, bad things growing wild. He felt the glamour slip from him, part by part—saw those closest widen their eyes as he shimmered and shrunk, gaze greening up, reddening from tip to tail. *Danger,* his mind sang out, *dangerdangerdanger—*

For *them*, Hell yes: danger aplenty. But not for *him*.

He was beyond that, and knew it, every fibre lit up with some deep, abiding grin.

"Wasn't no *joke*," he said, voice mud-thick, all uncaring who besides Ed might hear. "Not to me. And I ain't no vaudeville-hall act. Laugh at *me*, it's the last damn thing you'll ever do."

Then: more fingers—not Ed's, too small and soft by far—touched his. He wanted to peel 'em off, like leeches, or crush 'em, just to hear 'em squirt. But they slid down to encircle his wrists without trembling; his pulse hammered hard against them, a caged rat.

"Then they won't," said Yancey Kloves, simply. "Not anymore."

'Cause . . . I can do that.

It was her wedding, after all.

He swayed, pried his eyes open, but she was already gone, flitting through the crowd like a white-veiled wraith, as that damn refrain howled out all the louder:

Ohhhh, the Good Lord wrote the Bible, Lincoln freed the slaves,
But the Devil made Chess Pargeter to drag fools to their graves.
He made him small and pretty, as bright as any pin,
And set that red-head pistoleer to—

"'Scuse me, gents. *Excuse me!*"

Slipping her way betwixt musicians, one hip moving Toe-Tapper Joe aside so forcefully he lost his breath, Yancey waved an empty glass at the crowd, overriding their complaints with effortless cheer. "Can't tell y'all how much it means to me, and Uther," a doe-eyed glance at Marshal Kloves, owlishly a-blink at her from their table, "that y'all are having such a great time here! You've all been so kind and generous t'us, I wanted—" She hesitated; then her jaw firmed. "I *wanted*," she went on in a quieter voice, "to sing you something, in return. A song . . . my mother always loved."

As time grows near, my dearest dear, when you and I must part,
How little you know of the grief and woe in my poor aching heart.

'Tis blood I'd suffer for your sake—believe me, dear, it's true;
I wish that you were staying here, or I was going with you.

I wish my breast were made of glass, wherein you might behold
Upon my heart, your name lies wrote in letters made of gold;
In letters made of gold, my love—believe me, when I say
You are the one I will adore until my dying day.

The blackest crow that ever flew would surely turn to white
If ever I prove false to you, bright day will turn to night.
Bright day will turn to night, my love—the elements will mourn.
If ever I prove false to you, the seas will rage and burn.

On this last line, she let her struck-silver voice soften and fade away. And in the instant of silence before the hall erupted in praise, Chess let out a long, shuddering breath; he felt dazed, exhausted. The pull of the mind-web was a stabbing pain through his skull.

But Morrow's grip eased, voice kindly once more. "You all right?" he asked, words pitched low, beneath the noise.

"I will be, we can git, right this minute." Chess brushed at his face, impatiently. "That's always assuming you didn't break my damn arm, tryin' to hold me still."

"Very . . . pretty."

The harsh, low voice might almost have been Rook's; for one gut-wrenching instant, Chess half thought it was, before realizing it entirely lacked Rook's hypnotizing resonance. Yet it cut straight through the revel, sent the crowd spilling back over each other's feet as its owner reared up, just suddenly *present*, in their midst.

At the sight, Chess's mouth went dry, and stayed that way. Like he'd swallowed a mouthful of salt.

The man—whom nobody had seen enter—was tree-tall, broad-shouldered but lankier than either the Rev or Morrow, skin a-gleam with an ill patina like dried sweat, or hoarfrost. His hair made a crusted fringe, one short pigtail still left hanging; his torn and threadbare clothes were streaked with the same white that cataracted his eyes clear across, leaving him only the pinpricks of pupils to see through. And on his chest, where a lawman's vest once might have hung, the cross-cut icicle remains of a six-pointed tin star gleamed sharp.

That's not him, though; 'course it's damn well not. Man's dead, I saw it done. It . . . It just can't be.

"But, even so—" The figure lifted a lengthy hand Yancey's way, forefinger poised to shake, officious as any preacher. "—I'd far rather you'd let the *other* song reach its due conclusion, Missus."

Yancey, near as white as her own dress, swallowed hard. Yet managed, without visible qualm: "I . . . I don't hold with taking requests without some prior acquaintance, sir."

"No?" Impossible to tell, given his voice's ruin, if the question held any true amusement for him. "Then let me be known: My name is Love. . . ."

Sheriff Mesach Love, that was, as the gasp rippling through her wedding party confirmed; decorated Bluebelly war hero, gentleman born, his privilege shelved in favour of church-raising and homestead-building. Mesach Love, who'd been dealt a fate suffered by none since Lot's wife—widower to a murdered wife, father to a murdered son.

Late, in short, of Bewelcome township.

". . . and I have come a long and tedious way to seek out either Reverend Rook or his creature, Pargeter, recitation of whose life's works you so sweetly interrupted here—having sworn, no matter which of them I found, to deliver final judgement upon him."

At this, Kloves stood out—laid one hand on Yancey's arm, while the other sought for and found one gun-butt, sure as Christmastime.

"Even supposing you're who you say," he began, "might be your misfortune's got you all turned around. I'm Marshal for the jurisdiction; this is *my* wedding feast, and that's my wife you're speaking to. If the Rev were anywhere hereabouts, let alone his fancy-boy, I'd know it."

Love narrowed his praise-burnt eyes, and set his bitter mouth. "I *smell* them, Marshal."

A shrug. "I've no easy answer to that. Except to suggest how, sorry to say . . . might be your nose don't work too well, these days. Given all that's happened."

"That so?"

"It is."

"Hmm. S'pose we'll have to see, then."

Here Love made only the smallest of gestures—a brief figuring, equal-fit for blessing or curse. But a tremor ran party-wide at the mere sight of it, as though the very dust beneath came skirling at his call; not hexation, but the faint echo of some power far more oblique, implacable, sere. "God's will" writ small, and bent to another's service.

"O LORD GOD," the undead intoned, laying his skeletal palms together, "TO WHOM VENGEANCE BELONGETH; HEAR ME NOW, IN JESUS' NAME, AMEN. O GOD, TO WHOM VENGEANCE BELONGETH, SHEW THYSELF."

Chess heard the Rev read along, behind his eyes. Saw the words all but cast up and glinting, black sparks on bright:

LIFT UP THYSELF, THOU JUDGE OF THE EARTH: RENDER A REWARD TO THE PROUD.

LORD, HOW LONG SHALL THE WICKED, HOW LONG SHALL THE WICKED TRIUMPH?

. . . SHALL THE THRONE OF INIQUITY HAVE FELLOWSHIP WITH THEE, WHICH FRAMETH MISCHIEF BY A LAW?

"Psalm 94," Morrow whispered, eyes shut, his head half hung down—bent to Love's yoke, like he was more afraid of some damn quotation than the man's own black-miraculous spectacle.

But Kloves, unswayed, replied: "I want you *gone*, 'Sheriff.' Back to your own place. We've no need of you here."

"And I want Pargeter, or Rook. Give 'em to me, I'll move on. If not . . ." Love smiled, grimly. "THEY GATHER THEMSELVES TOGETHER AGAINST THE SOUL OF THE RIGHTEOUS, AND CONDEMN THE INNOCENT BLOOD," he said, to no one in particular—yet his voice wrung ever more horrid, 'til women clapped hands over their children's ears and a few weak souls doubled over, baptizing the floor. "BUT THE LORD IS MY DEFENCE; AND MY GOD IS THE ROCK OF MY REFUGE. AND HE SHALL BRING UPON THEM THEIR OWN INIQUITY, AND SHALL CUT THEM OFF IN THEIR OWN WICKEDNESS; YEA, THE LORD OUR GOD SHALL CUT THEM OFF."

A groan, a whimper—the crowd lurched all at once, aching to cut and run. Chess wondered, for a timepiece's barest half-tick, if he shouldn't let whatever was pending happen—he'd survive, almost certainly. But Ed's fists were closing, like he thought to throw punches at a man Death itself had spit up whole, and Kloves obviously meant the same. And Yancey cast Chess a single beseeching, lash-cut glance.

Goddamn all "good" people, Chess thought, with a sigh.

And let his glamour go altogether, with a plaster-rip wrench. In its wake he stood himself once more, purple-suited, to sneer back at the gaping faces which ringed him:

Yeah, take a look while you can; here I am, life-sized. Small-made, still, but that don't matter none. As you will see.

Sheriff Love might have his God, as always. Yet Chess had learned a thing or two 'bout gods himself, in the interim.

"No Heaven for you, Sheriff?" he enquired, conversationally. "And such a fervent sumbitch, too! You want me? Here I am."

Two guns to the Marshal's one, and a hand on either. Chess grinned at Love, mean as ever, 'til Love grinned back—equal-nasty in his own God-bothering way, and wide enough they could hear his salt-glazed jaw hinges crack.

"So you are, after all," he replied. "Praise Him!"

CHAPTER SEVEN

MISTER FREWER GAVE A slow blink. "By God," he said, finally, "if that *ain't* Chess Pargeter. Been there the whole time, I'd suspect." A pause. "Think Mister Chester knew it, all along?"

That Grey fellow replied, "Reckon so, if that's Chester over there; man's really named Ed Morrow, who used to be a Pinkerton."

Hugo Hoffstedt said, "Sheriff, Marshal—oughtn't you to *do* something, here? 'Fore—"

"You got any real kind of plan of attack on offer, Hugo, do feel free t'let it slip," Sheriff Haish shot back. And Uther, hand gone automatically to the empty place at his belt where his gun should hang, just blew slowly out through his nose—a bull, matador's cloak new-sighted, composing itself to charge.

In that instant, Yancey came painfully closest to loving him outright than she ever had before. *He's* good, she told herself, fiercely, *and that's the simple truth. Probably better than I deserve, given . . .*

Given how sadly complicit she was in what was happening—was *about to* happen.

Back stiff, she made herself look past to Lionel, who stood there gaping. "I shook his *hand*," he told her.

"I saw, Pa."

"Took it right in mine, and *shook* it, hard. Asked him how he liked the wedding."

"I *know*, Pa—I was there, same as you. Saw it all."

Her eyes slid back to Uther, guilt ably disguised as fright—or maybe not, since it wasn't like she *wasn't* verging on terrified, though not on her own behalf. So many people, such a small space, and all of 'em here on her say-so. All of 'em in danger due to her secret glee, now most securely fled, at having known what no one else did—of managing to avert, alone, a menace nobody but her even saw was there, in the first place.

Oh, it was true what the Good Book said: *Pride goeth before destruction, and an haughty spirit before a fall.* Facing Pargeter down had been frightening, but for all the little man's posturing, he was still human at his core; no different from dealing with the belligerent drunks she dealt with every night's end, no matter how off-puttingly careless he was in letting his power over-slop itself. Whereas Sheriff Love had been a righteous man once, or so folks said—but Yancey could barely stand to *look* at what was left of him: this glassine shell of ill-will that crackled as it moved, reeked like spoiled meat cured in hatred . . . by God, it was enough to make her stomach heave.

They cut a strange pair, posed before the company in pure dime-novel gunfight stance: Pargeter, stood up slim and straight in his purple livery, red-gilt hair lifted like burning corn, and an indefinite blackness a-hover 'round all his edges. About Sheriff Love, meanwhile, clung something white as paper, or leprosy—remorseless, comfortless. A hollow luminescence whose outermost edges tangled with his opponent's to breed something equally grey, debriding the world's God-given colours to dust and ash around them.

As Pargeter bristled, Love stood blanched and granular, dead skin slippy over a raw martyr's bone-mask. His eyes—so drily pearlescent they ate light—barely seemed to narrow against the hex-pistoleer's green glare, as though too well-burnt by God's own regard to find any other more than momentarily inconvenient.

Whatever I can do to help move this creature where he can do no more harm, I will, Yancey found herself thinking. *Even if I have to take Pargeter's side against him to do it.*

The very idea made her breath catch. But she knew it for truth, inescapably, as such sudden insights always proved to be.

Christ Almighty. This curse of a "gift," always showing a thousand terrible things converging, but not one damn hint of which way to turn in order to throw 'em off. She'd've passed the weight of it on gladly to anyone fool enough to ask, were it not still the only weapon she had: weak, inaccurate, impossible to control. The proverbial knife to a gunfight.

How in Jesus' name can I hope to save them, any of them? I can't even save myself.

Which was when another voice, softer-than-soft, came licking at her skull's insides, offering this advice: *Not for the present, no. But you know these guests of yours, little dead-speaker; good folk in the main, strong, and capable of much. If given opportunity, the right sort of push . . . might they not save themselves?*

Yes, she thought, not knowing who she answered. Deciding, on her father's soul and marriage-vow alike, to believe it—or act like she did, at least, 'til experience proved her right.

In front of her, at the same time, the stand-off played on—and whatever else he was, that mean-mouthed Mister Pargeter sure didn't seem to lack for courage.

"What say we take this outside, so nobody has to get hurt?" he suggested, back-shifting to balance on his heels, as though this whole unnatural paradiddle were little more than the prelude to a simple bar-fight. "This bein' a house of *God*, and all."

Love made a dry sound, half-hiss, half-snort. "Hadn't known you to be quite so particular, in previous circumstances."

"Yeah, well—that was with *your* people, you'll recall. And considerin' they'd all just finished kickin' the crap out of me, I think I showed undue restraint." This, Love didn't even deign to answer—just stared, his awful eyes level, prompting Pargeter to continue. "The rest . . . your wife, and such . . . that wasn't even my idea, anyhow. Was strictly the Rev's doin', all of it."

"You know yourself how that's an arrant lie."

"Not back then, I didn't."

Love's gaze went sliding right overtop the outlaw's head, to some far-off place beyond. "And what earthly good does knowing that fact do me now?" he asked, of no one visible. "Though it does beg the question—where *is* your whoremaster, exactly, 'Private' Pargeter?"

"Rev and I had us a falling out, sad to say."

"Ah." Love nodded, sagely. "Most sodomitical liaisons end likewise, I'd think."

"Oh, wasn't over *that*. But tell me, Sheriff, now we're all caught up: how's it happen you come to be upright again, exactly?"

"Through God's own bounty." He spread his long arms, palms lifting to the roof. "An angel appeared, and told me he had been sent to intercede, on *my* behalf. *Me*." An awestruck smile stretched the preacher's face, making salt powder down from his mouth corners. "For all my many missteps, my sins unforgiven, because I had further work to do upon this earth . . . I was spared. And sent back."

Pargeter thrust his thumbs through his belt, cocked his head. "Mmm. Sure it was *God* who made that particular call, Sheriff?"

Love took the implication full-face, producing a blank, inhuman immobility more terrifying even than Pargeter's killing grin. While, at the same time—

"You thinkin' what I'm thinkin'?" Uther murmured, to Sheriff Haish.

"How I'm just about to shit my britches?" Haish replied, just as low, eyes still fast on Love and Pargeter.

To which Uther opened his mouth again, to elaborate, only to hear Yancey chime in, before he could: "Long as they keep intent on each other, now might be a goodish time to start getting folks out the back."

This brought both men swivelling to scrutinize her, with Lionel a close third. "There's nobody can say my girl's not smart," her Pa observed, at last.

"Nobody damn well better try," Uther agreed. And crushed her briefly to him, searing her lips with what was only their second kiss thus far, but might well be their last.

MORROW DIDN'T KNOW WHERE best to put his eyes—on Love, that awful object? Chess, obviously poised to draw, making Morrow's fingers itch for the feel of his own shotgun? Or the Marshal and his lady, who seemed to be using this pause to lay a few plans of their own?

When hexes get to wranglin', plain folks should stick together, he thought, feeling helpless.

Though Sheriff Love'd probably take it as deadly insult to be named a *hex*, even now—drawing himself up once more, creaking like salt-crusted leather. To say: "God *does* provide, Mister Pargeter, even to the unbelieving. Why not to me?"

Over the Sheriff's desiccated shoulder, Morrow watched the Marshal, Haish and Colder Senior fan out through the crowd, tapping shoulders, bending ears; saw folks link arms, scoop up their children, backing away, quick and soft as their liquored-up feet would take 'em. While Missus Kloves worked her own way slowly forward, like she thought there was anything she could do to help. . . .

Go BACK! Morrow tried to mouth, without moving his face far enough to tip Love off. He suspected he must look somewhat like a fish caught in mid-hooking; that alone would've warned most folks away.

But not her, Goddamnit.

In front of him, meanwhile, Chess's smile took on a knowing edge. "Why indeed? But enlighten me, Sheriff: just who *did* this 'angel' of yours say he was, anyhow?"

Love's gaze dropped, just for a moment. "He said . . . your Enemy. Yours and your Reverend's, both."

Chess shot a sidelong look at Morrow, shared knot of memory flaring, a pine-knot cookfire-cracked: *ENEMY, by Christ*—

A plate-etching behind the eyes, bouncing from Chess to Morrow to poor Missus Kloves in turn—*I see him standing behind you,* she'd said, voice gone colourless. Huge, black; stone-stiff, knife-toothed, mirror-footed. That bottomless stare and that *name*, at last . . . the one he'd somehow let slip only to her, without 'em ever having met. . . .

(*Tezcatlipoca*)

Morrow saw Missus Kloves reel under it, gut-punched, before handing her way back up; damn but that gal had grit, even with her face gone white as her wedding veil. Caught her mouth shaping words in turn, and strained to read them—

Hold him . . . while longer, 'til . . . Pa comes back. Gone . . . get . . .

Was that last one "weapons"?

Morrow risked an "okay" sign with one hand, thumb set to forefinger and shook, hard; Missus Kloves nodded, just the once, but definite.

While Love repeated, harsh mouth a-twist once more—bitter as the salt that filled it—"*Your* Enemy. Yours. Just like you're mine, and God's. So, whatever else, that's good enough for me."

"Likewise," Chess snapped, eyes flaring. And clenched both gunless fists on empty air without fanfare or flourish, causing Love to burst apart suddenly, as though he'd swallowed a mortar.

Screams ripped up from the crowd; furniture crashed and fell, glass shattering, as those onlookers still left backed away even further. And the grey-white cloud that had been Sheriff Mesach Love settled slowly to the clapboard floor, pattering like rain.

Chess, meanwhile, simply stood there, admiring his own works, unmoved. As though he'd all of a sudden decided there was no point even pretending he was still pistoleer first, hex after—let alone the damn *god* that Enemy of everyone's had so often named him.

No need even to draw, let alone aim, or shoot; I think a thing, it happens, and that's all. Like it has *to. Like it's got no earthly Goddamn choice. Like I don't, neither.*

Well, that's one *way,* Morrow thought, numbly.

"HOLY CHRIST," WHISPERED HUGO Hoffstedt, so quiet Yancey wasn't even sure she'd actually heard it. Her eyes stayed locked on Chess Pargeter's terrible aspect, refusing even to flick away. Had she really so recently felt *sorry* for such a creature, back when the band's mockery brought hot blood to his face?

He'd been just a man, then, boy-sized, tough outside and bruised in-, wounded by love, then mocked for caring. Never having seen Reverend Rook, let alone his works, she'd almost envied him for having loved someone so much he was ready to cry—or kill—over it.

Yet love can be terrible, too, the nameless voice told her, sadly. *You have far too few words for so many things, granddaughter.*

Who is *that?* Yancey considered her life to have been far easier when she hadn't had to ask herself such questions.

Most 'specially so when the phantom intelligence in question didn't even pause, before replying: *No matter. Now watch—and be ready.*

For what?

Just like that, however, the voice was gone.

Pargeter, all blissful-unaware of this exchange, caught Yancey looking and sketched a mocking bow while Mister Morrow hurried to his side, muttering something Yancey couldn't make out. But right as he got there, his foot stepped awry, bringing him down heavy on one knee. Shock lit Morrow's face.

Pargeter grabbed his partner's arm in turn, as though to pull the bigger man up, half-pivoted in the same direction—and saw why.

For the drift of salt he'd made was whirling in a contracting spiral, vicious with energy; it scrabbled in on itself, mounding high 'til it abruptly plumed skyward, a miniature eruption that literally blew the top off the place, scattering shingles everywhere. Then fell back down, into an all-too-familiar shape.

Love stood there unharmed, exactly where he had a mere moment before.

The Sheriff slowly flexed his hands, which grated icily, giving off a great puff of skin-stuff. At the sound, a general moan went up from all around, desperate as wind through a graveyard.

"Fuck-almighty!" Pargeter burst out.

"Interesting," Love mused. Then added, looking up through what was left of the church's roof: "Thank you, Jesus."

Morrow clutched back, palpably a-strain to keep his body interposed shield-wise between 'em, apparently without thinking twice. "Chess," he gritted, "we need to *go.*"

"So he's got tricks. Think that frights *me*?"

"Know it don't, you ass. But what about the rest?'

Hell with those fools! Yancey could feel exactly how hard Pargeter wanted to snap the thought back, stacked cheek by jowl with how he *knew* he couldn't—and that was a change, one he found distinctly unwelcome. And here Hugo Hoffstedt broke in, pointing a shaking finger at poor Mister Frewer, as though *he* was the true cause of everybody's danger.

"*Told* you we'd rue the day we let these Mouth-of-Praisers in—hexation draws hexation, and that's the damn fact! And now look what's the result: two hexes, for the price of one!" His eyes skipped to Uther, already wending his way back. "Your foolish softness's doomed us all, Uther Kloves, you and your Jew father-in-law, too—"

"Shut your mouth, apostate," Love told him, absently. "Pargeter's the man-witch here, but *my* strength comes from Almighty God alone . . . *and you will not mock at me.*"

Hoffstedt's face turned even more purple; his eyes bulged. With a gagging sound his only accompaniment, he started a collapse, but hadn't quite completed it before Uther caught him, knotting one big hand in the tobacconist's shirt. "Sorry 'bout this, Hugo—" The other drew back and punched him, straight in the stomach.

Hoffstedt jackknifed, whooped a slapped-baby gasp, and puked out a sodden chunk of rock salt too huge for any normal throat to swallow, which skipped to lie before him, dripping. Yancey stared at it.

Salt, which Mala always said turned hexation aside, surer than any other known cure. *There's folks say witches can't cry at all, Yancey, since tears are saltwater; I've seen enough do so to know that isn't true. Yet salt does keep, and render, and purify. And salt throws off hexation, same as a rod does lightning—roots it down deep, so it'll make away with itself without causing too much harm. Same way as your Pa throws a spilled pinch over his left shoulder at dinner, to ward away the Devil.*

And the Sheriff . . . that was all he was *made* of, wasn't it, saving terrible grief, and a seeking after revenge? So even if he didn't understand the true whys and wherefores, believing it was the diamond-hard strength of his own faith that kept him safe, the result would be the same.

Oh, Jesus.

Not knowing to make the same connection, Pargeter just sneered, like it was all another bad joke. "Hell, preacher—if that's supposed to be a sample of *God's* work, then maybe you better go on and pull the other one!"

Mister Morrow was right, Yancey thought, soul-sick; *you should run, the both of you. For his sake, if not your own.*

But the devilish little man just wouldn't, obviously; wasn't in him. Might be he didn't even know how.

As Hoffstedt rolled onto his back, gasping, Pargeter neatly swapped his place for Morrow's, much as the other man tried to prevent it. "But that *is* some extra-fresh load of power you're carrying, one way or t'other," he continued, ignoring how being mis-called a hex twice in a row made Love's jaws grind. "And how you're puttin' it to use 'minds me most of . . . what the *Rev* could pull out his Good Book, you only pissed him off enough. Like back in Bewelcome."

"Don't presume to talk on that, you filth-piece."

"Oh yeah, I recall how you did pretty good in Round One, 'til he called on Lot in Sodom, and pimp-smacked your Jesus Christ holler like a two-bit whore."

"Be still!"

"Take a sight more than a shake or two of table-fixings to stop *my* queer-boy mouth, *Sheriff*—"

"*You!*" Love's voice almost hurt to hear, now. "*You* killed my wife, my son, my *town* . . . *you* and Rook, the both—"

Yancey shuddered, yet again. For they *had* done that, undeniably—and if Pargeter had not consciously chosen to do it, he had certainly delighted in seeing it done.

"Or *you* killed 'em, more like," Pargeter threw back, shameless, "by standin' against us." With a gunman's vaudeville flourish, he sent lightning crackling fingertip-to-tip, green as his eyes. "Took on 'cause you were too proud to hear the Rev 'blaspheme' your precious Book, though what-all it had to do with *you* I still don't know; thought to reap reward on our heads, and kicked your own house down doin' it."

Love drew himself up. "I did . . . what I had to."

"Likewise." Another grin. "'Course, I understand 'worship'— used to be the Rev I knelt to, in all senses. But since he made me *this*, I don't do nobody's will but my own."

"Don't flatter yourself, 'Private.' You're no god—not even a graven idol, like Moloch, or Baal."

"Oh, I'm a god, all right: the Flayed Corn King, He-With-No-Heart, somethin' new, and something *very* old. Responsible for every bad thing that happens 'roundabouts, too, they tell me—so who knows but that 'angel' you think God sent you wasn't my doin', somehow? All along. Ever think of that?"

If he'd expected this last shot to tell, it didn't, visibly. Yet Love's pale eyes slid sideways, fixing upon Morrow.

"I do note, however," he said, "that even without Rook, you still seem to have something left to lose."

At this, Morrow tried to push by, take up his protective stance once more—but Pargeter swept one arm out behind him, and the bigger man soon found himself abruptly up against the nearest wall, legs a-flail, 'til he lost his balance and fell to the same knee, with palpably painful impact. He'd already struggled halfway back up before an outthrust palm stopped him in his tracks—not more hexation, just a clear signal: *Stay back, Goddamnit!*

So he does *care for him,* Yancey thought. *Like I guess Love's counting on.*

Pargeter raked Love up and down, with fine contempt. "Threats on a third party?" he asked. "Don't seem very Christian. Better make up your mind. Is vengeance *yours*, or the Lord's? You want an eye for an eye, for real?"

Not waiting for Love's reply, Pargeter beckoned, seeming oddly happy at the prospect.

And snarled—"Then come take one of *mine*."

CHAPTER EIGHT

WITHOUT THINKING, MORROW SURGED automatically forward one last time, then felt the air around him slam shut, and ceased to struggle. Jesus *God*, he wished he had some sort of firearm handy! His shotgun, reckoned too long to conceal under Chess's imperfect glamour, he'd left behind in the Honeymoon Suite, with the rest of what little gear they retained. If Yancey's plan had actually worked, they would have had ample time to retrieve it.

But—*Sooner or later, Sergeant*, every *plan stops working—with the very first shots, more oft than not.* Colonel Stockwell's prissy-vowelled New York memory-voice, snapping back at him all the weary way from Marais des Cygnes. *The test of a true leader is how he deals with what he* couldn't *have planned for.*

Morrow's fists clenched. What he needed, by those lights, was a distraction, something to jolt Love off-guard long enough for Chess to whisk 'em both away and send the Sheriff rocketing after, leaving these poor people to their own devices.

As though she knew his mind, new-made Missus Kloves gave him a head-toss over toward where the church's back door was working its slow way open. And Morrow nodded back, schooling himself to not react as a hunched figure—her father?—crawled back inside, dragging a burlap sack heavy with what looked, even at this distance, like weaponry.

Get set, he thought.

YANCEY DIDN'T DARE TURN further, not and hope to keep Love's attention wholly fixed on Pargeter; to meet Mister Morrow's eyes, see the hope flaring there, was dangerous enough. Still, she could *feel* Pa's presence again, and her heart went helplessly out to him—a soul-scared man straining to act the part of brave father, convinced his daughter's life depended on him doing it. Which she could only hope it didn't.

Meanwhile, undistracted by any of the above, Sheriff Love bent his awful head over folded palms and whispered, like wind stirring gravel: "Go to now, ye rich men, weep and howl for your miseries that shall come upon you. Your riches are corrupted, and your garments are moth-eaten. Your gold and silver is cankered; and the rust of them shall be a witness against you, and shall eat your flesh as it were fire. . . ."

A deafening crack split the air, unseen thunderbolt-swift. Before his expression could twitch toward even the beginning of surprise, Pargeter went up like a roman candle of searing, blue-white flame.

With a yell, Mister Morrow lunged blaze-wards, only to reel off almost immediately—face shielded, beat back by waves of heat. The crowd moaned. Yancey fought all the champagne she'd drunk thus far back down.

Can't be that easy, though. Can it?

Seconds later, two only slightly pinkened hands thrust upwards from the inferno and spread apart, ripping their way free; the fiery shroud tore wholesale, shredded into streamers, rewove itself into twin whips of actinic flame dangling from Pargeter's palms. He stepped clear, no more high-coloured than usual, his imperially hued suit not even scorched.

"Good one," he said. "But I've heard better."

Not taking his eyes off Love, Pargeter whirled the fire-ropes 'round his head so they buzzed, trailing blue sparks. The very air above shimmered terribly, roaring as if cut, 'til he flung both Helllariats at Love headlong. They struck the Sheriff with a noise like two locomotives mating; Yancey braced herself against the crash— which never came.

For a heartbeat, Love glowed equally hot, if far less bright, as Pargeter's whips collapsed straight *into* him, sponged up. But the light faded, draining down into the floor, planks set a-flash like moonlit water. Once more, Love stared unblinking, untouched.

At last, Pargeter's grin faltered.

But, just in time . . . here came her Pa, creeping, weapons-bag in hand, to touch random crowd-members' elbows and handing 'em on toward escape, as though he were directing traffic. Catching hers, he bore her away to meet from Uther eeling his own way downstream, making for them with eyes glued fast on that swinging, faintly clinking bag of tricks. . . .

"Think your Satan-got might impresses me, you trousered harlot?" No brag in the preacher's dead voice, just plain, scornful fact. "I have the very Thrones and Principalities at *my* back. I have His Word, always, in my ear."

Pargeter shrugged. "Well, you don't *listen*, that's for damn sure."

But this insult lacked the usual venom, his glare gone narrow, calculating odds and means. Drawing an alarmingly long knife, he slapped its blade into his other palm, sliced fast, flicked the result Love's way; a fine spray of blood licked 'cross one bleached cheek with an audible sizzle, leaving a smoking trench behind. But Love simply raised his own hand and dug in, scraping melted flesh away as whitish sludge, like badly laid mortar. His teeth gleamed visibly through the gap, slate-grey, before his cheek reformed itself.

"HE WHO DWELLS IN THE SHELTER OF THE MOST HIGH WILL REST IN THE SHADOW OF THE ALMIGHTY," he rasped, wiping his hands. "I WILL SAY OF THE LORD, HE IS MY REFUGE AND MY FORTRESS, MY GOD, IN WHOM I TRUST." A long step forward. "A THOUSAND MAY FALL AT YOUR SIDE, TEN THOUSAND AT YOUR RIGHT HAND, BUT NEAR YOU IT SHALL—NOT—COME!"

Each of those last three words came with another unnaturally swift pace, closing the distance, taking him almost within his wiry little opponent's reach. Pargeter took a step back—Yancey felt Morrow's dismay, a cold shock in her stomach's pit, at seeing his fearless partner *retreat*—before groggery-brawl reflex took over, and he whipped his knife at Love's right eye.

The blade buried itself hilt-deep, which stopped Love for at least a moment; Pargeter seized this opportunity to circle sideways, opening up the field. And though his lips stayed peeled, Yancey sensed, for the first time, more doubt than anger behind this reflexive grimace as Love simply turned as well, resuming his opposing stance.

"Oh, what a vain, luxurious, vicious young coxcomb you are," Love declared, almost conversationally, pulling the knife free of his socket with a visible wrench. The eye that reformed was now completely white, unshelled to show the phosphorescent glow beneath, spreading in faint hairline cracks up to his very temple. "A walking canker, spreading fresh plague with every step. Yet God, who has made even you, has appointed me your cure." He looked down at his hands, brow wrinkling, as if he'd forgotten how the weapon he still held got there—then snapped it lengthwise, and tossed it to the floor.

Now it was Pargeter's face which went blank. "That," he said, almost too soft to hear, "was a gift. From a friend."

The black aura around him deepened, as though the edges of the world were peeling back. And the silence outside the church began to shred.

Something coming.

"Oh shit," Mister Morrow said.

Pa's head jerked, foolishly, as though primed to snap: *Don't think to swear in front of* my *daughter, you outlaw! Most 'specially not on her wedding day!*

But by then, Uther and Sheriff Haish had joined them; faster than Yancey could blink, they'd already upturned the coveted sack, doling out guns like party favours to Pa, Mister Frewer, themselves.

Love, intent on Pargeter, seemed utterly incurious as to the rising clatter and flurry behind him. But Uther, on finding Mister Morrow's shotgun at the bottom, snapped the stock, racked it—and tossed it back to its original owner, who plucked it gratefully from the air and levelled it over Pargeter's shoulder, straight at Sheriff Love's chest.

"Sheriff!" Morrow shouted. "You've got any of God's mercy in you, back off, 'fore this goes too far!" When Love glanced at him, though Morrow's voice cracked, his gun stayed steady. "*Think*, man! What's the fate of those who spill innocent blood?"

The Sheriff's other eye went white as well, while the entire air around him leached to the colour of dry-fissured bone.

"*I am,*" Love replied.

Then Morrow's finger clenched on the triggers, unleashing both barrels. Love's chest erupted; salt sprayed everywhere, flushing unwary eyes. But Love barely rocked back on his heels, pellets blazing merrily right on through, their momentum unabated. Along with yet more salt, sharp and pitiless, forged near-obsidian hard by passage through Love's furnace-hot heart.

Duck, Yancey thought, even as she yelled out loud: "Now, *now*, get damn well *DOWN!*"

But one burst nicked Haish's neck, drawing a mighty spurt—he spun, clapped a hand to the damage, looked drunkenly surprised. Fell to the floor, jacked and shaking, like cholera. The other neatly blew out the centre of Uther's left palm, instinctively upraised between it and Yancey, as though he'd dreamed it would shield her from lead. Luckily, her Pa shoved her headlong at almost the same moment, to sprawl face-first onto the floor 'midst the dust and splinters. Which, *un*luckily, left him—

Oh my Good God Jesus, Pa.

—looking down as she looked up, faces equal sick-white in the inconstant light. A flutter of ill-timed laughter spun inside her, trapped, a skeleton leaf in updraft. Like a flame-caught moth charred black, already dying.

"Gal," Lionel Colder tried to say, through a closed throat. And Yancey heard his lungs rattle as he toppled, juicy-wet, through that unmendable hole in his chest.

"*Shit,*" Mister Morrow said again, like it was the only word he knew. Like he'd forgotten how to say anything else, without bawling like a damn baby.

Not his fault, though. More Pargeter's, she supposed—but even now, lapped by this insane storm of destruction, he drew nothing from her but abstract alarm, mixed here and there with an odd pulse of pity.

It was *Love* who got the full brunt of her hatred, in a vitriol cocktail; Love who she wanted to see broken apart once more, reduced to crystals so fine they'd dissolve on skin. Blast him to particulates, and beyond. How dare he even mention God, for good or ill, when—

Eyes tear-burnt, Yancey felt blindly for her Pa's hand, which flexed in her grip, fixed and cooling. Closed her lids so tight they hurt against the sight of him, only to see his soul's skein bloom upwards anyhow—unwind from his mouth in a fine gold thread and out through the shattered roof, along with his last attempt at breath.

Took a second at most, probably less. Felt like forever.

Uther by her side, big as a house, stuck to her with sweat and blood alike; Uther, still trying to shield her with his body as he pried her gently loose, raised her to her trembling knees.

"Honey, oh honey," he said, tender as a stone-made man can be. "I'm so sorry."

Me too, she thought, but couldn't speak aloud. Could only choke on, dry, as though she were chewing a cud of blood . . . 'til from all around came a noise Yancey recognized immediately, though she'd only heard it described the once.

"What . . . the hell . . . is *that?*" someone, maybe Hoffstedt, whimpered.

A buzzing and clicking at the window-frames, as of a multitude of scrabbling legs. A reverberant hum moaning up through every breach, every crumbling mortar-lick. The floorboards juddering and splintering underfoot, sending those still trapped inside the church reeling, while Pargeter and Love both remained rooted. Jagged cracks lancing up through all four walls at once, filled with a tangle of red-stained green, a million dancing filaments tasting air: budding, seeding, blooming. Turning their hungry flower-faces toward the rigid purple-clad figure of their god, even as the plain wooden cross behind the altar broke free and crashed to the ground, crushing a handful of poor parishioners beneath it.

Yancey saw it all, through a hundred eyes at once: screams, tears, Pa and Sheriff Haish, Uther hauling her close.

But *heard* none of it, for her ears were blocked, admitting one sound only—that other voice in her head once more, dry, urgent—

This heralds your moment, granddaughter; be ready to make sacrifice—

Sacrifice? Yancey was barely able to ask.

You shall show them the way. Be ready.

A flicker of light caught Yancey's eye as half Pargeter's broken knife-blade leaped high into the air, tossed by a floorboard suddenly cracked in two; when it landed near her, and she squirmed to get one arm free, grab for it. The edges bit her palm, stinging fiercely.

With a splintering cacophony, Weed thrust up through every crack, spreading out 'round Love's and Pargeter's feet in a widening, slimy green and crimson pool. What Mouth-of-Praisers were yet present screamed in unison, rushing the church's doors and hammering on them, wailing, as the Weed spread ever further; the floor decimated, whole fresh ropes fisted every wall-chink apart at once, a barn-raising in reverse, brickwork crumpling outwards in a cacophony of shattering wood and billowing dust.

And through this fresh ruin the *itzapapalotl* (the foreign word sliding into Yancey's mind, bringing such a flood of similar jabber in its wake that for one reeling heartbeat, she feared she'd never speak English again) came swarming—a thousand thousand black glass butterflies on squeaking, jagged wings, each flap drawing blood.

They folded themselves sidelong 'round debris, grazing Weed

'til juice sprayed wide in their wake, and whirled ever inward in a glittering twister. The roar of their passage was like every sandstorm ever sighted bearing down in unison.

We're done for sure, Yancey thought, cleft palm cleaving to Uther's, a last hopeless parable of matrimony.

Yet even as she did, she heard that ruthless voice—*What should I call it?*—inside her answer—

Such discourtesy! I called you granddaughter, did I not?

. . . Grandma?

MORROW LUNGED TO HIS feet as a host of more natural insects—dragonflies like the Lady came cloaked in, mosquitoes and wasps, red-shelled ladybirds and a dozen more kinds besides—spilled in behind those volcano-born death-moths he and Chess had glimpsed above Tampico, gnawing through flesh and fabric alike. Flinging himself in their path, he gasped with relief when all of 'em went skittering away from him, as though he wore some invisible canvas tarp. Unbelievably, Rook had told the truth: he *was* protected from harm, at least indirectly; marked and bound, both for good and ill.

"Ed." Even Chess's voice had changed, resonant with echoes of the gap between worlds. "There." He pointed; Morrow followed his finger to where a young woman hunched over her screaming child—same one he'd seen Chess stare at, before?—with her whole back streaming blood. At the first sign of trouble she'd folded herself 'round him, just like you'd expect; now the butterflies were stripping her shoulder blades bare, drawing wet, red wings down her good gingham dress.

Morrow whipped off his duster, draped it over 'em both and hauled 'em clear, kicking past the maelstrom's swirling rings. Weed pulled at his boots, but let him go when he strained—as if it recognized that somewhere, deep down, Morrow had at last begun to accept his role as the Flayed One's servant.

The woman, her boy's screaming face pressed hard to her breast, could barely make her feet. "God bless you, mister," she managed, through bitten lips.

Morrow shook his head, and set one boot to her ass, as gently as he could. "Run!" he ordered, kicking the two further out of danger. "Don't stop. And don't look back!"

Then, much against his own misgivings, he turned to fight his way back in.

Back at the storm's core, Chess poured his anger out upon the preacher in entirely one-sided fashion, each finger discharging a six-shooter's worth of those roily little spell-loads, while Love simply stood angled slightly into the barrage, like it was no more than a stiff wind. No matter what Chess threw at him, it either soaked right into the man's skin or slid off harmlessly into the unstable bed of rucked and vibrating floorboards beneath, re-emerging as fresh new batches of Weed.

"Fuckin' well *die*, you sumbitch!" Chess growled. But Love simply shook his head, insects glancing off his face and body, leaving nothing behind but drag-marks.

"Unlikely, I fear," he said. "And you've only yourself to thank, for that."

With horror, Morrow saw Love move forward again, inexorably; whenever Weed reached up to snare his legs, the powdery flesh just broke apart and re-coalesced around it, leaving a trail of vines flopping like pulled veins in his wake. Missus Kloves gagged at the sight, like she was fixing to heave. Chess just stared on, amazed.

"There really ain't nothin' left of Bewelcome's big damn hero anymore, is there?" he asked. "Look 'round, Sheriff. Womenfolk, children, Marshal and Missus Kloves—'good people,' Goddamn *innocents*, caught in the crossfire. You could stop it, you only wanted to . . . but then you'd have to let me go. This what your God-botheration *really* amounts to?"

That got Love to stop at last, as nothing else had—to consider Chess directly, for almost the first time.

"Arminius's creed says we are justified by faith alone," he told him, "but sanctified by the Holy Spirit. And whatsoever the Spirit does is right, for it is the *Spirit* which does it."

All at once, those big hands flashed to seize Chess's throat, hauling him up by the neck—and everything proceeding from Chess's power-source immediately stopped dead. The Weed fell still, insects plummeting ground-wards with one great rattle, a glass-and-chitin hail. Chess's boots kicked useless, fingers scrabbling frantic, unable to find purchase; green lightning crackled from his fingernails only to disappear inside Love's body, like every damn thing else.

Morrow too collapsed, his own throat constricted, spots swimming before his eyes. The room darkened.

"And see." Love's voice had gentled, almost regretful. "Even thus is the Lord's vengeance properly delivered. With all your might, you're flesh and blood; no more, or less. Soon you'll be dead as Sophy, or my boy . . . dead as me."

Eyes bulging, lips blue, Chess choked out a final jibe: "Buh ahll—stih—*look*—behher."

The revenant nodded. "I'm sure you'll have fresh admirers aplenty, in Hell."

GRANDDAUGHTER—LOOK, NOW. SEE.

Yancey let her gaze slip back down to her own yet-dripping blood beading bright on what was left of the floor, the Weed's writhing bed. Where it landed, a faint scent and smoke rose up and the tide calmed, vine smoothing to wet grass, thick with possibilities. One incautious *itzapapalotl* flew over top and cracked down the middle, both sharp wings bisected, still fluttering even as they fell to smash below.

Remember what he said, your little Hataalii's travelling companion. Remember how it sounded . . . so plausible.

"The Weed eats blood, and dies," she whispered, eyes straying again to Mister Morrow. "You have to—cut yourself, and pray. In his name."

"Wife," Uther said, slow, from behind her, "what *do* you mean by that, exactly?"

Yancey held up her hand, brought the half-knife down again. "Watch."

The sheer keenness of the edge delayed the pain a moment, just long enough for her to begin to cry: "Mister Pargeter—*here*—" And then her hand was afire, her warning a wordless wail as much shock as pain, though both were almost equally bad.

The Weed sucked up her fresh-let blood swifter even than Love's pie-crust flesh had absorbed Pargeter's hexation, digging ever deeper, writhing as it fed. After which a ripple lashed upwards, twining tight about the man in question's purple-clad legs, and colour surged back into Pargeter's whey-pale face; he chopped one hand clean through Love's left-hand-side jaw hinge in a white-powder smash, so hard the Sheriff's head fair spun, whipping-top style. Yet Love's stranglehold did not shift, fingers thinning to circle Pargeter's throat completely and pull in sharp, a leathery, granular noose.

Not enough, Yancey realized, and clawed her way past the pain "More!" she screamed, to all those agape at her. "Blood kills the Weed, and that gives Pargeter strength—strength enough to put this *thing* down, where we can't hope to!"

Mister Grey, over by Haish's fallen body: "Hexation 'gainst hexation? Sounds dicey at best, if that's even what Sheriff Love is packin'."

Yancey waved his words away, impatient. "What other choice? If all of us spill a little, then . . ."

"Yancey, *no!*" Uther hollered, and grabbed for her wounded hand—trying to exert his husbandly authority, she guessed, much as it wouldn't do either of 'em any good, if he succeeded. But Morrow, rising from where he'd fallen, slit his own palm open to the meat, not even waiting to let it spill; reached down to grab the Weed straight-on instead, forcing it to his spurting wound. The soundless green pulse which erupted was near-visible, surging up through the Weed into Pargeter, who gave out a shout: high, wild, inarticulate. A wildcat's coital shriek.

Sheriff Love let go and staggered back, covering his ears. Cast eyes on Morrow, Yancey as well, like he was disappointed to his very core, and hissed: "Unbelievers! Ye have set up false idols and made worship unto them, as the Israelites with their golden calf, and God's judgement will be certain, swift, *severe.*"

Maybe so, Yancey reckoned. But her half-cooked plan was definitely working; 'round Morrow, the mess of Weed was already a tight circle of rich grass, so fast the change barely registered. His sacrifice even seemed to have boosted hers, retroactively—for she and Uther both now also knelt in a patch of vibrant growth, fit to pasture the best of livestock.

Here a new voice intruded, odd as Love's own, though in a far different way. It came from Morrow's mouth, though his dumbfounded face would seem to belie it, chanting—

> *"Now, oh friends,*
> *Listen to the word, the true dream:*
> *Each spring gives us life,*
> *The golden ear of corn replenishes us,*
> *The young ear of corn becomes our necklace.*
> *Blood of men, so precious—*
> *So flowery, like jade.*
> *Our flowers will never end,*
> *Our songs will never cease to be."*

This—prayer, one could only assume—rose up like a drone, lulling the townsfolk quiet. Beside Mister Grey, who knelt cradling the unconscious Hugo Hoffstedt in his lap, Mister Frewer arose and stepped toward Yancey, bending to pick up the blade she'd dropped.

Uther caught Frewer by the wrist. "You'd best not be thinking of doing anything foolish with that, sir," he said, low and flat.

Frewer blinked, shaking his head. "Fools is what we were. Tried fire, lost everything. This . . ." A shrug. ". . . it seems *right.*"

And it *did* feel that way, didn't it? Languorous, lulling. Sweet as smoke.

Yet one more voice she didn't know (and hoped to never have to, by its tones) intruding, to whisper: **Blood of men—and women,** *children, everyone: So flowery, like jade. Your precious, precious blood.*

"Uther—" Yancey reached to touch his hand, as she had Pargeter's, trying not to dwell on the similarity. "Husband: we've nothing else to try."

Though Uther's expression didn't change, after a second, he turned Frewer loose—and without a word of thanks, Frewer instantly took the blade to his arm, freeing a jet so fierce it fair made Yancey gasp with horror. *Not so much!*

But the other guests from Mouth-of-Praise still trapped within the church's ruins were also rising, all with that same absent look. Those who had 'em drew their own knives, while those who didn't went scrabbling among the wreckage for dining-ware, glass shards, sharp stones.

The air turned coppery; blood pattered down, like spring rainfall. And Morrow's voice rang out again, this time joined by near two-score others—each joining in with nary a stumble, as though they were reading off some invisible hymn-book.

> *The house of He Who Creates Himself*
> *Is found nowhere;*
> *But our Lord, our God, is invoked everywhere,*
> *He is venerated under every sky.*
> *He is the One who creates all things,*
> *He is the One who made himself.*
> *Not a single person here*
> *Can be Your friend, O Giver of Life!*
> *We, lost below, can only seek You*
> *As if for someone hidden among flowers.*
> *Your heart grows weary of us.*
> *The Giver of Life drives us mad,*
> *And no one can truly be His friend,*
> *Succeed in life, or rule on Earth.*

The Weed changed so fast it seemed to shimmer, its fragrance fiercely fresh, storm popping like a soap bubble. Yancey felt the power flood her, strong enough to taste, and heard her blood sing out in answer, hot and living and furious. Felt Sheriff Love's anger mount, equal fast as Pargeter's ecstasy, and revelled in whatever hurt it did him—merely academic when compared to the blow he'd dealt *her*, off-hand, simply by being what he was. But a passive variety of vengeance on Pa's behalf, nonetheless.

Two knots of passion fought within her breast, bisected: cold grief, sharp loss, a mounting general horror, set cheek-by-jowl with blind triumph and burning delight. And at the apex, magnet-pulled, her gaze lifted to Pargeter once more, his black aura now gone the same brilliant green of his eyes . . . which met and locked with hers, equal-strong, to flare with mutual recognition.

It's too much. He can't take it all in—can't let it go, either. And now, right now, is when it's gonna—

—blow, sky-high. The green broke apart, knocking Pargeter ass over teakettle, dazed, sickened. The backlash sent Morrow to his aching knees yet again, jackknifed, dry-heaving into the grass; townsfolk who'd bled to feed the Weed all staggered too, likewise released.

While Love rose up once more, strength and fury both surging back in a flood, boiling off of him like steam.

He turned his face on faithless-proven Hoffstedtites and Mouth-of-Praisers alike, roaring that God-sent final verdict he'd spoke of to the uncaring skies: "Ye have heaped treasure together for the last days!"

Moving so fast Yancey could barely track his passage, Love was on Mister Frewer before the poor fool had time to blink and struck him a backhanded blow that spun his head near clean around, bone cracking like a gunshot-load; Yancey felt the spirit blast from his body even as it fell limp, face down into the grass he'd helped pray into being.

"Behold, the hire of the labourers who have reaped down your fields, which is of you kept back by fraud, crieth to the Lord of Sabaoth—" A few steps more brought him to where Hugo

Hoffstedt lay, still unconscious, side by side with dead Sheriff Haish. Incensed beyond reason, Love lifted one boot and stamped down, crushing the complaint-fond tobacconist's neck so hard it near *sprang* from the body on a burst of blood that stained his salt-crusted boot crimson.

Jesus, Yancey's mind repeated blindly, returning under fire to the less apparently reliable God of her youth. For in those two dreadful moments, all her hexcraft-got "victory" had turned to dust in her mouth.

"YE HAVE LIVED IN PLEASURE ON THE EARTH, AND BEEN WANTON; YE HAVE NOURISHED YOUR HEARTS, AS IN A DAY OF SLAUGHTER!" Love howled out, joyfully. To which her dear Uther, suddenly bereft of friends, enemies and barely made acquaintances alike, shook his handsome head in disapproval.

"*You*, sir," he told Love. "Can just . . . shut the hell up. Your point is made, and you're frightening my wife."

Track-caught by such reasonableness, Love paused in his rampage, voice gone abruptly calm. "Well, as to that—your wife is damned, Marshal, I'm sad to say, same as every one've those she's enticed to give the Devil reverence, rendering this place anathema; it should be burnt, so that better people may start over. Burnt to the ground, and its ashes salted."

Though white-lipped, Yancey found the grace to snort, amazed by her own audacity. "Really. Answer me this, then, Sheriff: things only occur 'cause God lets 'em, as I recall . . . so if it *works*, and it did, who are you to argue?"

Those dead eyes swung back her way, two blasted moons in dull orbit. "Don't be sophistical, ma'am," Love replied. "It's unbecoming."

Uther took a step closer. "I'm the one gets to decide that, thank you. Now—people have had enough; we'll solve our own problems in our own way, thank you kindly. *Leave.*"

"I don't answer to you."

To this, Uther smiled, ever so slightly. "Oh?" he asked. And punched Love, hard.

It was a roundhouse hook to the jaw that would've floored any other man. But the former Sheriff was—*tacky*, so the Marshal's fist sunk in wrist-deep, then stuck. Yancey jumped to his aid, hauling on him with both arms 'til he tore free at last with a horrid sucking noise, sagging back against her. They were both equal-floored by the sight of his hand, skinned something nasty—a literal glove of blood, fingernails torn either almost to the root, or missing entirely.

"Oh, Jesus!" Yancey cried out, and Uther seemed happy to hear her upset on his behalf.

Started to say: "Hush, now—could be worse—"

But that was when Sheriff Love chose to haul off himself, jab Uther so rough he crushed in one eye like a popped egg, then backhanded him into what was left of the altar stone. Uther's temple struck the corner, skull broken open on impact, with a meaty crunch. One further twist, snapped-stick sharp, and he was looking back at her full-on, over his own shoulder.

Yancey screamed and clapped both hands to her face, as Uther dropped away. She heard him fall. And knew, at last, that she was all alone. . . .

Except for Love.

ON THE GROUND, ACHING all over, Ed Morrow came back to himself in a rush, slammed together once more by the whip-tail scorch of Missus Kloves'—*Widow* Kloves, now—desolate cry. For a split second, he thought on how it'd be to be made mateless and orphaned on the same damn day, and that supposedly reserved for celebration. How it'd feel to know it was your fault, too, for having brought the means of everyone else's destruction in through the door and handed 'em 'round like any other guest, thinking your will alone could keep 'em from acting like curse-laden skeletons at your unsuspecting husband's marriage feast.

A split second only, not a hair more. After which he forced himself up, grabbed Chess 'round his drunken-lolling praise-junkie neck and growled in one ear: "*Help* her, Goddamnit, 'fore that crazy bastard does her like he's done for the damn rest! It's the least you owe."

Chess's breath came huffing out visible, heavy with green-spiced vapour. "Don't owe that bitch nothin'," he snapped back, automatically. "Hell, *I* ain't the one wants to get up under her skirts. You like her so much, maybe you should take a swing at that crusty bastard yourself."

"Tried that already, remember? You were there. Didn't end well."

Before them, Love stood over op Missus Kloves, gesticulating like a premier Sensation Scene melodramatist: *The Preacher Transformed, or, God's Monster!* While she, a mere slip of a thing in her green- and dust-stained wedding duds, simply glared at him past her husband's corpse, grey eyes gone so hard you could strike matches on 'em.

"Well, sir," she said, with admirable haughtiness, "your work here seems done. Unless you're fixed to kill *me*, too."

Love thought on that, then shook his head. "No," he replied. "You knew what you did, but not why you shouldn't, so I'll trust God in his mercy to grant you time to reflect on your sins, and repent of them. For the nonce, therefore, I'll let you live, for our great Father's sake."

Missus Kloves drew her lips back, showing all her neat white teeth at once. And hissed at him, voice rage-thick, "*My* father is *dead.*"

For just a tick, Morrow saw Love's regained mask of sanity shudder, his leprous hands curl into claws. But with an effort, he appeared to thrust those impulses away from him, having already overindulged, to take the high road. Gave himself a species of all-over shrug, and turned away.

Only to find Chess right there, his fingers already dug deep in the "lapel" of that salt-skin-memory mélange Love wore for a coat.

"Time t'go, Sheriff," Chess told him. "Just like the Marshal said."

That same no-explosion, a barely there toll struck on the world's bell, and so Goddamn fast. Faster yet, every Goddamn time.

Chess and Love were there, then Chess was back, like he hadn't ever left. And Love?

GONE, AT LAST, IF only in body. Not like Pa, Sheriff Haish, Mister Frewer—poor, stupid Hugo Hoffstedt, laid low, never to return. Or Uther.

Yancey sat shivering in the street while Pargeter and Morrow, fellow architects in the destruction of everything she'd ever known, exchanged a look.

So easy, she found herself thinking, too bone-tired to even be angry. It'd've been just *that* easy for him to dispose of Love all along, had he only wished. Or rather, had he thought to.

Pargeter was still humming with whatever she and the rest'd poured into him, swaying slightly, stare glazed. It snapped in his already-green eyes, lifted his red hair, lent a greenish, motile tinge to his skin. His very sweat crackled, galvanized, in a way that both repelled and attracted. From the way Morrow stood, she could tell he wanted to touch him—and so did she, for that matter. To crawl into that fatal little man's too-bright shadow and curl herself 'round his legs like a cat, for just as long as he'd be inclined to let her.

There's nothing left for me here, she thought, without any particular emphasis. *Not one single thing.*

No, the voice in her head agreed. *You cannot stay. But . . . neither can he. For there is yet more damage to be done here, nonetheless.*

The Weed was almost entirely grass now, a jewel of fertility in a sore, parched land, not evil, but unnatural. And so long as Chess Pargeter was its anchor, it would only keep on spreading.

Removing him, however, might at least—disarm it, Yancey supposed. The way pulling bullets from a gun made it a different sort of weapon.

People would return. She owed them a place to rebuild that didn't have him in it, or her.

Though Pargeter was already turning away, Morrow's gaze stayed on Yancey, as she'd somehow trusted it would. And though a part of her rose against the idea of abandoning her husband of an hour's cooling side so soon, there was no point in staying to mourn; Uther Kloves would be equal-dead no matter where she went. No betrayal, then, just a cold urge, a horrid practicality—the realization that wherever Morrow and his half-god master went, Sheriff Love was sure to follow.

This is true, yes. You know it, granddaughter.

Yes. Not to mention how she'd need to know how to kill, as well, by the time their paths crossed once more. And killing was something both these bastards knew, intimately.

Painfully, she twisted already strained hips, raising herself to a clumsy crouch—at which point Morrow put out a hand to help, like the gentleman he no doubt hoped she thought him. Even now, with the wreckage of Pargeter's passage all 'round 'em, and her birthplace flattened like a bug . . . she'd've laughed, if she'd had that left in her.

"Thank you," she said, and let him draw her up. To Pargeter: "We need to talk."

"Don't see how."

"Don't you?" Yancey showed him her hand, her arm; saw his nostrils twitch at the blood that still ran there. "Yes, you're powerful enough right in this instant—but who's to say you won't need further reverence, in future? Can't leave without what remains of your congregation, Mister Pargeter."

To which Pargeter just gave her a look: green sunlight through a magnifying lens, piercing, painful. "Don't go affectin' any concern for me and mine, girl. Think I can't see the hate in you? I got time enough for one revenge only, Missus, and it ain't yours."

Morrow scowled. "Chess—"

"Not happenin', Ed. She'd be a millstone 'round both our necks."

"We *do* owe her, Chess." If Pargeter's gaze was fire, Morrow's was stone, utterly obdurate. "We brought this on her, in all its awfulness. As you damn well know."

"She brought it on herself. We'd laid low, left on our own recognizance—"

"—Love might've turned up anyhow, and killed us both. Like he probably would've here, she hadn't done that blood-trick of hers to save *your* ungrateful ass—"

"—and if my aunt had nuts she'd be my uncle, Ed; that ain't the fuckin' point, nohow." But the strange fire was fading, just a little, from Pargeter's eyes. He pointed at Yancey. "You know where we're going, what we gotta do; know what our odds are of livin' through it, too. You really wanna put her ass up in the sling with ours? That what it means to you, to pay her back?"

Morrow stared at him—then hauled him close and laid a full open-mouthed kiss on him, as much from desperation as desire. Yancey felt the tug of it in her own loins, sick with shame amidst all her loss; Pargeter fought to not react, albeit perfunctorily. But when Morrow released him, that stone-hard look hadn't much altered.

"I know," Morrow said, softly. "So do it for me, or don't."

Pargeter cleared his throat, then shrugged. Without warning, he seized Yancey's arm, sending an invisible rash of prickling heat through her body; smeared blood and dirt powdered off into the air. And then the flush sank bone-deep and snapped her stiff and upright, a wind-filled sail—her eyes widened, fingers splaying, spasming. Green light leaked from her mouth.

"Aw, hell—" Morrow's own big hand fell upon Pargeter's, gripping as if to pull it away, but Yancey felt Pargeter's power instantly snap-surge across into him as well, a spark jumping gap between metal and flesh. The supernatural cyclone whirled compass-wide, dizzying and queasy; Hoffstedt's Hoard shimmered, dissolving mirage-like, lost behind an undulating veil of power.

Stop it! Yancey called, her mind and Pargeter's abruptly merged, the way she'd never hitherto been able to with anyone but Mama; overrode his consternation completely in her haste, refusing to "listen." *Take us out of here, sir,* now! *Let whatever's happening work its tricks elsewhere!*

This time, Pargeter didn't even bother to argue, just let her rip: that same green blink, a cloth-wrapped hammer-hit, right 'tween the eyes. And then—

—Yancey came down, jolted enough to stagger as the sere earth turned under her wedding slippers, all previous tumult-stink instantly whisked away as clean, cool air licked her face. Strong arms caught her in mid-plunge; disoriented, she allowed

Mister Morrow to take her weight and gulped in deep, coughed out hard, stomach clenching painfully.

They stood high on the side of a long and shallow valley, with stunted firs and sagebrush for a nearby tree line. The next slope's centre was scored by a dry riverbed, low-set sun hanging mild above, sky speckled white as any hen's egg: all of it clean of anything but dust and weed, empty of threat. All of it utterly, wrenchingly unfamiliar.

"Where . . . ?" Yancey managed, eventually, but Morrow just shook his head.

"Seems somewhat familiar," he offered, at last. "But . . ."

Behind them, still aloft, Pargeter hovered a foot above the ground for one vertiginous moment more, before starting at last to sink. He touched down bootheels-first and smoothed down his finery, wiping all hint of battle-marks away, before marching right past them both, making for the canyon's narrow channel.

"Well?" he asked, impatient. "Two of you comin', or what?"

"You . . . ain't minded to rest?" Morrow called back.

"No time, no need." Pargeter snapped his fingers, sheathing them in lightning—checking he'd regained full control of his arcane faculties?—then snapped again, to banish it. "We're in the hill country, near as not to Splitfoot's; ten minutes should see us on their doorstep, well outta harm's way. So let's us stop dickin' 'round, and—"

But here he froze, reorienting: seemed to sideslip distance, suddenly back at Morrow's side, both guns levelled. Morrow turned too, Yancey following after, as a lone figure stepped carefully from the scrub. Felt her jaw drop at the sight, unladylike.

"Mister . . . Grey?"

"Truth told? Not entirely." The young man she'd known as Grey adjusted his hat and smiled, looking far beyond weary. To Morrow: "'Lo, Ed."

Morrow nodded back. Tonelessly: ". . . Frank."

Pargeter cocked both guns, probably pretty much for conversational emphasis alone. "*Was* you, wasn't it?" he asked. "The extra weight I felt, comin' out here. Didn't even feel you grab on—how'd you do that?"

Mister "Grey" indicated Yancey, with a wry smile. "Tryin' to keep her from getting pulled along, mostly," he admitted, "though that didn't exactly take, I guess."

"Looks like." The guns didn't waver. "So—you know Ed and Ed knows you, but *I* don't know you from sheep-shit; in my book, all that means there's only one thing you can be. Care to prove me wrong?"

Frank sighed, shook his head. "Think you well know how I can't, Pargeter."

He locked eyes with Morrow, passing some silent signal; in return, Morrow took a deep breath, eyebrows canting in surrender. "Yeah okay, all right. Chess—Miz Col—"

"Yancey," she corrected, quickly, unsure she'd ever be ready to hear either maiden or married name again. "Call me Yancey, please . . . Edward."

Which last addition sent things rocketing straight into the realm of awkward-forward, not that Morrow let himself be seen to notice.

"Yancey—allow me to introduce Agent Frank Geyer, of the Pinkerton Detective Service Agency. Sent here to bring us in, most likely."

Grey—Geyer—smiled again, this time more widely. "Not . . . entirely, no."

A pause ensued. Yancey glanced at her feet, just in time to see her wind-chased bridal veil go tumbling away along the canyon floor, smeared deep in bloody dirt, brief as some lost snow-ghost. And felt her past slip along with it, leaving her just another woman in a once-white dress.

I have to be someone different now, she told herself, resolving not to let herself think too deep about the choices she had to make from this point on, lest she quibble to make them at all. *Someone neither Pa nor Uther would recognize—me either, in days gone by. Do what I have* to, *in order to make sure that* thing *which laid them both low pays its dues. Fight fire with fire. So . . .*

Might as well start now as later, she supposed. If only for complete and total lack of any other option.

"Well, then," she said. "Better tell us all about that, hadn't you?"

"Yes, ma'am," Geyer replied.

INTERSTICE

Top headline in the *Californian* of San Francisco, for the first week of June, 1867:

STARTLING NEWS FROM OVER THE BORDER!
The Earthquake that Levelled Mexico City
Has Also Derailed Partisan Siege Designed to Oust Mexico's
Hapsburg Emperor
Offering Aid, Napoleon III's Troops Return
New Lease on Throne for Maximilian I
"He, At Least, Has Not Forsaken Us"

Still safely ensconced at their seat in Chapultepec Castle, from which the stately Paseo de la Emperatriz once issued forth, the Imperial couple—triumphantly reunited—announces intent to remain and govern the same country which lately threatened one of them with deposition & death.

"My wife and I, children of Mexico in our hearts, have determined not to desert her in her time of trial," the former Austrian Arch-Duke claims. "Indeed, this lamentable recent influx of <u>hexen-kriegskraft</u> from our beloved adopted land's distant past serves as reminder that the original War for Mexican Independence was led by Martin Cortes, son of Hernan Cortes and La Malinche, against the privileges of the conquistadors. Thus we must remain ever vigilant as Christians, seeing how our sins return again & yet again."

Those historically educated amongst our readers may recall that Chapultepec was once a summer retreat for rulers of the Aztec Empire, which itself gave birth in turn to Hex City's fabled "Rainbow Lady," the savage so-called goddess at whose feet most of the recent damage may be laid (with, we are sad to say, an American-born hex's foul connivance). Our sources inside the Imperial court claim that cultish shrines have sprung up where only lightly Catholicized peasants, conflating her heretically with Our Lord's own mother, go to spill blood in her name, by the bucket-full . . . often with such violence that fresh hexes arise in the wake of these orgies of witchcraft-influenced false penitence, only to then rampage through the devastated zone anew.

Of former President Benito Juarez and his ally Porfirio Diaz, once at the head of a rebellion intent on impeaching & executing his Excellency, little has been heard since the capitol fell. But Maximilian once more extends an offer of truce & amnesty if both will swear public allegiance to him & his heirs, the young Princes of Iturbide & Marzan. Meantime, the Emperor has renewed his alliance with Napoleon III of France, and offers any ex-Confederate soldiers who care to emigrate southwards the shelter of the Carlotta Colonies, should they value freedom from Union rule more than their loyalty to these re-United States. . . .

From the same issue:

STRANGE WEATHER, INSECT PLAGUES
Whole Towns Throughout Arizona, New Mexico Rendered Unfit
for Habitation
Migrants Head our Way, Seek Shelter & Occupation

A SECOND GOLD RUSH TO BE EXPECTED?

A ROPE OF THORNS

Californios Braced for New Upswing of Crime & Competition
Authorities of San Fran & Environs: "Anti-Foreign Laws in
Place for Good Reason"

Plus—from the busy pen of transplanted New Yorker Fitz Hugh
Ludlow—this travel-account from what is quickly becoming
America's most hotly disputed area of interest:

BLACK PILGRIMAGE
A Frightening True-to-Life Tale of
One Man's Journey by Stagecoach Across the Painted Desert,
Within Close Sight of
HEX CITY!
Magicians Received from All Quarters, with
More Arriving Every Day
Our Readers' Pressing Enquiries Answered:
Where Do Its Denizens Come From?
How Many Live There Already?
May Their Influence Be Avoided?

BOOK TWO:
EMPTY DAYS

June 2, 1867
Month Six, Day Eleven Movement
Festival: Etzalcualiztli, or Meal of Maize and Beans

This festival honours Tlaloc, Chalchiuhtlicue and Quetzalcoatl, all of whom are somehow identified with wind and rain. The drought is over—waters rise, and life begins anew.

The Aztec *trecena* Mazatl ("Deer") is ruled by Tepeyollotl, yet another form of Tezcatlipoca. But by the Mayan Long Count calendar, day Ollin ("Movement") is governed by Xolotl, the Twin Shapeshifter, Lord of the West and Double of Quetzalcoatl. Though identified with sickness and physical deformity, he nevertheless accompanied Quetzalcoatl to Mictlan in order to retrieve the bones from those who inhabited the dead world of the Fourth Sun and create new life from them, thus repopulating our present world, that of the Fifth Sun.

This is a day of the purified heart, a moment when human beings may best perceive what they are Becoming. A good day for transmutation, which arrives like an earthquake.

CHAPTER NINE

BLACK SHAPES OUTLINED IN spectral fire under a darkened sky, the air itself rent and somehow sparking, set abuzz like galvanized metal; it'd been a lamentably long time since "Reverend" Asher E. Rook felt the necessity of "casting" a spell, per se. Yet here he was, knelt down in the shadow of that first step-sided black ziggurat his dear, dread Rainbow Lady had raised up out of the cracked Arizona earth, which now formed the very heart of New Aztectlan—quoting his long-burnt Bible from memory, and hiding his perfidy in plain sight.

Hexes, beware hexation, he thought, intentionally misquoting Webster. *Not a one of us worth the trusting, to our very marrow. Yet we still all go on hoping, like fools.*

Gods on earth, writ large *or* small, still scrabbling desperately for love or lashing out in hate, same as the humans they used for dogs, for toys, for kindling. Still steered 'round by their nethers, in whatever direction least suited logic.

But as Chess had once remarked, on much the same subject: *As for me . . . I'm certainly no exception.*

For a second, Rook shivered helpless in memory's grip, feeling the print of Chess all along him like a scar. For *damn* if he couldn't use the contentious little bastard right now—him, or someone like him.

All around, the Blood Engine's fires burned low and sullen, smoke-towers just rippling the horizon with heat. Oil lamps, candles and witch-fire alike dotted up and down the temple's walls, outlining New Aztectlan's spreading borders in a malignant melanoma of light. From where he knelt—the roof of an empty adobe hut on its easternmost border, built a scant few weeks back, by some now-dead Redskin mage—Rook heard this place others had come to call "Hex City" murmur like a giant complaining in its sleep, troubled by dreams.

For lack of any better plan, he'd begun by drawing a charcoal circle, but that in itself had run the full extent of his preparations. Lack of the most basic training showing, yet again; with all his lore culled straight from the Old Testament and various gospels, what could he possibly hope to know of mystic sigils, names of power, sacred talismans?

But then again, how much did *any* hex truly need such thespianish trappings? Will and skill, that was all any of it'd ever been based on in his experience, no matter how spectacular the result. Fortune's favour, if not God's.

From an inner pocket, the Rev took a mojo bag much like that he'd once used to bind Ed Morrow; upended it into his palm, shook out a short-chopped, greying, mouse-brown lock and tossed it into the circle. A mental twitch of power was all it took to ignite the offering, rendering the immediate air acrid with burning hair-reek.

"The hand of the LORD was upon me," he murmured, as the smoke rose up and twined about itself, a snake trapped in its own coils. "And carried me out in the spirit of the LORD, and set me down in the midst of the valley, which was full of bones. And caused me to pass by them round about: and, behold, there were very many in the open valley; and, lo, they were very dry.

"*Ezekiel 37, 2 to 3.*"

In a cavern under the ziggurat, Ixchel (or the mortal woman's body she rode, at least—poor Miss Adaluz, that was) lay this very second cocooned in something part trance, part narcoleptic reverie. She had cast herself downward into dark water, as she did with ever-increasing regularity; seeking out the Sunken Ball-Court's slimy deeps, to commune with those same relatives of hers she aspired to pull back up into the light. And all the while trusting implicitly in Rook to do her business and keep her safe, according him roughly the same contemptuous parody of respect accorded any given guard dog.

Playing the part, he'd stood watch there a few hours, just to see what might happen. In sleep-death, her proud face slackened, she almost looked young enough to evoke an utterly unnecessary stab of protectiveness—but as attempts on her "life" by some of the city's earliest and least willing converts had proven, she was all but impossible to harm, even if Rook had thought to try.

Indeed, the longer she stayed embodied, more skin-out human she seemed, the more dangerous she became . . . her habitual lack of expression just one more mask, power boiling from her pores, that phantom cloak of dragonflies billowing behind her in a buzzing tide whenever she moved, so slow and stately, almost swimming. As though the desert air she cut through was black Mictlan-Xibalba-water, stagnant with a promise of plague.

Sometimes she bled, without seeming to know that she did so. Enthroned beside her, he often saw it come and go, unremarked: blood beneath her nails or streaking from the corner of one eye or the other like tears, to paint the black spirals on her cheeks; liquid carnelian rimming her areolae, or hung from the dark nipples themselves like extra jewellery. Blood welling up from somewhere inside her, spilling down those strong brown thighs to dye her ankles, well hid beneath her Chalchiuhtlicue-aspect's scaly skirt of writhing, hissing ghost-snakes.

Of course, Ixchel's vessel *had* been dead a good long time, at this point. So perhaps she was simply breaking the flesh down for parts, in anticipation of a second resurrection—soon-impending, at least by her personal calendar. And far more glorious.

"And he said unto me, Son of man, can these bones live? And I answered, O Lord GOD, thou knowest."

Then again, what amused Rook most was how these offhand

manifestations of hers now rang so interminably *routine*; for all he spent his days immersed neck-high in awful wonders, nothing disgusted or frightened him, for more than maybe a minute at a time. Which maybe explained why, for many of New Aztectlan's other hexes, *he* was just as much a figure of sharp fear and odd arousal as she . . . more so, perhaps, given they saw him far more often and had more immediate cause to fear what he might do, in his "wife's" unholy name.

For her part, she liked him to play fist to her glove, though the laws he enforced all came straight from her cyanose lips. Telling him, more often than not:

You know my mind, little priest-king husband, as is only fitting, since you are the lash I strike with, the mask I wear. My good right hand.

Like Chess was to me, Rook thought, *the person does for you what you yourself can't see needs to* be *done. If I hadn't done myself out of Chess Pargeter, he and I could've ruled this whole world, together. . . .*

Yes, if Rook had trusted him enough to bring him over from the beginning, or Chess had been able to grow beyond the limits of his own imagination without having to be pushed—why, they might have been twin mage-Presidents of America by now, with no deific aid necessary. 'Til they'd destroyed it, and each other, in the process.

He will *return,* ***little king,*** Ixchel would say, were she awake enough to listen. ***You know this.***

Come back here to die, you mean.

To die, yes. And live again. Perhaps adding, in that oddly softer way she sometimes had: ***I find I begin to miss him as well, if that is of help.***

Which he could rightly believe, given how important Chess had made himself to her plans. But knowing that wasn't much of a comfort.

From another pocket, Rook drew a smallish glass bottle. *Atwood's Jaundice Bitters,* the raised letters blown down one side and up the other proclaimed: *Moses Atwood, Cambridge Mass.* He popped the cork, up-ended it and beckoned the curl of hair-smoke inside, an Indian rope-trick in reverse.

"THUS SAITH THE LORD GOD UNTO THESE BONES; BEHOLD, I WILL CAUSE BREATH TO ENTER INTO YOU, AND YE SHALL LIVE. . . ."

There, done—one more whispered word 'cross the neck and the cork went back in, sealed with a curse. The charm, wound up.

"YE SHALL LIVE," he repeated, louder. "AND I WILL LAY SINEWS UPON YOU, AND WILL BRING UP FLESH UPON YOU, AND COVER YOU WITH SKIN, AND PUT BREATH IN YOU, AND YE SHALL LIVE; AND YE SHALL KNOW THAT I AM THE LORD."

The words of his mouth, a black-letter banner, spilled forth and up to roost like bats in the filthy twilight air. While something else took shape beneath 'em, man-sized in darkness: a far too familiar-aspected, scowling shade who, once coalesced, spoke just as gruff as ever, unimpressed by Rook's diablerie on simple principle.

And why don't this surprise me, said Kees Hosteen.

ROOK HAD RISEN EARLY, intending to walk back alone through Hex City's streets in these birdsong hours, usually the only time of day he could expect anything close to a genuine block of solitude. But all planning aside, it just wasn't to be.

"Reverend."

Rook turned to find one Three-Fingered Hank Fennig, late of New York City, leaning up against a nearby house's mud wall with his arms crossed (maimed left hand topmost, as befitted any southpaw) and regarding him over the rims of his ostentatiously expensive smoked-glass spectacles.

"Out early, ain't ya?" he asked Rook, amiably enough.

"Well, that depends. Don't look to me like you slept too long yourself."

Fennig was a viperishly lanky young buck, and his shrug travelled the length of him without much effort, since he didn't have breadth enough to interfere with the motion. "Oh, me? I ain't yet been t'bed, as it happens. Thought I'd take the air, instead."

The glasses, Rook knew, were far more than an affectation; having seen Fennig in operation a time or two against similarly foreign challengers, he surmised his hexation worked directly with the eyes, thus necessitating some sort of shield—that the boy could see *through* people, or even into 'em, discovering exactly which flaws to press on in order to force a break.

The results could be spectacular, as in the case of a provoking young witch from down Texas way—not an Injun, though certainly burnt brown enough to pass—whose elaborately coiled 'do had suddenly cut loose like an octopus knit from hair under Fennig's direct gaze, then ripped itself from her scalp and gone foraging, leaving her to bleed out in the dust.

"Surprised our infant metropolis holds any interest for you at all, considering where you're from," he told Fennig, drawing nearer.

Another shrug. "Oh, it's got a rustic charm, and these Territories is a prime place for them as likes to brawl, in general. A rowster could live easy here, once the cobbles was laid down and the jakeshouse row finally decided upon for sure, 'stead'a every man-jack just shittin' where he pleases."

"And not even kicking dirt over it, after," Rook agreed. "But I somehow misdoubt you've come to discuss the state of New Aztectlan's sanitation with me, Henry."

They strolled back together, Fennig with both hands kept carefully in his pockets, to defuse any appearance of threat.

"Back home, Rev, I'm what's called a Bowery B'hoy," he explained, as they rounded first one corner, then the next, "with my born 'legiance t'wards the Glorious Know-Nothin' Order of the American Eagle—Nativists, they likes t'name 'emselves, and pound down hammer-hard on any damn dirty immigrant sons of bitches wants entry t'their streets. 'Course, what a year or two out here'll teach you is, we all of us come from somewheres else."

"Go on."

"So . . . due to circumstances don't bear goin' into, here's where I find myself. And never before in all my life have I made my bed near so many other magickals, for fear of constant challenge—not that there ain't none of that either, mind. What interests me, though, is how what there *is* seems mainly by rote, from habit, not necessity."

Rook turned on his heel, his own eyes narrowing, thinking: *Smart fellow, this—someone worth the cultivating, perhaps, if his motives might only be clarified. Or the using, anyhow.*

Dangerous too, of course. But then . . . dangerous men were, ofttimes, the only kind of any worth.

Ah, God, he missed Chess. Like half his guts were gone.

"Gift horses and mouths, is what comes first to *my* mind," he replied, casually. "For myself, I know I'm right grateful to live someplace I don't *need* to scrap any more—'less *I* feel like it, that is."

Fennig gave a little nod. "True and fair. Hell, I spilled my claret and said your words quick as any, didn't I, when you and Her told me to?" A sudden flickering grin, cut with another sly, sidelong glance. "Still, it does strike me that—well—maybe things could go *further*, down this new road you've opened up."

"How so?"

Fennig paused, maybe thrown by the directness of the question, and gave it some thought.

Then swept one long arm in an arc, encompassing the whole of Hex City in at once, and began—"Like I said, we all of us come from elsewheres—all heard the Call of this place and answered it, to our costs; a long, hard road, full of toil and tribulation. And in return . . . gained entrance here, this town, a place where for the first time any of us's heard of, we can share space without drinkin' each other dry: outcasts and devil-spawn, the suffered-not-to-live. A place we can damn well call *home*."

Here Fennig turned to Rook full-on, eyes literally glowing; his smoked lenses, twin glass-sheathed lantern wicks, swum brim-full of bright blue light. "So why ain't we takin' more care in the building of it, is what I want to know? Why ain't we puttin' all our gifts together now we can—make something that'll last long after we die, 'stead of dryin' up and blowin' away?"

Rook raised an eyebrow, impressed despite himself. That anyone had finally asked the question at all was occasion enough; that it was this man was genuinely surprising.

"Bear in mind, Hank, never was a hex born took easy to another tellin' him what to do—which is why I don't foresee many folk signing up for latrine duty, sad to say. Still," he looked around, "city don't run itself, that's for certain."

"No." Fennig narrowed his eyes at Ixchel's ziggurat, as if measuring it. "Seems like she ain't quite taken that into account."

"That's my lady wife you're talkin' about, New York."

"Apologies, Reverend; I'd never get 'tween a man and his mutton." He visibly rummaged for the next few words, fitting 'em carefully together. "And yet—there's none'a the rest of you comes from a city upwards of two thousand strong, am I right? 'Cept maybe for her, an' I don't think *she* was the one had administration of it, or wanted such. That's why she's got *you*."

"Ain't all that many of *us*, either."

"Not yet," Fennig shot back. "But more hexes than ever dwelt in one place, more every day—and not hexes alone, either. You know a lot of 'em come in on the very edge of turnin', and them's the ones bring along sweethearts, kids. There've been others gone out to roust farmers and crafters from any town they can find, bind 'em into service. Hell, who d'you think's working the crop-plots, out where the Lady's gussied up the soil? My guess, we got two or three normal folk for every hex—and that's as like as not to go up, not down." A deep breath. "Pretty soon, the way we've been goin' on won't be halfway good enough, any more. And when that day comes . . . well, might be you need to delegate. Might be . . . we can even afford to trust one another."

He hesitated, considering Rook's impassive expression. "For now, at least," he added.

Rook thought it over. In silence, they turned down what had become, by default, Hex City's "Main Street"—a broad laneway run straight east from the open square before the ziggurat, so the knife-wielders at temple's peak looked direct into the sun each dawn. Its course was kept empty by something between divine decree and curse—any hex who thought to raise up a structure too near the road found himself suddenly struck down, all forgings collapsed to dust and glitter. Whether he lived long enough after to recover was dependent on Ixchel's mood, once the case was brought before her.

No matter how ruthlessly she policed her processional, however, the Lady was utterly indifferent to what might spring up just beyond. So instead of epic bas-reliefs and exotic marketplaces, canals to feed the farms beyond or elegant garden-set homes, New Aztectlan resembled some unholy mix of every foreign poor-folks' quarter Rook'd ever seen, infused with the wrecked, would-be grandeur shared by all too many Confederate towns during the War's dying days. But better and worse than both, because . . . well, look at who'd built it.

A transparent cube, walls, floor and ceiling all grown from something Rook thought might be actual diamond, with a twirling ribbon of multicoloured light spinning endlessly inside, was home to a barber-surgeon who used his keen-edged fingers for scissors and scalpel. A popular groggery-saloon boasted a façade as grand and glorious as any Parisian vaudevillery's—'til you passed at an angle and glimpsed it for what it was: parchment-thin, kept upright by hexation and nothing else, with a clumsy thing of sap-weeping planks hid behind. The domed brown blister kitty-corner 'cross from it was, Rook knew, a brothel run collectively by a half-dozen young women who'd masked their true talents in whoring, safe from priest or lawman alike, 'til the Call brought them here. Now they'd carved themselves a fresh business-domicile right out of the earth, with utter disinterest for stylish considerations; those in search of witch-pussy would just have to eat a peck of dirt, or go wanting.

And the general store where the fruits of raids and conjurings were offered for purchase seemed at first glance like a longhouse cabin, 'til a closer look showed every bark-clad log fused smoothly with its neighbour, stumps sprouting green leaves and threading knotted roots down into the earth. Scattered among the larger buildings, like warts on a toad's skin, were huts housing anywhere from one to a dozen citizens: those who'd staked a claim but didn't have enough power, as yet, to claim more territory.

It was all so unimaginative, Rook thought, with a spasm of disgust; even the most ostentatious displays were mere peacockery, mundane vanity writ larger, not deeper. As if the only thing these people could think to do, given power and freedom most could only dream of, was to ape the lives they'd left, substituting trade in raw magic for gold or cash.

"Right mess, ain't it?" Fennig commented, with disturbing acuity.

"Old habits, I s'pose," Rook allowed.

"Womenfolk like routine." Fennig glanced sideways at Rook's raised eyebrow. "Ain't you noticed, Rev? Near three of every five hex-workers in this town's of a feminine nature." He shrugged. "Plain sense, you think about it—power comes to a woman with her first bleeding, but only t'one of us if we're hurt near to death. Bound t'be more of them than us."

Fire blazed in Rook's memory, silent and searing: a haystack beneath a ladder upon which a poor boy with one square pupil was bound, his skin blackening, mouth open in a wail so soundless even the sparrow-marking God had not answered.

"Perhaps," he said quietly. "But that might be why they get caught so easy, too. Not to mention how witches bear witch-children, eventually—and more than half the time, both drink each other dry. We men are spared *that* bargain, at least."

"Except," Fennig countered, "here, we don't need t'be." He looked at the people beginning to gather along both street-sides, watching them pass: a hodgepodge of male and female, old and young, black and brown, red and pale, even a sprinkling of true Chinee-yellow, the sort Miss Songbird's pig-pale skin would never support. Plus various children, owl-blinking at their parents' elbows; Fennig nodded their way. "Some of those might be hexes-in-waiting already, but that don't mean we gotta be fearful. I could raise up a son, here, Reverend . . . you, too."

The truth of that shook him, twisting Rook's gut in a way he could never have expected. With numb dread, he thought: *What we do here has changed things already. Won't stop, either, just 'cause she don't see it happening.*

"A man wants to change his circumstances might do better to have no kin in tow, though," Rook observed, voice deceptively even. "One thing I've learned in this vocation, Henry . . . trust comes easier, when there's less to lose."

The three-fingered hand danced lightly up, making some mock-casual adjustment—and Rook felt the icy touch of Fennig's regard fix on him, peering inwards. For answer, he drew on his own mojo, like a lawman clearing his guns; force pressed 'gainst force a moment, as the air seemed to hush. Then Fennig let his breath out, dropping hand to belt, and Rook showed his appreciation for the gesture by returning the favour.

"Don't dream too big, son, is all I suggest," he told Fennig, without rancour. "'Cause Christ knows, this ain't no democracy, and it ain't our dreams take pride of place. That's the kind'a mistake leads a man to the Machine."

Fennig's jaw tightened. "There's some might be thinkin' to make that mistake, sure. But I ain't one of 'em."

"Just as well. Those risin' against *me* might have some chance. Those risin' against *her*? None at all."

"Well, laying any talk of 'rising' by . . ." Fennig waved his hand, dismissing all thoughts of conflict. "Don't see no reason we can't make some improvements, nonetheless. For all our benefits."

"Laudable goal, Henry. Others feel the same, you know of?"

"Not all of 'em, no. But we don't need *all*—some's bound for that Machine of yours, just like you said, no matter what they do."

"And more arriving every day," Rook agreed, echoing Fennig's earlier remark. Then, having reached the processional's penultimate length, "Temple Square" itself, he paused, then asked: "Care to help me welcome some more of 'em, Mister Fennig?"

"Rev . . . I'd count myself honoured."

WITH NO TANGIBLE WALLS to defend, travellers to New Aztectlan *could* simply make their way in from any compass point over the newly be-greened plain, straight for the city's heart—but only if they were a hex, or in a hex's company. Any Call-deaf mundane stranger got within a thousand paces was sent on his way, memory glamour-blotted. And when a hex found his way in at last, he was drawn to the square before the Blood Engine's ziggurat like iron to a magnet, knowing in his bowels to wait 'til the Rainbow Lady or her consort appeared to administer the Oath.

Ixchel had first taught Rook the Oath as a long invocation in her native speech, its meaning only made clear through shared hexation; Rook hadn't stumbled through it more than twice before substituting a shorter, English version, rightly sensing that the words mattered not nearly so much as the fundamental consent they articulated—a permanent locking in of souls.

Service I pledge to the Suicide Moon,
Obedience to Her High Priest;
Fellowship to the City's children—
This I swear, on my own power's pain;
This I swear, to loss of blood and life,
That the Engine fail not to bring another World.

Once voiced, the Oath branded itself scar-black on the brain, unforgettable, yet almost never truly understood. All its adherents knew was that on the Oath's last word, as they let their blood fall upon the Temple's soil with whatever was nearest to hand, both the aching pull of the Call itself and that maddening lifelong hunger they'd all carried simply *broke*, like a fever . . . washed away, its last remnants retreating deep within. And suddenly, they were free.

But that "freedom's" truth lay hid in the Oath itself, for those wise enough to parse it proper; the hunger was not gone, just transmogrified. Which left their pledge a hook sunk deep into every heart, key to an ever-leaking sluice gate that could be flung wide at any moment, emptying them of hexation and life both in one bright, fatal flood.

Might be that was why some balked at the last second, sensing the trap, and fought rather than submit—much good though it did them against Rook, let alone Ixchel. The Oath, once broke, drunk them up altogether, leaving their blank-eyed bodies to be bent backwards over an altar stone.

In New Aztectlan, blood was the key to every door: those leading in, and out.

INSIDE THE SQUARE, ROOK was met by a small crowd of petitioners, all of them murmuring requests while offering up small gewgaws, which straightaway disappeared into the many pockets of Rook's capacious black coat. He could never give as much help as he might wish, but he always accepted the gifts; taking someone's tribute meant you took 'em serious, and ofttimes that simple feeling of having been heard, acknowledged, was help enough. Priesthood was priesthood.

Fennig, meanwhile, was met by his own little knot of followers: three young women—two brunettes, one blonde, and none of them, Rook guessed, past twenty summers—who bestowed looks on him which ranged the full spectrum from worshipful-affectionate to outright exasperated. Shrewd face lit up by their approach, Fennig bussed them all with impartial enthusiasm, then turned back to Rook, beaming.

"Rev, it's my right and honest pleasure to introduce you to my ladies." Fennig spread his three fingers and twitched each in turn toward a girl, a mountebank's flourish. "Miss Berta Schemerhorne"— the first brunette, tall and willowy in dark green—"Miss Clodagh Killeen"—the blonde, a pert, freckle-faced miss—"and Miss Eulalia . . . Eulie . . . Parr." The second brunette was dark-complected enough to make Rook suspect some hopped bedsheets lay behind her distinctly English surname. "All of courage uncommon, and toughness unmatched by any dockside bingo-boy you could name."

Berta glowed; Eulie coloured yet darker; buxom little Clodagh scowled.

"Fine words, ye flimmery Nativist fancy-man," she snapped, "given how little the choice we any of us had in coming here."

"Aw, Clo—"

"Don't you 'aw, Clo' me!"

He raised his hands, but she slapped them away. And as she did—Rook glimpsed a spark pass between, skin to skin: Blue-white, bending the air, leaving an ozone whiff behind. The other two saw it, cutting eyes at each other; the Schemerhorne gal laid a calming palm on the small of Clo's back, sending some sort of shimmer pulsing forward to outline the restive heart beneath in light.

While Eulie, in turn, made a cat's cradle flicker with both hands, casting threads fine as spider's silk to pull Clo closer, hug her tight. Saying, as she did: "Can't take on so at every little thing, sissy, and you know it—now, don't you? Ain't good for the baby."

Rook straightened slowly, breathing suddenly difficult; those corset-stays of hers *were* loose-laced, now he looked closer. And set damnable high, to boot.

"You're—*all* hexes," he said, at last. "And . . ."

Fennig nodded. "Clo's caught short, yeah. So's you can understand my investment in makin' this place a true home, stead'a just once more room in Herself's house."

Miss Berta turned Rook's way, dropping a polite curtsey, to add—"We didn't suspect, not at first. Back in the Points, it was only Henry, and when he said he had to go, well . . . I wasn't too minded to stay behind, without him; thankfully, the others agreed. Then, on the road, it came to us each one by one: dreams at night, tricks and spells by morning, and then—" She looked down at her feet, which were bare but white, soles soft, as though she'd worn shoes most of the rest of her life. "It *was* hard to stay together, for a while. But we didn't want to leave Henry, no matter what Clo might say. *None* of us."

Sound familiar, Reverend? his own mind whispered, mockingly.

True, it didn't seem reasonable to think he and Chess had been something wholly unique in the annals of all hexation, but still . . . it hurt, more than Rook would've guessed, to see his own story played out again, threefold.

Three women, each equal-powerful. Three chances to speak plain, be heard and understood, be forgave your trespasses. A three-fold marriage without any of 'em harried by the thought of mutual damnation, or love turned to murder in a nightmare-swift eye-flick.

In that one instant, he envied Fennig and his pimp's roster of lovelies so intensely, it made him sick—so much so that were he a far worse man, assuming that was even possible, he would've gladly killed 'em all, and walked away whistling.

Fennig almost seemed to see it, too—the beginnings of it, at any rate. He angled himself subtly to nudge Clo back behind him, just in case Rook saw fit to strike.

Don't want it to come to that, if it don't have to, Rook was surprised to realize. *I'd rather by far have this one with me than against me—and his womenfolk, too.*

A moment only—less, perhaps.

'Til one second was split headlong from the next by a shout, somewhere by the southernmost intake gate—"*Reverend Rook!* I need words with you, *gringo!*"

And this, too, reminded him of Chess: the glad relief of imminent threat, distraction through destruction. So, shrouding himself in a tarry halo, Rook turned to defend Hex City and his lady's dubious honour against this latest challenger.

"Here I am," he said.

CHAPTER TEN

THE GROUP SET DEAD-CENTRE in front of him stood together, some fourteen strong, and only now did Rook see how their stance differed from the usual supplicants': shoulder to shoulder, braced and spread-footed, intently focused. Strangely, the clear leader—a leathery man in buckskins whose grey hair still showed streaks of south-of-the-Border black—was the one man Rook didn't recognize. All others had been Oathed weeks previous; a passel of young male hexes, most of 'em likewise Mex or part-Mex, with glyphs, fresh-smeared in red, shining from their worn serapes and dusty shirts.

A compact, then: some sort of coup in the making. And since Ixchel wasn't to hand, it would fall to *him* to crush it 'fore it got the chance to take root, let alone spread.

Not that the Mother of Hanged Men ever deigned to do much of her own hunting—even in those first days, when the City comprised no more than a few dozen citizens, she'd more often than not been content to name the offender to Rook, and stand back. But the few times she *had* taken a hand herself still loomed large. One offender—some white-bearded old English gaffer, strong as Rook and twice as crafty, who'd styled himself a true wizard—was lofted up by invisible talons into the air and boiled away to a cloud of shreds while Ixchel stood rock-still beneath, not even looking at the man as he died; just set her jaw and smiled, as the precious blood fell like sticky rain. Another, some N'Orleans voodooist who claimed to channel spirits more powerful than the Ball-Court's denizens, was shown her error when every fetish she wore exploded simultaneously, unravelling her from the ankles up.

Compared to further complicity in that sort of wanton slaughter, Rook was glad to assume the role of judge, jury and (unflinching, yet fairly humane) executioner—but intervene to slap down both challengers if a brawl not designed to oust the Lady broke out, just to make sure they didn't lose anyone too potentially useful. The best way to tame wolves, Rook had always believed, was to make them your sheepdogs. And though he doubted so soft an option would satisfy this particular shaman's honour, he probably owed it to the more peaceful New Aztectlanites—like Fennig, and his Missuses—to at least try.

"Some say mercy is nothin' but folly gussied up nice," Rook began, adding a touch of skull-echo to his best preacher's boom. "And while I'm not amongst 'em, necessarily, the law I enforce proceeds from far beyond me, admitting no quarter for defiance. So here's all the clemency you're likely to get, gentlemen: one warning. Stop, or be stopped."

The Mexican mage snarled, lips lifting back, and spat. Where it fell the earth turned to quartz, lifting free from the dirt with a sound like cracking glass.

"Squawk on, carrion crow,'" he replied, scornfully. "This is Mexica business, only—so bring forth *our* goddess, whose throne you have usurped. We would have what she owes."

Rook kept his rope-burnt voice placid, even as his temper began to rise. "'Fraid you've been misinformed, *Señor*—there's nobody talks to the Lady just for the asking, ancestry notwithstanding. You talk to me, *I* talk to her; maybe then, if you're lucky. But probably not."

"'Cause that's how you want it, huh?" one of the younger hexes called out, his coppery skin and broad cheekbones marking him more Diné than Mex. Rook thought of "Grandma," whose true name he still didn't know, and never would—that grim old shamaness who'd meant to educate him out of Ixchel's clutches, only to lose her own life for the offer's foolish softness—and felt his stomach twist with wary guilt, as the boy went on. "You get the Lady's ear, *Reverend*, and the rest of us just have to knee it?"

"'Cause that's how *she* wants it, fool," Rook snapped back. "I don't have any more damn choice in the matter than you do: *gods don't bargain*, as I've learned full well. So if you *truly* want her attention, do how she likes it best—throw yourself in now, and save me the bother."

The old mage snorted. "Think you're the only Way-walker's seen gods, *gringo*?" Something opened behind his anger like a second set of eyes, dreadful and hollow. "There's more moving out there than her, Rook, or that skinless bed-boy of yours. Something else is coming too, and soon—something you've got no measure of, not in your darkest nightmares."

"Yeah? Well, that ain't much of a surprise." Rook made his voice like a wall, massive, impenetrable. "I've seen things'd turn the rest of your hair white, old man—and we'll all see a whole lot more of such, before we're through."

"But you don't care to know what-all we got to say about it?" the Diné youth challenged.

"Nope. And since you still don't seem to understand, I'll elucidate." Without warning, Rook stomped down hard. A burst of black power detonated beneath his boot heel, shuddering the entire square in outward-arcing ripples; coupsters and citizenry alike grabbed at each other, just to stay upright. Only the great ziggurat stood unmoved. "See what I mean? Foregone conclusion. This place'll keep on growing, be New Aztectlan 'til it isn't anymore. Which is when them as ain't in on this will wish to Christ Almighty that they were.

"Now, you already drew your line in the sand just by comin' here, so your only real choice is to take the Oath, spill blood and keep to the right side of it, from now on. Or . . ."

"Or?" The chief mage said, expressionless.

". . . into the Machine you go. *Like this*."

Rook swung a backhand strike, lashing invisible tendrils 'round his opponent with casual ease. In his mind's eye, he'd plotted an arc ending with this interloper slammed down atop the Temple's highest altar, broken and bleeding. But when he hauled hard on the web of force, he staggered, as if he'd tried to lift the entire group at once. The snare fell away.

Too surprised for fear, Rook stared, while the younger contingent exchanged looks of shock and glee admixed—same as any greenhorn who'd just seen some long-loathed rival laid out with a single punch.

"You," the stranger told Rook, "are not the only one who knows what can come of making a vow."

As he swooped both hands up, Rook saw the shaman's co-rebels close their eyes, let their own hands go jerking skywards too, like marionettes. The old man clapped both fists together, sending a low *thoom* Rook's way that seemed to pull the air after; their impact was thunder turned inside-out, all but silent.

Then a tidal wave smashed into him, sent him flying back 'til he smacked the ground all stunned and aching, his shields shattering same as the spit-glass gone to dust under his feet. Rook fought to raise his head, fear beginning to push its way past shock at last— marked how the stranger stood watching, coiling the power his coterie had apparently willed through him 'round one arm, like a bullwhip. Behind, the younger hexes swayed in place, too discomfited anymore to grin; their faces drew tight, wincing, as Rook felt their broken Oaths suck at their sorcerously allied strength.

The Mex, however, had sworn nothing, as yet. *His* strength was untouched, though hardly strong enough on its own merits to do such damage.

Rook knew the feel of the Oath by now, could sense its constant shape: a green-black line heart-rooted in every sworn witch or warlock, then run down into the ground, to the Temple's Mictlan-Xibalba-sounding depths. Yet even through pain-blurred eyes, inchoate nerve-ends sizzling with frustrated power, he perceived now how each rebel bore *another* set of binding cords: a cat's cradle connecting comrade to comrade, 'til all spun finally back upon their leader, galvanizing him in a concentric circuit.

Together, Rook thought. *Working* together. *Lending each other their strength—or he's taking it, at the least, and they're letting him. How can that be?*

Here Grandma entered his brain, yet once more—had the bitch ever truly quit it? Reminding him of that black marriage she'd dangled in front of him, back when he'd still dreamed he could have his Chess without eating him: mutual cancellation, self-sacrifice. *They* may *live, but not as Hataalii. . . .*

They swore *to him,* Rook realized, numbly. *Another Oath, to share their power, so he could use it to break free of hers.*

God damn, if the mad old man kicking his ass this very moment wasn't some sort of state-uncertified *genius.*

The City's Oath ran far deeper, of course; within moments, the Mex's fellow coupsters would be drained, with no more power left to give—but within *moments,* they'd no longer need to. For the critical next few seconds, their collective was just too strong for Rook to beat, alone.

As the shaman stared down at him, sure of his victory, Rook mustered a last glare. "*Traitor,*" he called him. "We're all hexes here, Goddamnit . . . turned away by everyone, everywhere, 'cept here. So what if Ixchel's worship takes a toll? Blood ain't exactly in short supply. Spill enough of it, and she'd've made us free."

But the grey-haired stranger simply shook his head. "I already know your Lady, Rook—better than you do, for all you've shared her bed. She was one of my people's gods, in long-gone times; we fed her, fed *them,* 'til the earth itself was soaked, so foul nothing would grow. But did they help us, when the steel hats came? When *los conquistadors* raped everything in their path, leaving only sickness behind? When the *Christo*-shouters burned our books and bodies?

"No. They are hungry ghosts, not gods at all, *never* trustworthy. One is bad enough—but she wants to bring back more, doesn't she?

To raise each and every one of them up from where they squat in darkness, down under the water, so deep even the bone canoe fears to penetrate it."

Rook couldn't deny it, even if this phantom grip squeezing both his lungs flat would allow him enough breath to. The effort of lying wasn't worth whatever time he had left.

"Think you know her *that* well, you'd still best not be here when she comes lookin' for me," Rook managed, barely. But the shaman simply drew hard on the net once more, conjuring a fresh palmful of lightnings.

"Oh," he replied, "I fully expect to die at Her hand, now or later—as you do too, or should. You already know she will destroy this world to bring on hers."

"The Fifth ends in earthquakes—yeah, I heard. But the Sixth—"

Another head-shake. "No. Such creatures do not go *forward*, 'Reverend.' She seeks to sink us further still, to resurrect the Fourth World, which ended in floods when the Enemy, his brothers and his mother tore everything apart between them. When the earth itself was cracked like a bone and boiled, its marrow cooked sweet for sucking. And the Feathered Serpent was forced to steal our dust from Mictlan once more, afterwards, so that new men and women might be fashioned from it."

Fresh mill-grist, Rook thought, throat burning. *Fresh jaguar cactus fruit to be squeezed for its pulp, over a thousand rebuilt altars.*

"*This* is what she wants—the doom *you* have already helped her put in place. So *true* mercy, I think, would be for you not to have to watch it come to pass."

His hand swung down, straight into *someone else*'s deceptively flimsy grasp: four slim fingers and a thumb, all five nails cyanose, outlined in black blood. Dread Lady Ixchel stood suddenly between them, abrupt and upright, whole form ablaze with chilly lunar radiance—and at her touch the old Mex recoiled, gobbling, as Rook heard his wrist snap like a rotten twig.

"Old owl," Ixchel named him, tonelessly. "Foolish *nahual*. You claim to know me? Then you should know better."

So ice-cold and freakishly arousing at once, as always, stinking of death and barely clothed. Rook saw a thorn shoved through either nipple and some random jagged bone-shard bisecting her septum, leaving upper lip and cleavage crusted purple-red, a triangle of phantom claw-marks got in underground battle. But enough to make every prick in the place perk up regardless, and probably grease every pussy as well, to boot; never any call for Rook to think on someone else in order to give her her due and proper, and she knew it. He'd seen with his own eyes how the bitch could make even those queer-to-the-bone long to go digging in *her* charnel treasure-box.

(Chess's white face, lips set, teeth too gritted even to let out a proper sob of hate as she lowered herself onto him, while Rook did nothing but watch—breath held, heart hammering. Watch and await his own turn, with both of them.)

A man who beds with a goddess becomes a god, little king, or dies. Or both.

Her black blossom of hair lifted high, eddying. Behind her, the cloak of dragonflies billowed forth and rose up buzzing, a tinsel-winged plague.

The shaman's mouth moved like a fish's, gasping; his unmaimed hand gave one final tug at the cords binding Rook, only to see Ixchel send them snapping, severed, with a single finger-flick. As he dove back, momentum sending his gang sand-wards along with him, her gaze traced those invisible strands from body to body, following the lesser oath-web: a sloppy working at best, red-gold-gouting, fogging the air. Yet the nude bed where one eyebrow should have been did lift at the sight, if only slightly.

Clever, Rook heard her "say," abandoning outward speech entirely. *Clever peasants, clever dogs. Sons of a million* tlacotin-slaves.

The sheer strength of her contempt was hundred-proof at least, good enough to scour pots, and gave Rook the strength to power himself back upright. As he did, his eye fell onto Fennig and his beauties, caught up unknowing in the brawl's very heart—all three women had their hands linked for protection, a dim flame flowing to blanket Clo in particular, cupping her stomach's distention. Rook almost thought he could glimpse the child asleep inside, its tiny heart a-pulse with sorcerous potential.

The witch-ménage concentrated mainly on each other, a single unit, eyes downcast, so's not to attract undue attention. Fennig himself, meanwhile, was staring at Ixchel straight-on, sliding his spectacles down slightly in order to consider her over their rims. If he squinted, Rook could see an image of his queen-wife caught there, twinned on both corneas and clarifying under pressure, the way a daguerreotype takes shape. As though Fennig were somehow incapable of turning away—helpless not to stay and see what might develop, literally.

At the same time Rook regained his, the Diné youth—the only one of the shaman's donors still left upright—hauled out a knife and jumped for Ixchel's throat, coming at her silent, blindside-first. The dragonfly cloak parted to allow him passage, buzz-hum ascending to warning shriek; Rook found himself stuck in mid-automatic ward-stance, both hands up, fingers crooked to fire whatever his instincts deemed necessary. Though since he'd once observed Ixchel take a ball to the skull from Ed Morrow's pistol and still blast him backwards out of Hell, it was all probably pretty moot.

But it was *Fennig* who actually interposed: lunged in fencer-swift, using his cane like an *epée*, to send the Redskin somersaulting face-first into the nearest wall. Gravity, hex-augmented, was enough to snap his jaw one way, neck the other, with a furious crack.

Ixchel looked Fennig's way, and nodded. To which Fennig tipped his bowler, like she was just another skirt to flirt with.

"Least I could do, ma'am," was all he said, aloud. Adding, with his mind—*Seein' this is your city, after all. And you the reason, in the end, that me and my g'hals here have free run of it.*

Oh, I like this one, husband.

Times like these, Rook wondered why they ever bothered to speak aloud to each other at all, 'sides from so as not to lose the ability.

The shaman snarled, and wrenched a final helping of power from his bond-donors, who crumpled, curling around their guts. Knowing better than to strike at Ixchel, he sent it whipping at Fennig instead: an arc of liquid lightning, overcooked energies spinning off in all directions.

Fennig, however, simply stepped backward, allowing Berta, Eulie and Clo to join hands around him. Of a sudden, Rook could see the bindings netted between *them*, a living ward-circle: raw ghost-currents drawing only on each other, with not a single thread of the girls' own power—or Fennig's—reaching out to drink of the shaman's spillage. And as the spell broke harmlessly over their hunched shoulders at once, Clo's mid-section gave an all but imperceptible heave, shrugging the bluish farewell crackle 'round itself and folding it away, all neat and tidy, 'til it winked itself out like a stepped-on cheroot.

I was right, Rook realized, amazed. *The child, too. All of 'em, working in tandem. It's the Goddamn future growin' up, right in front of us.*

Then: *Time to end all this, 'fore someone gets hurt that shouldn't.*

Yes, little king. And so it shall be ended, now.

Ixchel turned hard black eyes back on the shaman and his donors. "Prostrate yourselves," she ordered, forcing the fallen hexes to splay themselves instantly flat, muscles spasming; blood broke from eyes, ears, noses, as choked cries of agony squeezed out through their locked jaws. To the Mex, in specific, she continued—"You wish to shed your precious water in my direction—make *chalcihuatl* from *nextlaualli* while seeking *xochimiquitzli*, the flowery death, as was your ancestors' right, and pleasure. How dearly I love to be reminded of these things, here in this new land! It is a great gift, and I accept it, gladly."

Oh, what a terrible creature she was, as Rook well knew already. Thinking, numbly: *But I'm the one who'll have to lie down with her, later on.*

Though he somehow thought any one of these fools would be right glad to trade places with him, to save 'emselves from what came next.

The smile Ixchel gave was beatific, dreadful as the sickly skull-fragment moon which hung above. "Feed me," she said.

For just one moment, shaman and followers froze, pain apparently ceased. Then their skins went purple—bloating, glowing—as their blood pushed out and upwards through every pore at once, heating to a boil in mid-rise, flushing a fresh-carved meat-stink throughout the air. Fanning her hands toward her face, Ixchel *inhaled* this sanguinary cloud in a single, impossibly long breath, 'til at last it dissipated, leaving behind a clutch of sinewy stick-figure mockeries: swollen-jointed and crumbly, already disintegrating, with black pits for eyes.

After, it took some effort for her to regain her stillness. Even as she turned and glided over to Rook's side, she had not mastered it perfectly; the *nox vomica* of pure power she'd swallowed danced behind both furnace-grate pupils, making her twitch.

For a moment, he was eight years old again, caught by his mother in mid-disaster, sick with suspense to learn his punishment. But the goddess who owned him only went up on her toes, so much smaller (and stronger) than him it fairly hurt, to kiss his sweating forehead.

"I have saved you, little king, yet again. Now, seeing I am past due thanks . . . it behooves you to come with me, and do me reverence."

As if all this had been nothing more than a trivial detail, absently settled. As if none of it really mattered.

We're dreams to her, Rook thought, *good, bad or indifferent. This was nothing, like everything else. A shadow-show between blinks.*

"Up in a tick," he told her, lips dry. "Wouldn't do to keep you waiting."

"No," she agreed. And was gone.

Left behind, the corpses powdered inevitably apart, then blew away on a rising wind. Clo let out a *whoosh*, and folded back onto the others, who murmured at her like doves. Fennig, meanwhile, gave her a quick comfort-clasp of the hand before once more pinning Rook with those oh-so-penetrative re-hid oculars.

"Knowing you're wanted elsewhere," he said, "I don't s'pose you'd care to jaw a while, if the ladies walk on."

Rook looked at him, face kept strictly unreadable, from half a year's practice. Did he really dare?

"Have to be quick," he said, eventually.

"As typhus, Reverend."

MINUTES AFTER, THEY STOOD side by side, watching smoke from the Blood Engine's stacks rise up forever. Even now, Rook knew, there were a horde yet of supplicants massing who'd need to be Oathed, 'fore they grew so weary from the Call tearing at their guts that they turned on each other, and had to be put down for the current citizens' edification. Ixchel hadn't thought much on *that*, obviously, when commanding he gift her with both his immediate presence and a workable cock-stand. But then again, such things meant equally little, in her ancient eyes.

"Your hex-work's in seeing," Rook said. "Which means you must've noted the same bindings 'tween our dead friends I did."

"Heard what the old man said, too. 'Power of an oath,' huh? *Any* oath—'twixt *any* hex? Or hexes?"

"Theoretically." Rook rubbed his chin, inquisitive mind stirring creakily back to life, with an oddly pleasant ache. "Practically, seems like the stronger the hex, the more who swear, the stronger the oath. Yet their vows didn't trump the City's binding."

"And drained 'em all the faster, for bleeding power twice-a-ways," Fennig agreed. "Maybe that's why it never struck Herself somebody else might try it, in the first place."

"Your g'hals are bound each to each too, though, from what I observed."

"Each t'each and each t'me, neat as any god-botherer's marriage-packet—and since that's what *Señor* Hex-no-more and his boyos seem to've done as well, the lesson *I* take is don't never try your strength outright 'gainst the City's, no matter how many you got webbed in on the same spell-rope, 'cause it's doomed to pull every last man jack of you down."

"Mmm. And yet . . ." Rook paused, brow knitting. "Maybe it'd've gone differently, had it *been* every man jack of 'em uprising in the first place, 'stead of just that one."

Epiphany's flash lit both their faces at once, small, but bright enough neither risked a glance at the other, for fear of snuffing it outright.

"A true Patriot's creed," Fennig said, approvingly. "All hexes created equal; no wonder she never conceived of it." His serpent's smile took on a fiercer edge. "Don't really grasp who-all she's dealin' with, hereabouts and today, do she?"

"No," said Rook, softly."To her, what swears to her is hers—full stop—and four centuries back, her subjects felt the same. Threw 'emselves headlong into the fire, and thought 'emselves blessed. But when an American swears to something . . . it's a two-way street. He expects to get what he pays for, and keep what he earns."

"He was *right*, 'bout her—the Mex, I mean. Wasn't he?"

Rook didn't quite allow himself to agree, he certainly didn't argue. Nodding to what little enough was left of the coupsters, by now: "You see what came of *that*, though."

"What I *see* is, if he knew more'n most, he didn't know near enough. Like . . . where best t'hit."

"And you do, I suppose?"

"No. But I will."

At the sound of those four small words, Rook felt a shiver of something fragile, almost hope-flavoured, so deep down he could've easily chosen to ignore it entirely.

Instead, he made sure to point out: "She's a god, you know."

"Oh, cert. But ain't we all, to some degree?" Here Fennig chuckled, only partly amused. "Philosophy aside, though, no God ever did nothin' much for me, Rev; you neither, I suspect."

Not for the first time, Rook wished (*devoutly* would be the first word to his tongue, had it not tasted so bitter) that he could still pray; that he had the right, let alone the capacity. Granted, he'd never gotten much of a reply, when he had. But given how, this time, it wouldn't be strictly on his own behalf—well. So odd a display of unselfishness from a career hypocrite like himself should really count for *something*, surely?

Apparently not, judging from the Almighty's characteristically unbroken silence.

"But there's a crack in everything, y'see, Reverend," Fennig continued, all unknowing. "You just have to keep handy to find it, keep quiet . . . and *pay attention*. So what I'll do is all the above-mentioned, while lookin' t'me and mine in the interim. And since you're the biggest dog I can count on to try and keep the Missuses Fennig and I out of Saint Terra, I'll stand by you as well, back you up 'gainst all comers. Sound fine?"

"*All* comers?" Rook repeated.

"Even Herself, needs be . . . eventually."

Again, there seemed not much to add. So Fennig touched his three fingers to hat-brim and specs-rim together, in half-salute. "Be seein' you?" he asked.

"Can't see how not," said Rook.

A final shrug. "*Bene.*"

And with a furl of his cane, he walked on.

WHEN THE MOON ROSE, the newest entrants were thrown a roustabout all up and down Temple Street. Like most Hex City hoys, it spun on the same discovery Rook and Chess had once stumbled on without knowing, to their mutual satisfaction: How, when jammed in proximity, the hex-hunger often became carnal rather than fatal, though equal-voracious and undistinguishing—meat being meat, after all, just like blood was blood.

Rook usually put in an appearance at these shindigs, partly to seed the impression his approval was required for them to continue, but he never stayed long, drank little, and refused all offers of companionship; stayed faithful to Ixchel, after both their fashions. Not that she cared if he had it off briefly with some light-skirt—or equal-light pair of britches, come to that—but to do so risked entanglement, accusations of favouritism, trouble. And more trouble, at this point, was the very last thing he needed to buy.

Were-lights of a score of different hues floated 'round the mob, throwing shadows in red, yellow, silver-white, green. Those folk whose craft ran to brewing and distillation set up dispensary stations on the crowd's edges, while on a platform raised up by a moment's impulse, a score of musicians hammered away with enthusiasm, englamoured clouds a-moil above. The hexes danced on earth, air, roofs, walls, indiscriminately; some put on and flung off new shapes, casual as most changed hats. And wherever the crowd fell away, sorcerously inclined revellers could be glimpsed . . . *taking* one another . . . in any and every sense one might conceive.

Tonight, however, Rook leaned down over the same balcony whose architecture he'd planted in Chess's dreams, while the Mother of all Hanged Men ran her icy little fingers up the inside of his naked thigh to cup him from behind. And damn if he didn't rouse at the pressure, still, to meet her halfway—purple-swole, dripping. Like any qualm-free monster.

Far beneath, he glimpsed a figure climbing onto one of the tables, and noted how the celebrants gathered 'round fell immediately quiet: Fennig's sweetheart, the gravid one, Clodagh. Who lifted her Irish voice in a familiar tune, snapping her fingers for accompaniment.

> *"Oh sis, come down by the water's side, sing I down, oh, sing I day—*
> *Oh sis, come down by the water's side—the boy's the one for me!*
> *Oh sis, come down by the water's side, the eldest to the youngest*
> *cried. . . ."*

She sang the lay incongruously upbeat, which was why it took him a fatal few moments to recognize it—too late entirely, to stop the knife from twisting in his gut.

> *"Sayin' I'll be true . . . unto my love—"*

"—if my love'll be true to me," Rook finished, beneath his breath. Feeling the full weight of what he'd done break over him, a salt-hot wave of regret.

Ixchel, always aware of his thoughts, touched her rough tongue to his sweaty spine, laving the middle-top vertebrae as though she longed to bite straightway in, to hear them crunch between her pointy jade-flake teeth.

He will come, husband, she said. **It is . . . inevitable.**

And she drew him down.

Though Rook's Hell would be hot enough once he got there, Ixchel's was cold, which explained why she so often needed warming. Still, it was an empty place, for all its passion, what with the Chess-shaped hole left forever open in its centre.

My bed. Self-chose—self-made. Nothing for it but to lie down, and keep on lying.

So Reverend Rook did his duty as the rowdy-dow spun on, marking mental time 'til he'd be able to get back to that other experiment he'd started, just before dawn. . . .

MORROW DID SAY HOW'S YOU had a lock of hair on him, tucked away in some dolly-bag, said Kees Hosteen's shade—dead these many months, from an accidental application of lead while doing the Rev unwitting service. Hosteen, who'd thought he was betraying one master to help another only to end up losing both, and himself, besides. *You keep a little somethin' from the rest of us, too? Or am I just special?*

"The latter," Rook lied. "Which is why, when I found I needed a favour . . . I naturally thought of you."

Oh, joy.

"One only, and important enough that when you're done, I'll slip the chain; you'll be free to slide off for wherever, with no further demands on your valuable time. Can't beat those odds."

Yeah, sounds just peachy. That how they're sellin' indentured slavery, these days?

"I could ask *less* nicely, you really want me to," Rook observed.

There was a pause, the barest flicker of something indistinct passing 'cross Hosteen's face—a sigh, turned inside out. Incentive enough to make Rook smile, and continue.

"Pinks'll be moving against us, likely soon. So we need intelligence, to give us some warning what to expect . . . it's a must, Kees. Old soldier like you knows that."

Hosteen still looked sceptical. *Would've thought you'd just conjure that up yourself, frankly . . . sleep with that Bible of yours under your pillow and pull prophecy out of your dreams, like Joseph. What in the hell d'you need me for?*

Rook held up a hand to show the never-quite-healed burn across his palm. "The Book's gone, Kees, a good while back. 'Sides which, there are factors which make it hard to act direct; Miz Songbird, for one. She's . . . got the taste of me."

A smirk. *Ain't that convenient.*

"No, Kees, it's very *in*convenient, in point of fact. But I did find a way to get around it."

It took Hosteen a beat, before his insubstantial face fell. *Aw, shit.*

"Indeed."

You do know she knows me too, right, Rev? From Tampico, when the Pinks came to pull Ed and Chess outta Mexico City, after it fell over. What makes you think I can slide under her notice, when you can't?

"'Cause she sees more ghosts than I do, every day of the week; don't draw attention to yourself, you'll be just one more shade amidst the throng. All I need you to do is find them, listen, come back here and tell me what you've learned . . . and then, soldier, consider yourself discharged." He held out the Atwood's bottle. "I break this, you're free—beyond my reach for good. Back to . . ."

He hesitated, lowering the bottle. The question seemed to spill up out of him, more of its own will than his. "Kees, I have to ask. What's it . . . like? Where—you were?"

Silence, for long seconds. Then: *You'll find out soon enough, I expect*, the ghost he'd once called friend replied. *Now: we done?*

"All but. Though if you were minded to look in on Chess as well, on your way back—" Rook broke off, shook his head. "No, bad idea. Forget I even said it."

For all Rook might wish different, Chess knew himself legitimately aggrieved and would seek the price, no matter what; let the world die screaming, so long's he had his vengeance. The man didn't forget, *never* forgave. To do so, he'd say, would be making himself a God he didn't believe in's bitch.

Chuckling a bit at this last part, the Rev glanced up to find Hosteen's phantom eyes upon him, full of something annoyingly unreadable.

He might not kill you, even now, he offered, *you only told 'im you was sorry.*

The very idea made Rook laugh full-out, long and loud.

"Oh, Kees," he said, eventually. "You know Chess, like you know me. So how damn likely is *that*?"

SURE AS NIGHTFALL, HOWEVER, the old Hollander *would* end up giving Chess a fly-by, if only for old times' sake—entirely of his own will, this way, with not a hint of Rook pushing him in that direction. Which really was about the only way he could hope to gain knowledge of Chess's current whereabouts, since if Songbird had had a taste, the once, then Chess had had . . . *all* of him. And still did.

Rook mounted the Temple's inner staircases slowly, his footfalls leaden. 'Til, at the top, he fell back into bed without even bothering to kick off his boots and slept at once, stretched out beside devastation's handmaid—a black, dreamless sleep, with darkness his only pillow.

CHAPTER ELEVEN

THE LAST THING MISTER Pargeter—Chess—did, before they came up over the final ridge, was to change Yancey's much-abused wedding rig to a set of clothes more boy-fit; denim breeches, a loose cotton shirt, wool stockings, black boots. Pointing out: "You plan on walkin' blind into a nest of no-'counts and raperees, I can tell you from personal experience how trousers are a sight harder to get off, 'specially if you fight back hard while they're at it."

Yancey hoped she didn't turn too pale at the thought. "Is that . . . likely?"

"Not while I'm around," Mister Morrow put in, voice dropping growl-low. Chess gave him a little eye-flick of amused appraisal, followed by a shrug.

"Let's put it this way, then," he told Yancey, "if you ain't got the sand to look after your own business, we ain't got the time to do it for you. Fair enough?" Yancey nodded. "Which reminds me—have to cut that hair, you want to stay inconspicuous."

Both hands flew to her head, like he aimed to do it right then. "No!"

Morrow again, sweet reason itself: "She can braid it up tight, stick it under a hat. 'Course, you'll have to conjure that for her, too."

Chess hissed in annoyance, but popped his own off and ran a sparking finger 'round the brim, making it subdivide like string-cut dough: two identical beavers, one of 'em already sized to fit Yancey's skull and top-knot alike.

"There," he said, tossing it her way—then turned back to the others. "She keeps her pride and glory; whoop-de-do. But once we're through Joe's door she'd better at least *act* the damn man, is all I'm sayin'."

Geyer opened his mouth, but it was Yancey who answered, thinning her voice as cold as she knew how, from years of wrangling drunks and settling bills. "A play-role *you* aim to coach me in, I suppose? If not, I suggest we get going." She widened her glare to include the other two. "And while we're at it, I'll thank you to never again discuss me to my face like livestock, *gentlemen*."

Scooping her disordered 'do into a twist, she jammed the "new" hat down over it and brushed past all three of them to climb the next hill, resisting the urge to hike up those phantom skirts no longer restricting her movements. Geyer tried to take her arm, but she threw him off (as gently as possible).

If I'm to be Adamized, there's no more reliance on men's kindnesses, lest I give the wrong impression. Chess doesn't play such games, after all . . . and he's far more cause to, given.

In her annoyance, she'd forgotten he could probably hear everything passed through her brainpan, he only concentrated hard enough.

So it was unsurprising yet blush-provoking when she heard him remark: "That's one tough little stargazer you've yoked yourself to, Ed."

Morrow huffed, legging it upwards. "She ain't, neither—and she's a widow now, too, so show some damn respect," was all he threw back.

"Marriage for money's not but one step away from outright whoredom, in my opinion."

Yancey stopped in her tracks. "*Excuse* me?"

Those green eyes met hers, cool and poisonous, even less human than before. "All right, then: you and that tin star of yours, was that truly made in heaven? Or maybe something your Pa dreamed up 'cause he wanted law as family, and you went along, 'cause you might as well raffle your maidenhead to the biggest gun in town as not?"

You, *sir, are a toad,* Yancey thought at him, bell-clear and deliberate, blush deepening. Meanwhile snapping, out loud: "None of your beeswax! He's dead 'cause of you, anyhow—"

"Oh yeah, that's right: *me,* not you, for thinkin' you could handle things on your ownsome. And you really do look like you miss him, too."

Geyer opened his mouth again, but too late, for Yancey had already punched the pistoleer full in his mocking face. "Oh my *Jesus!*" Morrow yelled out, and grabbed for her, bent on fending off whatever came next—but Chess just rocked back a tad, putting one hand to his split lip to taste the blood, before barking out a red-tinged laugh.

"Gal," he said, "I must admit I like you *better* this way, 'stead of all polite and persnickety; makes you seem like you got fire in your belly. Which you're gonna need."

"And I'm supposed to be flattered, I expect? Balls to that! You're a petty, heathenish deity indeed."

Chess shrugged once more, split lip already healed over. "Well, you're the one started prayin' to me in the first place—but since it's all the apology you're like to get, I guess you can either take it, or don't. 'Cause I surely don't give a damn."

A swish of dust, and he was out of reach. Yancey bent over a moment, panting harsh, sick with the helpless urge to kill: him, Sheriff Love, Reverend Rook and that Mexican blood-goddess of his, for gifting Chess Pargeter with such power when they *knew* him unfit to bear it. God Almighty.

Geyer scuffed the hill with his boot-tip, seeming more embarrassed than anything else. But Mister Morrow's hand fell on her shoulder, comfort-warm as Uther's had always been—and though she shouldn't've let it stay there, she did. "We'll be there soon enough," he told her.

"Wonderful."

"Chess . . ." Morrow gave a sigh, choosing his next few words with laudable care. "Listen . . . he knows he's done wrong by you, by all your folk, and it's makin' him hit out. But I know he feels badly, just the same."

"Really. How on earth can you tell?"

"'Cause you're still *here*, ma'am. 'Cause he didn't just throw you right back no matter how much you pled to come along, and be done with it."

They trudged along in silence a moment while Yancey mustered her own thoughts, 'til she'd become near-enough calm to voice 'em.

"'Feels bad,'" she repeated, eventually. "My father is *dead*, Mister Morrow—husband, too. The town I lived in my whole life torn ear to ear, with my inheritance pushed over and burnt to the ground. Your Mister Pargeter . . . from what I see, he's been mildly inconvenienced, at best. So thank you kindly, but I could give a horse's fat ass how that hex-slung son-of-a-slut *feels*, and that's a damn fact."

Geyer stopped short, amazed by her vehemence. "Miss Yancey!"

"Oh, I'm sorry—does my rough speech offend you, 'Mister Grey'? Besides which, his mother *is* . . . what she is, isn't she, Mister Morrow? Didn't object much to *that* part of the song, as I recall."

"She *was*, yes, like I said. She's dead now."

Yancey paused in her tracks, yet again. "Then I'm sorry."

But Morrow just shook his head. "Don't have to try and be, not 'less he asks you to. Which he won't."

Staring past her, he sought out Chess's bright purple figure far off in the distance, silhouetted 'gainst the sun. And Yancey saw him narrow his eyes, as though looking into either some unfathomable light, or some equally impenetrable darkness.

"He's not an easy man," Morrow said. "Not with himself, and not with anybody else. Only good part is, when you get riled enough to slap back, it does make him respect you."

"Don't doubt but you're right, given you know him best. Still, he won't get any more of a rise out of me from now on than he already has, if I can help it."

Morrow nodded, silent, while Geyer looked off into the distance, tracking Chess's progress by the spindrift he kicked up.

"But can you?" Geyer wondered, aloud. "It's hard enough for me to keep a civil tongue in my head, and I'm not—a lady, with those sorts of finer feelings t'grapple with."

Morrow cast him a look that all but shouted: *Stop your posturing, idjit.* "You do know he'd kill you stone dead, though, if you tried to kick up a fuss about it," he pointed out. "And that's equal-true for all of us, in the end."

Not for you, Yancey thought, remembering how back in the thick of Hoffstedt's Hoard's demise, Morrow had been the only one to rein Chess in. *Not really. Much as you may want to deny it, in front of me.*

And why might that be? Was Chess right, thinking he might have cause for jealousy from Morrow's eye straying in Yancey's direction?

Useful, in potential, a traitorous part of her whispered. *Now that I'm left to fend for myself in this world, robbed at gunpoint of all protectors, forced to choose 'tween bad and worse to get to what* I *need.*

Oh, she was starting to hate that Satan-practical little voice inside, the one she couldn't dare claim came from anywhere but her own fast-withering soul.

"Let's get a move on," she told both Pinkertons, and set her shiny hex-made boots back to the upwards path.

OFTEN AS HE'D DONE business with the Rev's contingent before, however, today Splitfoot Joe proved singularly uninviting.

"You get gone from here, Chess Pargeter!" he yelled from inside the saloon, while somebody else—more than one, probably—fired warning shots at them, out the barricaded windows. "You ain't welcome no more, not after what you done here last!"

"Can't think what *that* could've been," Yancey whispered to Morrow, where they crouched behind a handy rock—and Morrow found he had to think a bit himself to reckon the exact cause of Joe's antagonisms, given how many transgressions he'd seen Chess perform.

"Helped open up a doorway into Hell—*a* Hell, anyhow," he set on, finally. "Oh, and brought the Pinks down on 'em, too; that's all but a capital offence, 'round these parts."

Her brows knit. "But—don't they already know how you, yourself—"

"No, they don't, and I'd be right pleased you didn't enlighten 'em on that same fact, thank you very much. Frank too, I'm guessin'."

Geyer nodded. "He's got the right of it, ma'am. Tell, and our lives won't be worth a plugged nickel."

"Then my lips are sealed."

"Much obliged."

A yard or so away, Chess ignored all this—bullets popped off him like moths on a lantern, singed to powder in spark-showers, each one merely serving to spur his own ire higher. "That wasn't even *me*, you fools!" he hollered back, hands on hips. "That was the damn *Rev*!"

"Same damn difference!"

Chess's eyes blazed at that, literally; the glow was visible from where Morrow knelt. "*I* say there's a difference, then you need to take me serious—'sides which, ain't no way on earth you can stop me comin' in if I want to, save for setting yourselves alight and hoping I don't care to burn. So—what'll it be? Me, or the fire?"

"Word is, you bring the Weed, too. What you got to say to that?"

"Not a—" Chess began, but Morrow waved him silent.

"Word's right," he said, rising to his full height. "I've seen it done: Mouth-of-Praise, Hoffstedt's Hoard—all gone, wiped out, 'cause they didn't take Chess serious. You already know what he can do; really want to make him *want* to?"

Silence ensued. Then the door clicked open and Joe himself peeped out, looking stricken.

"I got customers in there, Chess," he said, half-apologetic. "*You* know how it is."

"Not really," Chess shot back, as he strode past him.

When those of Joe's trade who could still walk straight saw Chess coming, they mostly cut loose and scarpered, leaving the place denuded but for a few dozing drunks. Joe knew better than to protest—just set 'em up at a table Morrow recalled as his "best," while Chess paced and Geyer manfully fought down the urge to pull a chair out for Yancey, who did it herself.

"Whiskey all 'round, Joe," Morrow called out, to keep the man occupied.

"Sure." Rummaging behind the bar: "Truth to tell, them Pinks didn't even stick around too long, not after that Chinee witch of theirs figured you all'd been whisked off to Mexico. Left a few here to wait, lest you somehow magic yourselves back 'fore they caught up with you, but then those got pulled out too, once the Weed started spreadin'. So there was my payment for lettin' them badged-up fuckers in here in the first place, I guess."

"Just can't trust them Union types," Chess observed, audibly disinterested.

"I s'pose so. Here's your whiskey."

Morrow tipped his hat, but Chess waved his away: "Not for me; you know what I like."

"Uh huh, 'course," Joe stammered. "Just . . . we ain't got no absinthe on the premises; that stuff is awful expensive, and we ain't had the trade to merit it."

"Sure you do, Joe. Go look."

And there it was, right to hand, when Joe bent down behind the bar to feel for it with shaking fingers: a smallish bottle, green as any blowfly's back. He went to hand it over, then jumped a foot when it skittered 'cross the bar-top, leapt into the air, and slapped right into Chess's waiting palm. The cork popped out with a dead man's hand trigger-click, falling to roll, stickily, against the toe-cap of Chess's right boot.

Joe looked like Morrow felt, to see it. Even the Rev in his heyday had never spilled power 'round with such casual aplomb, wasting it on absolute nothings, for the mere pleasure of seeing how such a spectacle disturbed the non-hexacious.

Chess gave the bottle a pull, then licked his lips, pink cat-tongue faintly green-tinged. "Well, I'm for bed," he announced. "Best room's still at the top of the stairs, ain't it?"

". . . yes." Joe gulped. "I could, uh . . . clear it out. . . ."

"Oh, don't bother yourself." Raising his voice, ever so slightly:

"Reckon whoever's in there's probably heard I'm here, by now—and if they don't got the sense to be gone by the time I'm at their door, I somehow misdoubt they would've been smart enough to cover their bill; good riddance to bad rubbish, is what I say."

Up above, a great thump and scuttle, followed by the smash of a window wouldn't open fast enough; Joe almost winced to hear it, now white to the very lips.

"Sure that's so," he said, finally. "Mister Pargeter."

No call to scare the poor bastard like that, Morrow thought. It was an ill deed, unworthy of the Chess he thought he'd come to know, since Mictlan-Xibalba's toils. And when Chess's eyes swung his way, Morrow met his gaze full-on, refusing to call the words back. Adding in on top, as he did: *And let's see what you want to do about it, exactly, if makin' yourself a fearful object's so all-fired important to you right this very minute.*

"Nothing" was the answer, apparently. Instead, Chess simply swung away and mounted those steps, bottle drooping from one hand, the other perched on his opposite gun-butt—so characteristic a pose it brought a moment's salt sting to Morrow's nose, throat clamping down hard in memory of the man Chess had once been, rather than the creature he'd become.

At his elbow, Yancey said, quietly: "He keeps splashing it out on every little thing takes his fancy, he'll run through the rest of that power we bled into him back in the Hoard pretty quick—don't you think, Mister Morrow?"

"But he'd still be a hex, wouldn't he?" Geyer asked. "So perhaps the point is moot."

"Still be *Chess,* either way," Morrow agreed, slugging back his whiskey in one fiery swallow, and struggling not to cough his guts out. "Which is . . . no small thing, in itself."

Yancey ignored the glass Joe'd laid in front of her, watching Geyer take a far more moderate sip from his. Then, waiting 'til he'd drunk it down, she said:

"I believe it's past time for you to explain yourself, Mister 'Grey.'"

The man squared his shoulders, as though preparing himself to step face-on into a high, cold wind. He took a breath, and began.

"YOU HAVE TO UNDERSTAND, Ed, Miz—*Mister* Colder—"

"Kloves," Yancey reminded him. Thinking: *You were* at *the wedding, after all.*

"—by the War's end, for those of us who'd watched him work, Allan Pinkerton was a mythic figure—a second Odysseus using guile in the best of causes, managing to winkle a good portion of the Union in Horse-wise through the Confederacy's Trojan gates, even while the rest of the matter was decided on a battlefield basis. That's why I signed up with the Agency afterwards . . . why most of us did, I believe."

Morrow nodded slightly in agreement, possibly not even realizing he did so.

"When Mister Pinkerton went on the move, I stayed behind in Chicago, on Agency business," Geyer continued. "Not hex-related, in the main. The methodical centralization and science of crime as applies to *all* cases, that was our credo, which served us well indeed, since few of the magically inclined who take to crime wreak much more damage than the normal run of criminal. What they do is impressive, yes, but never let it be forgot: they cannot conspire. That, in itself, cuts their efficaciousness down substantially."

"And then?"

Geyer hesitated, as though still bound by the loyalties he was working hard to shuck.

"Professor Asbury, I reckon," Morrow said. "That would be where things began to change. Am I right, Frank?"

"You are."

This Professor, Geyer haltingly explained—not a bad man in his way, yet terribly single-minded—had been studying matters hexological at an Eastern university. He aimed to create a system of quantification which would allow him to distinguish the potentially hexacious *before* they came to full flower, and thus perhaps win them to the orderly side of things—create a matrix of nurture which would train them to accept mere human guidance, then set them as watchdogs upon their own kind. To use their natural hungers as a culling agent, in other words.

"Like cats on rats," Yancey mused. "Or . . . no, too dissimilar—dogs on coyotes."

Geyer shrugged. "If the dogs could pull fire from the air, or the coyotes bring inanimate objects to life and set them fighting amongst each other, then . . . I suppose so. It's all somewhat beyond my ken, Miss—ter, me being but a humble 'tec. So while I won't allow myself surprised to learn of Ed's mission after the fact—how Asbury and Mister Pinkerton set him to infiltrate Reverend Rook's gang, so's he might take Rook's temperature with that 'Manifest' of theirs—"

"Manifold, they called it; Asbury's Manifold."

"Thank you, Ed. It did surprise me, however—once reports began to filter up from Mexico, in the wake of *that* particular tangle—to receive a secret summons calling me into Mister Pinkerton's presence. I took an express train to meet him outside of El Paso, then hopped tracks and transferred to his private railcar, the one he often conducts business from."

"I know it."

"Have you set foot there lately, though? Changed, Ed—terribly so." A shadow hollowed out Geyer's face. "Much like the man himself."

Oh, enough, Yancey decided, abruptly; no matter how dear it cost Geyer to break his silence's sworn bonds, she'd no more patience for this waffling. *I need to understand this* now, *without annotation.* So she shut her eyes, bolted the whiskey, laid but a fingertip on Geyer's wrist, and—*opened* herself, wide.

(*See it all, then, granddaughter. As* he *did.*)

Yes, Yancey breathed back to that never-too-far phantom instructor, as the saloon's ruckus slowed to a drone—the very pocket of time she sat in popping forth like a cog, and slipping between ticks of the Pinkerton's pocket-watch, an oiled key in a sprung lock.

And then, with truly frightening ease, she was *there*, abruptly. As him.

MALE FROM HEAD TO toe, the centre of her gravity abruptly upward-shifted, and baking in the railcar's too-close air; she felt sweat drip down the runnel of "her" spine, soaking a patch at the waistband of "her" trousers so vehemently, she could only hope "her" belt was wide enough to cover it. The place was kitted out with all sorts of unfamiliar fripperies, reeking of ether and alcohol over not-faint-enough blood-stink, same as any more immobile sickroom. Chinese lacquer screens set up everywhere narrowed perspective 'til the fine gas sconces themselves seemed scarlet-tinged, while velveteen-print paper muffled the rhythmic clatter vibrating up through the floor, and unseen vistas rolling by outside the curtained windows played light off shade in ever-changing patterns.

Three figures occupied what space was left open, besides Geyer himself. A mild-faced old man with wandering eyes—Asbury, presumably; a frail girl wrapped in stiff brocade propped on a throne-chair twice her size, her half-blind porcelain face a malign doll's, veiled under the same deep red as her shot-silk draperies— *Songbird, they call her,* the voice put in, *little caged queen, maimed and poison-full since birth.*

And there in the back, someone Geyer knew well enough his heart leapt to greet him, for all he no longer looked a bit like his old self: Mister Allan Pinkerton, first of all Agents, looming massive even in repose, the ill effects of too much good food and too little activity swelling his already large form to cartoonish proportions.

A veritable twin for those infamous lithographs of Tweed, "she" thought, without recognizing whose face passed through Geyer's mind, *all bloat. My good God, boss—how could you ruin yourself this way?*

Even as the idea formed, however, it was derailed, horrifically. Pinkerton moved forward into what passed for the light, allowing "her" to see what now passed for his face.

"I'm main glad ye could come, Frank," this object said, its voice one thunderous beehive snore—Scots accent rendered parodic, r's rolling like cannonballs. "Yuir rate of travel did ye no damage, I trust?"

Geyer swallowed his shock, with a dry click.

"No sir," he said. "Haven't been out of Chi-Town for some time now, as you know. It was . . . restful."

The gaping tear laying Pinkerton's jawbone almost open showed a high, wet rim of teeth through his cheek's fine-flayed meat, a fascinatingly awful image. Was it creeping *from* his lip's furled, necrotic sneer, or *toward* it? And that knot of sickness pulsing at its apex, half bruise, half tumour—had that once been his *ear*?

"Ye'll wonder how I manage tae keep mysel' shaved, I suppose," Pinkerton said, noting Geyer's attempt to not react with dry humour. "Well . . . no' very well at all, as ye can see."

Yancey felt something hot on "her" own face—more sweat, if she were feeling kindly. Or simply an understandable response to the startling notion that Pinkerton's unkempt tangle of mutton-chops, beard and moustache might hide further damage still.

"What happened?" Geyer asked, at last.

To which Songbird gave a vicious little smile, and replied, "Chess Pargeter happened. Did he not, Mister Pinkerton?"

"Shut your foul mouth, ye Chink-eyed hooer," Pinkerton ordered her, without rancour.

Doctor Asbury shuddered, hastening to try and mediate. "Miss Songbird, Mister Pinkerton—please! A modicum of sympathy might be accounted an amiable gesture, between allies."

Songbird snorted. "He deserves none."

"Don't I, madam? That wretched invert shot me in my face—"

"As you all but dared him to. Call yourself a general? You are unfit, on every level."

As if conjured, a gun appeared in Pinkerton's hand (probably dropped from a spring-loaded sleeve-rig; Geyer had seen such back in Chicago, amongst the gambling set). "It's a prerogative of generals," he rasped, "to execute traitors—or incompetents. Was your witchery simply too feeble to match Pargeter's, or did ye let him loose on me a-purpose?" To Songbird's disdainful raised eyebrow: "Oh, I've seen ye stop shots before. But bear in mind my . . . condition—and the rate of Dr. Asbury's progress. Are ye so sure we've no surprises for ye?"

Songbird sniffed. "Mechanical *niou-se*," she replied, dismissively. "My arts are not to be encompassed by such trifles. You may test his tricks against mine, at your convenience."

Geyer cleared his throat. "Gents, lady—this all strikes me a mite counterproductive. Surely, Pargeter's threat enough we should probably deal with him first before settling private scores, let alone moving on to Reverend Rook and his . . . whatever she is, after."

A moment passed, and Pinkerton re-holstered; Songbird looked away, petulant rather than angry, danger dissipated, leaving Asbury to cast Geyer a grateful look.

"This 'Weed' the dispatches tell of," Geyer asked him. "Some natural plant augmented, pure hexation only, some hybrid of the two? And how does it play out, exactly, in this game?"

Flipping his black-covered notebook open, Asbury showed Geyer a sample stuck beneath waxed paper: dried reddish-brown oval leaves and long trumpet-shaped flowers affixed to a corded vine, the whole gone a green-beige colour, like mouldy parchment.

"As it manifests within Mister Pargeter's vicinity," Asbury began, "the Weed appears a heavily mutant version of *Datura inoxia*, a species of the family *Solanaceae*—known locally as thorn-apple, moonflower, Indian-root, *nacazcul*, *toloatzin*, or *tolguache*, and so on." He used a cunning little pair of tongs to pluck one leaf from the page, holding it up so the hair-like tendrils covering it, fine as down, shone in a greyish halo.

"In its natural state," Asbury continued, "it contains a number of powerful hallucinogens, explaining the near-universal reports of visions on encounter of its hexaciously altered form; many savage tribes used this plant to engender religious deliriums, in order to enter their so-called 'spirit realm.'" Asbury replaced the leaf once more, disquietingly careful. "Expert herbalistic skill was required to ensure safe dosage, since its variable potency easily induces coma, or even death. But the Red Weed *itself* has not directly killed anyone, that we can verify—neither through exposure, nor even ingestion."

Songbird made a sound in her throat, possibly risible, or merely exasperated. "As always, *gweilo*, you study much to say little. We workers know that plant for what it is: a casting line fishing for deeper prey, death for any of our kind to remain within its reach too long."

Asbury inclined his head, stiffly. "Miss Songbird is correct, of course," he admitted. "The hexacious do seem mortally vulnerable to the Weed, given sufficient proximity. Which is due, I believe, to its secondary aspect—the fact that it serves as a power collector, and transmitter channel, for Mister Pargeter's own magical energies. Consider a spiderweb, spun naturally wherever the spider comes to rest, by which it traps the insects it feeds on. After enough time— and larder stock—such webs may achieve a density that changes their environs. For Mister Pargeter, I believe the Weed serves this same function: a manifestation of his magic, evoking *and* altering this plant into a medium of transmogrification."

"Transmogrification . . . change?" repeated Geyer.

"In the land itself, Agent Geyer. Fed by spilled blood, as tradition commanded the old Aztec and Mayan deities be reverenced, the Weed changes whatever area it covers—the natural soil and flora— renders them green and fertile, and transfers power into Pargeter as it does so. I speculate this confirms that the god-aspect bestowed upon Pargeter by his sacrificial ordeal is a fertility or "year-king" deity; from descriptions of the ritual itself, most likely the god named Xipe Totec—"

It was Pinkerton's turn to clear his throat, now; a sound both forceful and sickeningly liquid, as though something in his larynx were decaying. "What Asbury's sayin' is, Pargeter brings the Weed along with him, then makes sure it digs in deep. He's changin' Arizona and parts adjacent to something else entirely—and soon, we'll have no chance of stoppin' him."

Ducking down, Asbury unrolled a map of the southwestern States. Across the southern part of Arizona, spilling over the nexus where it met New Mexico and Old Mexico beyond, clouds of red ink dots were scattered, while dates written nearby confirmed a rough schedule.

"Self-evidently, the Weed follows Mister Pargeter's route northwest-ward, after his Tampico escape," he pointed out. "Yet in addition to Pargeter's clear line of travel, Weed also manifests spontaneously—as far north as Utah, by some reports, as well as in Nevada and California. And despite Arizona bearing the heaviest concentration, one area remains curiously untouched." With his thumb, he touched a circle in the state's northern territory, surrounded by red on all sides; Geyer knew it at once, even done to scale.

"Hex City."

"New Aztectlan, they call it," Asbury corrected. "Several miles from the township of Bewelcome, thaumaturgically destroyed by Reverend Rook in '65—a devastation enhanced by Pargeter's own incipient manifestation. Whether as an after-effect of that destruction or not, the Weed appears incapable of manifesting on Bewelcomite soil; samples brought there desiccate in minutes."

"Samples? You've more of it, then?" said Geyer. Asbury nodded. "Alive?"

This brought an unusually long hesitation. "As it can be," he said, eventually. "*Datura nacazcul* appears sustained by human blood alone, which limits our ability to raise it. But it has proven valuable nonetheless—since, as a hex-engendered species, it has a certain capacity to treat certain . . . conditions."

"Mine, he means," Pinkerton explained, without equivocation. "We make tinctures of it; helps keep this God-cursed affliction at bay, to a degree. Ye can smoke it as well, though like wi' the Indians, getting the right dosage's devilish difficult." His wounded face spasmed, eyes gone oddly dead. "Turn the De'il's spawn against the De'il, and God will laugh outright."

Yancey felt Geyer's dismay and fright bone-deep, though she knew his face would've no more moved than Morrow's, under similar circumstances—and abruptly, she pitied them both. To never feel free to give way, vent one's worst feelings to the wind . . . she couldn't imagine it, living that way.

Chess Pargeter and I have that in common, at least, she thought.

"Thiel," said Pinkerton, abruptly. "I told you in my missive, Frank, Thiel is . . . unreliable. Hence your summons."

"Sir, that simply cannot be true. I've known George Thiel for years; if there were any man less likely to betray—"

But Asbury, one hand lifted as if to shade his face against the light, was shaking his head in tiny, frantic movements behind its shelter. Songbird only looked amused.

Pinkerton put one fist down on the table and left it there, no further emphasis needed. "Yuir loyalty does you credit, Frank, but I've sources of information you don't. Leave it at that, and be content." Adding, to Geyer's open mouth: "Now is the time for orders, not talk. Will you obey, or no'?"

Geyer could only nod.

Pinkerton jabbed a sausage-like finger at the map, flicking Asbury's aside. "Along wi' the Professor's theories, Miz Songbird's Celestial scryings suggest a reason for why Rook chose Bewelcome to raise his New Babylon next to: the place is dead. No' just of life— of magic. Which may suit it to our needs."

Asbury leaned forward. "If my calculations are correct, any fully wakened hex entering that area will soon have only what strength he takes in to work magic with. Once exhausted, he will not be able to replenish himself, until he leaves. With more exact data, I believe I can construct a mechanism to exploit that effect, neutralizing hexation completely within its boundaries—an invaluable property for a base of operations against a city of hexes, you will appreciate. Logically, this should also produce full neutralization of Reverend Rook's summonings, so those hexes who *do* choose to serve our cause may be free of that distraction."

"A weak term," muttered Songbird, "seeing how from dawn to dusk, it hooks at my skull so I must spill half my power each day to endure it."

Since Pinkerton and Asbury gave no indication they'd heard, Geyer decided to pretend likewise. "All very impressive, Doctor, but I'm—"

"—no hex, aye, Frank; we ken," Pinkerton interrupted. "That was no' a problem for Morrow, either, 'til he commenced to let his britches do the thinking." The light in his eyes was back, exultant. "A short trip wi' one of the guid Doctor's devices, a day or two in observation, and we shall be in a position t'meet ye not far outside the ruined land itself."

Geyer glanced back down, following the red dots' swathe. "And Pargeter? He's clearly on his way to Hex City, moving faster than any mundane transport could take him—what do I do if he turns up?"

Pinkerton smiled. "Agent, if ye should chance to encounter Chess Pargeter, then run, fast and far as ye can. If possible, before he sees *yuirself* at all."

But here Yancey stopped listening, the big man's voice abruptly falling to a buzz in the middle distance. For her guts had suddenly clenched up at the sight of the name on one black dot, not yet marked in red, sitting defenceless in the path of that encroaching tide—innocent, blameless, and utterly unaware of what would come upon it.

Hoffstedt's Hoard.

Then—Songbird lifted her head, as if she heard noise from another carriage; glanced around suspiciously, almond-flesh eyes already narrowed against even this dim light and squeezing further, almost to slits. Yancey gulped. She held her thoughts still inside Geyer's head, breath slow; Songbird's gaze passed over "her" as if Geyer was not there, but did not alight. Lightheaded with fear, Yancey followed that gaze, wondering what it saw.

A near-fatal mistake. The mere alignment of focus seemed to trigger a snapback of mystical forces, and for an awful second, Songbird's vision *was* Yancey's: she saw shimmering veils of power spark and flare outside, cloaking the train in invisible fire, as it thundered across the landscape. But clinging to that veil, peering like a street urchin sneaking a furtive peek into some knocking shop's back windows, was a burly man with a coarse grey beard, transparent as dirty glass.

Songbird reared back, shrieked a fast and furious string of Chinese, backed up by power's whiplash; Yancey felt her hand slice air and ether alike, slamming both window-ward. Caught in its path, the bearded spectre outside distorted lengthwise, like smeared ink—

—AND YANCEY SAT BACK into her proper body, still locked upright at Splitfoot Joe's table, muscles stiff as a day-old corpse's, while a dizzying chill swept her from head to toe. Released, her hand fair flew from Geyer's wrist, movement alone appearing to transmit somewhat of the same sensation to him; he gasped out loud and stared at her, rigid, like she'd grown another head.

What gave you the right to rummage 'hind my eyes, Miss, when I've tried to treat you kind? he thought, so theatrical tin-thunder sharp she winced, trying to block it out.

"That ghost, on the train's side," she said, out loud. "Songbird . . . *knew* him."

Morrow frowned. "What ghost? And—how d'you know *that* name, anyhow?"

The information came rattling out headlong through Yancey's throat, unstoppable: "Little Chinese witch, barely more than a child, works with—" *Don't say Pinkerton's name!* She had to remind herself, forcibly. "—your boss, and Doctor Asbury . . . there's something wrong with her, more so even than the usual. Bone-bleached, eyes so weak she can't see properly in any world but the spirits', can't bear the light of the sun or walk outside without two veils and a parasol."

But now they were both regarding her with a similar pitch of horror, which finally stopped her in her tracks.

"I'm sorry," she said at last, weakly, eyes avoiding Geyer's. "I just needed to know. What you knew."

The Pinkerton swallowed. "Are you . . . you're a hex?"

"No. Hell, no."

"Then how—"

Yancey felt a hopeless lurch; the innate Goddamned impossibility of telling him anything acceptable suddenly fell on her all of a piece, with all the dead weight of grief deferred.

"There's other things in this world, Mister 'Grey,'" was all she could manage, finally, "and I'm one of them. That's all."

But then, you should understand that, *given what we left behind us. Sheriff Love, and all his godless Man-of-God works.*

And maybe he *could* hear her still, hard as she was labouring to make it so's he couldn't. Because with that, Geyer nodded his head, looked down at his hands, took a great fresh breath—and started over.

"She did seem to see something, though I didn't; left quick enough, afterwards. The boss and Asbury just let her go. I thought . . . well, I had other things on my mind, at the moment."

Mister Morrow broke in, impatient: "Hold on here, let's go back a minute, 'fore we outpace ourselves. *What* ghost?"

Yancey described him, and watched Morrow's face fall.

"Sounds like Kees Hosteen, to me," he said. "He was in Rook's gang; last man standing, really, after Mictlan-Xibalba. I sent him to get help, before we left, but we were gone when he got back. Died in Tampico, walkin' into a bullet meant for—someone else."

"Can your Reverend Rook raise the dead?"

Morrow snorted. "Don't doubt he can, considerin' how much there is of it in the Bible."

They sat, ruminating on the concept. 'Til Geyer said, slowly, "If I'd been more attentive, I might've known what to expect later on at the Hoard, 'specially after noticing how the . . . remains . . . of Sheriff Love were gone from Bewelcome square. But I was so engaged in taking Asbury's readings, it simply never occurred to me—not even when I saw tracks leading off into the desert, and that mystery light poor Mister Frewer described off in the far distance, moving faster than any human eye could follow."

Love, travelling quick, as the dead tend to do.

Morrow frowned again. "Readings? He gave you the Manifold?"

"A Manifold, yes. To take the data he needed."

"'A'—hold the hell on, Frank. There's more than one, now?"

And with that, they were off again, Geyer sinking back into a lengthy explication of Asbury's various achievements: a whole tiny Manifold factory ensconced in one boxcar of Pinkerton's king-train, churning out fifty of the things a day (Yancey caught a flash of the one Morrow'd once carried from his mind, spasming painful 'gainst his waistcoat pocket-seams as a heart attack in progress). Geyer drew it out, flipped it open with a thumb-tip, and they all admired the way its needles clicked immediately roof-ward, toward Chess—the single most magic-charged object to be found, doubtless, within several vicinities.

"Didn't even guess you had that on you," Morrow said, amazed. Geyer shrugged.

"Much good it's done me, considering they let me go without any real instruction. But it's like George Thiel said—now the die's been cast, this machinery of the Professor's *will* change the world as we know it, for better or for worse. There's no stopping it."

Like so much else, Yancey thought, the cold feeling in her guts returning.

"Mister 'Grey,'" she asked, "why was it your boss thought this Mister Thiel unreliable?"

Geyer's eyes met hers yet again—this shock was softer, though still potent. Something he'd carried without examining, for longer than he'd had time to feel guilty over.

"A long story," he said. "Suffice it to say . . . someone had, indeed, been *gravely* misinformed."

"Pinkerton?" Morrow asked.

Geyer shook his head, sadly. "No," he replied. "Me."

CHAPTER TWELVE

AFTER GEYER'D DIVESTED HIMSELF of the rest of his tale, laid out the full extent of his and Morrow's mutual former employer's perfidies in fine and horrid detail, he sat as though gutted. The fire burned down, reddening the darkness 'til everything around them hurt somewhat to contemplate—or perhaps that was just Morrow's skull, which had begun to pound, erratic as that tooth old Doc Glossing had "painlessly" pulled, what now seemed like fifty years before.

"He's a man of parts," Morrow said, finally, of Pinkerton. "Well suited to make hard choices, as needs must. From what I've seen, though . . . can't quite believe he'd be capable of all *that*."

Geyer shook his head. "Nor I, Ed; nor I. And yet . . ." He winced, as though Morrow's ache were catching.

The conversation ran dry once more, with little hope of revivification.

"I'm for bed," Geyer said, finally, bolting the last of his drink. To Yancey: "Would you be willing to share with me, Mister . . . Kloves? I'd take the floor, of course, in practice."

"That'd be right kind."

"Then . . . should we both go up now, together?"

She hadn't even been looking Geyer's way previous to that, just contemplating middle-distance, but this last broke her free, and she made a regal little gesture of demurral. "Not just yet, sir; I need to speak with Mister Morrow awhile. Then he can escort me, later on."

"Without makin' it look like I *am* escorting her," Morrow assured them both. "Us all being fellows together, like we are."

"Yes," Geyer agreed, and rose, stiffly. "Goodnight, then . . . gentlemen."

Geyer climbed the stairs, leaving them alone but for Joe, who busied himself where he stood behind the bar with haphazardly polishing something below eye level. Once upon a time, Morrow might've feared it was a shotgun—but he was honestly tired enough from a day and night of hexacious combat plus magickal travel, followed by a bunch of secrets he'd frankly rather not know, that he could barely rouse himself to care, either way.

From the corner of his eye, he observed Missus Kloves run a nail up inside the sweaty band of her beaver. To distract her, he leaned forward and inquired, low: "So . . . how you like it so far? Bein' took for a man, I mean."

"It's different. Not so bad, I suppose, apart from having to wear this."

Morrow shrugged, touching his own hat's brim. "You get used to it."

"Do you? Well . . ." She shot a look over at Joe, who made sure to be staring elsewhere. "If it's all the same to you, I think I'll doff it."

Joe's canny, not blind, Morrow felt like saying. But instead, he allowed: "Your call."

She sighed. "Yes."

A breath of a pause, which Morrow almost felt catch in his throat, and the decision was made—she lifted the offending headwear free, letting what was left of her marriage-day braids swing loose along with it, then dug in with both hands and unravelled them further, fluffing the solid mass out briskly. It fell to frame her face, two fistfuls deep, softening the pert lines of her jaw 'til her true sex was unmistakable—and Morrow took the thrum of it like a blow to the chest, Joe's clear gasp echoing the one he feared to make.

Missus Kloves turned in her chair, lifting her eyes to Joe's once more—and this time, he met them. "Ma'am," he said, voice dry.

"Sir. Can I rely on your discretion?"

Joe considered this a second. Then: "Spring out for another bottle . . . real cash, this time . . . and it's a deal."

She raised an eyebrow. "Believe you'll have to spot me, then," she told Morrow.

"Guess I could stand another drink," he said.

THE "WHISKEY" WAS ROTGUT, which Morrow appreciated, since it meant Joe was letting them off cheap. Missus Kloves—*Yancey*, he reminded himself, God *damn*—took only the barest sip, visibly strained to withhold a coughing fit, then slid hers over.

"Your Mister Pargeter . . ." she began.

"He ain't—" Too fast; he bit the words off, re-thought a bit. Carefully: "I got no real claim on Chess—we travel together, is all. He's his own, if he's anybody's."

"I truly meant no disrespect. Just that . . . people assume things, I'm sure."

Pink touched up the apple of one cheek, shading to crimson; her eyes had already flicked away. More blushes all 'round, tonight, than at a church ladies' sewing circle.

Deny it, right to her face, his nethers suggested meanly, *and you still might have a chance. Chess won't mind—ain't like he's Jesus, or you Peter. You don't owe him everything.*

Man'd been first to say it himself, after all: *I somewhat think you like that gal, Ed.* Like he was all but daring Morrow to do something about it.

"I can't lie," he said, finally. "I do count myself his friend, and we have been . . . friendly. But though I maintain there's more things in him to admire than he'll give himself credit for, I'm not his kind, which we both well know. So far, there's been one man only for Chess in this whole world, that I've seen—and that man ain't me."

"So you *don't* love him, then." When Morrow didn't answer, she went on, feeling her way: "Or . . . it's a different sort of affection entirely, like me for Uther—for I *did* care, enough to honour my vows to the end, no matter what Mister Pargeter might think. Brotherly, perhaps?"

Morrow drained the extra glass fast, muttering, "Be a damn bad sort of brother, if it was."

Giving thanks to Christ, at the same time he said it, that she'd never yet had occasion to touch *his* skin the way she had Geyer's, much as part of him might want her to. Because that meant she wasn't already privy to a whole host of chancy recollections, each with Chess's name firmly attached: The flash of sweat between his freckled shoulder blades as Morrow hammered down hard into him, urged on by raucous cries; feel of his red beard's slide in inconvenient places, mouth blazing a wet trail, as pleasure spilled over into pain. Or even the taste of last night's breath mingling come morning, turning bad to good, fast as two pricks jerk upwards.

"He's brave," she allowed, obviously noting his continued embarrassment, yet blessedly unaware of the specifics. "That counts for something, I suppose."

"Counts for a whole damn lot, in my book."

"But is he trustworthy? That's what I'm asking."

"So long as *other people* are, around him . . . I'd have to say yes." Morrow's eyes sought hers, held them. "I mean—you're trustworthy enough. I like to think I am."

"Some would say you used to lie for a living, Mister Morrow."

"Couldn't've been too good at it, then. 'Cause I sure lost *that* job."

At this, she gave a tiny grin followed by a snicker, and he paid her back in kind. Wondering if she saw anything at all whenever she happened to glance his way, 'sides from a fool twice her age, with unsteady morals and odd habits.

I'm an idiot, Morrow thought.

Yancey sighed. "So he means well at heart, according to you, no matter how rudely he behaves," she said, as to herself. "Very well: I'll take that as wrote, if I must. But like I said, if he keeps on spendthrifting that extra hexation we gifted him with on trifles, tossing it 'round like Katy-bar-the-door, we'll be trouble-bound long before Sheriff Love catches up with us."

"Which you think he will."

"Think?" Another smile—wider, and far more fixed. "Mister Morrow . . . I pray for such a meeting, devoutly. I *count* on it."

Though he'd figured her for being able to take care of herself long before her wedding-rout, the look that came into her eyes as she said this near froze him to his seat. Her initial grief and shock had given way to something darker—a thing he only now realized he'd feared might happen, all along—and Morrow found himself somewhat pitying the next person who might get between her and the next opportunity to work vengeance on Sheriff Love's salt-cured corpse.

Again, he tried to turn her thoughts in another direction. "We can just pray more power into him, I reckon, we have to . . . you being his high priestess, or what-have-you."

"Is that what I am?" She considered the idea. "No, I doubt that: anyone's shed blood would do just as well to feed him, from what we witnessed."

"Not without you to pray over it, it wouldn't."

"But . . . you prayed too, Mister Morrow. So . . ."

"Might be it's *both* of us that's needed, to work that particular trick," he finished, without thinking. And got another little kick in the ribs from how his heart leaped to see her string the truth together equal-swift, forehead knit in concentration, like somebody'd taken up an invisible stitch between her fine, dark brows and yanked, hard.

"It's a puzzle, all right," she said. "And we don't have much time."

Morrow cast his mind back to the Hoard, how he'd felt the sheer force of his and Yancey's worship spin almighty-powerful Chess between 'em like a child's whipped top. A double possession dragging alien words from both their lips—rendering centuries-old jabber-squawk to English, while the power they'd unwittingly harnessed went surging forth through the newly greened ground, fighting its way up into Chess like a flooded river spilling its dam. It was the sheer responsiveness of the tremendous energies they'd dallied with that scared the bejesus out of him, even now. Yet in the end, Morrow knew none of the power was his, or hers. It had been placed under their temporary command for one purpose only: to render it up to Chess, even as Chess fought it off with every last particle of bone and sinew.

A sick breath out of the dark, memory-borne stench of cold draft and wet rock walls: "English" Oona Pargeter's raddled whore's pan, opium-cooked from the inside-out, cured like meat. A woman reduced to nothing but need, just dead flesh still teetering upright, wrapped like Hell's own candy in hate and poison.

The only thing Ed Morrow knew for sure Chess Pargeter feared, in life or death, was the thought that he might be likewise helpless one day before a similar hunger. So to find himself a hex, after all that—and not *just* a hex, either, but a damn blood-drunk god of hexes, power magnified beyond all comprehension alongside the clamouring jones for more, ever *more*.

If Oona had ever thought to put a curse on him, that'd've been a doozy, right there. And seeing how hexes bred hexes, who knew? Having met her the once, Morrow certainly wouldn't have put it past her to try.

But now he blinked free of contemplation, realizing Yancey was repeating something. "I'm sorry?"

"I said, I've drunk my fill; looks to me like you have, too. Time to retire, for both of us."

"Probably best, yes."

Now even Joe was gone, leaving the whole place vacant. As they paused on the landing, poised to go their separate ways, he asked her (again without thinking, as seemed to be the pattern): "You'll be all right?"

Fresh ridiculousness piled on top of a whole heap, enough to make him grit his teeth 'til they squeaked. But she didn't even seem to notice.

"Don't rightly know, Mister Morrow," she replied. "I'll have to, I expect."

Then, quick as a fawn, she had already crossed over to her room—Geyer's, rather—and clicked the door to, shutting him in the hall.

Inside "his" suite, meanwhile, nothing stirred, though Morrow doubted Chess was sleeping; he didn't appear to need to, these days, no more than to eat or drink, dress himself, or keep track of his possessions. Whatever he wanted for, he could conjure—just like anything he *didn't* want could be as easily disposed of, with even less warning.

Inside, the moon paled things so they looked almost clean. Chess sat cross-legged on top of the bed, still mainly dressed, back turned and staring out the window, apparently unaware he was no longer alone. His boots lay shucked on the floor, puddled all over with silverish light; the same light touched his hair, and rimmed his sideburns with frost.

But when Morrow came up sidelong, quiet as he could, he realized that Chess might as well not be there at all. Deep in some sort of trance, his green eyes were open but empty, pupils invisible. His skin, cool as a too-deep sleeper's, barely dented to the touch.

The most amazing thing, seeing him this way, was to realize once more just how *young* the most ruthless off-hand killer Morrow'd ever met really was—barely older than Yancey herself.

No play tonight, he thought. *Just as well, given . . .*

So, with a presumption born of long-stood intimacy, he stroked Chess's eyes shut to save them from dust and pressed him prone, then crawled in next to him and cuddled up, one arm flung 'round him for warmth; no earthly way to tell if that was how Chess wanted it, so why not? They could debate it in the morning.

Ed Morrow let his own eyes close, heavy as though individually weighted—felt his breath slow, 'til his lungs barely seemed to strain.

THEN, IN THE DREAM he hadn't even guessed was creeping up on him, he opened them once more . . . only to find himself perched on a ludicrously tiny, filigreed bench in the rock garden out back of Cold Mountain Hotel, with Yancey sat up next to him: ankles crossed delicate, hair neat-dressed, wearing the exact same clothes as when he'd first met her.

"This is where my Mama's buried," she informed him. "Where she *was*, anyhow, if it's still there. I wonder where they buried Pa?"

"I'm sure someplace just as nice. People liked Mister Colder."

"They did, didn't they? I always thought it was more for show than anything else, since there were some at the start—Hugo Hoffstedt amongst 'em—who claimed having a saloon in town invited dicey elements. But after Mama passed, I believe that softened folks toward us." She wiped at her cheek, briskly. "Knew all along I'd outlive them both, of course; it's no tragedy, like being forced to bury your children. I just . . . hadn't thought it would come so soon."

"I'm sorry for that," he told her. "Truly so."

"I know you are." A pause. "She was born into the Hebrew faith, I think; him too. Don't quite know what that makes me, considering I was married in a church."

"Never cared too much on religion, myself. The Rev used to say all it was good for was reasons folks could kill each other over, and I suppose he'd know."

"What was he like, Reverend Rook?"

Awful, he wanted to say. The sun struck hard against those neat-laid border stones at their feet, picking out the quartz, and dazzled him; there were tiny green sticker plants growing in between, furled and succulent, like thorny roses.

"Gave a fair impression of being good, sometimes," he made himself reply, "and Chess did love him, in his way. But to tell you the truth—I hope to hell you never have to find out."

"Am I dreaming this, Mister Morrow? Ed?"

He'd been wondering that himself, somewhat. Beyond the garden, the Hoard's main street shimmered slightly; the garden's dust glittered like mica. Yet Yancey stayed cool and fresh, her calm eyes infinitely inviting. Morrow yearned to watch his reflection fill them up, like little grey mirrors.

"Well . . ." he began, slowly. ". . . I know *I'm* asleep."

She nodded, yet again. And then, as though that'd decided the matter for her, she climbed up onto his lap, too quick for him to do much more than rock back in surprise—the weight of her plopped astride, pressing hard down on him. One small breast seemed almost to lunge itself into his hand, nipple scarring the palm, as she traced a thumb 'round the shape of his lips like she was measuring his mouth for size, or trying to sell herself on what might be the best thing to do next.

"No need to be over-formal, in a dream," she said, carefully.

Through a suddenly dry mouth: "Guess not."

Though he couldn't've told what she tasted of, he somehow knew it was the exact same way he'd always hoped she would. As they kissed with lips and teeth, messily, Morrow thrust his other hand up under her skirts, only to meet with no real resistance; everything just peeled away to his touch, skinned itself the way a flower drops its petals. There was a fine dusting of hairs all up and down the insides of her thighs, dusky-silky, to match the thatch on her innermost parts; when he slipped two fingers inside, a smell emerged both fresh and salt. He groaned at the feel, out loud, and loudly: so long, so damn *long*. . . .

With a last sticky nip, Yancey sat back, both breasts unlaced and blushing prettily. Said, breathless, "I'm unsullied yet, Mister Morrow, if you'd wondered. Uther and I never got so far; he was old-fashioned in some ways, which I found charming. Still, I'd take it as a great kindness were you to relieve me of that particular burden, if only in metaphor, before waking."

Morrow blinked, stupid. "Oh. Yes?"

"Yes." She sat forward, solemn: "Ruin me, Ed."

"I'll . . . do my very best."

A twist, a tumble, and the bench fell away, the garden itself dissolving around them—sand turned to silk, sheets on a phantom bed slipping down 'round both their hips. And they were naked, too—conveniently so, scrabbling and grabbing at each other, with him pressing forward, she straining to widen herself around him. He was simultaneously surprised and not by her apparent understanding of the act, for wasn't this what dreams were for? To play out in full whatever actions the day's demands had denied them, truncated by duty's call or time's restraints?

One leg wrapped 'round his, calf to calf, while the other arched up and back, so she could hook it 'round his hip; he sunk deep, drawing a double gasp. "Oh God," she said, through her teeth, as the movement lit them both up from inside out. "God, sweet Christ, good God Jesus—"

(*good God almighty, go on and* hit *that*)

What?

(You *heard me, Edward.*)

Hands in his hair, digging. Her breath in his ear, a bite grazing the lobe. While the whole of her clamped down on him, back locked in spasm, wet and hot and glorious as spilled blood.

"Harder," she told him, voice rising and sinking both, a fucked cat's mean-ass squall. "Harder, *harder,* Jesus *God*, who's the Goddamn faggot here, 'tween the both of us? Stick it in, twist it like you *mean* it, motherfucker, do me 'til it damn well *hurts*—I said *hard*, you dumb ox, *HARD!*"

"Gah! What the shit-fuck son-of-a-*gun*—"

MORROW WENT LEAPING BACK, pecker out and near to spitting, from Chess's violent embrace. Chess bolted upright too, mussed from the bottom up with his customarily immaculate hair sweat-stuck every which way, face red as his wilting prick. To spit out, mouth caught in a betrayed half-snarl: "Were you screwin' that damn girl in your *dreams*?"

Morrow clutched at himself, instinctually modest, though it wasn't like the two of 'em hadn't seen everything the other had on offer. "What's it to you, if I was? You even think t'ask *me*, 'fore you started using me for entertainment?"

"I didn't think I had to!"

"Then we both know somethin' new, now, don't we?"

For all he knew, Chess'd been dreaming too, and couldn't really help it. But still, Morrow found, he'd genuinely believed they were past all that—how he wasn't simply some muscle-bound toy for Chess to amuse himself with, some handy object to rub against, but . . . a *pal*, Goddamnit. The way he most-times felt Chess was to him, these days.

Poised to spit out his ire, Chess abruptly seemed to think better, and let himself settle. Allowing, finally: "S'pose I might'a surprised you."

"Oh, just a tad."

"Though it ain't like you seemed exactly reluctant, at the time."

Morrow made his voice gentler. "*Dreaming*, Chess. Just the way you said."

Those green eyes flared. "Dreaming of *her*, is what I *said*."

"I think she somewhat started it, comes to that. But—yes."

"That's right. 'Cause, I mean . . . you don't even want to *be* here, with me. Do ya? Not really. Not anymore."

"I . . . don't *not* want to."

Chess sniffed, dismissively; gave Morrow's dick a combination of flick and twist, running his nail 'round its uncloaked head just hard enough to hurt, yet still set it humming. "If you're talkin' 'bout *this* thing, I guess not. But don't tell me you don't wish I was her."

Spoiling for a fight, 'cause that always was easier than talking things through—but Morrow wouldn't be provoked. Instead, he schooled himself enough to answer, fairly amiably, "Which only makes us even, seein' how *you* wish *I* was the Rev."

Chess didn't bother to deny it.

"True enough, Goddamnit," was all he said, at last.

Thinking, so hard Morrow could trace the shape of the words: *He put a hole in me, so deep—deeper than my chest, by far. And I only* wish *he'd done it with a bullet.*

Once, Morrow'd thought it impossible for savage little Chess Pargeter to have a heart, let alone one that hurt him, even on occasion. Now that Chess was genuinely heartless, however, pain leaked from his every pore.

Morrow sighed, and opened his arms. "C'mere."

"I can see inside your head, Ed. Don't you dare try to pity me."

"Just come *here*, you damn porcupine. Or take yourself back off on devil-godly business somewheres else, and let me get some sleep."

Chess set his jaw, mutinous, before folding himself inside the larger man's embrace. And Morrow hugged him fast, not holding back: all tight sinew, a contentious gift-box packed full of awful wonders. Or simply a man, fair and foul and singularly made, capable of great harm yet oddly innocent at the core; a man too young to have loved but twice and been sorely disappointed both times, to the cost of everyone else around him.

"It's all changed," he half-felt Chess say. "Used to be I was good at *this*, at least. . . ."

"I always thought so," Morrow agreed, stroking the back of Chess's skull. "And you still ain't no outrager, for all you might've used hexation to work your will on me, that first time—hell, you *gave* me the chance to say no, and I didn't. So don't worry yourself about that."

Chess shook his head. "We both had our fun, as I recall. It's just . . ."

Here he fell silent, swallowed, as though he couldn't widen his throat enough to let the conflicting flood of words out, or bear to make himself pick and choose between 'em. So, since he had the option . . . he opened his mind, instead, and let the whole tangled mass come sliding into Morrow's, with a convulsive wrench.

Just I was out there for hours with my skin left behind, roaming 'round after Sheriff fucking Love, and after all that I still can't find him, one dead man made of salt in the whole damn world, and it's like he fell through a crack down into THERE, that place, oh Jesus I don't want to think about it like someone's hiding him from me, and who would that *be, I wonder—*

Not Rook, Morrow thought back, head pounding—Chess's rageful fear hammering behind his eyes, the world's worst hangover magnified thousandfold. *And not her either, or you'd know, wouldn't you? Three of you being bound at the neck like you are, in slavery-marriage to this world-wrecking plan of hers.*

No, Ed, that's right. Which means it must be—

—that other fella—

Black-faced and huge, hunched like a crossbones corpse, locust-grinning: The Enemy, Night Wind, He By Whom We Live, Smoking Mirror. And all of it underlaid with Yancey's trance-took voice, sounding out the syllables of that alien name—

Tezcatlipoca

—that'd be him, yeah—

Thought so, Morrow made himself "reply," throat filling up quick with bile, 'til his back teeth burned. Then added, out loud and hoarsely: "Think we could maybe switch back to talkin' with our mouths, 'fore I have to puke?"

Okay, Christ! Pure jolt of annoyance, stomach-punch harsh, that everybody he dealt with couldn't keep up on a playing field so un-level, it might as well be a cactus patch cut with horse-crippler. Followed by this frankly startling afterthought, given who it came from: "Sorry, Ed. Sometimes . . . I forget."

"I know you do," Morrow said, gulping acid, and held him closer.

Cold wind crept in over the sill, drying their sweat together tackily, while a great clumsy grey moth blundered past, in hopeless search of some candle to singe itself on. Out in the darkness lurked all manner of threats, momentarily invisible: Weed seeking to lay itself lovingly at Chess's doorstep, *itzapapalotl* flocking, the widening crack down south and the gathering storm up north, with as yet undiscovered trouble no doubt massing to the east and west, to boot. Plus Hex City's constant lure, casting baited hook-lines in Chess's direction—power calling to power, tempting him same as any other devil.

"He's always whispering at me, you know," Chess said, of the Enemy. "On at me all night and half the day, 'bout all manner of mystic shit—stuff I am, stuff I owe, stuff we're gonna have to do together. Like I even give a good Goddamn *what* happens so long's I can hold that bastard Ash Rook's beating heart in my hands, take a good big bite, and show him how it feels."

A shiver moved through him, sickly uncontrolled, raising Morrow's neck-hairs in sympathy. "What're you really scared of?"

"Not one fuckin'—"

"Oh, *enough!*" Snapping, as Chess stared: "You can read my mind, right? That's gospel. And guess what? You're leaking like a sieve, same's whenever you get riled—think *I* can't hear? Sure, you'd rather die than admit it . . . but the fact is, this fear you feel ain't for *yourself* at all."

Chess bit his lip, clamping down hard on a swift *That's how much you know, motherfucker. . . .*

Yet the images bled through nonetheless, etched in pure sensation: nightmare sketches of the valley scorched, Morrow dead with a hole 'twixt his eyes, Yancey and Geyer in similar poses; Joe took into custody or swung outright, his whole place burnt down. A flood of Pinks, Songbird pulling spells from the air like unpicking silk 'broidery, Asbury with his sparking pain-rope wires, Pinkerton's maimed grin.

Or, if nothing else—Sheriff Love appearing, inevitably, over the same hill they'd climbed to get here. Hoffstedt's Hoard again a hundred times over, a hundred times worse.

And each and every part of it consequential not just to what Chess'd done—*'cause I've done a heap of shit merits killin', Edward, before* and *after*—but because of what he *was*: a walking plague, a cursed object. A God- (and gods-) damned hex.

"That was never anything you could've done something about, though," Morrow said. "Not even if you'd suspected. Hell, you could've shot yourself in the damn head the minute Rook told you, and all that'd've done was bring it on the faster."

Chess gave a long sniff, mouth twisting. "If you're tryin' to make me feel better, it ain't working."

"You're not the worst thing ever happened, son, is all. No matter how you like to think different."

"Tell that to the Marshal, that other Sheriff, those yokels from Mouth-of-Praise. To Y—that girl's—damn Pa."

"So you're scared, like I said; no shame in it. You know that already, from the War—fear's what keeps you upright, keeps you human."

"Too bad I ain't, though."

"You ain't *not*, either, fool. Not completely."

"I can see how it's going, even if you can't," Chess said, at last, his voice all but toneless. "It's gonna be like the Hoard was, soon enough—everything, everywhere, all 'cause of me. My own damn fault. And though I can do every other fuckin' thing, I can't do a thing about that. Can't even start to know how to *try*. . . ."

He winced again, caught in another breath, curdled in his throat like a half-choked sob.

"No," Morrow told him, simply. Then leaned in and kissed him, hard; wound Chess's arms in his, pressed him back and down, felt him strive against it 'til familiarity took over, one last time . . . that struck tuning-fork tone echoing through both their bodies, opening Chess's mouth, his legs. Rousing both their cocks like a carnal magic trick and fitting each to each, slick-sliding, stiff and ready to rut.

No, Morrow thought, *this is nothing I could feel for a brother. Thank whatever Lord watches over such foolery, above or below.*

They went at it with a will, chasing distraction hammer-hard 'til it finally surprised them both, drawing a mutual grunt and holler. And if either might've been picturing another at the peak, they knew each other well enough (at this point) to keep that fact a secret.

In the last few seconds before red faded fast to black, however, Morrow realized not only that he still hadn't told Chess what Geyer'd let slip on Pinkerton, but that Chess—attuned to others' thoughts though he might be—hadn't sensed enough of that lingering echo even to ask.

No point in hurrying bad news, he thought, dimly. *Always gets there too fast for comfort in the end, no matter what.*

Chess, meanwhile, his most immediate hungers well-met, was already snoring.

EVENTUALLY, KEES HOSTEEN'S GHOST came to stand a while by the rumpled bed's side, watching their twined bodies sleep; some time after, he made a stroking motion over rather than through

Chess's curls, as though unable to accurately judge the distance between objects from the real world and wherever he was, no matter how close the one might impinge upon the other.

Then, as the sun began to rise, he bowed his head and let the various parts of him eddy away, leaving no trace behind.

CHAPTER THIRTEEN

IT TOOK WHAT FELT like hours for Yancey to find her way back to sleep, after her dream of Edward Morrow—the shreds of which, even now, flushed her skin hot and pounding—broke with a force that vomited her out into the darkness of her room, shuddering and sweat-soaked under her quilt. When fatigue finally stole back over her, she slid under with the dim thought that at least, with no chores to do, she could lie abed as long as she needed in the morning. But lifelong habit bred betrayal, and with the sun's first light Yancey found herself wide awake once more, blinking at the room's ceiling.

She lay still, only half aware of a soft rasping sound she finally identified as Mister Geyer's snores; the ghost of an ache, more mental than physical, lingered in places she hadn't realized could pain her. At length, she forced herself to her feet—stepping over Geyer where he lay rolled up in the moth-eaten rug, wadded coat pillowing his head—and went to the washstand to splash tepid water over her face.

The air had that same peculiar stillness as a thousand mornings in the Cold Mountain, making memory seize her throat and eyes like venom. She had to brace herself against the washstand, choking, 'til the burn of it subsided.

Presently, she wiped her eyes clear, wondering if there was some other source of fresh wash-water to be found, since she'd only doffed her boots and stockings for sleep, and her conjured clothes seemed the equal of any more mundane garb for soaking up sweat and dust. On the landing, a window showed a hut out back: obviously a coldhouse, from its planking's thickness, the heavy tarring in every seam and condensation stains along its base. Beside it—thank Christ—a pump.

Continuing down into the main room, she found Joe behind the bar, recombining what dregs he could save from mostly empty bottles into new ones. "You do know that's as surefire a way to spread fluxes, coughs and colds as you could ask," she offered, noting he did at least make an effort to only mix spirits of a similar type.

Joe merely shrugged. "Folks like the all-sorts; crowd here's pretty rough, and I ain't got stock to waste. And spirits ain't so contagious as you'd think. Hunting up a wash, am I right?" Nodding to the left, behind the bar: "Door out back. Screen and a bucket by the coldhouse, you want some privacy." His mouth skewed oddly, yellow teeth shown in something she couldn't quite read as a smile. "Anybody you don't mind joinin' you, they come a-lookin'?"

The dream slammed back into Yancey's skull, face erupting with fresh heat, so she took refuge in dignity. "I hope, Mister . . . Joe . . . that you don't think my current company is any indicator of my nature."

"Hard to know what to think." He began putting the newly filled bottles away on the shelves, pushing the empties aside. "Only know I ain't never seen but one kind of person ride with Chess Pargeter: all monsters, one way or another."

"Is that so."

"It is." He turned to contemplate her straight on. "Man ain't right," he continued, voice pitched low, no doubt for self-preservation. "Never was, not even back before, with no hexation in it. I know why that other fella cleaves to him—he's sotted, same's the Rev used to be. But you . . . you seem nice."

Yancey swallowed. "Might be I'm *not*, though. Ever think of that?"

"Sure. Maybe you're already broke past the fixin', I dunno. But—"
He sighed, and leaned against the counter. "Gal, I've seen a hundred
men swear blood-revenge in here, for you-name-it. Half of 'em, it
was just bluster over a bottle; half again got bored, or dead, 'fore
they ever came near the ones they wanted. But some found who
they were lookin' for, and ended 'em. Men shot, stabbed in the back,
throats cut." His gaze flicked to Yancey's feet. "Almost where you're
standing, I saw one get his belly sawed open, guts spilled on that
floor like offal. Man who did that died himself three weeks later, in
a botched robbery up Utah way."

"If there's a point to your discourse, I'd be much obliged, you
were to arrive at it," said Yancey, hating the way her voice quavered.

"Point bein', ma'am—only men I ever saw didn't come out the
worse for takin' revenge were like Mister Pargeter. The ones who
were already as bad as they were gonna get."

"Think that means you've seen me at my worst, Joe?"

Yancey whirled; Joe turned more slowly, his general sallowness
now outright sickly. Chess leaned against one side of the doorway,
arms folded, hat rakish—and while he too was smiling, the gleam in
his eyes presaged nothing good.

"Means I've seen enough to know not to cross you," Joe told him,
voice admirably steady, "and that's why I don't propose to. So . . .
what can I do you for?"

"Nothing. Young *Mister* Kloves, on the other hand . . ." Though
Chess didn't quite sneer, Yancey felt herself flush, all the same. "I'll
be needing you outside, missy."

"If I might inquire—for what?"

Without hesitation Chess cross-drew—and tossed his sinister-
side gun to Yancey, connecting straightaway with her upflung palm,
an instinctually perfect catch. She stared at it, mouth open.

"Heard you might want to learn to shoot, is what," Chess said,
shrugging. "'Cause Joe's fine words notwithstanding, there are men
out there need killin', and you've got as much claim as any to do it.
So you may as well learn the trade right."

"I need to clean up, first."

Chess inclined his head. "I'll be waitin'."

WHEN YANCEY CAME OUT, hair still damp and clothes clinging, she found Chess lounging against the hob-rail used to tie up mounts, where a score of Joe's empty bottles had been carefully set up. He raised one eyebrow at the gun in her hand, which she had chosen to carry by the cylinder, rather than gripping the handle. "Christ, gal, don't you even know how to *hold* an iron?"

"Why would I have had cause to learn that particular skill, Mister Pargeter?"

Chess snorted. "What fool *wouldn't* teach his kin to shoot, out here? A dead fool, that's who." At Yancey's look, he rolled his eyes. "Aw, don't take on; dead Pa's the human condition, far as I can see. Ed's got one—Rook, too. Hell, mine's probably dead, for that matter."

"The plain fact that you don't *know* makes that a singularly useless statement."

Chess laughed. "Uh huh. Now get over here, and show me what I got to work with."

As Yancey crossed to his side, Chess took her arm, guiding her to a stance some thirty feet away. "Most fights blow up inside ten yards," he said, without preamble. "So if you can hit a target this close, you'll be good for all manner of shindigs. First thing, hold it proper—straight out from your shoulder. Keep it up there, long as you can." He stepped back, and watched.

Minutes passed; Yancey's arm began to tremble, but something in Chess's eyes warned her against relaxing. Finally, he leaned in without warning, grabbing the gun back. She gasped and let her arm fall, rubbing at her wrist.

"Not bad," he said. "You'd let it drop, I'd've pasted you a good one, just to learn you different." Chess gave her a shrewd look. "Or did you pick up on me planning that?"

"No—I didn't think to."

"Maybe you should. You got an advantage. Use it."

Yancey nodded. "True. But all that was about the gun's weight, wasn't it?"

"Get you trained to how heavy it feels—that's absolutely right." He touched her arm, causing her to start; fatigue vanished in a greenish flicker. "Ready to go again?" When she nodded, he put the piece back in her hand, turning her toward the bottles. "Now. This here's Colonel Colt's 1861 six-shot Navy Revolver, thirty-six calibre, and if you put a ball from it most anywhere in a man it *will* drop him. Got a kick like a mule and makes an almighty noise, so brace yourself."

Yancey gritted her teeth, selected the left-most bottle as her target, lined up the barrel's sight and tried to squeeze the trigger, which took a startling amount of effort; she ground her finger tight, tighter . . . then relaxed, lowered the gun, eased the hammer down, and after a second's examination found the loading switch that let her break the weapon open. Wordlessly, she held it up before Chess's face, showing empty chambers.

Chess clapped, sardonic-slow, but his expression was unlike anything she'd seen before—surprise, amusement, genuine *pleasure*.

"Always," he said, "*always* check your weapon. You got no idea how many idjits couldn't get that through their head, in the War— and believe me, under fire, that don't pay." He took the gun back and loaded it for her, deftly practiced, showing off how the cylinder ratcheted as each round socketed home. "I used to pack a loader for speed," he said, "'fore . . . well, before." He snapped it shut, slapped it back in Yancey's hand. "Okay, no more tricks. Go wild."

Yancey closed her eyes, breathed deep. Then—without giving herself time to think—she raised the gun, sighted, braced herself, and bore down on the trigger with everything she had.

The crack of the shot was louder than anything she'd ever heard, spiking straight through both eardrums like an awl. Wrist on fire, she screamed and staggered back, stench of cordite flattening her lungs. But she kept the gun up somehow, though her arm wavered crazily. And in the second before her eyes squeezed shut, she saw something she hadn't expected at all—the bottle exploding, a haze of shards.

Chess recoiled slightly himself, more at the scream. But as he straightened he saw the burst bottle, and clapped a hand to Yancey's shoulder, bracing her 'til she'd got her breath back.

"I suppose," she managed, ears still ringing, "you'd call that . . . beginner's luck."

"Sure. But some beginners are luckier than others." He stepped back. "Now, let's try again—without the ruckus."

BY THE TIME THE last bottle was disposed of, Yancey's arms burned equally—Chess had made her practise with both hands, together as well as separately. Her palms felt raw, ears humming tinnily, an acrid cordite stink permanently rooted in her nostrils; the growing heat had plastered her shirt to her back, pulling stickily as she moved. But the gun itself now felt disquietingly familiar. Chess soon stopped reaching 'round to adjust her arms, or pressing clinically upon her waist or shoulder to shift her stance, and the last three or four bottles—some of them not very large—had needed no more than one shot apiece to hit.

Chess pulled his hat off, raking back his hair. "That was . . . halfway decent."

"Only halfway?"

She'd meant the question honestly, and was startled to see a sudden grin split his beard, white on red. "Hell, Kloves—what're you doin', fishin'? I've seen blooded veterans couldn't learn a new firearm quick as you just did."

Yancey looked down, trying to quash her feelings of absurd flattery, without much success. "It doesn't seem a . . . demanding weapon, exactly."

"Yeah, but 'seem' is the word makes all the difference." Chess sobered. "Standing targets on a range is one thing. When the lead starts flyin', though, that's somethin' else entirely, and I'll tell you this much for free: you got any foolishness in your head about 'fair fights,' put it right out, for good. Brawl starts, you'd best be ready to *finish* it—whatever it takes, fast as you can. 'Cause that's how it goes, for such as us; womenfolk, I mean. And—"

"—men . . . like you."

"Oh, I seen flat-out queers far more man-made than myself, missy, believe you me. Killed 'em, too, when they made the mistake of underestimatin' me just because I have my habits writ large all over. Big don't mean shit, if you ain't prepared to either put one wherever's handy and run, or put one in the head, and walk."

"Not sure that particular lesson's going to come as easy as the rest did."

"Naw, you got the instinct, never fear. Anybody can learn gunplay, but the will to kill? That's a whole other matter." He examined her. "Then again, maybe it *is* that thing you got makes all the difference, after all. Like with me."

Yancey moistened her lips. "Uther . . ." she began, and swallowed. "He used to say talent was like a poker hand. No matter how good a draw you got, you still had to learn how to play it to make it mean anything." She held up the gun. "This is yours, like it was forged with you in mind, and no other; I can *feel* the heft of it, all that time and skill and practice. And that you did all on your own, no matter what else you brought to the table."

Chess lifted that creepish-lit gaze of his, and fixed her with it. "How long you known what you are, gal?"

Yancey let out a breath, remembering Mala—yet more hurt, older but somehow fresher, a pressed wound. "Most've my life, I reckon. Why?"

"Know when *I* knew?" Without ceremony, Chess pulled his shirttails clear of his belted waist, showing where a scar wormed its way beneath his breastbone like some leprous smile, the whitish-pink of raw haddock. "When Ash Rook pulled my heart out through here and showed it to me, and I didn't die."

"That's when you knew for *sure*."

It was out of her mouth before she could think of calling it back, and Chess's lips thinned at the taste of it. But they both knew it for truth.

"Lesson's over, for now," he said, finally. "Have a drink with me."

"I don't—"

"You do today."

More absinthe, naturally. Chess pulled it from his pocket with a mountebank flourish, took a swig and held it out, clearly expecting Yancey to match him. With a sigh, she took a pull, then almost spit the result back out onto the glass a-sparkle at their feet.

"My Lord," she managed, choking down foul liquorice-moonshine dregs. "This is dreadful stuff! And you *prefer* it?"

"Got to, eventually. 'Course, there ain't all too many others ask after this particular swill. So that means whatever stock a place happens to have of it, it's pretty much mine."

Yancey took a second shot and coughed, yet kept it down easier, this time; Chess grinned, like he relished the thought of changing her tastes. *Perverse as a cat,* she thought, knowing he'd pick up on it, and was rewarded by the grin becoming an outright chuckle.

"Strategically thought out, on your part," she said, at last.

"So take another."

"Oh, I don't want to deprive you."

"What of? I can always make more."

A near-unassailable argument, though Yancey suspected her faculties were already somewhat disordered. Above, the sun drew high and beat down bright, while wormwood's mounting poison lent everything around her just the faintest rainbow tinge; "a lucid drunkenness," some customer had once described the effect, when trying to sell her Pa on the idea of ordering a bottle or two. But given the difficulty of keeping its colour undecayed, not to mention the unlikelihood of cultivating a bohemian clientele in New Mexico's wilds, he'd ultimately decided against it.

In the distance, she saw a few of Joe's regulars come wandering out to squint in the noontime heat, while others arrived on foot or by horse, glancing their way only briefly before recognizing Chess, and finding something elsewhere to stare at. A mixture of fear and embarrassment 'cross their faces made Yancey frown; the former she understood, and sympathized with. But the latter?

"Might be they think I'm after what's inside your pants," Chess suggested, idly. "Or vice versa, which'd be even funnier."

"Little do they know."

"Ha! You got *that* right."

They both had a snicker, at the very idea. Yet when he looked at her again, she saw an ever-so-slight softening in his fierce stare—almost apologetic.

"You know," he said, "Ed might've misspoke somewhat, back in the Hoard. Bein' raised up as whore-get means you don't see nothing *but* women the first few years, and for all we're made to follow after the same meat, I don't *despise* your kind, as such—they just ain't got much use for me, and I mostly return the favour." He paused. "I did hate one woman, that's true enough . . . but I loved her a good long time, 'fore I finally figured out she hated *me*."

Yancey blinked, unsteadily. "That'd be your Ma."

"It would."

"Then why are you still alive?"

"'Scuse me?"

"Babies die, Mister Pargeter. Happens lamentably easily—I've seen it close up, twenty times or more. So . . . she'd really wanted you dead, you would be."

"That don't mean nothin' but she looked to cut her losses, make a return on the investment. Money always was the only thing that bitch ever held in esteem, just like the only useful thing she taught me was how high to charge."

The absinthe had wrapped her in cotton wool awhile, putting up a sugared screen between her and his more outrageous—effluences: half-heard thoughts, half-glimpsed memories. And now things were definitely starting to push up against that screen's edges once more, to intrude 'emselves in at the seams, forcing Yancey to watch them pool and sharpen. That girl with hair like Chess's, a fox-faced minx with ragged skirts and broken teeth, wavering back and forth at her mind's keyhole between part-bloomed youth and early age . . . wreathed in smoke, doling out slaps and caresses, screaming hoarse-vowelled gutter abuse. Good lord, but she was just so *present*, yet and always, yammering at the corners, constantly bent on resizing Chess the outlaw back to Chess the kicked cur, the object of barter, the cold and lonely child.

What kind of a mother acts in such a way? What kind of a man has that for a mother?

"And she never loved you, ever."

"Gal, you didn't *know* her, for which you should give thanks. She stabbed me in the neck one time, hoping I'd die bleedin', after she already sold first crack at my ass to the lowest bidder. I'd go to kiss her, she'd spit in my damn face. And *then I learned better.*"

She shook her head. "I can't understand it."

"That's your look-out."

Such a sleek little man, Yancey thought, to contain so large a load of high-coloured nastiness. She could all but taste his bile from where she sat, and it made her want to spit.

"You ever wish it was different?" she ventured. "That she—that *you*—"

"'Wish in one hand, shit in the other, see which one fills up the faster.' That's what English Oona used to say, savin' the Limejuicer tang." But when he saw she was still intent on him, he snorted. "What's it matter? Things are like they are; we act accordingly, or don't."

"That sounds almost Biblical. Like something Sheriff Love might say."

Chess laughed again, harsher. "That Bible-belting son-of-a-bitch and me ain't got nothin' in common, as he'd be the first to tell you." He cast her a piercing look. "So what, he's on your mind? See him comin', do you, in that crystal ball you call an idea-pan?"

"I don't have to. There's but two names on his list, saving the occasional heretic, and we're still between him and Hex City."

"Which works out well for you, since I hear you're all for giving him another go-round. So I guess you'll be wanting this one, too—for a matched set."

Before she could protest, he'd already slipped his remaining gun's butt into her empty hand. The doubled weight was yet one more shock, though it also somewhat steadied her, like being fit for chains.

"But . . . you'll be left unarmed."

"Hardly. It's a dirty joke, considering all that time I put in, 'cause turns out? I don't need either of 'em. Never did."

He waggled all ten fingers in front of her eyes, making the air itself snarl and buzz. The sound was far-away lightning, or something raked almost to tearing—big and small at once, and far too close for comfort.

"And I'm to be your back-up?"

"You, Ed, that Pink in there: cannon fodder, more like, considering what the Sheriff and me got to throw around. Still, ain't like you don't want to be here, is it?"

"No. But if you're truly trying to convince yourself you don't need us at all, why couldn't you've just handed him his hat back in the Hoard? Without any extraneous help from us pitiful hexless folk, that is."

Again, she saw that weird appreciative flicker cross his face. *For you sure do like to have your wounds pressed on, don't you, Mister P.? Which only makes a sort of sense, seeing how they're all that's left of the man you thought you were. . . .*

"Also," she continued, "I'd be pleased if you'd stop making grand ethical comparisons between us. 'Instincts' aside, the only man *I've* ever felt like killing is dead already."

"And you don't think you could bear to give him company, it came to that? One way to find out."

Too quick to equivocate with, he steered her right-hand gun up, sighting it at one of Joe's customers through the saloon window—a largish, shaggy man whose silhouette seemed so familiar that, addled as she was, Yancey felt a moment's fearful clutch it might even *be* Edward Morrow. Chess wouldn't allow that, though, would he?

"Easy 'nough," Chess said, his tone surprisingly convincing. "Child could do it. Just make certain you got a bead, and . . . pull."

"No."

"He's nothin' to you, *Missus*—nobody is. What folk you had're all halfway to rotten, 'less them that's left decided they weren't worth the burial."

The inherent addendum, equally contemptuous, even in silence: I *saw to that, with your conniving*. The sting of it went from ear to hand and back up again, faster than telegraph-wires; before she'd formed the idea, Yancey saw her other barrel connect 'gainst his temple, tiny bone-thud impact dwarfed by the click of her thumbing the hammer.

"Goddamn *no*, is what I said."

"Oh ho! Brave notion. And just what d'you think would happen, if you tried?"

Now it was her turn to grin, just shy of a snarl. "Care to find out?"

They traded glares, wind surprising cold around them, there in the noonday sun—'til a third voice intruded: "Hey! What the hell're you two playing at?"

Yancey's heart did a rabbit-kick. *Oh thank God, it* wasn't *him.* A beat after that—this being the first time she'd sighted the man since their last night's . . . converse, in the flesh or out of it—blood rushed to her cheeks, hot and quick. Mister Morrow seemed a tad thrown himself, probably for similar reasons, while Chess noted the back-and-forth, approvingly.

"Just making a point, Ed," he said. "For what little that'll help her, when the real shooting starts." Adding, to Yancey: "'Cause we've at least established you'd shoot Sheriff Love or *me*, if only to prove you won't shoot nobody else, on the off chance they're guiltless. And also 'cause you're halfway sure it wouldn't do all too much, anyhow."

Son of a . . . Maybe I will *let fly, just to wipe that smug damn look off his face.*

"I was beginning to like you, Mister Pargeter," was all she allowed herself to say, at last. Which simply made him roll his eyes at Morrow, and grin all the more.

"Your error," he told her, coolly. "But keep the guns; I fancy the look of you with 'em, if only for amusement's sake."

When he turned to go, however, Morrow grabbed his arm, hard enough he couldn't. But it was Yancey he glared at, sending a fresh run of prickly heat from head to toe. "Out here playin' Goddamn William Tell with real rounds for so long *Joe* had to tell me where you two were—and did you even once think t'tell Chess 'bout what . . . Grey . . . said, last night?"

"You're the ones share a mattress. Did *you*?"

Morrow took it full force, blinking rather than flinching, while Chess, caught in the crossfire, looked one to the other like he longed to slap 'em both.

"What *about* what he said?" He demanded.

"YOU KNOW HOW PINKERTON'S working with hexes already," Geyer told Chess, all four of them up in the pistoleer's suite— Morrow and Yancey arranged on chairs flanking Geyer, while Chess set up his usual back-and-forth pace in front of the window. "That hellion from San Fran to start with, Madam Yu, or Songbird—"

"We've met a time or two, yeah, and she likes me same as she probably likes how a dose of clap lowers her home-stable's tone. So?"

Geyer sighed. "Well . . . as per their initial agreement, the Boss had been letting her sniff out other hexes to sign up or suck dry, most often the latter—but the Hex City Call interfered, drying up their lines of supply by sending all expressed witches and warlocks scurrying off toward Reverend Rook and . . . that other lady. But then Doctor Asbury began to manufacture copies of his Manifold, issuing them to ranked officers, each inside cases fit with a scale to match their readings to." He flashed his own Chess's way, netting little response. "Which means . . ."

". . . they can do what they were jawing over when last we saw 'em, remember?" Morrow asked. "Hunt up them as *could* be hexes 'fore they have a chance to blossom, then raise 'em housebroke to leash and collar?"

Chess huffed. "So they got a *passel* of just-bled bitches like Little Miss Fuck-You-Hard on their side—what's that to do with me? They don't get in my road, they won't get hurt; they *do*, then they will. Day I can't get shed of a flock of witch-girls, you can lay my ass out and throw dust in my face."

"It's not only young ladies, Mister Pargeter—not by a long shot." Geyer leaned forward. "That train of his . . . last Morrow and I stepped aboard, it was a regular steam-car made commonplace time, and now it can go from Chi-Town to Mexico in under three days. Doesn't even need rails, nor an engine; it can go through a *mountain*, if that's what's on order. And you know how that's done?"

"I don't doubt but you're gonna tell me."

Morrow, now: "By rounding up folk who ain't yet come to it wherever they run across 'em, Chess, and packing 'em away in its freight cars like cattle—men and boys, old and young, who've been lucky enough to dodge the rope Rook didn't, or that battlefield harm old Kees Hosteen was talking about, back when the Yanks tried to make a Brigade out of new-minted hexes. Then they ask 'em if they want to serve their country, and if they say yes . . ."

His voice trailed away, run dry at the sheer horror of it, especially from a man he'd once admired. But Chess didn't take the hint.

"They what, hexify 'em 'gainst their will? Poor damn babies. Bound to've happened sooner or later, and if they're so dumb they *still* turn Pink after, then—"

Yancey sat upright, her final straw snapping. "Oh, let *me*," she said.

Her hand darted forward, snaring Chess by the sleeve and pulling him so close it made him startle, like she came loaded with some particularly female complaint he might catch through sheer proximity. "Whoa, now! Just 'cause you and Ed been flirting . . ."

"Hush," she said, severely, and kissed him on the lips.

Purest intuition, same as going skin-to-skin with Geyer had

been, the night previous—but she couldn't fool herself there was no small shred of payback in the gesture, either. If nothing else, it certainly shocked Chess silent.

Both their minds broke open, pulled right on back to Pinkerton's conclave, together: so close-sat between the predatory trio of Asbury, Songbird, Pinkerton and Geyer's memory-self it seemed insanity no alarm was roused. The former agent looked uppercut, dazed.

"But . . . these are citizens of our nation, sir, not enemy operatives; fellow veterans, some of them. I thought our charge was the *protection* of such innocents."

Pinkerton's dreadful maw quivered, as though striving (yet failing, miserably) to knit itself back together—and it shocked Yancey to realize how shocked *Chess* was by the sight, his unwitting handiwork made flesh.

"We are nane sae innocent as tae be sinless, from Eve's womb on," Pinkerton replied, shortly. "But what America stands on here, Frank, is the precipice of a far worse division than that which almost sundered us—one which must be avoided, at all costs."

"I'm still not sure why that necessitates forcing the unprepared into custody, ripping them from wives and families, subjecting them to—"

"A cocktail of the same sacramental Weed Pargeter sows behind him, only," Asbury assured him, "creating delirium, followed by a mere shadow-show of impending grievous bodily harm: threat of fire, or approaching bombardment . . ." Hastening to add, as Geyer gawped at him: ". . . and then, once the deed is achieved, sedation via heroin—a housewife's cough remedy!—or gentle gastric lavage. It is done with all possible delicacy, Mister Geyer, leaving not a speck of permanent damage; we have no wish, or need, to go further."

"Yet these medicament-aided vaudevilles of yours must ring convincing enough to make the change occur," Geyer shot back, "which confirms the whole offensive matter as torture!"

Asbury reddened, from his collar up. "Our processes, however traumatic, allow these recruits to *avoid* such Mediaeval nonsense, sir! No more burnings, hangings or pressings, no more 'spectral evidence'—no hysteric, misinformed massacres, in fact, such as that which lent Salem its legendarily ill name."

Unable to restrain herself, Songbird giggled behind her fan, drawing Pinkerton's roar. "Be still, both o' ye!" To Geyer: "I *must* ha' men around me I can trust, Frank, *sincerely*, and not worry over. If you canna play that part for me, then tell me now, and we'll ha' ye back Illinois-way on the instant."

"I . . . that wasn't my intent, boss, by any means. It's simply . . ."

He shook his head, amazed, while Pinkerton merely shrugged. "Aye, it's a conundrum—how tae comport ourselves as true Christians, gi'en what we deal wi'? We can't do much tae hurry the lassies along, and setting one hex to make another is a witless errand, for they eat 'em right after, or at least try damn hard. Savages!" Songbird laughed again. "But the Professor here's figuring a way tae keep 'em in line."

And here things froze, a print-run newsbill settling from ink to image. Cutting out the middleman, since they were there already, Chess turned directly to Geyer's shadow-self, and asked: "What's he on about? Those grounding-wires the Doc uses to suck up magic?"

First Yancey'd heard of such a thing, but Geyer-of-the-past—perhaps somehow combined with his current self through hexological miracle, so that the "person" they spoke to was as much Geyer as its original?—nodded quick enough, like it was familiar business. "Says he can boil it down into a spring or cog and add it to the Manifold's next generation, so's we won't even need the whole rigmarole with casting a circle or dispersing the result—just point and shoot, and the thing takes more the more your target tries to fend it off, 'til they run plumb dry."

"For permanent?" asked Chess.

Geyer shrugged, blankly. "Asbury says magic's a natural force, like gravitation, so no . . . every hex can take a charge of it, like running electricity through metal, which means it'll build up again, eventually. But the rest of that stuff he talks of—build a machine that can *extract* magic, let alone store it so any normal man can use it, later on? That's like sayin' you can build an engine that flies to the moon, or a bombshell fierce enough to level an entire city. No, if the last century's taught us anything, such foolery is the province of hexation alone."

"So what broke you free of Pinkerton's sway, exactly, and sent you chasin' after me?"

Geyer looked down, abashed. "He sent me away with George Thiel, his second-in-command 'til then—doing work Pinkerton no longer trusts himself with, be it purging Weed or rounding up potentials. He feared Thiel's loyalty was slipping, that the man intended to form his own Detective Service Agency, in direct competition to our own. So Pinkerton told me to ride along with him on a fact-finding mission up Bewelcome way, watch for my chance, and—when I saw it—act."

"Back-shoot the fucker, in other words."

"I said: 'Given provocation?' To which he replied: 'Provocation's a thing can always be decided upon, after.'"

"Wouldn't expect any better, from the same man had agents dress like ghosts to scare a nut-house confession from Alex Drysdale."

"No, no." Geyer shook his head fiercely. "That was justice, however rough. But how could I follow his orders after that, knowing he held a loyal man's life in such disregard? Worse still, when I broke the bonds of silence to warn George, he was unsurprised—he'd known it was coming, and made his plans accordingly. Fly north and east, back to the government, and tell them first-hand what hay Pinkerton's been making of his authority . . . convince them how vitally important it is not just that Hex City be overthrown, but that Pinkerton *not* be its conqueror, lest he use such victory as an excuse to seize power for himself."

"Shut up," Chess ordered him, turning back to Yancey, who braced herself. "As for you—that was a dangerous game you just played, missy. Last woman who kissed me . . . well, turnabout is fair play, or so I've heard. . . ."

Before she could ask what he meant, it was his lips on hers, tongue tracing the seam in one hot, abrasive lick. The charge of it broke outwards, sweeping Geyer, Pinkerton and the rest clear, and what followed came as a series of blood-tinged blinks, viler than anything Yancey'd ever dreamt on: all limbs and motion, a serpentine coiling, pinned hands and feet, imposed desire and vivid rage co-mixed. Chess lay trapped in its midst, prone and horrified; a looming man-tower she could only assume was Reverend Rook stared down on his humiliation, purring, with horrid affection: *Soon be over, darlin'. Just let her have her way.*

At the very centre of this storm, meanwhile—his tormentor, the cyclone's bride. The aforementioned Lady.

Her real name is Ixchel, Chess told Yancey, dispassionate. While his own memory-self, bound fast as Leviathan, struggled against her toils with everything he had, only to prove it wanting. Thinking furiously, with the only part of him left free: *Oh, I'd kill you right now if I could, scatter your bones and dance on 'em, in a fuckin' instant. Bite your lips off, bitch. Rip out your lyin' tongue, and hang it for a party favour. Just kill and kill and kill—*

And her, nodding, black hair 'round his face like a curtain, funereal flag of some overthrown nation. Thinking back, in vaguely amused return—***If you could, yes. Yet you cannot; you are made for this, little* ixiptla, *my husband's husband. It will happen.***

Chess bucked and writhed, but in his mind's eye alone. He chewed at his own tongue 'til his teeth almost met, and still she rode him down through the storm, the rainbow's black core, a cauldron of hissing dragonflies. Rode him 'til an ending of sorts lit up the hollows of their skulls, and all their eyes turned black.

Motion through darkness, vertiginous downward plunge, and Yancey hit bottom at last. That dreadful female form had absented itself, along with the Reverend's ghost; the two of them were left alone, nose to nose, and the weight of what she'd inadvertently done to Chess pressed at her chest like some massive iron bell's clapper.

"I'm so sorry," Yancey said, eventually, knowing it made not a whit of difference. "I didn't . . . I couldn't've . . ."

Thankfully, all Chess's anger seemed to have fled in transition, leaving only gruffness behind. "'Course you couldn't. Just don't do it again—not without warning."

She hesitated, then ventured: "You must truly hate me."

That irritable spark flared up once more, though no longer directed her way; a flare of insight blooming, uncomfortable, undeniable. Snapping back: "Jesus, what for? You ain't her, just 'cause you got a few of her particulars—ain't my Ma, either. You're—"

—something different, the like I've never seen, with your clumsy-true aim and your high moral quackings. More akin to me than not, even folding in your choice of where to lay a roving fancy. Though he was with me last night, in the flesh, and don't you ever forget it.

More an ally than an enemy, in other words. One of the current gang, so tiny there was no point in either mistrust or rank, beyond the barest rudiment: Chess in front, the others behind, for protection—theirs, and his. Shedding blood in his half-deified name. Watching his back.

Hell, even I can see that.

Close as they were at this moment, the thought could've come from either, and still be just as true.

CHAPTER FOURTEEN

NIGHT'S HOUSE ROSE EVERYWHERE. From horizon to horizon, the desert filled with its whisperings.

To the west, a train powered by anguish rode ghostly rails, heading swift and sure for a certain hidden valley. Inside, its master dozed, sedated to a less immediate level of pain. His partners sat in the dining car, one watching the other throw a series of three coins over and over, noting down the results, which were—unsurprisingly—always the same.

"Your divinatory scholars call this the *I Ching*, I believe," Asbury said.

Songbird did not bother to nod, let alone look up. "When Fu Xi first compiled them, the hexagrams were cast using a handful of yarrow stalks, but that method has been lost for centuries. The Han gave us coins instead, which serve."

"And the outcome?"

The bleached girl-witch bent lower, studying the latest compilation of broken and unbroken lines. "*Tui* above, the joyous lake. *Sun* below, a gentle wind through the wood. Weakness outside, strength inside—a situation out of balance, extraordinary, dangerous. Such a condition cannot last; it must be changed quickly, or misfortune will result."

"I thought that was the path we were already embarked upon."

Her weak eyes flicked to rake him, visibly unfocused, yet too sharp too evade. "Did you? This is Pinkerton's crusade, Professor, as you well know, though you raised no objection—but then again, neither did I. I keep my own counsel, with the *Book of Changes* as my advisor." Colourless lashes drooping, as she quoted from memory:

Nine in the third place:
The ridgepole sags to the breaking point.
Six at the top:
One must go through water that goes over one's head.
Misfortune, but no blame.

"Meaning?"

"There are things more important than preserving one's own life, so long as the right prevails." She hissed through her teeth. *"Ai-yaaa!* Such foolishness. Yet the true reading is plain. If anyone is doomed to sacrifice himself to rebalance the whole, it will be English Oona's son, not anyone sworn to *our* cause."

"Why cast these runes at all, then, if you see the future they speak of so clearly?"

"Because luck can change, always; that is its nature. And always in more than one way."

Asbury nodded. "Indubitably. And yet . . . in a world containing both science and hexology, surely we have no need for such antiquated concepts as *luck*?"

Obviously, Songbird did not feel this last observation worthy to be dignified with any sort of response. Instead, she let her red veil swing closed like a door, returning to her efforts; Asbury sighed, reaching for a fascinatingly appropriate yellow-backed dime novel he'd picked up at their last stop: *The Salten Town, or, Outlawry Aplenty at Hex City's Door!*

"It's a hard life you lead, for one so young," he said, as though to himself. "All . . . this. Were you not—" Here he glanced up again and hesitated, finding her dim gaze returned to him, even more off-putting than before. "—what you are, I mean," he finished, weakly.

"Were the sky not blue, perhaps, or the moon and sun exchanged? Old fool! What *should* I do, play with dolls? A hundred generations went to make me. I am a warlord born—an empress reduced to a brothel figurehead, sold alongside peasant girls in a muddy pigsty. More than match to any full-grown *American* sorcerer. So what matter, if I rail against time's cage on occasion, or find myself intemperate?" He saw her fingers flex and tremble in their gilded sheaths, perhaps with the effort expended to *not* hex him silly.

"Please—I meant no insult."

Songbird sniffed, suddenly cool and remote once more. "*Gweilo go-se shifu*, elevated undeservedly by cleverness—you have not substance enough to insult me. In the Forbidden City, they would have made a eunuch of you."

"And we have made you a whore. Is that so preferable?"

"We each use the other for our own ends—you give me shelter from Reverend Rook's accursed Call, and I lend power, as needed. If that counts as prostitution, I am hardly the only whore in this compartment."

Asbury flushed. "Nevertheless," he went on, doggedly. "I am not unconscious of your position's injustice. I sought only to offer you freedom, or the best version of it I can give; a kind you may not yet have contemplated, perhaps."

"What . . . freedom?"

Diffidently, Asbury placed a Manifold upon the table where the coins of the *I Ching* yet rested. Beside it, he laid a delicate bracelet made up of a dozen interwoven rods; its metal looked like silver, but the dull *clank* it made on wood lacked silver's chime, sounding somehow dead. Songbird narrowed her eyes further, as if both objects might be scorpions disguised by glamour.

"You know the latest iterations of my device can drain away the hexaciously gifted's accumulated power," Asbury said, tapping the Manifold. "But this—" his hand moved to the bracelet "—is the next step. By donning the guard, composed of the same alloys that ground thaumaturgical forces, the hex's affinity is blocked—he no longer draws in such forces to replenish himself, nor feels any hunger to do so, nor provokes such hunger in other hexes. With one simple bracelet, he can deny altogether the responsibilities of a never-asked-for burden." He leaned forward, urgent. "You'd be free both of the Call and of any obligation to us. Without your power, Mister Pinkerton will have no need for you, and you could return to—well, wherever you want. San Francisco, far Cathay . . ."

Songbird lifted her gaze. "And this 'guard'—is it always made so, removable at will?" Her voice went softer yet, a silken rope noose-coiled. "Or are other forms of it yet more . . . permanent?"

Asbury grew pale, stammering: "But surely, you see there are those of your kind who cannot be permitted . . . who are not . . . *safe*."

But here he broke off, realizing that thin squeaking he heard was her nail-sheaths grating against themselves.

"Old man," she said, "take care how you speak to me, or to any other *ch'in ta*, for that matter. I do not want your pity, or your 'help.' Your devices mean nothing to me—less than nothing. For even if they do what you claim they will, it cannot be made permanent."

"I *beg* to differ—"

"Beg all you wish. Do you truly think you can cure this sick world, wracked to its very core, by 'curing' me? I have a part to play, like the spider, the wolf, the carrion crow. And because I *know* this, because I am not stupid enough to deny it, I am already so far beyond your grasp that you should truly be afraid. Just think how much further even than that such as Chess Pargeter, Reverend Rook or his Lady of the Long Hair must be!" She smiled, revealing kitten-teeth. "Especially so, since—on your employer's orders—we now travel *toward* them, rather than *away* from them."

Asbury swallowed. "You're at risk too, then, as much as we, if not more. For all three will be hungry, when we arrive."

"Yes. But I, at least, will either conquer or die, doing what I was meant for. And *you* will not deprive me of my chance to do either with this manacle of yours, unless you wish to be cut a hundred times in a hundred different ways: denied *xiao* by *ling-shi*, both in this world and the next—*all* the next worlds, from Mictlan-Xibalba up through each and every one of the Ten Thousand Hells my *amahs* promised *me*."

Again, she met his eyes, and it was all he could do not to recoil from the sight. For now they were crimson as the veil that hid them, solidly, from sclera to pupils—Mars doubled, a study in vermillion. Until, having received the response she must have wanted, she blinked, and they returned to "normal."

"Now read your silly book, and do not dare to address me further," she told him, dismissively. And returned to her endless scrying, flicking his offered jewellery aside like some errant lump of dung.

BLASTED BY HEADACHE, YANCEY retired early, ostensibly leaving the men to hammer out some sort of accord, though she knew in her heart any immediate agreement on strategy was unlikely at best; two former Pinkerton men and a man who thought Pink-killing admirable sport made for bad bedfellows, even with one of 'em being exactly that.

Funny how huge this cramped room seemed, when empty. For a single heartbeat, Yancey wished Morrow was here to fill it up, then resolutely pushed all such imaginings away. *He's spoke for that way,* she told herself, *even if his natural bent sometimes takes his mind— elsewhere. And I suppose I don't want to . . .*

Impose? Come between them? Deprive Chess Pargeter of what few minor comforts his life currently held—that horror of a man, impossible and unpleasant, his irreverent soul packed full of sorrowful rage with no other method of surcease?

I do like him, more fool me, she understood, ruefully. *My Goddamn error, indeed.*

Easing her boots off with a sigh, Yancey sat back against the headboard, let her lids droop 'til all she saw was the veins decorating their backsides, and counted breaths like sheep.

Until: *Granddaughter,* a voice said—that *same* voice, bearer of bad news and good advice alike. *We must talk.*

When she opened her eyes again, red-purple light striated the dream-sky above like a bruise. Yancey got to her feet, soil gritty under her bare soles. All around, scree-lined slopes rose up to an edged ring of stone. The air was thin and dry, cool with altitude, though the earth still held the dying day's heat. A harsh scent of ash scored each breath she took, underlaid with something fouler. At the centre of the bowl, the dead grey-black embers of a fire sat, and beside them, oh, beside them . . .

The Yancey of but days ago would have retched, and even now, she had to gulp down bile. Yet it was not the mere appearance of this ruined corpse that so revolted—albeit leathery and shrunken, it was less repugnant than the contents of most renderers' carts. But the miasma magnified tenfold as she stared, coating her throat with tar and decayed fruit.

"It is a *Hataalii's* murder you smell, granddaughter."

Though the words were in no language she had ever heard, she understood them without effort. Yancey closed her eyes again; at once, the revulsion shrank sharply. "You've called me that for some time now," she said. "And I'm mindful what courtesy you might mean by it, for which I thank you. But my mother was Mala Colder, born Mala Kiraly Lukacz, and though I didn't have the pleasure of knowing *her* mother, I have no other. So, respectfully: use my name or any other title you please, 'cause I'm no kin of yours."

She braced herself, not daring to open her eyes, 'til dry laughter filled the air.

The woman who stood unwavering on the crater's edge, steady-balanced as if weighted, was both squat and unlovely: a frog-faced Indian squaw of no tribe Yancey knew—Apache, Sioux? Her long white hair stretched down to her belt in two slim braids; the shawl wrapping her was woven in complex, interleaving stripes of colour, sole bright thing about her, other than her black eyes' predatory shine.

"And this," she announced, to no one in particular, "is why *this* one may be worth the talking to."

Smiling as she said it, but with nothing that looked like kindness. And the red-purple light of the sky clung to her, its power palpable as a forge's heat.

This, too, a days-younger Yancey would have found near-paralyzing. But after Chess Pargeter, and Love, and the feel of her blood going into the Weed, a steel she had never thought possible had woven itself through her spine. She met the woman's gaze without flinching. "All right. Now . . . who are you, really?"

The smile fell, a discarded mask. "*Bilagaana* dead-speaker," the woman called her. "Why not *make* me tell you? You could, if you tried."

It was true, and Yancey suddenly knew it, the way she always did. And though the rush of that certainty was dizzying, she held onto herself, hard.

"Yes. But why would I?"

A moment, then another; the woman's scowl relaxed. "You would not," she admitted, "since you are no *Hataalii*. For which I am thankful."

Yancey's eyes slipped back toward the dead fire pit's awful companion. "That's . . . yourself, lying there," she said.

The woman spat. "What was left behind, after Reverend Rook betrayed me to his *Anaye*-wife. *Ai*, that I was foolish enough to be merciful! But he was a man in love, though not with her." She folded her arms and shook her head, bemused. "And for all that men say women do foolish things for love, a lovestruck man will let the whole world burn, or burn it himself."

Yancey thought of the scar underlining Chess's breastbone, and fought down a shudder. "Love's . . . not what's between them, now, it seems."

The woman sniffed. "*Seeming* is nothing; you yourself told that red boy as much, just today. Now—come up here beside me, dead-speaker. See what lies waiting."

Yancey calmed herself with a deep breath, then climbed the loose scree of the inner slope 'til at last she stood perched on the top edge by the woman's side, where she was surprised to realize herself a good few inches taller than her mysterious mentor. Then she looked out—eastward, since the sunset was behind her—and caught her breath.

Nightfall lay thick over the land, lights sparking up here and there, sadly separate. Slowly, Yancey realized she must be seeing for miles and miles, far beyond what the horizon should have permitted: Towns, cities, states, territories—near the entire West, maybe even far as the Mississippi. But this darkness was something more, Weed's onslaught the merest surface froth of something far more corrupt.

Like rancid oil at the bottom of a mud-darkened puddle, Yancey could trace the currents of wrongness that eddied over the world. Within seconds, she had linked them back to their thickest points— the blurred, half-real edifices of Rook's hex-town; the quake-flattened wreckage of Mexico's capital, hundreds of miles south; and most of all, the salt-flat, white-glowing husk of Bewelcome. Black cracks pierced each place like broken cinders, producing a rushing vertigo in her stomach.

"Once, when things were not so pressing," her not-grandmother said, "I would have wasted time—cajoled, flattered, offered instruction, as I did with Rook. But I have been longer than I expected fighting my way back from the Far Places, and things are grown so bad it seems best to speak plainly, if only to avoid misunderstanding."

"Likewise, and most decidedly," Yancey said, unable to turn away from the horrid sight.

The woman sighed. "I have sent dreams to my own tribe's dead-speakers, but they are too far away to be helpful. Still, they in turn have sent emissaries to their nearest enemies, reminding them we share a common foe—worse even, in its season, than *your* kind has been to us, ghost-face girl. A threefold menace, each branch sprung from the same tree of bones: the Weed, and who it follows after. The risen city, and those who rule it. The crack, and what comes out of it. All bent to one abominable purpose."

"To destroy us?" Yancey guessed. "Or . . . everything?"

"Grandma" shook her head, sharply. "Merely to thrust this world on toward the Sixth would not appease she who drives this monstrousness, or serve her ends. She wishes to *undo* a destruction—force time itself backward to restore what she remembers as her followers' glory, before your people meddled in their affairs."

"*My* people?"

"Those who overcame the Mexica—steel hats, she calls them. *Los conquistadors.*"

"Um—conquistadors were Spanish, I believe." At Grandma's look: "But lay that by. . . . This'd be Reverend Rook's 'Rainbow Lady,' I take it?" She'd almost said the name outright, but stopped in time, remembering Ed's palm making harsh contact with her jaw to keep a similar name from possibly summoning its owner. Though what lingered was not the pain of the blow, but the stricken look in his eyes, immediately after.

Grandma spat. "She thinks herself fit to overturn Balance, who is nothing but a shed snakeskin of venom and folly. And for that, she has loosed such horrors upon the world. . . ."

She seized Yancey's arm, pointed at the throbbing void centring Bewelcome's whiteness. "It has reached further down now, to the Ball-Court's lowest levels. Past the Mexica host, presided over by Mictantecuhtli and his fleshless lady Mictecacuihuatl, into the realm of One and Seven Death and all *their* nightmares." Grandma's voice fell into a mesmerizing rhythm, and with each name, images flashed before Yancey's eyes—too quick to be truly seen, too ghastly to forget. "Jaundice Demon and Skull Sceptre, who cause the flesh to sicken and fall. House Corner, his sharp teeth bared. Lord of Rubbish and the Stabbing Lord, who attack from the blind side. Packstrap and Wing, whose victims die struck from above on the roadway, alone, with the dark wind blowing past.

"And in their company, neither leading nor following, something that has been here already for longer than we dream—enjoying their progress, pointing them the way—"

Yancey felt it in her gut, a landed punch. "The Enemy."

"We know him by many names, dead-speaker, and sometimes he

seems to care for us, if only because we keep him busy. But in this form he is the Trickster without care—the King who Eats Himself, playing his flute on a staircase of human skulls. And this crack he keeps open will be the root his Bone Tree grows from."

So what does any of that mean? Yancey choked back the urge to yell. As Grandma'd said, the hour was getting late—terminology hardly mattered, considering it all sounded equally bad.

"Why don't you tell Mister Pargeter all this," she asked, instead, "seeing he's the only one might be able to *do* something about it?"

"Because he cannot hear me—*will* not, perhaps. He is a stubborn fool."

"I can't disagree."

"So it is, when a man hates his own mother—the earth opens up under his feet, one way or another. Women live in your warrior's blind spot; he cannot see them, or see them coming. How else do you think the Rainbow Lady was able to take his man even as he lay beside him, right out of his very bed? How was she able to make *him* come panting at her call, though it goes against his very soul to do so?"

I do wish you hadn't made me remember that, Yancey thought.

"Suppose he'd say . . . 'cause she's 'a damn hex-god,'" she replied, out loud. "'Cause she's not like you or him, or Reverend Rook, either."

"No. She is *exactly* like him, and me, and every other of our kind— puffed up with stolen blood, writ large, gone bad. For whatever she and her Enemy are now, they were once as I . . . as you, even. And though she refuses to see it, her time is already done; what she and Rook have worked with Rook's little killer proves as much. Gods sleep within us all, waiting to be prayed alive. And gods can kill other gods."

She turned to fix Yancey with one eye, head cocked like a carrion bird's. "*You*, meanwhile, the red boy needs, along with his travelling companion—that one man who stayed with him for friendship's sake, even after knowing what he really was. Which is why he begins to mistrust you both, as he fears anything which might make him weak."

Yancey frowned. "He isn't, though. He's *crazy* strong."

"Tell him that, then. Make him even stronger. Or he will drive you both away, and ensure all our dooms."

She turned once more to the horizon, where Hex City cast its weird light upwards, deforming the stars behind. "Something is happening there, in that city Rook's perfidy helped her build. I did not see it coming, while still in my body; it was as yet hidden in time's creases, even when looked at through the weave of Changing Woman's own loom. But now I am bodiless I see my vengeance is less important than the seed these two have sown. Properly nurtured, it will benefit all *Hataalii*, no matter their blood . . . and therefore, though it galls me to say so, it must be preserved."

"Now you've lost me, ma'am."

The old squaw hesitated, as though she almost feared to speak the words. "In that place," she said, at last, "we—*hexes*—can work together."

"That . . . just doesn't happen."

"Nowhere but there, dead-speaker. Do you understand me?"

And here Yancey took her own pause, jaw set, frankly afraid to admit that she really didn't.

"So you need us kept together," she said, instead. "Is someone coming to help us? One of your—*Hataalii*?"

"*Hataalii*? No. None could stay close to your red boy now, without risking death-duel. Yiska, the one my people sent to, would be a full medicine woman already, if only she could give up her love for weapons—born Diné, but she rides with the Na'isha of late, since all is fallen into confusion. A spirit-talker, like you in some ways . . . in others, not." She pointed out over the plain, now gone completely black. "She and her band travel quickly, but they do not have the capacities your red boy does. Expect them soon."

"And until then?"

"Delay, child. For as long as you can. I have other plans to set in motion; impossible things, under any other circumstances. But here, now, between the crack and that woman's 'New Aztectlan' . . . yes. I think they can be done."

"And if I do . . . what's in it for me?"

Grandma stepped back, blinking—the first purely human expression she'd worn. "Do you *bargain* with me?" she asked, then snorted again. "*Bilagaana*! You do not know even to respect the dead."

"Mayhap, but since you're not *my* dead, I owe you no particular restitution. Where I come from, we expect to be paid for our labour, 'specially if it could get us just as dead as you."

"What is it you want, then?"

This, at least, required no thought at all. "Sheriff Mesach Love, under my grip. Close enough for me to dig my muzzle in, 'fore I plug his dead heart."

A slow smile spread over Grandma's ugly face, darkly gleeful. "Ah, you are brim-full with hate, little dead-speaker. But in this, our wants coincide—for where *the* Enemy goes, *your* enemy shall surely follow."

"A preacher and the Devil—someone else's devil, anyhow." Yancey shook her head at the very idea. But Grandma gave only a shrugging *hmph*, unimpressed as any town biddy.

"*Nothing worse, in this whole world, than a bad man who knows his Bible.* So Asher Rook once said, faithless blackrobe that he is, opening his prayer book only to find fresh curses. And as for your Sheriff Love—if he was an honest enough man before Bewelcome's fall, now he dances to the Enemy's tune, knowing all along his newfound power comes from nothing good. But like you, he does not care who he treats with, so long as he gets what he seeks. And in the end, this will be his undoing."

"How so?"

"When he fought with your red boy at your wedding, the town itself was levelled, your husband and kin cut down. You yourself might have died, or either of the Pinkerton men. But did any blow one monster dealt the other do lasting damage? No, because each draws from the same source. It was *as though they fought themselves.*"

A sudden understanding lit Yancey's brain, from ear to ear. "Was the *Enemy* brought Love back, not God at all . . . he said as much, when Chess quizzed him on it. So—if there was some way to turn him back, to undo what Rook preached on his homestead, with Chess's syphoned-off hexation as connivance—"

"I knew you would see it, eventually."

"Not being stock-stupid? Thanks, ever so. But . . ." Here the flash gave out, leaving her once more in darkness. "What I don't know is how that even *could* happen, let alone how to make it come about."

"Of course not, for you are no *Hataalii*. How fortunate, then, you have at least spilled your blood to feed one."

The clear implication being: *Chess Pargeter could, given enough incentive—enough* sacrifice. *Just like he helped Rook turn Bewelcome to salt, he could now turn it back, on his own hook; get him there, pray into him extra hard, see what happens. Unless . . . no, wait . . .*

Something was scratching at her, some piece too jagged to fit. And then, all of a sudden, it dropped straight down into her mouth.

"Doctor Asbury says Bewelcome's a dead spot; no magic gets in, or out. Same for the Weed, and since that's what Chess gets his mojo from—"

Again, that fierce smile, darker by far than the lips which shaped it.

Your doctor does not know everything, Grandma said, without using her mouth, for extra emphasis. *Not even the half. Like too many* bilagaana, *he thinks this world works by machinery alone—that it may be solved like a puzzle, written down, re-written. Between the two, you would do better by far to follow our Enemy's counsel.*

Yancey bowed her head. "All right, then, ma'am; I'll do that. Thank you kindly."

The hex-ghost considered her a moment, and Yancey thought she could almost see something close to affection in those stone-obdurate eyes. But perhaps it was simply a reflection from one light source or another—strange things moving under the surface, a fish's maw in a murky pond, invisibly toothed. For the dead did not give up their secrets, ordinarily, without great pressure—more than Yancey had thought she'd brought to bear, so far.

But then again, perhaps the pressure just *was* great, all on its own, without Yancey doing a thing. Perhaps things really *were* just that bad for everyone, whether dead or soon-to-be.

By God, she sure hoped she was wrong, even as the insight bloomed. But the look on Grandma's face said otherwise.

Since you do not wish me to claim kinship, I will not, she replied. *But you should wake now, child. Things are already moving toward their conclusion.*

Above them, the dark sky had begun to boil, cones forming along the horizon—sheet lightning dervish-dancing attendance with such frenzy it threatened to let loose a near-mythic deluge. Yancey shivered in the ever colder wind, though Grandma did not.

And that feeling itself, nervishly incontrovertible, was what began to shake her free of the dream at last—to bring her steadily upwards, fingers clutching, legs kicking like a swimmer's.

YANCEY'S EYES OPENED, GUMMED deep with sleep, to find Geyer pulling her up and out of bed, while Morrow himself knelt to wrestle her boots back on—and oh, it was a cold joke indeed that never in a thousand years, before the Hoard's collapse, would she have thought to find her rooms full of strange men. The strangest of all, naturally, being Chess Pargeter, who stood peering out the window with both arms tight-crossed. It was still night by all appearances, maybe the earliest sort of morning, with that gathering storm from her dream-consult casting watery shadows, as though the walls themselves wept.

"You need to wake up now, honey," Morrow was saying, unaware how he echoed Grandma's words (while *He called me honey!* was all Yancey's sleep-stunned mind could yammer happily, in return). "Something's happened, and we've got to get on."

At the same time, Geyer looked 'round, the hand he wasn't currently using for Yancey's support falling to his weapon. Telling Morrow: "Boots, good. You see her coat anywheres 'round? Her gun-belt?" To Chess, meanwhile: "Where're *your* guns, by the by?"

"Gave 'em to her, this afternoon, for shootin' so well. Don't you boys *talk*?"

Yancey pulled herself further upright, shaking the last of her torpor off, along with Geyer's grip. "Move on . . . why?" she asked Morrow. "It's the Weed? Weed's found us?"

"Somewhat worse."

"*Worse?*"

But before he could elaborate, another voice intruded—from outside, borne on the roiling air, low and booming enough to mimic distant thunder. Sheriff Mesach Love yelling full-on into the wind, syllables breasting it like knives.

"Chesssss Paaaaaaargeter!"

Yancey staggered to Chess's side, trying her level best to figure exactly what he was staring at, but the darkness defeated her. While he stayed right where he was, surprisingly unsurprised.

Remarking to her sidelong, with admirable calm—"Never did think it'd happen, back when notoriety was a fair trade for bein' talked up in every bandit hole from here to Tlaquepacque . . . but I'm gettin' *damnable* sick of the sound of my own name."

CHAPTER FIFTEEN

BACK IN THE WAR, Rook had known men from the Ozarks who boasted of those mountains' caverns' glories: pink and green crystals force-grown in silence, pools of icy milk-white water, great fluted columns of salt-crusted stone and ropes of glassy quartz. Blind fish whose luminescent guts pulsed visibly under their scales. Though Rook half-dismissed such tales as typical soldiers' puffery, the images proved strangely persistent, prompting him to wonder what other beauties might lie underground, waiting to be discovered.

The meditation chamber Ixchel had dug out for herself beneath New Aztectlan's temple-pyramid, however—six-levelled, in either mockery or reverence of Mictlan-Xibalba's own interior path—revealed none of them. Having been told more than enough times how this journey's stages were supposed to go, Rook could easily map it out in his head. The Dark House, then the Rattling or Cold House, the House of Jaguars, House of Bats. The Hot House. The House of the Razor . . .

But no. Only the first and fourth were in any way true—empty darkness, supernal stillness punctuated by the steady drip of water. A rough-cut stone room hung with flapping, rabid rodents who plumed up and outwards, chittering, every sunset.

From a corner of their bedchamber, you touched a certain brick and watched a portion of the wall ripple backward, stone flexing like a curtain. The stairs thus revealed spiralled ever downwards, for a long, long time. And at the bottom the passage wore on, the track of a giant worm through rock, 'til it ballooned into a hollow underlying the great ziggurat where a sourceless shaft of light whipped ghost-columns of dancing dust 'round Ixchel-Ixtab-Yxtabay, Lady Serpent-skirt herself, lying death-still atop a black obsidian slab. Rook's breath hissed in his ears as he approached this altar, reflected off unseen walls—a wool-packed sound which reminded him of nothing so much as that other impossible place between worlds, the Moon Room. . . .

And all at once, what sprawled before him was someone entirely other: slight and lean and masculine-flat, naked and seeping, bloody from head to toe. Chess Pargeter, splayed and betrayed, empty ribcage cracked open and spilling organs like a blood-eagled Viking's, his absinthe-coloured eyes glaring green fire.

You son of a bitch, you went and left me behind.

Rook flung up his hands, gasping—then paused, half-expecting to hear laughter ridiculing such a foolish show of weakness. But Ixchel remained wrapped in breathless sleep, and there was no one else about to comment . . . not unless you counted ghosts like Kees Hosteen, who floated in the shadows just behind him.

Guilty conscience, Rev? The old man's shade asked, coolly.

Grimly, Rook forced himself forward, ignoring the commentary. He knelt before the altar, bowed his head, and murmured: "Suicide Moon, Lady of Traps and Snares, Your unworthy consort calls You home. Bestow upon those who crawl before You the gift of Your Presence."

The response *this* drew was utterly familiar, not to mention expected: a dry, soundless snort. *She really* buys *this kind'a ass-kissing, from* you? *Really?*

Not bothering to answer, Rook gestured him to silence, and genuflected again. "Mother of all Hanged Men, it is Your chosen son who calls You. Return, You who are also Tlazteotl, Coyotlaxqhui, Chalchiuhtlicue—"

An ague-clammy palm lay suddenly flat against his forehead, with no whiff of air to warn him. Rook froze. Standing above him, Ixchel smiled, her jade-flake teeth like thorns. "No need to stand on ceremony, my husband," she murmured. *"For it is written that a man shall leave his family and cleave unto his wife, and they become one flesh—"*

"Please don't."

She laughed, that same silver, plucked-sistrum shiver which once haunted his worst nightmares. "Very well, then." Her gaze swept to Hosteen's ghost, where he stood at Rook's side. "Who is it you bring leashed here before me, to do me worship?"

Hosteen, boggling: *'Scuse me?*

Rook raised a pacifying hand. "Kees, be good enough to fill in Lady Ixchel here about all of Allan Pinkerton's latest anti-hexological embellishments, would you?"

To her credit, the ghost-goddess listened silently while Hosteen did so, her barely inhabited skin giving off its usual icy glow, a lit corpse-candle. Allowing, finally: "But I fail to see how any of this should trouble me, or mine."

"They're on their way to Bewelcome right about now to test the damn thing out, probably on Chess. And from there, it's just a hop and skip over to *our* doorstep."

A boneless shrug. "He will defeat them. They have no notion of the forces they tempt."

"Will he, though? 'Cause much as I hate to say so, darlin', last time I looked he'd almost no notion of what he was juggling, either. And didn't particularly want none."

They both paused here, recalling in tandem Chess crying out in the wilderness, his dream's desert: *Goddamn you both! I will* not *do what I won't!*

"But he *must*," she said. "He is the Year-dancer, and the year is almost up . . . his very existence has shuffled the calendar, moving us too quick to stop toward the *nemotemi*, the Empty Days. That time when nothing should be done, because everything is possible."

"Well, you *could* try just tellin' him that, I suppose, and hope he jumps which way you want to push him." She threw him a cold black stare, which he was pleased to realize he now found hilariously easy to ignore. "But lay that by. How goes it down below? Manage to invite any more of those relations of yours to join the fray on our side—dig up a few that're awake, at least, anyhow? Or likely to become so?"

"Do not address me this way, Asher Rook."

"But how *else* should I think to address you, honey? Intimate as we've become, like you just pointed out." He returned her original smile, with interest. "So . . . they're all a-slumber yet, is what you don't want to cop to. Which, in terms of full-fledged gods currently in play, would leave it basically just you . . . and him. The Enemy."

"As it has always been."

"Well, in terms of steering Chess where he's wanted, your God K has a hellacious head start already. So might be it's time for us both to take a more direct hand."

She nodded, a queenly dip of her back-sloped forehead, from which dead Miz Adaluz's locks were creeping steadily back, restoring her original Mayan hairline.

"He must Become, completely," she agreed, "and whatever help we can give him to do so will aid all three of us, in the end. Yet perhaps we should not discuss such matters of true import in front of your . . . pet."

Oh, don't mind me none, Hosteen began, only to have her round on him in full terrible aspect, dragonfly cloak whipping out every which way, to fill the tomb with buzzing choir music.

"Silence, creature!" she snapped. "You have no right to insult me with speech at all, let alone so informally!"

If ghosts had shoulders, Hosteen would've been squaring his, fists rising like he thought the two of them were like to settle the issue with an all-out bar-brawl. *Silence your damn self, Jezebel! 'Cause with me, you're pretty much none for none: I ain't a hex, never took your Oath, and you already got me killed.*

"If you truly believe yourself somehow outside my power simply because you are *dead*, old soldier—"

Rook interposed, smoothly. "Kees . . . consider yourself dismissed."

The bottle appeared in his palm at a finger-snap, Hosteen's hair-smoke coiling aimlessly inside. Immediately, his former friend's sad imprint accorded it the entirety of his attention, like a pointing dog; Rook almost thought he could see the semblance of his grey mane rise, ruffling the way a vulture's crest puffs in anticipation of something nicely rotten.

I can go now, that's what you're sayin'? he asked, understandably suspicious.

"With my blessing."

Keep it. But—if you happen to get the chance, tell Chess—

Hosteen stole a look back at Ixchel, who barely seemed aware he hadn't left already. "Tell him what?" Rook prompted, gently.

A raft of emotions flickered 'cross the dead man's face, all equally truncated. At last, he merely shook his head, and sighed: . . . *nothin'.*

Rook cast the bottle down, heard it pop, and watched what little was left of his third-in-command blow out, a windless wind-gust, leaving nothing behind but those next uncertain steps along his future's bleak road.

'Round and 'round it goes, Rook thought. *Like a mill wheel 'cross the threshing floor. And the grain is ground into chaff, good and bad likewise, so one from the other is rendered indistinguishable.*

"I'm thinking we might leave Three-fingered Hank in charge, while we're both gone," was all he said out loud, however. "Him and his ladies, that is. Makes for four pairs of eyes watchin' our backs, 'stead of just the one."

"As you see fit."

"Should probably go up and tell 'em, then."

"Yes," she replied, utterly remote even as she reached for his hand, fingers cold as ever in this deep-set chamber pot of a place; rough with wear, slick with something he could only hope was sweat. One lavender fingernail seemed ill-set in its bed, peeling upwards, perhaps about to detach, so he covered it with his own lengthy index, fist engulfing all her stolen digits like a mitt.

My bed, he reminded himself, repeating the words incessantly, a caltrop rosary. And folded her to him, allowing the hiss-winged swarm-cloak to carry them both away.

YANCEY WAS WELL-BRACED to see Sheriff Mesach Love's leprous salten face again, once she, Geyer and Morrow followed Chess down to the saloon's front door. Yet she hadn't at all expected what Chess did next, upon that threshold: stopped short, one hand thrown up, warning them all back—a former soldier's gesture, ripe with uncharacteristic caution.

"You know how the Sheriff out there and me first met, Ed?" he said, not turning back, as contrast between harsh light outside and gloom within made a haloed silhouette of him.

Morrow hesitated, before admitting: "Read the Agency report, yeah. Like everybody else."

Chess nodded, raising his voice to include Yancey herself—even Geyer—in the juice of the tale. "He was gonna lead a posse 'gainst us, which meant we had to set an example, so's others wouldn't get similar ideas. And me, I'd've just snuck in and killed the fucker, but Ash Rook wanted to make a production of the whole to-do, 'cause that's how he's bent. So I went along, like I always did. . . ." He paused. "Still, only now occurs to me—at least Love really *believed* what he preached back then, dumb bastard. Was more'n willing to die over it to defend his kith and kin, which's pretty funny when you think about it, 'cause all of them was equal ready to die for *him*, too. That woman of his, who wouldn't leave his side no-how, no matter what he said—got saltified the exact same way, God's favour or no. And when she went down, she took their baby along with her."

And I laughed at her, while it happened, Yancey alone heard inside her head, Chess wondering over his own actions, as at a stranger's. *Laughed at all three of 'em, like my sides were fit to split.*

"You did him a terrible wrong, that's true enough," she agreed, out loud. Thinking back, at the same time: *And that'd be 'cause you're a bad man, I reckon—selfish and angry and unforgiving, if not downright wicked. Though you've suffered, too, and pain makes us all human, more or less.*

Yeah, well, he replied, internally, *that's the part ain't debatable, like I told the Rev, back when he was moral enough to care. So I still* don't aim *to debate it.*

Adding: "Hell, gal, think I don't know what-all I got to be sorry for? Used to be, though, I wouldn't have cared; I miss that."

"You can't just not *care*—"

"*I* can. Could." Here he finally turned, again seeming to address them together. "'Cause fact is, it don't do any earthly good to feel bad over what the gun's pointing at, when it gets to be time to draw. All that'll ever do is get you killed, right along with the ones you pump a bullet in."

Yancey drew breath to disagree, but Love already was bawling out his challenge once more: "Pargeter! You gone deaf or what, you heathen creature? Don't cower there in the dark with your entourage—come face me on this cut-rate Megiddo's field of battle, like the *man* you purport to be!"

"I'd tell you to come over here and say that," Chess called back, "but . . . hell, guess I can probably screw you up just as easy, you stay right where you're standing."

And with that, he stepped free, shrugging his jacket back from his belt as he strolled into range: sheerest habit, both holsters being empty. While Yancey stepped straightaway out behind him, fast enough that Morrow and Geyer were hard-pressed to follow—only to halt, mid-stride, when she saw what Love had brought along with him.

"Lord God of Hosts and all his angels protect us!"

She felt herself stagger, caught up one more time by Ed Morrow's welcome arm; clutched close to its warmth for comfort, finding none. Because—those figures arrayed 'round Love, just waiting— she knew them . . . *had* known them. They hung as if by hooks through the neck, all their weight dangling limp, blank eyes staring off to a dozen different quarters. And woven over it all, pallid flesh and dirty rigs alike—sewn through the muscle, covering bone where it showed, blossoming crimson pods at every cheesecloth-skinned joint—a net of Weed throbbed and knotted, a hundred thousand marionette cords grown thick and juicy, hideously animate.

Morrow tensed like he wanted to throw punches, but didn't know where to aim. "Oh, you crack-walking son of Goddamn Perdition," he said, in much the same tone Yancey'd just used.

Love simply shrugged, and spread his arms out wide—unconsciously cruciform—to encompass the army he'd brought along with him. Yancey's eyes followed them as though magnetized, helpless not to recognize faces, along the way: poor Sheriff Haish's remains, neck wound packed full of leaves that fluttered with each heave the Weed forced out of him, like soft green gills. Hugo Hoffstedt to his right, even worse—torn-off head held precarious atop his body, wobbling with each step, by tendrils wound 'round neck stump and skull alike. Mister Frewer, so cadaverous in life, now looked sucked almost dry; his head bobbed loose as well, seeming to float on a fan-like growth of fronds that strung 'emselves through jawbones and cheeks, rendering his entire brain-pan a ball balanced between invisible juggler's fingertips.

Everywhere Yancey looked, yet another of her murdered wedding guests stood repugnantly upright, Hoffstedt's Hoarders and Mouth-of-Praisers reforged by death into a more tenuous fellowship. On all too many of them, she saw livid slashes where they'd shed blood to feed Chess, far too late to benefit from their sacrifice. And finally, to either side of Love himself . . .

Both Yancey's knees gave out, so quick she barely felt them go—but this time, she caught herself in mid-fall and drew up back up sharply, hands falling to what were now *her* gun-butts. Using her own rage as fuel, she gladly allowed it to eat her anguish 'til nothing remained but a genuine will to shoot 'til she could shoot no more, no matter *how* many bullets it took to put these apparitions down for good.

And then you, Sheriff. I'll see you ground into parts so fine you poison the earth you stand on 'fore I allow any more of this *disgusting offence 'gainst life itself, Goddamnit.*

Her father, chest-hole thick with Weed that swelled and beat like a second heart; Uther, green filling out the grisly wounds deforming his half-pulped skull like a mask, right hand a sticky glove, hiding the hole Yancey knew had been blasted through it. He still wore the remains of the same suit he'd spoken his vows to her in.

And then, as if her recognition-spark had jumped the gap from living to dead, Uther Kloves' lone remaining eye slid snail-track slow 'round to hers, and blinked.

Nothing in there to call "alive", not any more. But God, oh *God*, all the same—

"They're *screaming*," she heard herself say, core-stricken. "Inside, deep down. Almost too deep to get to, for anybody but me."

Each in turn, the rest all cocked their heads, bringing their dead gazes to bear—Haish, Frewer, Hoffstedt . . . Pa. Their soundless shrieking went up forever like some Hell-made alarum, setting her whole skin to sizzling.

"Missus Kloves," Geyer said, "we can't hear a thing, really—"

"What's that to me? Point is, they're still here, some tiny part of 'em at least. And they just damn well *shouldn't* be."

Abruptly, Morrow turned on Love. "Who is it told you could do this, you bastard? Goddamn *God*?" She felt the rage beat from him like heat, in waves. "You lay those people *down* again! They're dead, and they got the right to stay that way!"

Love seemed unimpressed; Yancey thought there probably wasn't much could even startle him, these days. "But this isn't *my* doing, Agent Morrow—only miraculous Word I know's our Lord's, and unlike Reverend Rook, *I* employ it correctly. As Mister Pargeter's Enemy told me to tell you, this is all *his* fault, and only likely to get worse." Those dry eyes narrowed. "But see, I almost didn't need to, for he knows it already. Ask him to deny it, if he can."

Chess spat. "Why would I? Just admitted the same, not twenty seconds back."

Love nodded, as though this only went to prove his point.

"No," he repeated, "wasn't *me* threw these poor souls into purgatory. But if He's given them to me for use, I'll certainly point them in whatever direction He sees fit to lead me."

"That 'He' you're talking of—that wouldn't be God, now, would it?" Yancey hurled the words at him, hands settling into proper, draw-ready grip on her hand-me-down shooting irons. "*Our* God? Or don't you even pretend to be doing His work anymore?"

"What good would that do me? I'm damned no matter, Missus, by *this* malefic creature's hand." Indicating Chess, Love gave a smile so bitter his lips wrenched apart in sections. "Yet if I cannot pull myself back up, I can pull *you* all down here with me."

"I *knew* it!" Splitfoot Joe yelled from an upstairs window, startling all concerned. "I damn well *knew* it! You're the fuck-all bad-luck king, Chess Pargeter!"

"Oh, shut your pie-hole!" Chess shouted back, shutting Joe's window with a flip of one hand—then smashing the shutters closed over it, for good measure.

Love looked up, over Chess's head, and raised his gravelly voice, calling out: "That's sadly so, innkeep—you'll burn just as long and bad as this creature here, for harbouring him and his. Though if you turned against him, joined the side of Right for once in your miserable life . . . well, things, might go different. You have my word, as a man of faith."

Chess's bark of a laugh was oddly steadying, for sheer familiarity. "Damn, Sheriff. How almighty stupid you think that man *is*, anyhow?"

"Given he sold *you* room and board, even at gunpoint? I'll take my chances." Love shifted his gaze to Morrow; the big man paled, but didn't flinch. "Maybe you're thinking to buy the sinners dwelling here time to flee? You're soft enough to care more for them than yourself, I reckon, however much a waste it is." To Geyer, meanwhile: "And you, a Pinkerton man yet, standing in the whirlwind's path— allied with oath-breakers, demons and inverts. Will you die in their defence?"

"Stand by a friend, when I have to. Seems the thing to do."

Love shook his head. "Foolishness. You know Pargeter won't stand by *you*, any of you. Not if he thinks it'll cost him." Moving his dead, salt-white eyes back to Chess: "For that's all you've ever done, even before you met Rook. Kill and steal, and run when you're done. You leave nowhere better for your presence. Even the green growth you sow is poison, unnatural, as you always have been. Invert. Faithless. Worthless."

Chess's fists tightened; the power-mist about him drew in, like shoulders hunched against a blow. When he answered, his voice fair hummed, wound whiplash-tight. "I pay my way, Sheriff. And I pay my debts."

"When it suits you, yes. When the whim amuses you. And when you do pay, it's not in gold but with others' blood, or whorish sin— others' corruption, even if the means of it doesn't seem corrupt to you. Muddy everything, kick it all down and crow over the ruin . . . *real* companionship, love, *family*." Love's face warped, as though some torrent pulsed beneath it. "So prove you have some worth, Chess Pargeter. Your heretics would gladly spill blood to see you thwart me once again; refuse them. Face me *without* that Hell-borne potency, if you dare."

Chess said nothing for a moment that became so appallingly long, Yancey's stomach clenched up. *Oh, no, he can't be thinking—*

Luckily, however, he obviously wasn't.

"Opinions aside, one thing I *ain't* is a fool," was all Chess said. "And since I well remember how our last fight went . . . this time, we're gonna try somethin' different." He turned his head just slightly, not so's he had to take his eyes from Love, yet just far enough to throw a nod in Yancey's direction. "Missus Kloves, if you please."

Before he'd even finished, both guns were in Yancey's hands, muzzles already bead-drawn. The first bullet went straight through Lionel Colder's forehead, freeing a burst of jellied blood and pulped matter, along with something brighter—something nobody but her saw, feeling a whip-crack of grief-struck joy as that final soul-shred rocketed upwards. Uther went down a second later, double-load of loss and relief splashing past as his vine-ridden corpse crumpled. With both blasts, Love howled, clapping hands to his head like *he'd* been shot.

And then—the fallen bodies stirred. Dragged themselves clumsily back up, empty puppets now, tools turned weapons. Yancey kept the Colts level, unwavering.

Love straightened too, almost as slow. "Pointless," he rasped. "The dead cannot be killed. And I cannot be stopped by pain."

Yancey cocked the guns. "Maybe not. But it's worth the effort, just to try."

'Cause I sure do like that sound you make, when I do.

As she opened up again, a cold prism dropped over it all. Time slowed. Each trigger-pull felt leisurely, the possibility of missing a bad jape. Brains flew like sap. To either side, she Morrow and Geyer stepped to follow her lead. Their combined shot-storm chewed its way through the corpse army's ranks, knocking them spinning. Yancey cheered each released fragment as it leapt upwards. Though she realized she was weeping, she kept blasting away—watched Love, fallen to his knees, arch backwards in agony, his own screams lost in the deafening roar.

Then her pistols ran dry; a second later, Morrow and Geyer ceased fire as well. Yancey gasped, breast heaving, barely able to breathe for cordite stink. Grey-white clouds of smoke rolled away. The dropped Weed-revenants stirred still, a ripped-raw fan of carnage, fresh shoots knitting back together with dreadful inexorability. Yet Yancey only had eyes for Love's own feebly shifting form, her eyes swollen yet heart exultant.

Though it might well be her life's last act, by God, she had *hurt* him, finally—made him know pain for what he'd done. And that was worth something, certainly.

As though she'd spoken, Chess's eyes slid back her way, with no mockery at all in them for once, only respect. A look even one without her gifts might have read as meaning: *Yes, that's right. Now you see. Now you understand.*

As a few revenants made what was left of their feet, Love pushed himself up as well, even though his face's very shape was beginning to soften. Salt sprayed wet from his mouth, guttural words nigh-incomprehensible: "*Daaammnashun*," he croaked. "*Ghaaadzss Judzhh . . . ment—!*"

One half-melted hand lifted. At its cue, the Weed-corpses trudged on toward Chess, who watched them come.

"Not that I'm lookin' to *hurry* you," Morrow muttered, hand rising protective to Yancey's shoulder, "but it'd be useful as all get out, to know what you're fixed to pull from that trick-bag of yours, if and when."

Chess raised a finger. "Not just yet, Ed—wait a minute. Hold position."

"This ain't the front lines, Chess!"

"Ain't it?"

Even Geyer's hard-won calm was starting to crack. "Um—*no*?"

Chess paused, eyes gone abruptly narrow, like he'd spotted something off in the distance—then grinned broadly, half born killer's incipient battle joy, half boyish delight. "Here it comes," he said.

Here what *comes?* Yancey wondered, reloading frantically.

Seconds later, however, the question was answered: A vast hoof-clattering overbore the ringing in Yancey's ears, while a high-pitched whooping rose above, nearly drowning the general riot. At the valley's southward entrance, a bright yellow dust-plume mushroomed—and a gang of riders came streaming up over the edge of the rise, long black hair flapping, armed to the teeth with bows, rifles, pistols. Wide-set young men with fierce eyes sported head-scarves and war paint, riding saddle-less, using their knees to steer. At their head rode a yet more unsettling figure, to all appearances another handsome brave with a haughty, knife-blade nose, copper profile subsumed 'neath the powder-black outline of a grasping hand . . . 'til "he" drew closer, vest flaps twitching apart, and Yancey saw how *her* breasts moved free beneath her shirt.

This startling figure paused as her followers milled about her—
'til at last her gaze met Yancey's square on, cleaving fast with a
passion that quite took Yancey aback, which only made *her* smile . . .
and *wink*, too, by God. Like they were flirting 'cross a crowded room,
'stead of fending off the risen dead, or leading warriors headlong
into slaughter.

Ah, I see you, a voice said, at the same time—some mix of Savage
tongues sliding fast to echo-chamber English, setting Yancey's
already-spent head tolling. *Too young, untrained and out of bullets, as
the Spinner said you'd be. For you must learn to hold your fire 'til the anger
passes if you want to do true damage, little* bilagaana *dead-speaker.*

Like you, Grandma had said, in last night's dream. *But . . . not.*

And what *was* that name the old hex-woman'd called her by,
when she'd claimed she was sending aid? Started with a "Y" as well,
Yancey recalled.

From inside the building, another muffled yell from Joe, peering
through the shutters: "Aw shit, is that *Injuns*, now? Might as well set
the damn place on fire, then rebuild from the bottom up!"

"You see me tryin' to stop you?" Chess threw back.

But the woman on the ridge was already singing out a fresh cry,
eagle-harsh—"*Haaaah!*"—and urging her companions forward,
whipping out a tomahawk whose blade shone a rich and burnished
brown, fashioned from the jawbone of horse or stag. Her fellows
armed themselves similarly and set those dreadful weapons to
whirl and plunge, breaking over the Weed-creatures' back-ranks
at full gallop. Bone blades sheared through spongey new-grown
limbs, popped the lids off skulls, split spines without seeming to
break a sweat—mowing Love's army down wholesale once again,
with the quotidian, brutal efficiency of reapers cutting grain. Love's
resultant yells almost set Yancey to giggling.

"Just who *is* that sumbitch?" Morrow demanded, backing up, like
he thought he might get splashed.

"I think that sumbitch's a woman," Geyer replied, doing the
same.

Yancey nodded, gulping back her mirth. "Name's . . . Yiska, that's it. Navaho, though she rides with the Kiowa—the Apache, we call 'em. It means . . ."

". . . 'The Night Has Passed,'" Geyer filled in, snapping his fingers. "Hot damn! This might be a bit of luck, after all."

"Sounds like you know her pretty well, for a bitch you've never met," Chess said.

Geyer shrugged. "*Of* her, sure—Agency's got five hundred on her head in New Mexico alone. That squaw's the very definition of a Bad Indian; robs, scalps and burns wherever she can, 'specially if the Army's involved, plus cattle-rustling and gun-running. And that's without even goin' into those *other* rumours—how she's either a shamaness or somethin' too close to tell the difference, and wears those trousers 'cause she likes meddlin' with the ladies, to boot."

Here he had the grace to break off, no doubt suddenly remembering just who it was he'd been talking to, in the first place. But Chess surprised all three of them by barely seeming to acknowledge he might've had reason to take offence.

"A queer hex, huh?" He commented. "Can't have *that*, now, can we?"

More howls rose up, as Yiska's band pulled up sharp and swung 'round in the opposite direction, coming in so fast and close that this time Love was actually able to grab one horse by its mane and tug, hard enough to snap its neck. The stallion plunged dirt-wards headfirst, catapulting its unlucky rider free. But an odd updraft caught the Apache mid-fall, twitching him deftly free of gravity's trap—set him screwballing straight for Yiska, who swerved and flung her free hand out, all but plucking him from the air to slam down on her mount behind her. Her horse whinnied in surprised discomfort at his abruptly doubled load.

"*Cricona de mujere!*" the brave yelled back at Love as they swung by, just out of his range; Yiska roared with laughter. Love snarled, casting Chess a particularly foul look, to which Chess simply fluttered one hand, fingers waggling dismissively.

Two more braves pin-cushioned Love with arrows, which he ripped free, spraying bits of himself everywhere. But none bothered to target the Weed-creatures directly; instead, they stuck to sweeps and darts, slicing and hacking, leaning out dangerously far to strike blows and ducking clumsy swings and grabs in return, all with the casual ease of long-practiced technique.

They've done this before, Yancey realized. *Fought things like this more than once—had to've done. Which means . . .*

More dead than hers walked this land, now; anywhere the Weed had conquered, most likely. Which in turn made her think on just how far the Weed must have already spread, and feel sick. The horizon seemed to blur, sky gone tissue-thin.

Maybe these *were* Last Days, after all. Maybe Sheriff Love's terrible cry of "*Judgement!*" had been only the rawest of truths.

Right in the path of one galloping horse, vines exploded up out of the earth to whiplash about its legs, snatching the screaming stallion to earth so fast Yiska had no chance to intervene. Cartwheeled through the air, its rider somehow managed to come down legs first, with spectacular agility—might even have survived if he hadn't tumbled right into a good five or six of the Weed-things. They fell on him with the fury of starving wolves, all shambling lassitude utterly gone, and commenced ripping him skin from bone. His shrieks spurred two more warriors into a futile rescue attempt; they turned their mounts straight into the horde, only to go down too, creatures seizing at their belts, vests and weapons all at once. Blood burst over the frenzied melee, unleashing a cacophony of horrible tearing noises.

Yancey felt the rush of released power surge against her body, heading straight for its favourite recipient. She glanced back at Chess, and saw him swaying like a drunk, eyes narrowed until a green-glowing thread sewed his lashes together. Spilled blood was spilled blood, it seemed—no prayers necessary. Perhaps they never had been.

At Yiska's shouted command, the circling braves broke rank, peeling back from the spreading tide of grue-gorged Weed even as its avatars marshalled fresh speed and strength. In the centre, Love stood tall once again, his unmarked face almost human to look at—always saving the blind white eyes which followed the riders' path, of course, merciless as bone.

"They keep this up, they're only gonna get themselves butchered," Morrow said.

Geyer, preternaturally calm even in his fear, agreed wholeheartedly. "Yes. And I'd very much like to forestall that same eventuality in our own cases, Ed."

Back on the ridge, Yiska hauled her mount to a stop and twisted to catch Yancey's eyes again. That same tug wrenched at her mind, leapfrogging language: *We do what we can, dead-speaker, so you may do what you must. If the red boy is willing, tell him—*

But here Chess's own presence irrupted into the connection like steam-heat, hot enough it made Yancey want to gag.

Just tell me yourself, you snatch-lickin' squaw. Thick with blood-glut euphoria yet oddly calm, hazed by intoxication yet strong, so strong. Merely hearing it so close, with no particular effort invested, shot viselike pains through Yancey's mind; she could feel them echo straight through, into Yiska's. *Give* me *orders? You came here to help, then* help.

As you say. But will you listen?

I'm listening now, ain't I?

Challenge the salt-man once more; ask him to name a final ground. When he does, bring him there. We will follow, and quickly, for we know it already—the only place he may be beaten.

Yiska turned away, breaking the connection; Chess nodded, and let Yancey go as well, focusing his whole attention on the Sheriff. "Love, you too-dead shitkicker, you're wasting both our time!" With a single stomp of his boot, the earth seemed to ripple, half-seen waves shocking the Weed-army rigid. "Care to settle this right now?"

Love turned to look, Yiska and her braves immediately forgotten. "If you're so inclined."

"Then you name your place, and we'll finish it—together." Chess spread his empty hands, green light-haloed. "Just you, just me."

Your word's no good with him, surely, Yancey thought; *he'll throw the offer right back in your face.* But apparently, this was a day for surprises.

"Bewelcome," Love named, without a second's hesitation. "The very centre of your iniquity, Pargeter. As you'd already know, were you but honest."

The response came so quick that Yancey *knew*, with utter certainty, how Love had all along sought to herd Chess back to the scene of his crime, so's the Sheriff could take proper vengeance. Had all her suffering been nothing but a *gambit*? Her life, and theirs, no more than pieces sacrificed in some unspeakable game?

But Grandma knew as well, she reminded herself. *So . . . might be you've already done yourself a disservice right there, you bastard.*

Chess laughed, low in his throat. "Well, dead man, if you're itchin' to get your ass beat there twice, then *come on.*" He glanced back over his shoulder, half-saluting the poor, hex-belaboured drink-groggery behind him. "Thanks for the booze, Joe. Don't expect I'll be back this way again."

A dim holler, from inside: "Suits me!"

Chess laughed again, then raised one hand, twirling it elaborate. Immediately, the wind kicked up heaven-high, dust and stones flying fast. Yancey hunched instinctively into the shelter of Morrow's body, both unable to tear their eyes from Chess, or from the twister taking shape above his head.

Morrow had to bellow to make his voice audible. "So—what's the plan? We gotta . . ."

Chess shook his head. "Not 'we,' Ed."

"*Chess—*"

"I said *NO!*" The yell left Chess red-faced enough he switched to thought-talk halfway, with a pissed-off shake of his head. *Wanted me to care—well, this is that, God damn you. I've cost you enough already, and I don't aim to run my tab up further. So now I kill him or he kills me; either way, he's done, and you're safe.*

Tears poured down Morrow's face, torn from him by the wind,

along with a bafflement so deep, Yancey's heart twisted at the sight. *"Chess, you stupid son of a—"*

What'd I always say, Ed? Truth's no insult. I know what she was. And I think— Chess glanced at Love, then back. *—I know what I am, now. Or what I can fix to be.*

He lifted his hand, palm out, an unmistakeable command. *Stay, the both of you. Ride's been fun, but it's over.*

Chess closed his eyes, cyclone's roar intensifying, staggeringly loud; the air itself began to warp, writhe, and tear apart above his head. At the same time, Love approached, false clothes untouched. They locked stares, equally unimpressed: green kill-flash against level cataract-pale, two halves of one incomprehensible sum, inexplicably balanced. The moment hung, then broke as Chess hauled down hard, as if pulling a rope.

Blackness ripped open at the base of the twister's cone, a lightless void. Chess stepped toward it, Love at his side. Together, they lifted their feet over the threshold . . .

. . . as Yancey lunged forward, one arm hooked 'round Morrow's waist, for once. But found him already on the move, as though he'd read her intent, without knowing it.

They both grabbed hold of Chess's purple sleeves at once, holding tight. And the twister's fury skirled sky-bound, a vast hand made of air and anger which caught all four of them up in its palm, shaking them invisible.

THE TORNADO UNSPOOLED ITSELF, dissolving as it went; where it touched down, the Weed mounded high about fallen revenants and Kiowa alike, trembled, then collapsed. Dead flesh shrank and withered, sucked dry in an instant. Within moments, the battleground was nothing but a sea of gently pulsing Weed, what few remains could still be spotted ancient-looking, as if left over from some long-gone, unremembered tragedy. Geyer stared first at it, then back to the air-hung rift which was only just beginning to narrow closed, with dreamlike slowness.

A rapid clattering canter brought Yiska and her surviving band to his side, jumping the Weed incautiously as though it were mown hay. Yiska looked down at Geyer, who—ridiculously enough—had to work like a demon to keep his eyes from wandering to those unstrapped breasts of hers, one brown nipple poking careless through a rent in her blouse.

"Feeling wounded, Pinkerton man?" she asked, in English hoarsely accented, yet crudely accurate. "Sad, I mean—to be abandoned?"

He shook his head. "Happy to be alive, more like."

"Well, the sun has not set." Yiska grinned, so broadly Geyer found himself smiling back. Then she, too, glanced at the rift. "To ride the Bone Channel leads to death, in our stories."

"Always?"

"For someone. And yet—" the grin flickered back, lightning-quick "—there are few better ways to die than as legend." She gestured at a horse which wandered off to one side, its rider lost. "Mount up, Pinkerton man, if you dare travel in bad company!"

Geyer hesitated. The impulse to follow was near-irresistible. But he had other duties, long neglected during this side trip with Pargeter's haphazard crew, and now found himself freed—at last— to return to them.

You're my friend, Ed, always, he thought. *But you got friends of your own—and I think you maybe like 'em better than is useful, at this juncture, to the interests I seek to serve.*

The choice weighed painful enough on him that he said nothing, but Yiska seemed to read his decision anyway. "So, and so, and so. *Hiyaaah!*" This last cry went over one shoulder, to the others; they yodelled back, and she kicked her mount forward, plunging straight into that ever-closing Hell-smile, seeming to vanish even before the darkness covered her. One by one, the others galloped after her, hooting and hollering and waving their bloodied weapons, like boys racing each other to the best sport in all the world.

As the last of them barely got through, the air knit itself closed, fading away. Geyer stood alone, shaking his head in wonder.

A strange age, he thought, *that's for damn sure. And only bound to get stranger.*

Minutes later, he caught up with the wandering Kiowa steed, gentling until it seemed calm enough to mount—clumsily, without a saddle—and begin guiding it northward.

CHESS AND THE OTHERS were borne by competing currents, snatched and mouthed, torn headlong from one moment to the frenzied next—then expelled at the other end as if shot from a cannon, plummeting face-down into Bewelcome's town square. To every compass-quarter silent figures flanked them, hands upraised in unheard prayer, worn faceless and contorted. The wind moaned through broken walls, and a few sticks of what had once been the church where Sheriff Love hoped to preach his fiery Nazarene sermonage still flung, broken bone-sharp, to scratch at a blackened sky.

Yancey retched up a mouthful of salt. Beside her, Morrow crouched with both hands to his gut, like he'd just been nut-kicked by God's own boot. But Chess lit feet-first, like the cat he so resembled, and found Love already planted likewise upright, as though he'd grown there. Which, in a way . . . he had.

"Okay, then," Chess told him, trying to ignore the two idjits at his feet. "You 'bout ready to get it done? Or did you want to *pray* a bit, 'forehand?"

Love shook his head, neck grating slightly in its socket. And might have got around to answering, had a fifth—most unexpected—voice not rung out, from an entirely different direction.

"Gennnnnlemehn," it began, Scots burr blurred to the point of slurry incoherence. *"'Tis main guid tae sheeee yeh, boath, e'en in thessse unforrrrtunate, ehhhh . . . ciurrrcumstances."*

CHAPTER SIXTEEN

ALLAN PINKERTON, SELF-ELECTED king of all Diogenes Boys, stood at attention on his hex-powered train-car's back deck, with Songbird at one elbow, Asbury at the other—having made far better time than Chess or Love, probably for lack of distraction. With his unseasonable fur coat buttoned high enough to mask the bottom half of his face and a short-nosed pepper-box revolver in one hand, he loomed like some Russian bear drilled to stand on its back heels: a bit unsteady, a bit ridiculous. Completely threatening.

Songbird, predictably, seemed to glean both thoughts at once, plucking them deft as any pickpocket from Chess's ill-shrouded brain. And gave that crack-toothed little grin of hers, at his discomfort—same one made him want to slap her hard enough she'd lose a matching set of choppers on the other side, kiddy-moll or no.

"We have been waiting here for you, English Oona's boy," she told him. "This fool—" and here she nodded at Doc Asbury, who hung on Love's and Chess's every move with equal fascination, happy as a kid on Christmas, "—tracked you easily, plotting a course from that village you helped level. We did allow you *some* time to recuperate in between, at least . . . though, knowing you as I do, I do not expect gratitude."

"Apparation," Asbury murmured to himself, at the same time.

"Transit of objects from one place to another, through willpower alone . . . but not within the confines of some Spiritualist séance, no. And across *miles*, not mere inches."

Chess ignored them both, instead tracing the train's path with his eyes—a long trail of parallel gouges, scoring the earth like giant twin fingers drawn idly across a child's sandbox, which lead back from the vehicle across the white salt flat, the scrubby ground beyond, and out of Bewelcome's canyon-set valley entirely. For all Chess knew, they led straight back to the Pinks' home nest in Chicago itself, though he couldn't see this floating nightmare rolling down some fancy Eastern city street. Under the train's wheels, the gouge-tracks ended in sprays of sand and salt, pushed aside by some faint shimmer that twisted the eyes; the original wheels were still set inside, blurred as if by liquid glass. Chess's skin itched, watching it; had a *tone*, like a chigger-whine gone so high it could only be felt, not heard.

Six cars, and none of them an engine: a passenger carriage, black Pullman dining car, plus four rust-and-brown boxcars, the latter three padlocked tight. Chess could *feel* the power packed dense within these, cramped as contortionists wedged into an impossibly small space, invisibly a-smoke with misery. Around the fourth, meanwhile, a full squad of armed and uniformed Pinks had deployed themselves, shotgun and rifle muzzles levelled steady. It said something for the sick and fevered menace that boiled around Allan Pinkerton, where he stood on the train's caboose, that these men—Chess's favourite prey from childhood on—were one of the last things he'd noticed.

A moment later, he realized, with so little dismay it was a shock in itself: *Aw, hell. They look like Ed used to.* He tried to summon the old hot hatred—a hundred tales of authority abused, slight well worth killing over—but felt it slip right through his fingers, and soon found that even that failure wasn't enough to spur him on to new fury.

God damn, he raged to himself, *don't I get to keep anything I used to love doin'?!*

All the frenzied activity and panicked flight, all that forward-seeking heat and dust and motion, all the destruction left behind, and *this* was all it got him, faced off like he'd been in that Tampico hotel room six weeks ago, with the exact same suspects: Pinkerton, the Chinee bitch-witch, that idjit tinkerer with his gadgets. And poor Ed for collateral, along with young miss Yancey—would one of 'em go down, like Hosteen had? Both?

This *was* different, though; bone and blood told him so. The light itself seemed scarred, imparting a skew to everything, making the salten ground under his feet ring fragile as a canvas scrim. All of it *tilted* somehow, threatening to tear clean through.

I shouldn't be here, he thought. Then surprised himself by following that already surprising statement up with: *Nobody else should, either.*

"Mister Pinkerton." Ed staggered to his feet, bringing Yancey up with him. "You've no reason at all to credit my word, not now—but if you stick your oar in here, it'll cost lives don't need to be lost." He turned to Songbird. "And you, lady . . . you must've seen what went on in Mouth-of-Praise and the Hoard for yourself, in your scry-mirror; you need to *tell* 'em what they're facing. Before—"

"What we *face*, Mister Morrow," Pinkerton's tar-and-gravel voice boomed out, making an obvious effort to regain intelligibility, "is renewed war wi' Mexico, over the devastation of their capital by yuir invert sorcerer allies! Do ye no' ken how fierce President Johnson is tae avoid another conflict, wi' our own nation still in tatters?" Pinkerton leaned forward, febrile eyes ablaze. "I've been given carte blanche to deal wi' them as I see fit—to purge this hexslinger-birthed rot from American soil. The garrison at Yuma has already been ordered in, plus a full detachment of the Treasury's Secret Service Division; the Army's strength is mine, too, for the asking. We'll start here, and then move on tae Rook's hex-haven, razing as we go."

"Johnson? The man's a fool and a double-crosser, as you well know, from his conduct during Wartime!" Though Morrow aimed his words at Pinkerton, Chess could tell he meant them for the men below, whose eyes had begun to flicker sidelong, looking for certainty in their fellows, and not finding it. "Don't let yourself be *used*, sir. Don't throw yourself—your men—away."

From Pinkerton, no response at all; from Songbird, only a delicate yawn. But from Asbury—a slackened jaw, cut with dismay. Chess watched him look Pinkerton up and down as if truly seeing him for the first time, and saw that dismay deepen.

"A man might truly believe ye meant only the best for us, Edward, after all," Pinkerton scoffed. "But then again, seems ye've found an innocent of yuir own tae protect." The collar shifted, hidden smile beneath rendered awful by exclusion, as his regard fell on Yancey.

Songbird snorted. "No innocent, this one, Pinkerton-*ah*. She has her own minor witchery, steeped in Pargeter's taint. Not that it is any match for mine."

"I don't recall giving you permission to speak for me, little girl," Yancey told her, coldly. To Pinkerton: "Experiance Kloves, sir; widow to the Marshal Uther Kloves, of Hoffstedt's Hoard, who gave his life against—that thing, over there." She indicated Sheriff Love, who just stood there with fists clenched, fuming at the interruption. "So I think I've as much right to a say in this matter as any of you."

Pinkerton's brows might have lifted just a notch, while Asbury's cheeks reddened further. "We . . . we deeply regret the suffering visited upon you, Madam, as on all unwittingly placed in the path of this chaos," the Professor said, weakly. "But surely, that only shows you how Messrs. Pargeter and Rook *must* be contained, before they cause more of the same, to others."

"Aw, name of Christ Jesus, stop lumpin' me in with Ash Goddamn Rook!" Chess shouted. "We ain't joined no more, at the hip or elsewise! I'd spill his blood sooner than any of you!"

Pinkerton, with high disdain said, "Yuir arrangements are of nae interest tae me, Pargeter. Will ye cooperate peaceful, or must we assert oursel's? An answer is all I require."

But it was Love who replied, finally roused to action.

"Then I believe you'll all just have to *wait your turn*, to get it," the Sheriff said, and whipped eel-quick to the front of the line, past Chess, Yancey and Morrow alike; his passage's gust whipped up salt-crystals in every direction, drawing blood and breath, while Chess and his companions just stood fast.

'Cause we're used to it, Yancey thought, with grim humour.

"We're taking Pargeter in, Sheriff," was all the prime Agent replied, however. "That is the fact of it." Adding, as if he'd only that moment remembered: "And we've a raft of charges tae append to you as well, while we're at it."

"I'm surprised you use my rightful title."

"Why not? They've no' elected anyone else in your stead, since Pargeter and Rook laid ye low."

"No, 'cause there's none left to vote on the matter. And where was this private army of yours when Satan's minions made sure of *that*, I wonder?"

From Asbury, hastily: "Mister Pinkerton can't be expected to maintain a presence in every homestead, surely, Mister Love! Besides which, it was your own . . . misfortunes which caused him to send to the Department of Experimental Arcanistry, leading to the engagement of my services."

"To do what? Take reckonings, *measurements*, while my flock wears away by degrees?"

Asbury blanched, unable to keep his eyes from jittering to a nearby triplicate entanglement of what had once been men, uppermost of whom Chess thought he recognized: Same fucker'd held him down and broke his nose for him while the others laid on the boots, before Rook finally joined the party. Now he was missing half his own beak, left-hand eye socket hollow. And the oddity of it was, though Chess would usually have had to kick himself to rouse even a semblance of sympathy, he now found he felt . . . quite the opposite.

Like I'd have to work hard not *to care 'bout what that sumbitch brought on himself,* he thought, panic rising in his empty chest.

"No' our charge," Pinkerton threw back, unmoved. "From all

reports, I'd've supposed ye a man well capable of looking after yuirself, let alone yuir kith and ki—"

"You shut your damnable mouth."

The sound slid in, so low Chess felt it in his joints and skull-plates, a sickeningly deep roar. Without thinking, he put forth his own power, rooting himself to the ground; Morrow and Yancey, not similarly anchored, clung together, swaying. The hex-run train jolted, cars sent crashing up against one another; thin-voiced cries skirled out from inside locked boxcars. Pinkerton gripped the caboose railing hard as Asbury lurched beside him, wide-eyed. Songbird, meanwhile, merely lifted off, scarlet-lacquer parasol shifting neatly to block the sun as she hovered mid-air a few inches above the planks, staring down.

And the Pinks, all thirty or so, howled rage that turned swiftly to terror as waves of salt—liquid-flexible yet still stone-hard, and heavy—came flowing up their boots and legs, encasing them 'til only their fear-maddened faces remained free. Then put forth yet another delicate membrane at Love's command, and sealed over the men's mouths, silencing them.

"There," the Sheriff said. "That's better."

Between the paralyzed Pinks and Chess's fellow travellers, three mighty columns reached high, then bent over, ends splintering to a dozen sharpened points—each of which bore down on a different target: Pinkerton, Songbird, even Asbury, now gone a truly sick-looking grey.

"You will *not* interfere with my appointed retribution," Love stated. "Your men have no power over me, and your allies, Mister Pinkerton . . . like yourself . . . stink of hexation, as the Devil breathes sulphur. Whereas I have divinity at *my* back. So here's the choice, plain and simple: let Pargeter and me settle this, and live— or interfere, and face God's judgement."

Songbird said, "A god, yes. But which one?"

Love's face tightened in a snarl. Perhaps only by contrast, he looked strangely more human than Chess had seen him, since— well, before.

"*Any that'll answer*," he ground out, eyes roaming from figure to motionless figure. A faint skitter of powdered salt blew harsh over the granulated crystalline ground. "This is *my* place. I raised this town. My people, my wife, my boy stolen from me, hand over fist—" His ash-and-grit voice almost broke, but not quite. "If such reckless injury was wrought upon Union Pacific, would you do less? No. So I *will* have full measure. I will have what I am owed."

In front of him, the air shimmered. For a moment, Chess almost feared *he* was crying, and felt aghast—but no. It was more as though Chess could see time itself peel back, by five years, by ten. The town it had been, unpolished, but reared with dedication; Love and his woman Sophy, hugely gravid, laughing over their work; the empty plain of grey-green scrub and grass, waiting for Love's arrival. And then . . . something else again, *incomprehensibly* old, a wild moonscape of shale and sandstone that knew no human footfall at all roared softly with a phantom slosh and moan, melting wax-cylinder imprint captured from the memory of some aeons-gone sea.

Over and above one another the images wildly slid like shuffled cards, the heart of this gutted place anchoring everything to its dead centre. Past overlaid present in bare, dark-on-dark fragments, atavistic shadows reared up behind muslin hung to dry, lizards bigger than grizzly bears that jostled and snapped at each other, with nothing on what passed for their minds but kill-or-be-killed carnage.

It was this *place*, itself. This place had always been weak, a sore in the world's hide that never wholly healed, only broke open again and again beneath time's ceaseless friction. The crack through which both light and darkness seeped in.

As Love turned to face him, Chess wondered whether the Sheriff had *chosen* it for that same weakness—knowing he heard his God so much clearer here, yet never thinking to ask why.

Or maybe it'd just been Goddamned shitty bad luck.

The laughter which exploded out of him caught even Chess by

surprise, stopping Love flat in his tracks. Even Songbird frowned.

"*Silence!*" But Love's cry was too cracked for real power, his clenched fists impotent. "You *will not make a jest* of this! His Judgement—" As Chess drowned him out with another helpless squall, the man's bloodless face looked fit to explode. "STOP *that!*" he screamed.

"Muh . . . *make* me, ya fuckin' puppet." Chess had to brace his hands on his knees, whooping deep gasps. "Still think you're some kind'a holy vessel? God's Left Hand? Only if his Right don't know what you're doin'!" Eyes swimming, he forced himself to straighten. "You want payback, then take it in your own name, and spare me the God-botheration. Hell—" He grinned, and Love visibly recoiled. "I always figured whoever took me down, it'd be someone had good reason to be pissed—and you do, for sure. So just end it. Now."

For half a second he thought Love might actually refuse.

The sheer unlikeliness of that idea turned to laughter once more—an uncontrollable gout of it—and Love's expression changed, accordingly. The need to be morally in the *right* was gone. Only the need to hurt remained.

Chess watched with an almost euphoric detachment as a fourth spear-headed limb of salt burst up out of the ground, circling to orient its razor-sharp tip upon him. *Come on, you bastard*, he mouthed, *come on, come on—*

NO.

Yancey's warning struck him like a slap; he spun, and her eyes met his, as angry as Love's had ever been. *I haven't hurt him how he merits, yet*, she complained, lips unmoving. *So if you won't fight of your own choosing . . . I'll damn well* make *you fight!*

And with that, the reckless bitch sunk her teeth into her own wrist.

"Jesus!" Morrow yelled out, as blood welled up and spattered down, soaking swiftly into the salt-crust, and Chess felt the power explode back into him, hitting every internal pleasure point at once. Head thrown back, he was unable to prevent the sheer brutal ecstasy of sacrifice from swirling into him; he felt green light flare from his pores, reflecting off every salt-crystal, as Love's spear broke apart like icing sugar. And the feeling only got better when Morrow snatched out his knife, cut his own palm open and wrapped it 'round Yancey's wound, a flesh tourniquet.

Up on the train, Pinkerton's eyes caught that same green glare and drank it in, his unwieldy coat going up like tinder; heavy wool was scorched by green fire, crumpling away from Pinkerton's body like parchment. Eyes wide, Songbird spat some incomprehensible Chink oath and lofted herself even further, safe out of reach, power-halo cocooned. And Chess just stared, understanding at last what he'd sensed all along—why that feverish power bleeding off Morrow's ex-boss had felt so familiar.

Because . . . it was *his*.

That last moment of the Tampico confrontation came back, daguerreotype-sharp: cross-drawing his empty guns and firing all the same, loaded at a blink with nothing but spellcraft, and driven by the same instinctive rage Bewelcome had fallen to. *Breaks outta me and busts through you like the ball I made of it*—Chess could almost *see* it happening—*then dashes itself to pieces, same as any other ordnance, leaving a shred of itself behind in the furrow . . . a seed.*

Taking the top off the Scotsman's ear had birthed an unnatural, gangrenous infection in its wake, eating into body and mind alike: Chess's magic, worming its way into Pinkerton first as something fought, then embraced. Hexation treated with hexation, breeding a taste for the same. Thus making this—disease of his the issue, come to term in a storm of pure man-witchery.

From that one moment had come all the lunacy that followed: paranoid mistrust of his own underlings; support for Asbury's projects, from mass-produced Manifolds to this train itself, driven by hexes chained up like Roman galley slaves; the mad determination to destroy any obstacle in his path. The obsession which had brought him here, setting him on a collision course with Ash Rook, the Rainbow Lady, Hex City.

All my fault, Chess thought, and Christ, he was so tired of that not-so-simple truth. *Just like every other Goddamn thing.*

Pinkerton's coat was gone, the collar concealing his face burnt away. What lay beneath was awfully familiar, in both senses.

Chess remembered his Ma, droning away—*Oh, the drip's bad enough, Christ knows, or them itchin' bloody warts, but the Germ? The French Complaint? Might as well save up for a bullet an' shoot yerself, do yerself a friggin' favour. 'Cause that's one case where the cure really* ain't *worse than the disease, by 'alf.*

Lion-faced, lips and nose all blurred together with sores, an inward-seeking pit that ruffled with each breath; his spit welled up silver, like Pinkerton had taken the mercury dose already. Ore cinnabar rimmed his single nostril, furled bat-snout lips, the exposed top teeth. And those piggy little rogue-elephant eyes, so full of rheum and ire . . .

Asbury made the single most ridiculous sound Chess'd ever heard a grown man let fly, a squeak muffled behind both fists—all but threw himself back against the railing, as if trying to push his way right through it. Seeing his reaction, Songbird whirled in mid-air, red skirts belling, and though she made no sound, her shock showed equal-fierce: her shield-aura blazed up, too bright to look at. Morrow took a stumbling step backward, jaw similarly slack; this time, it was Yancey's turn to support him. To knit her hand with his, and let their blood fall where it might.

"Boss . . ." Morrow rasped.

"*This* is what yuir comrade made of me, Edward." Gluey decay permeated Pinkerton's voice, yet it rang with good cheer, as though abandoning any attempt to still sound human was purest relief. He was bigger than he'd been, too, shirt all but buttonless, braces strained over swollen shoulders. "Dinna fret, though—it's no' nearly so unpleasant as it appears. I barely sleep; my perceptions are clearer, keener. And I'm strong now, Edward—*so* strong, it beggars belief!" Ham-hands closed on the ironwork railing before him, and tore it out of the caboose's frame with a screeching snap. Contemptuously, he cast it down, then hopped out after it. With one fist, he smashed the base of the nearest salt-spear; it burst like cheap porcelain, gone to dust and powder in an instant.

Sort of behaviour'll sure change your image of a man, no matter how "good" you reckon 'im, Chess mused, seeing how the salt-trapped Pinks' eyes bulged, on finally glimpsing their leader in the altogether. *Or maybe 'specially so, you were dumb enough to think that well of anybody, in the first damn place.*

Love stepped forward. "Thought as much," he spat. "You wish him kept alive because his Devil's might sustains *you*; you crave it all, for yourself. By God, that shall not be!"

Pinkerton laughed, gooily. "I'll concur with Mister Pargeter in one thing, Sheriff: God plays nae part in these proceedings. And so . . ."

Faster than Chess would have believed such a bloated, heavy thing could move, Pinkerton's bunched fist swung at Love's jaw— only to slap cold into Love's upflung palm, and stop. Green lightning billowed, backlashing into Pinkerton, who roared in agony; surprise flattened his already truncated visage into something truly ludicrous. As Love clamped down with all five fingers, the salt that was his substance flowing halfway up Pinkerton's arm, his opponent's mass began to shrink, collapsing. In turn, Chess felt that awful pull in his own guts, as Love's dead essence drank up the power of Ed's and Yancey's blood with greedy delight.

Instinct took control, prompting a near-fatal mistake: Chess flung out both his own hands, double gun-stance style, and spasmed as the power-drain's ripping agony only redoubled. Love turned, slow as minerals forming—ground-salt rippling upwards along his body, coalescing into plates and spikes that sheathed him like whitish-grey slabs of armour, a lime-crusted stalagmite grown head-high in seconds—and smiled.

"Foolish," he remarked, probably to both of 'em. "Yet not unexpected."

This loss of contact seemed to snap their link; the lightning died, and Pinkerton dropped back onto his ass with a grunt. Chess buckled to all fours, gasping for breath. At once, every ounce of strength was gone from his limbs; it took all the effort he could manage to keep from simply falling flat on his face. He felt the ponderous, trudging steps as Love came closer, 'til two encrusted boots finally placed themselves before him. Even as he watched, their salt and the ground's flowed into each other, eddying back and forth.

If there was any sympathy at all in Love's dead voice, Chess was deaf to it. "Here is your sin, Pargeter—all around you. Bitter shall be your portion."

Those too-long fingers passed over Chess's face, stroking scratchily along his lips. A sting struck his tongue, and suddenly he was heaving so hard he couldn't breathe. Black and stinking blood, sparkling with tiny crystals, splashed over the ground in a foul flood, hollowing him out. He spewed and spewed, vision darkening.

IT FELT LIKE ANOTHER tornado, suction-rush tearing strength out of Yancey in hot spurts, each surge of weakness matching one of Chess's. No sense to it, especially since the ragged bite she'd taken out of her wrist was already closing over, not losing near enough blood to provoke such a sense of shock. But this could never be about mere flesh; it was something in the place, working against her, sucking at her like a sink-hole. A quicksand of salt.

She was on her knees before she knew it, fighting not to get up but to keep from keeling over, tongue ragged, tasting blood. So cold. *Not in front of Love*, she prayed. *Don't go letting him see you falter.*

And then Ed Morrow's strong arm encircled her, warming her, if only for a second. He bent close, contorted face all a-blur, though she couldn't tell if the water was in her eyes, or his. "Yancey, honey," he whispered, "you gotta cut free of this, *please*."

She shook her head, waved a feeble hand at the knot of monsters triangulated upon each other, kitty-corner at all angles of Bewelcome's disaster-emptied main square. "'M . . . part of it, like them . . . all together. *Linked.*" So clear to her now, the warp and woof strung between all three men: power, immediate and inevitable. A literally fatal web. "So maybe this's . . . *s'posed* to happen."

"Not you." It came through grit teeth. "Goddamnit, not *you*, too!"

"Let it ride, Mister Morrow," said Love, of all people, only his face still showing semi-human through a wealth of salten plate; he tossed his head at Chess, like he still had even one pigtail worth flapping. "She chose her end, by standing with *this* monster. It's time for you to walk away."

Morrow said nothing; his face didn't even change. But Yancey *felt* his decision, a punch to the heart—tried to grab at his arm, but slipped her purchase. At the same time, Morrow's knife slashed down, twice over: once to rip the sleeve, once to lay open the big vein in the forearm. More blood, steaming fresh, to water this unholy ground.

And what crop might yet grow, thus irrigated?

He raised his voice, then, too—and Yancey knew she must be close to crossing over some final threshold, because it seemed she could hear *other* words beneath his, not even in English. Yet clear enough, for all that . . . clearer by far than the tumult gathering 'round her, massive swirl and grind of some salt-sandstorm looming up between sky and ground, blocking the sun so it shrank pinhole-dim.

"*Nomatca nehuatl, ni*   (*I myself, I, Quetzalcoatl,*
            Quetzalcoatl,

   niMatl / ca nehuatl niYaotl,   *I, the Hand / indeed I,*
                        the Warrior,

niMoquequeloatzin—atle ipan   *I, the Mocker—I respect*
            nitlamati . . . ."   *nothing. . . .)*

"*Tla xihualhuian, tlamacazque!—*   (*Come forth, spirits!—*
   tonatiuh iquizayan, tonatiuh   *from the sunset, from the*
            icalaquiyan . . . ."   *sunrise. . . .)*

> "*in ixquichca nemi*   *(anywhere you dwell*
> *in yolli / in patlantinemi . . . ."*   *as animals / as birds. . . .)*

> "*in ic nauhcan*   *(from the four directions*
> *niquintzatzilia ic axcan yez . . . ."*   *I call you to my grip. . . .)*

> "*tla xihuallauh, Ce-Tecpatl,*   *(come forth, knife,*
> *tezzohuaz titlapallohuaz—"*   *to be stained with blood—)*

> "*Tla xihuallah.*   *(Come forth.*
> *Tlatecuin."*   *Cross my path.)*

Without wondering how, she knew the words were pouring into Ed from elsewhere, and that he did not care. She felt the land beneath the salt rouse to Ed's sacrifice with ten times the strength it had for hers—unsurprising, really; she'd spilled blood for spite and fury, to drive Chess into battle, while Ed's had been for love and grief, out of a determination to save lives.

(*Balance, granddaughter.*)

The ground quaked, juddering them both painfully. Dull reports echoed, crack of dry ground, stone fracturing, snapping. With crashes like dropped clay pots, the salt cells binding the Pinkerton agents broke; to a man, they bolted, shouting as they fled.

A wall of green thrust up, vine and Weed-tangle slamming through the valley's topsoil. It blossomed in a perfect circle, tendrils twining frantically inward but unable to cross the salt-lip, straining to reach Chess 'til its overspill latched onto Pinkerton's hex-train—probably the largest other source handy—and began drawing fiercely on *its* power. It swarmed monkey-quick over the carriages, kicking up sparks and bursts of lightning like a firework show gone all askew. The train shuddered and crunched down, its enchantment-driven wheels suddenly gone the way of all spells.

All dignity forfeit, Asbury screamed like a colicky baby. In turn, Songbird let loose with a furious kettle-shriek, terror only thinly overlaid with anger. The force-grown crackle of leaves nearly drowned the Weed-flowers' chitter, a flock of maddened birds intent on devouring whatever might be unlucky enough to lie in its path.

Yancey felt Morrow pushing harder, pouring all of his determination to save her—and Chess—into the sacrifice. The potency at work painted everything in ghost-shapes; all she could do was knit her grip with Ed's and haul all the harder, throwing a last whisper of thought Chess's way: *God damn you, you irritating little man, get* up.

No response—not audibly. But amidst the dead white glow of the salt, her spiritualist's lens showed her Chess, bright green and red with blood, his shoulders shaking. And she knew that he was laughing.

Seconds later, the entire Weed-mess let fly a mutual blast of pollen, every seed pod rupturing at once and hurling its cargo into Bewelcome's air. Chess sucked in a deep gasp, swallowing it down like burning whiskey. Thus sustained, he plunged his hands down, tearing into the crust of salt, rendering bloody meat-gloves of them in moments, though the hurt of it seemed to register only briefly before he found raw soil, and buried them to the wrists.

As with the best of Chess's black miracles, a soundless pulse went off in all directions, turning his whole skin the pulp-green of a cut stalk. Love's remaining spear-pillars shattered under their own weight, while great gouts of crackling lightning came off the train's locked boxcars; the wood split, heavy planks splintering like balsa, iron chains gone to rust and dust in an instant.

Yancey couldn't quite make out the figures who spilled from the wreckage—some alive, some grievously injured, some beyond all pain—but she knew what they were: hexes, trapped in some unimaginable way, kept from feeding on one another by Asbury's black science and forced to drive Pinkerton's train where he would, defying geography. Those who could rabbited fast as the Pinks before 'em, stumbling toward the mouth of the valley, earth still a-rumble beneath their feet: more screams rose up, weak with despair. Beneath them, pounding thuds, growing steadily louder. Nearer.

But moments before the first of the escapees reached their goal, he came skidding to a stop, backpedalled frantically, urging those following behind off. Because of this concern for his fellows, or perhaps because he stood (all unknowing) on the edge of a sheer and sudden drop, whoever-it-was couldn't see the monstrous shape which reared up right where his eyes had formerly rested 'til it darted its huge head down and *bit him in half*, snuffling him up like a dog with a bit of cheese.

"What . . . ?" Morrow breathed.

To each side of the valley's entrance, great beasts pulled themselves free of the stone like downed birds from mud, aeons-dead bones clothed anew in flesh, albeit incomplete and rotting. Green fire outlined their eye sockets. A dozen of them? A score? Yancey felt their tremendous weight pound the earth beneath her. Reptilian, elephantine, creatures of an older sun, these thundering lizards hammered toward Bewelcome's heart, their horns and teeth all set for Sheriff Love.

Cool-headed to the last even when set in sorcerous mayhem's path, Love took advantage of the rout to snatch up Pinkerton's discarded pepper-box, discharging it straight at Chess's face. But Chess merely opened wide and swallowed the shots down whole, not even bothering to gulp.

"Lose more bullets that way, don't ya, Sheriff?" he asked.

"Oh, don't *dare* mock me, you nasty creature. Sinner from a line of such, born gallows-fruit—"

"All that, yeah; still not ashamed. So what's your point?"

A sigh. "Only this . . ."

Love closed his eyes, bringing his fists together. His lips moved. Yancey could hear nothing over the beasts' approach, but the words went straight to her brain: *For one last jolt of strength I ask you, who have named yourself Chess Pargeter's Enemy; be you angel or no, fallen or otherwise, I beg your favour.* The prayer went tumbling into that void Yancey could feel yawn wide, beyond this world. . . .

And something answered.

Behind Love, above him, the air turned smoke-dark. A figure took slow shape, intangibly immense, shoulders wrapped in a mantle of blue fire. Its face remained featureless, for which Yancey, her skin crawling, offered devout thanks. Love bowed his head, letting this phantom form flow 'round him; his own seemed to blur and stretch accordingly, as though viewed through water. Until he towered erect once more, furiously large, long lines dreadfully magnified: Sheriff Love gone almost entirely, leaving some new creature entirely— neither the Enemy nor Love, but some obscene mix of both—to stand, swaying slightly, in his place.

Then he lunged forward and dealt the creature leaping upon him a stunning blow that knocked it sideways, popping its jaw clean off. Yancey felt the punch in her own mouth—sheerest agony, though it meant she had nothing left with which to scream. So the undead creature screamed for her, 'til Love wrung its too-long snake-neck like a chicken's. Some vital current of power snapped; the thing collapsed, disintegrating as it went, reverting to fossilized bone dust. Love did not stay still to watch. He spun, and charged another creature, seizing it by two of its three horns and forcing its nose deeply enough into the ground to suffocate it. Smaller monsters swarmed him; he shrugged them off, insultingly casual.

Pinkerton lay curled into a foetal posture, shuddering spasmodically, jerking with each impact; Chess joined him, staggered with the shared pain of his grisly satellites. Ed, too, curled inwards—half-hiding Yancey, half attempting to hide himself *in* her, as his blood-loss finally exacted its price. It took all the little strength Yancey had left to lift one arm, touch his cheek.

If this was the end, right here, no one could say they hadn't fought it every damn step of the way.

CHAPTER SEVENTEEN

THE BLOWS HURT, AND then some. Chess could feel power torn from him with each new strike—but in a strange way, this was more bearable than anything that had gone before. One thing Oona Pargeter's only son knew how to do was take a beating.

So he let himself flex on the backhand, loosening his focus, and let his mind hiss like hot metal in the tempering quench, spinning his conjured pets 'round Love in a distracting flurry. He could draw this out, but to what point? No matter how much blood Ed and Yancey spilled for him, Love's emptiness would eventually devour it all, choking down Pinkerton and him alongside; the man seemed made to be his natural undoer. Yet this here was the only place Love could be put down, or so that Sapphist Injun—Yiska—had claimed. If hexation wasn't the answer, what was?

A voice came back to him then, brimstone-hoarse, once beloved, warning: *Magic ain't a gun, Chess. Can't treat it as such, or it'll blow up in your hand.*

Power he had in spades, so it wasn't that. What he needed was *knowledge*.

He didn't bother trying to form clear words; couldn't've kept them together under this sort of pressure, anyhow. Instead, he flicked a sharp mental slap 'cross the inside of Asbury's temples, hard enough to bust his hysteria. Minds met—Chess had a dim sense of labyrinthine lattices, incredibly complex, though choked with terror and confusion—and the clash threw up a memory: the Tampico hotel room, where Songbird's and Asbury's different expertises combined to trump Chess's dead-god mojo hand.

As predicted, Asbury seized on the idea, a lifeline in a drowning sea. Spinning, he shouted: "Miss Songbird, listen; this is simply the same magic you once countered, writ larger, all connected—and therefore it *can* be stopped, if the circuit be broken somewhere . . . anywhere!"

"Foolish old ghost!" she shouted back, shield-muffled, her halo gone thick to stave off flying bone shards. "I would as soon be able to stop the Yang-t'se in full flood! Why should I even try?"

Asbury hesitated, 'til his eyes fell on Pinkerton's fallen form. "Because you're the only one who knows how—and you've taken Mister Pinkerton's money."

Songbird closed her eyes tight—then lofted herself yet still further up, as Love round-housed the last of Chess's whatever-they-were so hard it exploded. Twisting to face Chess direct, he heard her start to chant, and froze, like she'd pulled his key out: a high, atonal keening, incomprehensible to Chess, whose Chinee ran rudimentary at best. As her pale hands sketched ideographs on the air, red robes swirling about her, Chess saw patterns rise through their folds, arcane embroidery coming to light like flaws on a blown coal: Black dragons, silver phoenixes, silk-trapped and squirming to be free.

Love pointed up at her. "Keep back, you pagan necromancer!" he hollered. "I'll brook no interference in my—*aaaagghh!*"

He broke off, mid-tirade, as the shadow-shapes on Songbird's robes suddenly all came free, swooping down on him in a gouge-happy swirl of talons, spilling powdered salt like blood. As he beat at himself in annoyance, batting her fetches away like so many mosquitoes, Songbird's incantation was already complete. She spread her fingers wide, and shook the resultant spell-net out over the whole battlefield at once.

Memory possessed Chess again, lighting him up from the inside: crouched at Ma's ankle in the red lantern-lit dimness of

Laugh-Laugh Sally Yee's, watching two Chink zither-players "duel" by tossing phrases back and forth, each adding a bit more flair to the last improvisation: one repeating the other's notes in perfect reverse, each pitched to be a precise harmonic counterpart of the other. And between the two, audible only in the echoes, a single pure note resonating, more felt than heard—the exact midpoint, caught between mirrored melodies.

Good call; he threw the thought her way like Hosteen's knife. *Get him right 'tween the eyes for me, and hard—and don't stint just 'cause you'll be getting me on the backstroke, neither.*

Ai-yaaaa! As if I would. And the instrument in question is a gu zheng, you garbage-eating dog of a whore's crotch-dropping!

Won't get to paste me good 'n' proper 'til you're done with him, though, will you? So just hush up for now, you pompous bitch, and keep on with what you're doin'.

I will, if you let me!

As Songbird's spell slid stiletto-smooth into the magic-flood torrenting from Chess to Love, he heard that same tone once more. Two patterns meeting, one reversed—matching and cancelling like ripples, flattening each other out. The current collapsed with shocking speed, and stayed pinned down—a cessation of pain so sudden, it dizzied Love actually fell to one knee, while Pinkerton blinked and slowly uncurled, his once-monstrous face now only slack and jowly and old, beard and hair gone white as Songbird's own.

Chess, meanwhile, found his balance, glancing over at Ed and Yancey. *Have to be fast, 'fore the storm's eye passed over.* Should he try to reach her, plant an order so deep she thought she'd come up with it? *Might still be possible to save 'em both—*

Too late, red warrior-boy, yet another mental voice told him—not Yiska's, though similar. Older, and far more knowing.

Aw, horseshit, Chess cursed.

Love snarled. He fisted his hand in the ground, salt coagulating 'round it like it was wet clay, and pulled it free—then threw it hard, straight up. Magic-sink that it was, it passed straight through

Songbird's shields and smacked her 'cross the face, sealing her stillborn scream shut.

A half-second's suffocation was all it took. Chess saw her resolve snap, smug sorceress collapsing back into a hysterical girl. Panicking, she clawed at the rigid mask, lost all control—plunged like a rock, hitting the ground at Asbury's feet with a *crack* that meant the fall'd cost her at least one limb.

The binding-spell stuttered, then snapped outright. Chess roared and doubled over, power-drain opening up again—and this time Songbird, too, was set thrashing in its grip, magic leaping from her in streaks of pink-green lightning to vanish into Love's body, just like Chess's hex-blasts. She'd brought her own power into the circuit, and now it had closed once more she was trapped, 'long with the rest of them. Her body smoked and steamed; a horrid flush swelled the edges of her face, puffing 'em 'round the mask, like it was eating its way inside.

Chess swayed, everything he had left bent on keeping upright. Damned for his sins he might be, but he'd be damned twice over if he died on his knees.

The only warning was a jewellery-latch click, followed by some massive, indeterminate flare—instantaneous, blinding. Then the power-circuit burst apart, every mote of hexacious might flung away into the air, concussion knocking the train-cars on their sides and Love down too, back-first. The cyclone winds went slack, airborne dirt and rock pattering ground-wards. Songbird's salt-mask poured off, leaving her to whoop a great gasp, double over and puke more salt into Asbury's lap; her white hair, released from its confines, hung down like a second veil. And the Professor held her all the while, tender as though she were his own granddaughter.

"Oh, my dear," he told her, with pleased relief, "do you know? I wasn't entirely sure that that would work."

It took Songbird a few seconds to regain awareness, after which she tried to stand but cried out, falling back into Asbury's arms. Twitching the robe back, the injury became plain: her leg was indeed broken, bent where no joint should be. With a snarl, she contorted her hand arcanely over the injury, Chink-speak spilling from her lips.

Nothing happened.

Face shocked blank, she repeated the spell, again to no result; a third time, a fourth, faster and faster. Similarly amazed, Chess only noticed the trinket responsible at almost the same time she did: a silver-coloured bracelet of interwoven metal rods, closed over her wrist. Songbird froze, staring.

"What have you done?" she whispered. Then, twisting to face Asbury: "Old idiot, what have you *done*? Put it back! *Put it back!*" She clawed at the bracelet futilely, but it seemed locked in place: too tight to slip off, too strong to break. "*Release my* ch'i, gweilo *bastard!*"

"It was the only thing," was all he whispered, in reply. "The circuit had to be broken, and . . . you were there, nearest to hand. The only one on whom I *knew* this would work." He gazed at her, imploringly. "I meant to save your life—!"

Songbird screeched, and clawed him 'cross the face, screaming again at the jolt to her leg. Spent, Asbury made no attempt to get back up but merely lay blinking, gouges trickling thin red down both cheeks while she dragged herself close enough to do more damage, bracelet-side hand clenched in a tiny fist, like she was fixing to hammer this frail old man to flinders. And Asbury, regret-paralyzed, might just have let her—had Pinkerton not grabbed hold instead, hammer-sized grip encircling Songbird's wrist completely.

He pulled hard and clenched, cracking metal like tinsel, then stuffed the bracelet-shards headlong *down his own gullet*, swallowing hard; pink-green lightning burst from every pore, rimming him head-to-toe. His skull flared, briefly visible inside his skin, free-swung jawbone clear as day. Then the light grew so blindingly fierce, even Chess had to shade his eyes—and when he *could* look, he found Pinkerton changed, yet again.

All final traces of corruption gone, face intact, healthy, flushed with life; even his bulk had tightened, fat sloughed off to reveal a leaner, more muscular build. And the great height he'd kept, with that moose-sized beanpole Love—feet regained—only coming up to his shoulder. Shirt and shoes and stockings had burned away, only the barest tatters of his check trousers preserving any semblance of decency. Pinkerton's chest rose and fell, a pure delight glowing in his grin, as he turned to look down at his now-crippled former comrade.

"Never did quite grasp yuir taste for this," he remarked—and hell if even his voice wasn't healed, clear and resonant once more. "Damnable heathen cannibalism, 'specially when practised on yuir ane. But now. . . well, madam." The grin widened. "I can only hope ye enjoy never havin' tae worry o'er anyone doin' it tae yeh again!"

Songbird rolled her face in the dust, giving out a funereal keen: "Ohhhhh, thieving *wu ming shao jiu* scum! Yet I will regain my power, all of it, now that trinket is removed; I *will*! And *then*, we will see—"

Pinkerton shrugged, grin vanishing. "Maybe, maybe not . . . but one way or t'other, ye'd do best tae gie it a rest." He turned to Love, slapping his hands together. "Now. Where were we?"

For all that look of bemused wariness was probably near as Love could come to fear, nowadays, it was still oddly heartening to see. "Nowhere, Mister Pinkerton, my quarrel not being with you. You remain entirely irrelevant."

Deliberately, the Sheriff turned his back—but the king of Pinks couldn't leave it at that, obviously. He half-raised one fist, already ghost-fire-rimmed, only to see Love deflect the result with a single palm contemptuously raised over one shoulder, not even bothering to turn around. The blast caught Pinkerton himself on the rebound, knocking him unconscious. Asbury squawked; Songbird, too exhausted to laugh, showed her teeth in malicious glee.

"*By their own hands shall they perish,*" Love quoted, to himself. "Glorying in iniquity, they shall be hurled from the window like Jezebel, and eaten by dogs."

Asbury said, "Perish? Now, see here—"

Love swung 'round—but the old man was already struck dumb, mouth stoppered by Songbird's unmaimed hand; the girl glared up, seeming to will him quiet. And Asbury bowed his head, gaze dropping: became prim, meek as any small desert creature playing dead, to ward off predation.

Love's faith-burnt eyes turned in Chess's direction next, locking fast. And right that moment was when it struck Chess how Mesach Love might be weary of all this foofaraw as Chess was, if not more. Even the hatred he could still feel burning at Love's core had guttered, while what remained around it was . . . worn thin as the walls of this place, bleached like bone left too long in the sun. As if all the power he'd consumed, from Chess and Pinkerton and Songbird alike, had done nothing but flood straight through him, wearing him away as it gushed back into the black, where something shrouded in dark fire grinned.

You know, don't ya? Chess thought. *Came back as a puppet, and that's all you've ever been, all this time—an' not one doin' your Lord's work, neither. Never His. Never even your own.*

He cocked his head. Asked Love, out loud: "Was I worth all this, just for a measure of payback? Think hard."

Love considered. "Were our places changed," he said, after a moment, "how would you answer?"

Hmmm. Good point.

Chess must've smiled somewhat at that—grimly at best, but enough to make Love's ashes flare up one more time. 'Cause the next thing he knew, he was blindsided by a salt-slap, pressed down face-first with the Sheriff's sodden-grainy boot hollowing itself 'round his neck.

Love leaned in close, hissing: "Time to get ready, Pargeter. To die, at last—alone, forsaken, while my wife and son watch every last hurt play out, if only from Heaven's gate. For where's your beloved 'Reverend,' now he's most needed?"

Like Songbird before him, Chess breathed in salt and coughed out bile. Tried to say: *Hex City, dumb-ass—where'd you damn well* think?

But he couldn't, and hadn't really expected to. Everything got gun-barrel narrow, and he found he felt—not resigned, as such, nor exactly content . . . never had been yet, after all. Not even in far less onerous circumstances.

But he did find himself wishing Asher Rook was somewheres nearby, if only to see how dying twice wasn't really so bad, when you didn't give a good Goddamn. Or maybe just so he could spit blood his way one last time, hoping it went deep enough to sting.

Crazy thing was, though—he almost thought he could hear him. Saying, amused, *Aw, c'mon now, darlin'. You don't really think I'd let matters 'tween you and me close out like* this, *did you?*

Look up, my husband's husband. Rise.

AND SUDDENLY, CRAZILY . . . he found he could do both.

The sun's fire seemed to darken, filtered through smoked glass. The air felt molasses-thick, dragging on him as he turned to take stock: Songbird sat motionless, one white hand still over Asbury's mouth, while the Professor's blood sat unflowing on his gouged cheeks, filmy eyes saucer-wide. Though Love's alien stillness seemed no different, at least, the space beneath his boot where Chess had lain was empty—and the boot itself *still curved*, like it rested on something mid-vanishment. Pinkerton was a wax sculpture stretched limp on the chalky ground, Ed and Yancey lying prone too, nearby—and how long had it been since he'd last seen either of them move, anyhow?

What time is it? Chess thought. *Don't know how long we've been— shit, this light, can't hardly see no more. Salt's eating it, like dust. It just— it looks so, damn*—familiar.

He looked down, hazily, head swimming; looked up again. Saw the sun pop like a pinhole, bright white against grey. Saw it waver and blur, colours spectrum-skipping. Yellow sun in a black sky. Black sun in yellow.

Water lapping up at his heels, cold, gelid. The shadows of knives falling, like unclean rain.

As his left hand rose to wipe his brow, mouth painfully dry, he all at once saw something set down on it—narrow, bright, its head all eyes, both fixed and fragile wings glittering with speed, so fast they gave off a buzz. A dragonfly.

Of fuckin' course.

For way off in the distance—but growing ever closer, like cream turns under a witch's stink-eye—a whole hissing cloud made from more of the same was on the convergence: devil's darning needles loud as locusts, swirling like faceted snow. Numberless wings dirtying the sky, the ground, thinning the skein between Above and Below 'til Mictlan-Xibalba itself peeked through. 'Til a shape like a massive seed-pod humped up from its very centre, far too large to hold only one occupant—first one hand out-thrust, then another, pulling the swarm aside like a pair of living curtains. Left hand slim and fine-fingered, burnt sienna-toned, with black-flushed nails and a spattering of tattoos 'cross its palm; right one square and manly with a reach put Pinkerton himself to shame, big enough to hold a fellow down by his throat while the other worked its will on him, probing hot and sweet and evil from head to Goddamn toe.

"Neatly done, darlin'," the Rev observed. "Why, that was almost . . . strategic."

The flush of seeing him enfleshed once more ran Chess's length like ball-lightning, shameful-invigorating. But all he said was: "So it *is* you—late, like always. Somewhat wondered if you were even comin'."

Rook smiled back down at him, like he was too happy to see him to trust himself to speak. While by his side, arm threaded possessive through his elbow's crook, stood dread Rainbow Lady Ixchel with her long hair blowing and her snake-skirts a-ripple 'round her ripe hips, scales rattling dry as dead leaves. Blood ran from both bare teats, streaking her belly like war paint, to drip dark spots on Bewelcome's salted ground.

The sheer raw force of her was dismaying, as ever—but now Chess could peer beyond that force, or into it; see how the mortal substance of the vessel she wore was eroding, slow but inexorable, Bewelcome's thinness straining under her weight. And Rook looked little better, his long black coat dusty, collar frayed to a wisp, face both harsher-carved and looser at the jaw-points than Chess remembered it, with marks of worry, strain and weariness cut deep.

And to think how easily all that might've been avoided, Chess thought, *if only . . .*

Rook gave a tiny shrug, the movement hardly visible. *"If only's" a fruit lamentably easy to cultivate, darlin', though it travels badly. I mean, it ain't like you'd really accept any apology I tried to make, is it? However grovelling?*

I might, at that—if you was to just go 'head and try me, you smug sumbitch.

At this, Rook looked taken aback, like he almost wanted to answer. But it was her voice spoke instead, making Chess's muscles twitch in fury: lilting, mock-affectionate, each vowel etched in the stone knife-sharpening sounds of a long-dead world. A voice he mainly knew from nightmares of being rode hard and put away wet, without even what little pleasure he might've got from the process left behind, in recompense.

Then consider it said, she told him, smiling her sharp green smile. **It is your time, after all, little year-king. You have seeded plentifully, marking a trail for others to follow, a net of power trawling New Aztectlan's territories for due tribute. But your reign is done, and here we are, to collect. Now comes the time... of harvest.**

"I wasn't talkin' to you," Chess told her, knowing she'd ignore him. Switching over to Rook: "Hey, Reverend—what is this we're in here, some sort'a time-hex? You slip us 'tween seconds on a watch-face so's we'd have the chance to jaw our mutual complaints out, that it?"

"Something like that, yeah. For them, this's an eye-blink—less than. For us—"

—an eternity, if need be. Until our matters are settled.

Chess laughed. "Hell, we could do that now, you pitiful damn rag-'n'-bone show object. I already spent the whole damn day so far fightin'—bit more won't make no never-mind, unless you got something I never seen before hid up that skirt of yours."

Her eyes narrowed. **You truly believe it would be so easy?**

"What, 'cause you're a god? The hell you think you made of me, bitch?"

Something of the sort, yes—but only in its season. And your season is almost up.

They bristled at each other, air 'round them both starting to twist and crackle 'neath the strain, 'til Rook sighed, raising both his hands. "No need for all that, is there? Not yet. 'Sides which—Lady, have you ever seen Chess here take the easy way out? Even back 'fore he knew what he really was?" She looked away, one bare foot stirring the salt impatiently, toes raking up its crust like claws. "Well, then."

He looked back to Chess. Said, quiet: "I am glad to see you, though. 'Cause in the end . . . there's no one else on earth I'd rather get myself killed by."

"Yeah? Well, there's no one I'd rather go down tryin' to kill, myself." A jerk of his head toward Ixchel: "'Less we fold in your Missus over there, 'course."

At that, both Rook and Ixchel, grinned like their mouths were tied to the same puppet-strings. "Wouldn't expect it any other way," said Rook.

Unable to face that smile, Chess took in the scorched earth of Bewelcome township once more—salted inhabitants, wreckage of the Pinks' train; Love, Pinkerton, Asbury and Songbird; finally, Morrow and Yancey. The sight of his own guns, still holstered on Yancey's belt, warmed him, if by no more than a jot.

But it was Morrow he looked at, as he voiced the question he'd sworn never to ask: "Why'd you do it, Ash? And spare me the bullshit 'bout savin' me from Hell, for Christ's sweet sake. . . ." He sent a glare Ixchel's way, over his shoulder. "I know what *she* wants—some grand rollback to when she and hers ruled the roost—but how is *this* shit supposed to help?"

Rook sighed again. "Chess, this world that's coming . . . it ain't a place where 'why' holds much water. We do what we do because it's what we do, and that's all there is to it—like askin' why the sky's blue, or water's wet, or things fall down, not up. You spread chaos and the chaos *itself* is the point, like you spread the Weed to show the people what the new world runs on: spill blood, and prosper;

hoard it, and die. You . . . and Ed, for that matter . . . just did what it was in both your natures to do, and the rest followed naturally on." Looking at Love: "Though to tell the truth, I never would've expected you'd keep a personal grudge 'gainst anyone other than me goin' quite so long. I'm almost jealous."

"Oh, you ain't got cause to be—you're top of my kill-list still, that makes you happy. But don't think to use my given name again, *Reverend*."

He'd thrown the words out thoughtlessly, as ever, only to feel a painful gut-clench of angry regret roil up from deep inside Rook, as they landed. Still, he shrugged it off, vising himself tight around his own hurt. If Rook thought Chess weak enough to forgive him, just 'cause *he'd* suffered too . . .

But Ixchel was laughing, skin-crawl silent, effortlessly recapturing his rage-focus. **As you wish, Our Lord the Flayed One—for that is most truly your title now, in any event.**

"And who asked *you*, exactly?"

Ungrateful! she exclaimed. **And after we came such distances, froze Time itself to save you? Unchecked, the White Christ god-babbler there would have left nothing of you for the vultures. But there will be time enough to defeat him once we three have undone what the One he serves has made of this world.**

Chess snorted in disdain. "Shows all *you* know." To Rook: "What d'you think that is inside Love, eatin' up everything I throw at him like chuck? Sumbitch got hold of some portion of my power, without me even feelin' it!"

Rook scowled. "From who? Sheriff don't truck with any but God, as I recall. . . ." But here he trailed off, sniffing the air, frown deepening. "What . . . what *is* that?"

Ixchel's face went dead, as if her incarnation had never been more than a lie, badly told. And the word whispered out from her, like a hot wind.

Him, she said.

Something else stirring in the not-darkness, a fourth point to the triangle, rendering it square; a certain . . . obscurity crossing the day's face, scarring it to artificial twilight. Something turning on a dime, impossibly huge, showing itself to have been there all along, only biding its own sweet time. Huge as a house, thin as crossed bones, pitch-black . . . and *smoking*.

Come out now, brother, Ixchel told it, with surprising respect. *Husband, son, all—everything, and nothing, my only woken equal. I acknowledge and invoke you.*

Yet you still hesitate to name me, sister-mother-wife, the Enemy's too-familiar voice replied. *Why would that be, I wonder?*

Blue fire blossomed over Love's statue-still head and shoulders, billowing up and up. Beneath it, the smoke-like form the Sheriff had taken on in order to destroy the revenant thunder-lizards swelled out of him 'til it stood free, grinning. And that bone-shutter pulse filled the literally timeless silence, thrumming up through Chess's boots like rail on a rotten bridge, unsafe at any speed.

You have always had . . . so many names, Ixchel said, finally.

Yes. And I did not even have to eat my own kin, to gain them.

Four faces in one, always changing, that other voice at the back of Chess's skull supplied—some old lady's voice he suspected might be the same one that'd called him "warrior" and "boy," not too long previous. *The black Tezcatlipoca, Smoking Mirror himself: a ghost, a skeleton, a dog with human hands, as we see him. The red Tezcatlipoca, Xipe Totec, who raises up the corn and is ground down to make more; that would be you, little red-hair, 'til your next sacrifice. And this new* bilagaana *Bible-worker, in his salt coat: he would be the white Tezcatlipoca, Quetzalcoatl. The other God Who Dies, waiting to play out his part . . . but only once you play out yours.*

*You should listen to her, **pelirrojo***, the Enemy advised. *For here is wisdom made only greater after death—and how I love you talking monkeys for this! You who remake yourselves, over and over, without any sort of ritual at all.*

Chess shook his head, trying to clear it—stole a glance over at Ixchel, who didn't seem to've heard the first voice at all. And saw Rook rock back on his heels just a scootch beside her, like he recognized them both.

Black, red, white . . . and one more, too, if I recall correct. But then that means there's a Number Four, don't it? Chess thought. *The . . . blue, though damn if I know what he's for. And him we ain't seen, just yet.*

The Enemy smiled at that, or seemed to. Hard to tell, with no real lips to cover all those teeth.

That is a fine city indeed you've made for yourself, my sister, he said to Ixchel, shrugging northwest. **Though perhaps inexpertly founded, built as it is on sand. Do you yet recall the Doom that came to Tollan, for similar arrogance?**

Now it was her turn to shiver a tad beneath memory's lash, and Chess couldn't claim it didn't warm his heart to see it.

The blue Tezcatlipoca is Huitzilopochtli, that other voice told him, meanwhile, soft as shifting dust. *He who was born from lightning in a ball of feathers, He Who Tore Apart the Moon. And his province . . . is war.*

Ixchel drew herself up once more, pale and full, lambent as a lit corpse-lantern. Throwing back—**You lie, brother-son-husband, always; I am not frightened. You scheme and trick. What you cannot lay claim to, you wilfully destroy.**

Mmm, and I create, too. Nothing comes from nothing.

Then build, with me. Build it all up once more—the right way. The way things were, and should be once again.

The Enemy looked her full in the face then, with what almost seemed to be—sorrow? Amazement? An odd sort of affection, the kind which endures long after everything else—all the more violent emotions—is finally burnt away. Chess knew it to look at, having seen it often enough in the Goddamn mirror.

Our time came and went, sister, he said, gently. **Let gone be gone.**

She shook her head, hair falling to hide everything even vaguely human about her. Replying: **No. This world will end, as all worlds do. What I have set in motion you cannot stop.**

I do not propose to.

The fuck? Chess thought.

Something kicked him 'tween the ribs, hard as a horse, making him suddenly so dog-tired over this hopeless slog of a conversation he wanted to weep out loud. These savage deities with their stupid rules, their endless high-button shoe courtesies! What was the Enemy fixin' to do, jaw the bitch to death?

Rook'd probably tell him asking a god's favour was best done on bended knee—but Chess somewhat doubted it, given the god in question. So he rounded on him instead, hands sparking green, all pretence at politeness torn clean away.

"Why'd you even come, then?" he demanded. "Just t'have fun at our expense? What kind of damn god you call yourself, exactly?"

Not yours, obviously. So if you wish to interfere, that is on your head, not mine.

"I'm any part of you, means it's on your head, too. Or don't it work that way?"

It does, and yet . . . what you must understand is that I do not care what happens, overmuch, one way or the other.

"And I do?"

Now, yes.

Never was raised to . . . care for nobody, his own voice murmured from memory, God alone knew how long a span of time previous—a year? Two? History folding back on itself, spindled at its core; how long ago since the camp and its gallows, the twister? Since the War itself ended?

Standing naked in the desert with nothing but his scars for finery, smiling like a fool as he let Asher Rook draw him close; feeling his dick slap up 'til it left a hot smear of juice on both their bellies, biting into the bigger man's lip like he wanted to make a hole large enough to fit himself inside, and knowing the days of lovelessness were over, for good or bad. For *ever.*

"No," Chess said, shaking his head, fighting hard to not cast a glance Ed's way—or Yancey's, either, damn it all. And knowing, as he did, the only one he was fooling was himself.

Here came Rook himself, meanwhile, looming in deliberate, voice rumbling low: "Deific help set aside entirely, though, strikes me there might be a way out of the Sheriff's clutches yet, for everyone.

You need a hefty jolt of hex-shock in order to shake free from that back-and-forth the two of you got goin', not these drips and drabs that Ed and his lady friend can afford to spare you. Something so big it's impossible to stop—or take back."

Chess crossed his arms. "And just what the fuck am I supposed to take away from all this yammer, 'sides from you really do dote on the sound of your own voice? 'Cause frankly, I knew *that* already."

Rook flushed, aura snapping like a whip. "Now, listen here—"

For once, however, it was Ixchel who put in, helpfully: ***He means that it is blood alone which pays for blood, little god-king—true currency of all worlds, one which can never be devalued. Which is why you must let it to get it.***

"Christ you ever stop t'hear yourself? You're worse than a Goddamned fortune teacake." To Rook: "What's that s'posed to even mean?"

Rook shook his head, gently. "Darlin'," he said, ". . . you *know* what it means."

The answer seemed to pop out onto his tongue, sharp as any thrown stone, so painful-true it was almost like he didn't even *need* that other voice to confirm his suspicions—though it sure enough did hasten to, all the same.

He means you must make sacrifice, red boy, as you were once sacrificed; choose someone you care for, to die in your stead. For only thus can this place be brought back to the way it once was, when your Sheriff Love was a man only . . . a man with a town, a wife, a son. A man who, because he was willing to die for them, might allow himself to be killed.

As though they both understood and approved Chess's realization, Ixchel and the Enemy nodded, in unison. Their not-voices overlapping, the rise and fall of waves on some awful sea.

Jaguar cactus fruit, jade earthquake ball, repository of thought and blood alike. Red cornerstone of all houses, centrepiece of all wheels, turning. The key to the Machine.

Chess swallowed, throat choke-full of vile juices. "I cut out somebody else's heart and that puts Bewelcome to rights—that the idea?" A beat. "Like who?"

Now it was Ixchel's turn to shrug. *It hardly matters. All lives are forfeit, in the end.*

Just as all lives are due to us, always, the Enemy suggested, idly. *Or so we were always told—eh, sister?*

I never saw you rush to repudiate those strictures, she replied. *Not when your* ixiptla *mounted the steps at Tenochtitlan alive, playing his flute, to the adoration of all . . . and not when he came back down riding the high priest's body, a mere skin suit with hands flapping loose at the wrists, his face a mask for glory.*

The reality of it swelled up blunt behind Chess's brows as that tumour'd killed one of Oona's bunk-mates, back in San Fran—pushed her left peeper out 'til it near left the socket and she died raving, gaze permanently divided, each eye turned to a completely different pole. A thousand years of men just like him, cut down in their prime to keep these two greased and happy. Children girt with gold and chucked down wells to drown in the dark; gals kept virgin 'til the knife plunged in, a black glass blade their only lover. Once upon a time, their suffering would've made him chuckle, like the woes of everyone he'd killed in battle and the myriad more woes each death had sown in turn—weeping wives, desolate kin, mothers and fathers he'd never known, and spat on the very idea of.

But now he saw it straight on, for the dreadful tree it was: a tree of bones hung with flesh and watered on blood, growing up out of Mictlan-Xibalba's sewer to breach this world's skin and pull it wide, releasing every sort of horror.

This world's a shit-pit, he remembered telling Rook, too matter-of-fact to be sorry over it. *Just dogs fucking and killing, where the strong eat the weak and the weak get eaten. And for all that Bible of yours's good for hexation-fuel, you know your own damn self how that "good God" you preached on's nothin' but a happy horse-crap lie.*

Choose one to die, so Bewelcome could live. But which?

Songbird, her witch-wings clipped, lying in old Doc Asbury's arms. Asbury, trembling like the rabbit-heart he'd always been, 'neath his hoity calculations. Pinkerton, or whatever monstrosity a dose of Songbird's stolen magic had made of him. The slave-hexes who'd pulled his train, already run halfway to Hex City, if those *things* Chess'd called out of the canyon walls hadn't done for 'em first; same for most've the Pinks, he reckoned, with what few still lurked amongst the rocks hardly worth his time.

Or Yancey, driven by revenge and sentiment alike, like he'd always been. The one thing in skirts he couldn't call a bitch or a whore with a clear conscience, whatever *that* was.

Or Ed.

Turning a cold eye on Rook, and thinking: *'Cause that's who you meant to point me toward, right, Ash? The tool that turned in your hands, lived long enough to cleave to someone else right in front of me, so you think jealousy'll make me yearn to settle his hash. Which I might, if him and her weren't the only living souls who ever helped me for no gain at all on their part, only loss and heartbreak. Who've stuck with me when no one else would . . . and why?*

Goddamned if I know. Which must mean, in the end . . . it doesn't much matter.

So simple, from one breath to the next: he saw things as they were at last, unimpeded by lust or hate, like everything else had dropped away—everything. Even himself.

Especially himself.

Chess looked at Rook, whom he'd once loved and did still, to his eternal foolishness; the two outrageous figures flanking him, one human-sized, the other anything but—remnants of one bloody age, turned harbingers of another. And as he did, it came to him how they all of 'em *deserved* to be defied, their grand plans laid waste to. Hell, they needed to be took down and knocked out loaded, laid so low they'd never get back up again.

Should be possible, too. 'Cause if their power and Love's power and his own power really were just different brands of the same . . . well, Chess probably might not be able to kill *them*, any more than he'd been able to kill the Sheriff, no matter how diligently he'd tried.

But this much I do know: I can for damn sure kill myself.

"Oh, fuck all y'all," he told Rook, sighing. "Think I'm gonna save myself at someone else's expense, just 'cause *you* tell me it's the only way? Like you know me so damn well? If you still think that, after all you've done . . . all both've us have done . . . then maybe we never really knew each other at all."

Rook took what Chess remembered as a heartbeat to compose himself. "C'mon, darlin' . . ." he began.

"No, *you* come on. Think I can't surprise you? Watch this."

He missed Hosteen's knife, almost much as he missed the old Hollander himself. It'd've been so easy, that way: blade's metal would only feel cold for a moment while crossing his throat, edge so sharp the sting would be rendered something faint, faraway, forgettable. And then the liquid heat would explode out and down as Chess closed his eyes in relief, savouring the triumph.

Still, it was like his hands knew what to do. Slip down, slide in, reach far as you can go . . . haul hard enough to prise the whole breastbone up like a lid, with a horrid, gelatinous crack, to let what little was left inside come spilling out.

He saw Ixchel and the Enemy both close their eyes at the same time—mouths hung open, tongues teeth-caught—while his precious blood went up like February firecrackers wrapped 'round with sweaty dynamite. Saw Rook go down on one knee with both arms out, mouth forming a mammoth *No, God, Chess, NO!*, and wanted to laugh out loud. But his mouth was blood-stoppered; his teeth ground together, frenzy-caught, gnawing into his own tongue like they'd been designed to tear it out by the roots.

All I wanted was my heart back again, he couldn't stop himself from thinking. *That's all, Christ shit on it.*

Such a weak-sounding whine of a final idea, given who it came from.

We all want something, grandson, that other voice said, without a shred of comfort. *Now sleep.*

So Chess Pargeter closed his eyes at last, feeling the pulse of a spell too vast to be undone bear him away, bodily, in every direction at once.

CHAPTER EIGHTEEN

So the little warrior can care for someone other than you, my husband. Truly there is no end to wonders. . . .

YANCEY FELT THE TIME-SLIP spell without suspecting what it was, planet jerking sideways under her like a crashed train and the shadows snapping around. It was enough to jolt her free of her daze, blood- and soul-loss admixed; she tried to push herself up, but couldn't—Ed's weight too much to move, weak as she was. But she could twist herself sideways, just enough to bring the field of battle into vision.

And saw Chess dropping to his knees, chest one tremendous wound, as more blood spilled down out of him onto Bewelcome's salted earth than it seemed one human being should be able to hold. While his hands lifted high, red-shining, fingers streaming fresh tissue. . . .

Oh sweet Christ he didn't he didn't *he DID!*

"Oh, shit, Chess!" Ed bucked awake as well, fought to gain his feet and failed with no more strength left in him than her, though it didn't stop him trying. "Chess, what the *fuck*—"

Beyond, Sheriff Love whirled and stopped dead, his pole-axed look near-comical. He had only a moment to stare before the ground whiplashed again under all of them, a crack of force and heat exploding outwards; it knocked Love yards backward through the air, coming down so hard his salt-armour shattered, shelling itself in chunks. Yancey and Ed themselves were tossed like toddlers on a blanket, slamming heavily onto the ground some feet apart, shocked stupid. Yancey blinked up, black spots bursting in her tunnelling vision, wondering why the earth under her back felt so strangely . . . soft.

Then the sky turned green.

MORROW SAW CHESS'S SILHOUETTE etched sharp against the light-cataract pouring through him, before the radiance blazed up too bright to bear; shading his eyes with one arm, he braced the other on the ground, and felt it change: salt cracking, resolving itself to dust, and further. Until it became a moist brown soil, worm-full and slick, so rich it tingled.

Morrow jerked his hand back and saw fresh new grass boiling upwards, swallowing his palm print whole.

The green light was a warm wind stroking every inch of him, even through his clothes. Morrow yelled wordlessly as a spurt of burning pain corkscrewed through his arm, then turned to euphoric heat; viridian fire went crawling through the still-open sacrificial gash, sealing it over with pink new skin. The weakness washed away. Twisting, he saw Yancey sit up in another patch of spring-fresh foliage, goggling, as her own wounds' slate was wiped similarly clean.

Following the blast's path, grass bled outwards, ripping up through the salt crust and devouring it. The wave swept over Asbury and Songbird, leaving the China-girl's leg suddenly straight and strong, the Professor's cheeks blood-clean. Pinkerton, his hurts far less mundane, glowed fiercely alight a moment, as if lightning-struck, before the power sank inside; his often-altered form resolved once again to the mere man Ed remembered from that fateful train ride, two Novembers ago.

As for Love, meanwhile: white flakes and shards cracked off the Sheriff, crashing down, a snowstorm of grey and white rubble that uncovered flesh, skin, hair, patch by painstaking patch. The uneven pigtails Morrow dimly remembered from a pre-mortem sketch had given way to full, flowing locks: Love's face, clean-shaven in its time-stopped revenancy, now bore a curly beard so matted it made Morrow's own face itch to look at, while what semblance of clothes his undead salt-flesh presented had dissolved headlong, becoming mere rags and tatters. Before Morrow realized it, the transition was complete. Mesach Love stood reborn, gangly as a new colt— barefoot, bare chest heaving—amidst the wreckage, staring at his own long-fingered hands like he had no earthly idea what they could be.

And still Chess burned on, a verdant holocaust, pouring so much life into that ruined town it repaired every ravage it spilled over. Of the face-fallen statues choking Bewelcome's town square, some cracked apart into shapeless piles, then flared up green, recapturing their original forms. Before Morrow's stunned eyes, the salt literally burst off them and people emerged, staggering forth. Like Love, their clothes were frayed as if they had worn them all that time, hair and beards ridiculously overgrown, yet skin and eyes baby-clear. Cries of shock, wonder, joy began to rise. The eroded shapes of buildings sketched themselves anew in chartreuse lines, resuming their substance: beams and bricks, mortar-laid stone. Even those dwellings that'd been no more than canvas tents reared up, raised once more.

And all of it green-tinted in Chess's backwash, but real, its own natural shades restored. Not a hint of salt's awful greyish-white was to be found, anywhere.

The regenerative wave-pulse slowed, now, reaching the town's borders, well outstripping the original zone of devastation. As it did, the green light faded, thinning, a reservoir nearing empty. Morrow turned back, squinting, trying to distinguish Chess's form—only to catch sight of him just as he folded backward, collapsing bonelessly to the grass.

"Chess," he whispered, lurching forwards. Strangers blocked his way, shouting questions; he shoved them aside. Some struck back in bewilderment and anger, and suddenly Morrow found himself seized by a dozen hands at once. He thrashed, grunting, too desperate for anger . . . until a woman's voice rose above the crowd's babble, so full of joy and anguish and disbelief it shamed everyone still.

"*Mesach!*"

". . . Sophy?"

YANCEY WATCHED SHERIFF LOVE push his way through, so tatterdemalion a figure she could barely connect him with his previous terrible aspect. Then his eyes lit on the one who'd screamed his name—a well-formed blonde with a dark freckle marking her wide brow, just off-set of centre, clutching a wailing, shawl-wrapped baby—and his face seemed to melt with joy.

"Sophy! Oh, my Lord Jesus, thanks and all praise be to Him and His Name—"

He ran to them, tails flapping, and seized them in an embrace so tight it seemed he meant to swallow them whole. They clung to each other, shuddering as they wept.

So young, Yancey thought, blinking away her own tears. *I never saw how young he was. So young, so happy.*

Like Uther was. Like I was too.

Still sobbing, Love's woman pushed him back a bit, staring up into his face. "Mesach, how? How did all this, this . . ." She gestured vaguely round. ". . . come to be?"

Love hesitated, but was finally forced to admit, in all fairness: "Rook's boy—Pargeter." And turned away, to fix his gaze where Chess had fallen.

When Sophy Love saw what he was looking at, she actually screamed a little. Though the blood-sheet's bulk had boiled away, fresh spurts still gouted, if ever more slowly and weakly, from the uneven V-shaped gash that traced Chess's breastbone and ribs—one unhealing wound in this whole town. A mere man would have been long-dead already; in truth, Yancey could barely believe that even Chess could still be alive, let alone still able to rasp:

"Fuck. Fuh, fuh, fuh . . ."

Trailing off in another liquid burst of coughing, Chess tilted his head, eyes shifting to seize on Love's approach. With Sophy at his side and the other Bewelcomers gathering adjacent, Love shook his head, slowly.

"What you did, Pargeter . . ." he said.

Chess's face contorted, sneer and snarl at once. Spraying blood down his chin, he spat.

"Dih'nt . . . do ih . . . f'*you*," he replied.

And then, the light went out. Chess's head relaxed, horribly slowly, to one side. His limbs spasmed, insectile, locked in death's final jitter.

"*CHESS!*"

Yancey twisted again, finally spotting Morrow where he lunged against a dozen Bewelcome men's strong arms; struggled and bucked, to get only a punch in the gut for his pains. Another man struck him on the back of the head, open-palmed, yelling: "Let him rot, the little bastard! You know who that is, stranger?"

"Better than any of you ever will, motherfucker!" Morrow shouted back, thrashing. It got him another slug, this time 'cross the face.

Sophy Love, her initial shock gone, ignored it all, continually tracing her husband's face, as if unable to keep from touching him. "Seemed—forever, an eternity. Like I was dreaming, save I couldn't wake. What's happened, Mesach?"

Love held her by both shoulders, smile boyish-wide. "You've been restored, girl; He saw you through, like I said He would. You were always so strong in your faith, Sophy—stronger than me, by far, and that's what saved you. Saved all of us, to be together again at last."

"Sheriff Love?"

Perhaps it was the almost toneless diffidence of the question that disarmed him; Yancey would never know if Love might've reacted more warily to anything louder. Simply that as he turned to face her, on sheerest reflex, she lifted one of Chess's Colts—and put a shot neatly through his bare chest, just below the breastbone.

Yet again, Love plunged to fetch up on one knee, supplicant;

Sophy shrieked, dragging a wail of fright from her babe along with howls of shock and fury from the watching crowd, all of which slid over Yancey like water off tarred canvas. Without haste, she walked to where he knelt, and placed the other gun against his forehead.

"Draw," she said. Knowing full well he had nothing left to do so with.

Love gasped, paralyzed as his followers seemed to be, utterly aghast by the situation's impossibility. Then the shock in his eyes gave way, like seasons turning over: Yancey saw fury, then memory, guilt, regret. Eventually, at the last, a bitterly sad acceptance.

"'S fair," he managed. "Wasn't . . . the True Lord at all, who aided me. I knew that. But since . . . I got what I wanted, I'll . . . pay the price . . . gladly."

"Glad or sorry, I don't much care." The coldness inside her had eaten everything, leaving this one last task to complete. "Goodbye, Sheriff."

She pulled the trigger.

YANCEY'S FINAL BULLET WENT in at an angle, came out the same way—took half of Love's nice new skull along with it, from what Chess could glimpse. He'd've liked far more to see it done closer up, and taken his time enjoying the view. But he felt his spirits lifted just a tad by the shot's echo, that oh-so-familiar refrain.

Little Missus Kloves served out her apprenticeship and joined the fraternity of shoot-to-kills, blooded herself in anger, leaving the table well-set for a nice long dinner of revenge served cold. Not too shabby, for some chocolate-box flit in skirts probably never expected to get ten miles out from that dust heap we found her in.

As though Chess hadn't been just as much the death of that damn place, in far more direct fashion than even Sheriff Love himself. But it didn't much matter now, he reckoned; enough that he knew the truth, and owned it. Wouldn't be long, either way.

Oh, and everything really was going now, eaten 'round the edges like a rag on fire—fast, *fast*. So Goddamn unremitting.

It amazed Chess how he'd really believed, almost all along, that there was nothing he'd miss, leaving this world. *Only the whole of it, you ass-stupid fool.*

Every bit, the living and the dead, and then some; hot sun on his back, the wind and the rain, full-out galloping into battle, feel of his guns in hand, a good hard fuck. Getting drunk—on absinthe, anger, blood. Stomping twice on some enemy's face for good measure, and laughing while he did it; the sound of Asher Rook's voice preaching, or Yancey's, singing. Ed's heartbeat under his cheek.

Old Kees Hosteen ribbing him 'round the campfire, taking slaps just to stay close, and never faulting him for it. *Just the way you are, and we all know that, Chess. God damn, you're a mean little man.*

Friends.

More than one by the end of it, yeah, and not *all* of 'em paid for in blood, or favours. Whoever would've seen *that* comin', back in his San Fran gutter days?

Ed's face again, a-swim in the gathering darkness, struggling against his captors—was that raw pain on it *for* Chess, or because of him? He hadn't ever looked to see anybody mourn over him, dead or alive. Hadn't ever looked to care if they did, or didn't.

Yancey'd been snatched up too, now—pinned at the wrist by one man, the waist by another, grimly wrestling with a third over her firearm. Love's woman swayed, mouth an open black wound in a pink-and-white mask, while that brat of hers screamed on. Between them, the long-limbed collapse of Sheriff Love had finally resolved itself into a heap of fresh meat, his zealot's eyes gone blank and cooling, rolled to the sky. No one seemed to be paying all that great a mind to it anymore, considering; far more intent on Yancey, who they looked like they were fixing to rip apart, for having connived his doom.

Which maybe explained why none of 'em paid any mind to the greasy blackness Chess saw—felt?—boil off Love's flesh, seeping out through his gaping mouth, his nose, his ears, the very pores of his skin. The Enemy, shucking its busted-up cat's-paw like a popped butterfly-bag and eddying Chess's way once more, wrapping itself 'round him coil by loving coil 'til it was close enough to whisper through his skull, like it was a broken bone flute.

My sister spoke truthfully. You are at the very end of your cycle—a sacrifice once more, bringing life out of the dead land but saving none for yourself. Your wound is one you cannot hope to heal.

Noticed that, yeah, thanks.

Yet I can save you, still. If you accept my help.

Chess almost tried to laugh, but thought better on it. *Oh, sure. 'Cause trustin' some fucker offers you your life at the Reaper's doorstep always works out so well.*

Do you want to die, pelirrojo?

And now the laugh *did* bloom, painful-pleasurable as he'd expected—a firework bubble of spite crowding the rest out, if only for a mere half-second before it popped, spraying his insides with paraffin.

Ask you that myself, he barely managed, *'f I only could.*

I know you would, little brother. Ah, how I do like you for it!

So you've said, Chess said—all his anger suddenly gone flat again, exhausted by every last part of this yammer. Too tired even to turn away, assuming his abused body would've allowed it.

The Enemy looked down on him, hole-eyes barely narrowed in a dust-black face—a death's head reversed, if you could say that of someone who'd never died, or been born at all.

Were this world once more the way she wishes, it told Chess, with a nod in still-hidden and time-locked Ixchel's direction, *no one like you would be allowed anywhere near my ixiptla. They gave me princes—youths raised to love me since birth, cultured, educated. Kings-to-be who yearned to die in my place, to have everything I gave them stripped away in an instant of awful ecstasy. To be shucked like corn, a red pain-flower, and rolled down the temple steps afterwards, one more corpse on a pile.*

They were idjits, then. Got what they deserved.

Another nod. *"Heretic!" they would have cried, and fought*

each other to the death to kill you for saying so. But I . . . find I somewhat agree.

Chess felt the Enemy wrap him close, lift him up, effortless. Those vast no-eyes peering further into him, unblinking, 'til their empty expanse was all he had left to see.

Now answer me, truly, before the end. Do you want what I offer?

. . . depends . . .

On what, little brother?

Though he didn't in any way need to, Chess made himself take a long, ragged breath. Not enough blood left in him to fill his mouth completely, but he felt it slick his dry tongue, leak to paint his lips 'til they matched his beard.

And replied, out loud, his throat grating each word like it was rock-pile dust, ". . . can yuh gih me . . . my 'venge?"

On who?

With his very last bit of vim, Chess rolled his eyes 'til they all but crossed, snarling (inside his head): *Your bitch "sister," numbskull, and that snake she calls husband. Who the hell'd you think I meant?* Wasn't but halfway through the first sentence, though, 'fore he heard the Enemy chuckling again, as though he'd just made the second-best joke in all creation—which made him long to paste it one, and it laugh all the harder.

That don't bode well, he knew, mist deepening 'round him. Finding he could barely remember anymore what those words meant each on their own, let alone when run together.

so do it then, Jesus, do it do it, while I'm still

the end, this is it, no more

going, going

go

Oh, yes, something said, at last, as he plunged downward, fingers straining helpless toward an infinitely retreating bottom he feared almost worse than death itself to reach. *It would be my pleasure.*

Another pulse hit, bright *blue* this time: turquoise, robin's egg, faience glass, bell-sounding water crashing on a white cliff's brake.

Trip-hammer hard. Ball-lightning bright.

The hairs on Chess's body seemed to crisp at its touch, skin flushing azure from head to toe; his eyes flooded with a black so deep everywhere he looked was midnight, while the creatures gathered 'round him lit up from within, instantly rendered messy clots of flashing bones and circulatory systems redone in yellow, green, bright pulsing red, faces shrunk to featureless blanks, indistinguishable absences. Each one of them perfectly substitutable for every other one, with no distinction made except as to their relative strength or weakness, the ease or difficulty with which they might be singled out, struck down, torn apart.

Brother, wake. Brother, I call you forth.
You who were the New Corn, now completed.
You who were Red, now made Blue.
You who are Lightning's son, who sets One against Another.
Adorned with Hummingbirds, fashioned from Amaranth.
You who will Lead the Charge.

A smoke-finger pressed down on either lid, heavy as corpse-coins. The Enemy's breath hot and foul against his face, a slaughterhouse baptism.

You who I name . . . Huitzilopochtli.

His province is war, *grandson.*

Bright, blinding: Chess coughed it out, but more welled up, shrinking what he'd always known as *himself* to a point, a speck, a tiny, vanishing seed. Something so small, it could only be made to be swallowed.

Don't I ever get to be myself again? he wondered, despairing.

Teeth chattering in his mouth, abruptly sharp-filed as Ixchel's own—but not green, not jade-flaked, he somehow knew. Black glass, a flock of *itzapapalotl*-wings flapped in unison, volcano-hardened, sharp enough to bite through sin.

Sharp enough to tear a whole city's throat out, however hexacious.

The Enemy smiled back at him, its own teeth equal-razored. Told him, gently: ***Sleep, little king. Your part is done; I will speak for both of us, from now on. Rest well, in the deep places, 'til I call you forth again.***

No way to fight it, not this far along. Nothing left to fight *with*—it'd seen to that, Goddamnit. But Chess tried anyhow, like it'd known he would.

"You said . . ." he got out, as his lips went numb, "yuh . . . didn't care enough 'bout what she was plannin' . . . to try 'n' stop it."

Mmm, even so.

Black and blue, lids stroked closed, the ground opening up, swallowing him down. Crushing him, and everything around him, silent.

All but the Enemy's voice one last time, licking at his inner ear: ***Yet as you yourself have said . . . I lie. The same as every other god.***

And worse.

CAME A POINT, AND quickly, when Ed Morrow just couldn't fight his way any further toward what he suspected might be Chess's body—too many Bewelcomers in between, jockeying to show the all-too-recent Widow Love they had her best interests at heart.

"Surrender your weapons!" one of 'em howled at Yancey, close enough to sluice a bit of Sheriff Love's bright blood-spray off her cheek with his spit, where she stood holding a double-draw stance on what had to be fifty or more opponents. "C'mon, woman—we'll make it quick! Can't expect to just stroll into town, shoot down the man founded it and stroll on out the other"

"You *shut your mouth!*" she threw back, voice froze near to cracking. "A year or more you've been salt—maybe things ain't all they seem, ever think of that? *He* knew what he'd done, and said so!"

Another shout, bristling with insult on the dead's behalf. "Sheriff Love was a great man, you outlaw harlot—a man of *God!* 'Spect us t'believe that could ever change?"

"Why should I care *what*-all you think?"

"Because you claim to be a widow, wife to a murdered man, like me . . . and if the one means something, so should the other. Don't you think?"

Sophy Love stood there, dry eyes riveted to Yancey's face. Hugging her boy to her with both arms as he fretted and wept, and gone so white-to-the-lips pale herself, she might as well have been rendered salt again.

"A pity we can't ask him to confirm your tale, though, ma'am," she pointed out. "Seeing how you were the only one close enough to hear this . . . confession of his, beforehand."

Yancey swung a muzzle toward Missus Love's face. "You calling me a liar?"

"I don't know what to call you, frankly."

Yancey shrugged, looking far more Chess-like than Morrow'd hitherto given her credit for. "Good enough," she said. "No need for us to be friends; my business here's done. So you'd best get out of my way, for I *will* keep on shooting—didn't come all this distance to swing on any tree but the one outside my father's hotel, if I aim to swing at all."

"You may not have much choice in the matter," Sophy Love replied. To which Yancey gave a singularly bitter laugh.

"I'll put a ball in my head myself, *ma'am,* it comes to that," she assured her.

Morrow didn't know if he believed her, yet suspected Missus Love did—and he'd lost what little liking he'd ever had for taking chances. But he'd been seized far too securely to interfere. Even the panic thudding through his heart was lead-heavy with exhaustion, and with Chess gone, there was nowhere to turn for a hexacious escape, either.

So he closed his eyes, took the deepest breath he could, and howled his former boss's name as loud as he had left in him: "*Mister Pinkerton!*"

It was strong enough to quell much of the noise, though it left Morrow gasping, and the rest of the outcry died away into mutters of confusion as Pinkerton sauntered up. In his wake came Asbury, surprisingly hesitant, while Songbird sat motionless where she'd fallen, not even bothering to lift her parasol. Beneath her unbound white mane, her porcelain face had already begun to redden.

For all his comparative undress, Pinkerton bore himself like a king, and Morrow recognized the aura radiating off him—whether born of his ordeal like other hexes, or stolen via Asbury's science, Pinkerton's hexation was beyond denying now. He made him a genial nod, then folded his arms, in such a way as to brook no opposition.

"Wi' the Sheriff dead," he asked, "who speaks for this township?"

More or less as one, the crowd's eyes turned to Sophy. "Sophronia Love, sir," she said. "And you, of course, would be *Allan* Pinkerton, of the renowned Detective Agency."

"Charged with keeping *law*," Morrow interjected, "in those parts where civilization has not yet grown to custom. *Law*, and justice—a proper court, and a proper trial, and an advocate. To speak for the accused."

Pinkerton's mouth twitched. "And am I right tae guess who ye'd have in mind to speak for, Edward?" He looked back to the crowd, taking in Yancey and her guns, Love's and Chess's fallen bodies. To Sophy, with some regret: "Missus Love, though I well ken ye've no taste tae hear this, it must be said. Yuir husband was . . . no' undeserving of his fate."

"No, I don't believe that. My Mesach was a good man—a *kind* man—"

"The kindest turn most brutal, given a sufficiency of suffering." Pinkerton glanced at Chess's body, lying in its massive, drying bloodstain. "God knows Pargeter dealt out pain wi' a free hand, before and after turning hex. By reports, yuir husband caught up to him in this young lady's home town—" he nodded at Yancey, who didn't move, "—and left quite the field of desolation in their wake. Making her actions, in return, wild justice . . . but justice, naetheless."

The crowd was silent. Yancey stared at Pinkerton. Morrow held his breath.

Pinkerton shrugged, continuing: "Yet . . . tae deal such opens one tae receive it, also, and she's more than old enough to answer for her own deeds." He turned to Morrow, spread out his hands, mimicking Pontius Pilate's classic gesture. "She's a guid enow lass I'm sure, Edward, but she's nane of mine."

"And that's the end of it? Walk away, leave us both to swing—?"

"Oh, I said nought of leaving *you* here, Ed." Back to the Bewelcomers, voice battle-captain loud: "This man *is* mine—and though his crimes require no less judgement, I claim that privilege for myself, as his employer and commander. Does any here dispute me?" The question was bland enough, but Pinkerton lifted one hand as he spoke, allowing it to flicker with bluish-green were-light—cold and searing—which stilled any further protest. "Then I ask ye to release him to my custody."

"I won't be threatened in my own home, sir," Sophy Love replied, admirably uncowed. "Especially not by a man who claims to represent these United States' government, while at the same time wielding Satan's might."

"As ye say, madam. It's *I* who's the law's due representative, even here. While ye're but a lawman's widow—new-made, tae be sure, and tragically. But without any real power, except what public sympathy may deed ye—temporal, or otherwise."

Another flash, no doubt designed to punctuate his argument. Instead, it sent whispers spreading throughout the crowd behind her, equally mutinous: *Pinkerton's a hex? When'd that happen? Are we t'be plagued with these creatures forever?*

Sheriff would've seen to it we wasn't, he hadn't been cut down, by her over there. Which makes him just as guilty, that other Pinkerton man, for bringin' her here in the first place.

Morrow looked to Asbury, desperate for any further aid, but the old man only shook his head; his will was broken, at least momentarily. Back to Yancey, whose frozen fury had finally begun to melt, revealing fear beneath; no immediate solution there, either. Begging might not help, but it was all he had left—and for her sake, he was not too proud to do it.

"Mister Pinkerton," he began, "*please.* Missus Kloves doesn't deserve—"

"There's blood on her hands, Ed; the price is clear." Pinkerton came closer, lowering his voice. "Now, if you dinnae wish tae swing alongside her, you'll come right quick, wi' nae more struggle." But here a frown knit his brow; he straightened, turning, toward something only he could see. "And what in hell's own name might *this* be?"

Morrow felt the rumble before he heard it, and looked up—just as, on the far side of the open square, the air ripped apart like a torn silk scrim to expel a cold, wet gust of wind, a sodden northern night-storm's air. With a yodel of alien song, a whole platoon of copper-coloured riders poured through the black gash—arms presented, arrows nocked, with an immodestly open-vested Apache shamaness at their head.

Yiska.

Some woman—not Missus Love—cried out from the crowd's backside, like she was seeing the Last Days 'emselves dawn bloody, red skies and all: "*Savages?* Oh great God Almighty, what *next?*"

A fair enough question, Morrow recognized, though he knew himself sadly inoculated against the miraculous these days, whatever stripe it was.

Yiska reined in her horse with a yip and a flourish, almost at Pinkerton's feet; he stared up at her, arms pugnaciously re-crossed. Even to the uninformed eye, they certainly seemed to know each other.

"'The Night Has Passed,' is it?" Pinkerton said. "Bad day in a bad few years tae go raiding, I'd think—and a damn strange place tae target, too. Unless ye knew somethin' we nane of the rest of us did, in advance."

Yiska shrugged. "Only that when two gods fistfight, things are not often left the same, in their wake." Her eyes narrowed, appreciatively. "But then, you are not quite what you were either, are you—you who I last saw in the second *Naahondzood,* the Fearing

Time, after we helped win that War of yours for you, only to be driven from our homes like cattle."

"Ye've come back since then, I see—gathering in force, armed tae the teeth, as the Indian Act forbids."

"I see no Agents here but yours, *bilagaana*. And you are but a hex new-made, if that." She sniffed, then wrinkled her nose. "Ah, chah! Not even. A sham *Hataalii*, stuffed with stolen might. *I* am more fit to wield it than you, fool."

Pinkerton's brows drew together, beetling. "Ye know . . ." he began, calmly enough, "one thing I'm gettin' main sick of, these days, is the sound of Chink and Injuns frails callin' me *fool*."

His hands drifted together, all but met, conjuring an even stronger reaction: a minor conflagration, hot enough to make all the non-hexacious step back a tad, dancing between both palms like some captured *djinn*. But Yiska merely sneered.

"Hear me," she said, raising her voice slightly—not even deigning to address Pinkerton directly, but rather her band, who grunted and clicked their tongues in appreciation. "It is as Red Cloud of the Oglala spoke: *We have now to deal with another race—small and feeble when our fathers first met them, but now great and overbearing. Strangely enough, they have a mind to till the soil, and the love of possession is a disease with them. These people have made many rules that the rich may break, but the poor may not. They claim this mother of ours, the earth, for their own and fence their neighbours away. We cannot dwell side by side. My brothers, shall we submit, or shall we say to them: 'First kill me, before you take possession of my lands.'"*

Pinkerton shook his head. "A pretty speech, indeed. But it'll no'—"

"Be quiet," Yiska snapped, with such natural authority that almost all engaged parties did just that, at least for a second; she cocked an ear, listened hard, then laughed out loud, as though she had heard something she liked. "Hah, yes! The Spinner has not forsaken us, after all; she pulls her threads, shaking the web from sky to sky. *This* is far more like it."

"More like *what*, yeh daft squaw?" Pinkerton demanded, purple to his very hairline.

Yiska gifted him with a smile like a wolf's, all teeth.

"Change," she said, happily, throwing back her head. And *howled*.

WHILE, AT THE SAME TIME:

This is a forked path, dead-speaker, Grandma's spirit whispered, so low only Yancey might hope to hear. *The fabric turns in my hands. Help me, so I may help you.*

Since your advice's always been so *good on the whole, thus far—that* right? Yancey wanted to say, but merely shook her head, instead, drawing an odd look from Sophy Love. Given the drama currently playing out between poor Ed, Pinkerton, and the Diné woman, however, it was only a matter of time before the woman turned away again, distracted—allowing Yancey to ask, mentally:

How?

Let me come into this world once more, and act, for both of us. Lend me your witch's strength, freely.

I . . . my Ma said that wouldn't be a bright idea, for either of us.

And she was right, under most circumstances. Still—have you a better plan to offer?

To hell with all hexes, alive or not, Yancey thought, hopeless— then, as Yiska's howl split the sky, tightened her finger on the left-hand gun's trigger, sending a bullet into the ground. It kicked up a distraction's worth of noise and dust, scattering just enough of the crowd to cut her a clear path. She twitched her other barrel away from Sophy Love's blank face, getting barely a blink in return for this last misguided spasm of mercy; annoying, but not so much so as to keep her around. Because for all these fools might be fixed to lynch her, she told herself, she really had come here to kill one man only, in the end. And now that that job was done with—she found she didn't aim to kill more, no matter how much they might pique her. Not 'less she absolutely had to.

Sprinting faster than she'd ever thought she could, Yancey

barged past the men who held Morrow pinned, kicking one of them square to the back of the knee as she went and breaking his hold; from the corner of her eye she saw Morrow duck under the other's wild haymaker swing, moving neatly sidelong to let him lay his own already wavering buddy out. The ensuing chaos sent Sophy Love scurrying back toward her husband's body, one arm flung out as though to ward off further damage, the other keeping her baby shielded as best she could. Those near enough to see closed ranks around her, while the others joined the general tangle: Pinkerton and the Bewelcomers, Yiska and her braves, a swirl of sand and flying hooves, fresh gunfire blooming wild in her single shot's wake.

She was almost to Chess's body, boot-soles already tacky with his blood. A length behind her was Morrow, whose eyes met hers on the back-glance, apparently trusting she had some plan in mind. That one look was sufficient to make him spin on his heel and take up a defensive position, unarmed but game, to block any comers.

A good man. She could only hope he'd come out all right from this, whatever "this" might prove to be.

Hope we both do, come to that.

"Any time," Yancey said, shutting her eyes; *Indeed*, Grandma replied. And she felt something *pull* at her, inside and out, with such force it made her want to scream, fall face-down, be violently ill 'til she passed out. Like the cosmos itself was treating her as its personal spool, winding everything she had and more out of her at once 'til she felt turned inside-out.

And just like Ezekiel's spinning wheel, their differing degrees of power rose to meet and mingle in the middle of the air.

MORROW KNEW HE SHOULDN'T have been able to hear anything over the ruckus Yiska and Yancey had kicked off; the Na'isha riders had responded to Yiska's howl by breaking into yells of their own and sending their mounts into a wild, circling gallop around the flummoxed, infuriated Bewelcomers. For all Yiska's threatening, he couldn't help but notice that none of her followers seemed actually to be striking lethal blows—they kicked and slapped, whacking backsides, heads or shoulders with the butt-end of tomahawk or spear, but never drew more than a solid punch's worth of blood.

Meanwhile, the enraged Pinkerton began trying to lay Yiska out, to no very good effect, raw whiplash arcs of power slashing from his hands—but she, in turn, struck the hexation aside with swift slaps, shrugging it off as she danced her mount aside using only knees and thighs. Something like what Sheriff Love had done himself with Rook, Morrow supposed, right here in the fight that had first set everything in motion. For a moment he had a disorienting feeling of vast, slow-spinning circles coming back round to their starting points; a dreadful sense of futility and inexorability overwhelmed him.

Then Yancey made one of the worst noises he'd ever heard, something that should by all rights have gone utterly missed in the chaos: a small blurt of breath, a whimpering grunt, that reminded Morrow of nothing so much as the surprised gasp of a man gut-stabbed—but far far worse, for being in Yancey's clear voice. Even as he spun back round, rushing to catch her as she folded, he wondered crazily if he'd heard it with his ears at all. She was grave-pallid, face drawn tight as if in agony, though her eyes stared blindly and all sound but the faint gasps of her breath had stopped.

Of themselves, his fingers moved, stroking a damp lock of hair back from her forehead . . .

. . . and Yancey's hand flashed up, seized his wrist with shocking strength. The world *shifted* as Yancey's sight slammed into Morrow's own brain, dizzying him. Without transition, there was another Injun woman standing before Yancey: a squat, white-haired old squaw with one hand extended toward the girl and the other pointing skywards, above the moiling crowd. From Yancey's midsection, a glowing silver thread spun with flash-flood speed into the squaw's hand, leapt to the other and then into the air, where it gathered in a swelling knot over the Bewelcomers' heads. And beyond, off to one side, watching with looks respectively of remote, amused interest and drawn, battered grief—

The Rev, by all that wasn't holy. And his Rainbow bride, too.

Morrow's hand clenched tight on Yancey's, memories backlashing down the link to her like a lightning-strike, and both of them instantly knew what must've happened to Chess during that lost moment of time, when it looked like Sheriff Love had him pinned. Some final confrontation with his ruiner and his transformer had driven Chess to make any choice at all, rather than allow more destruction—and from the grief on Rook's face, perhaps it'd been the only choice that would truly hurt the other man. For whatever consolation that might be, now, to him . . . or them. Or anyone.

That is as may be, soldier, said the squaw. *But I have no time for lovers' quarrels. I care only that Rook and his* Anaye-*wife be stopped, for good and all. Your dead-speaker girl has promised me her power to that end in return for Yiska's aid. Interfere with me at your peril.*

"You're killing her," Morrow said.

No, the girl is stronger than you know, and I have worked such medicine before. I know my arts. The squaw glanced up at the knot of light in the air, and nodded.

She made the same snapping motion Morrow had seen Songbird do, as if breaking off a thread, and the silver strand of light parted in her hands. Yancey instantly drew in a massive, choking gasp, colour flooding back to her face; Morrow pulled her close, steadying her. Looking up, he saw the silver knot burst, lashing streaks of light out to a hundred different points.

Wind whirled up, still refreshingly cool with the surge of new life, and spun into a circular wall of air and sound. With such instant speed and coordination that Morrow knew it had been prearranged, Yiska and her braves broke off, flooding away from the panicked Bewelcome crowd—and before Pinkerton, still a-rage with lightning, could give chase, the wall of wind had begun to fill second by second with flying shards of bone and tooth and stone.

Around and around these spun, thickening, 'til the squaw yanked hard on the thread-end of silver light she still held. The wind shifted in a flash, fossil shards funnelling upwards into the air, then downwards onto *her*, covering her the same way a snuffer does a candle flame. In bare moments they had piled head-high, then twice that, boiling like stew-pot clay. And then they collapsed inward, locked solid—revealing a giant grey manlike figure, rough-hewn, dragon-toothed and clawed, which towered over the crowd, swaying slightly.

More screams, total panic: Bewelcomers poured backwards, leaving only Pinkerton behind, who glared at this thing as though he found it personally offensive. The giant paid no attention to any of them. It turned, steps sledgehammer-ponderous, and aimed what vaguely resembled its face toward the twin figures of Ixchel and Reverend Rook. Lifting one three-fingered taloned hand, to point, it roared—Diné words instantly made clear to Morrow too, through Yancey's interposition.

"YOU! YOU WILL . . . BE . . . STOPPED."

Shit-fire, Morrow realized, *that's* her *in there. Hex-ghost riding a lizard-bone Merrimack, looking to pick a fight with a Goddamn god.*

Never could say you lacked for entertainment 'round these parts, could you? He found himself musing, grimly.

In reply to the old lady's challenge, meanwhile, Morrow saw something he'd genuinely never expected: a look of true shock, and real fear, on the face of Reverend Asher Rook. But Moon-Lady Ixchel simply threw back her head and laughed, inaudible at this distance— her mirth only redoubling as Pinkerton, exactly as frustrated as Love'd been by the prospect of being ignored, charged headlong at the giant *thing,* hurling blast after blast of hex-bolts, only to be sent flying a half-dozen yards with one backhanded slap.

Morrow felt Yancey stir, and relaxed his hold, without releasing her entirely. *This what you expected?* he asked silently, link still vibrant-clear between them.

Her own laughter, far gentler than the Lady's, washed back over him like water, cold and sparkling. *Stopped "expecting" anything a long time ago, Edward,* she answered—and this time it was she who tightened her grasp in return, on him. *Still and all, though, might be we should try to clear out of here, too . . . together, if you like.*

He caught his breath at the last words, whose meaning could

not possibly be mistaken. And drew breath, intending to agree, out loud. . . .

But before he could, a hand fell on his boot—small, strong, blue-tinged, gripping like a vise. He whipped round, just in time to see the "corpse" at both their feet gift them with a feral grin, eyes gone night-black, his every tooth an obsidian dagger.

Morrow's breath flew back out, so fast his throat felt raw.

"Chess?" he managed.

The thing shook its head, managing not even a bad imitation of humanity.

"No more," it replied.

WHEN CHESS STARTED TO move again, Rook's heart all but *leapt* haphazard in his chest, bruising it from inside. Yet the illusion was only momentary—and that terminal realization landed deep indeed, a barbed harpoon.

No no no, that ain't him at all, Goddamnit—

Beside him, he felt Ixchel shake her head in sympathy, serpent-skirt set hissing. **Indeed it is not**, was all she said, mouth twisting like it was full of sour corpse-juice, puckered too fierce even to spit.

The figure's chest looked well-healed, like it'd never been rent at all, and the rest of him seemed similarly intact—spanking, horridly new: blood-red hair and beard, bright blue skin, eyes burning green, but with an iller light than any Rook had ever before seen, even in Chess's most killing fits of passion. One that came from somewhere absolutely *other*.

Both Yancey and Morrow were staring at him as well, apparently equally revolted, though Rook knew damn well that of the two, only the girl could possibly guess what she was looking at. Or . . . no, maybe not; they *were* joined at the hip and elsewhere, meaning her sight must be leaching into poor honest Ed through his skin, everywhere they touched.

Which meant he knew exactly what she was saying when she blurted out, "Oh sweet Jesus, it's . . ."

Thrown bits of broke stone bells, landing like mines in all

directions: each syllable was a blade, a club, a lit chunk of pitch. And even that gross vehicle Grandma'd fashioned for herself out of the thunder-lizards' detritus, that stomping bone reliquary, had to stumble and shudder under the whole name's dread weight.

. . . *Tezcatlipoca*, Ixchel sighed in his ear, so close—so *cold*—her undead tongue crisped the skin of his lobe.

Yes, sister.

Those lips Rook'd once hung on, kissed and bit 'til they were sore as bruised fruit. The mouth that'd cursed him a hundred times over, first in jest, then deadly earnest. That skin, that face, that body—all of it Chess, *Chess*, and nothing like. A ghost-god's puppet. A walking devastation.

It turned its dead black eyes on him, now, and laughed at how he flinched.

You yearn to break her hold on you, conquistador—regret your choices so sharply, back to the very beginning, that you might wish yourself hanged and rotten away to dusty bones, if only this one I wear still ran wild through the world. Yet here I am now, your lover reborn, to make all your dreams of freedom real . . . if you only break your oath to her and bow down to me, in her stead.

Ixchel watched for his reaction, curiously incurious. And if his head-shake made her happy, he—in turn—did not care enough to want to know.

"I might, at that," he allowed, "you really *were* him. But you ain't."

And here Ixchel laughed yet once more, icy-rippling as ever. ***You see***, she told her Enemy, ***I chose well after all, when I made this man my mate . . . a traitor so far forsworn already he would never break faith again, at any price. Not even with me.***

One more smile greeted this proud assertion, dreadful as the rest. And yet—might that really be something else Rook saw underlying it, almost too dim to glimpse, the way even the dirtiest water still throws a reflection back?

Perhaps, the Black Trickster replied, thoughtfully—crossed-bones king of Smoke and Mirrors alike, spreader of indiscriminate chaos. Then was gone, along with his blue-skinned Chess-body, completely as a rock dropped through the same stagnant pond-skin.

"Nice to finally know what you *really* think of me, honey," Rook told his awful wife, without rancour.

To which she simply shrugged and snapped her fingers, summoning the chittering dragonfly swarm 'round them once more, and threw back: ***Am I to be jealous, knowing you have preferred your little warrior from the start? We are king and queen, husband. Our business is to conquer, to build, to rule.***

"Won't be doin' much of any of that, he does what he said and lays his wrath down on us, like at . . . what was that place?"

Tollan, City of Jade. They insulted him, and paid dearly for it.

"Like Sodom and Gomorrah. Or . . . here, when me and Chess were through with it."

And look what has happened since. She wrapped him up, digging her bony chin into one collarbone's curve, so sharp it was like she aimed to piece him through. ***All wounds may be reversed, no matter how deep, if blood enough is shed to pay for it.***

"So you say, but here's what I *see:* the only other one of yours in all creation you've managed to shake awake, coming to knock our gates down with both guns blazin'. How's that anything but bad?"

Oh, husband. You must learn to trust me, eventually.

And before he could reply, she enshrouded him completely, flapping her hands—like bleached-blind bats—to flutter them both away.

IN THE WAKE OF SUCH outright insanity, Yancey and Morrow clung fast together, too shook to move. But then, all of a sudden, Grandma's suit was yelling something at Yiska—and before they could wonder what, with a yelp of acknowledgement, the Navajo-turned-Apache had already swooped in to grab Yancey up out of Morrow's arms and boost her 'cross her saddle, then take off for the hills at full gallop, crew at her heels. It all transpired so damnable swift, Morrow couldn't've hoped to draw a bead after any of 'em, even if he'd still had a gun to do it with—so he was left spot-rooted, howling after Yancey, as she went out of sight.

"Hold on, girl, hold on! I'll come for you, I swear on a stack of Bibles—I *will* find you, Goddamn it all to Goddamn fuckin' *hell*—!"

In the opposite direction, meanwhile, Songbird—still dazed from her ordeal—came to just in time for that lumbering dustpile to scoop her up, kicking poor Doc Asbury aside like trash, and go barrelling after Yiska and company; she was borne away likewise, weakly flailing. Soon, there was nothing left behind but tracks, the Chinee witch's screams echoing away into the night.

"*Yancey!*" Morrow yelled out again, in despair. And fell to his knees, head bowed, expecting nothing but a bullet for his pains—well-deserved, wherever it might come from.

Above, the sky stretched out blank, an endless darkening bruise; the wind blew cold, ruffling 'round Bewelcome's reassembled edges, and he thought he could hear the stealthy steps of its returning citizens, none of whom he figured wished him well. But Ed Morrow stayed right where he was, not even bothering to sigh over how just how badly his life—already precarious—had gone, in these last few seconds, to complete and irretrievable shit-pudding.

If Chess was still here—the real *Chess—he'd've made sure it turned out right, somehow,* he found himself thinking, foolishly certain. Knowing full well just how insane the very idea of that belief would've struck him, just a scant year or so past.

"Aw, pull yuirsel' together," Pinkerton said, briskly, from behind him. "For there's no sight quite as wracking as a grown man gone womanish when there's work tae be done in Justice's cause, and vengeance aplenty tae be taken, along the way."

Here their eyes did meet, at last, with a flinty little spark— and Morrow was somewhat startled to find his former employer rendered either once more human or mostly so, as though the stolen hex-fire were already draining from his veins. Even that accent of his seemed considerably less accelerated, the man himself re-sized to fit Morrow's memories of him, from the days when both had held each other in good opinion.

"Thought it was me you wanted to wreak justice on," he said, "not so long back."

"Did I say that?" Pinkerton asked, with a shrug. "Well . . . might be I overspoke, a trifle. For war's on its way, and we'll need every last man standing tae make our assault—and courage in battle washes all clean, or so they say, no matter *what* mistakes a fella may have made, previous."

Morrow looked down at the dirt once more, then clambered to his feet a bit unsteadily, and paused to dust his knees, before replying: "This vengeance, then—would it apply *to* Missus Kloves, as Missus Love surely still desires, or be exercised *for* her, along with everything else?"

To his credit, Pinkerton didn't lie—not right then, at least.

"Uncertain, as yet. So . . . are ye amenable?"

". . . I am," Morrow said, finally. And reached, shoulders squared, to willingly shake the best-known devil in the current angry mob's affably outstretched hand.

EPILOGUE

Somewhere else, entirely:

CHESS CAME TO BY slow degrees, marrow-cold, with something unfamiliarly hard—and wet, and rough, and dirty—incising his cheek. Opened his eyes on darkness and squinted just the same, like he expected that to be any help.

Hollow echoes all 'round him, a great sigh and clatter, congregative. The clop of hooves and grate of wheels over—*cobblestones*, was *that* it? Like he'd heard tell they had in New York, a layer of pavers set 'neath the usual street muck and sluiced clean every half-year, shallow enough to be dug up and thrown in a pinch?—plus a distant, mammoth thrum and clank of engines, furnaces burning black, throwing dirt up into the skies.

And now, eking through that stinking yellow fog he'd thought was just his eyes, a whole city street arrived: buildings dilapidated and promiscuously overhung, jammed hugger-mugger as a junk-fiend's teeth. Half-glazed cataract windows staring down, where they hadn't been shattered wholesale; stagnant gutters and hinge-fallen doors; a sketchy crush of humanity loitering or roaming, wreathed in grime, ignoring Chess in the grip of their squalor. Raggedy skeleton children ran free as roaches, relieving themselves indiscriminately.

I know this place, Chess realized, a slow hollow birthing itself in his gullet's lowermost pit. For God alone knew he'd heard it described, a thousand times over—the worst of all possible bedtime stories, told by one who'd been born there, only to steal and screw herself passage to what she'd dreamed was a far more exotic continent.

But this couldn't be *that* place, surely—not after the Enemy'd stuffed him into some infernal belly-hole, prisoning him inside whatever tiny outpost of the Sunken Ball-Court that betraying sumbitch of a deity carried under those swinging slatted ribs where *his* heart should be, from which to pluck and don the faces of the dead.

All of 'em are mine, no matter 'oo. And all of 'em find their way down 'ere to me, eventually.

Chess's hands slapped leather, automatically; no guns, of course. Not even holsters.

"Hell, then, one way or t'other," he said out loud, resisting the urge to shiver. "Must be."

"The 'Oly Land, more like," somebody corrected him, from perilously nearby. "Or Seven Dials, they calls it, up-town. But close enough."

A woman stood on the corner, angled toward him with a sort of hunger, as though she'd been following his trail far longer than either of them could calculate. Her hair was a sodden red tangle, grim smile in a fox-sharp face, skin pallid even in darkness, an uneven thumb-print smear—and the voice, Christ Jesus crucified. That bloody, bleedin' *voice.*

"Don't you know me, then?" she asked. "For I do know *you,* believe me, no matter 'ow long it's been. I'd know you anywheres."

As she spoke, all the anger flowed out of Chess at once, blood from a cut throat; the hollow at his core had swelled so large now he felt empty, a mere shed skin. Unable to stop himself from replying, though he well knew the error of it.

"Yeah, I know you, all right . . . *Ma.*"

He said it tonelessly enough, bowing his head down, almost like he meant to pray. And watched "English" Oona Pargeter's nasty grin widen steadily in return—almost comically so, albeit without a touch of genuine humour—'til she went the whole hog, and dropped him a mocking little curtsey.

"Oh, that's what *you* fink, sonny," she replied.

TO BE CONTINUED in *A TREE OF BONES*

ABOUT THE AUTHOR

Gemma Files was born in London, England and raised in Toronto, Canada. Her story "The Emperor's Old Bones" won the 1999 International Horror Guild award for Best Short Fiction. She has published two collections of short work (*Kissing Carrion* and *The Worm in Every Heart*, both Prime Books) and two chapbooks of poetry (*Bent Under Night*, from Sinnersphere Productions, and *Dust Radio*, from Kelp Queen Press). *A Book of Tongues*, her first Hexslinger novel, won the 2010 DarkScribe Magazine Black Quill award for Small Press Chill, in both the Editors' and Readers' Choice categories. *A Rope of Thorns* will be followed by the final Hexslinger novel, *A Tree of Bones*.

Find out more about her at http://musicatmidnight-gfiles.blogspot.com/.

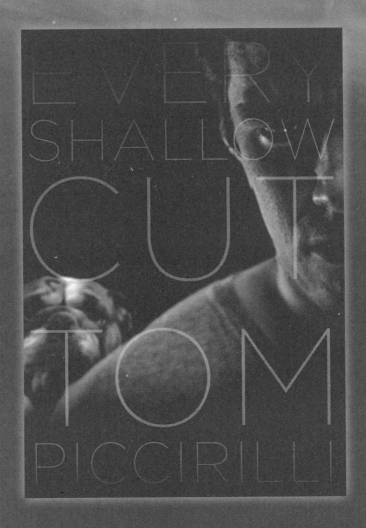

EVERY SHALLOW CUT

TOM PICCIRILLI

AVAILABLE MARCH 15, 2011
FROM CHIZINE PUBLICATIONS

978-1-926851-10-5

3

NAPIER'S BONES DERRYL MURPHY

AVAILABLE MARCH 15, 2011
FROM CHIZINE PUBLICATIONS

978-1-926851-09-9

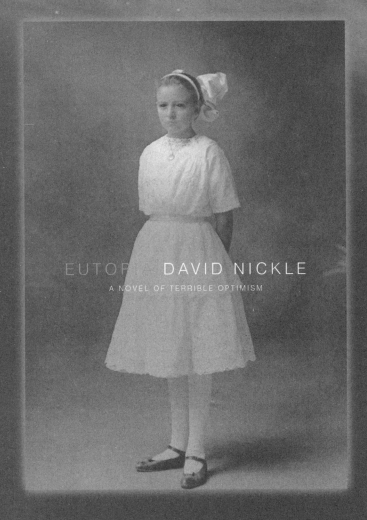

EUTOPIA DAVID NICKLE
A NOVEL OF TERRIBLE OPTIMISM

AVAILABLE APRIL 15, 2011
FROM CHIZINE PUBLICATIONS

978-1-926851-11-2

THE DOOR TO
LOST PAGES

CLAUDE LALUMIÈRE

AVAILABLE APRIL 15, 2011
FROM CHIZINE PUBLICATIONS

978-1-926851-12-9

FROM THE AUTHOR OF *FILARIA*

THE FECUND'S MELANCHOLY DAUGHTER

BRENT HAYWARD

AVAILABLE MAY 15, 2011
FROM CHIZINE PUBLICATIONS

978-1-926851-13-6

EDITED BY SANDRA KASTURI & HALLI VILLEGAS

2011

IMAGINARIUM

the best canadian
speculative writing

COMING JULY 15, 2011
FROM CHIZINE PUBLICATIONS
AND TIGHTROPE BOOKS

978-1-926851-15-0

978-0-9812978-9-7

TIM LEBBON

THE THIEF OF BROKEN TOYS

978-0-9812978-8-0

PHILIP NUTMAN

CITIES OF NIGHT

978-0-9812978-7-3

SIMON LOGAN

KATJA FROM THE PUNK BAND

978-0-9812978-6-6

GEMMA FILES

A BOOK OF TONGUES

978-0-9812978-5-9

DOUGLAS SMITH

CHIMERASCOPE

978-0-9812978-4-2

NICHOLAS

CHASING THE DRAGON

"IF YOUR TASTE IN FICTION RUNS TO THE DISTURBING, DARK, AND AT LEAST PARTIALLY WEIRD, CHANCES ARE YOU'VE HEARD OF CHIZINE PUBLICATIONS—CZP—A YOUNG IMPRINT THAT IS NONETHELESS PRODUCING STARTLINGLY BEAUTIFUL BOOKS OF STARKLY, DARKLY LITERARY QUALITY."

—DAVID MIDDLETON, *JANUARY MAGAZINE*

EMB
RACE
THE
ODD